Nina Milne has always dreamed of writing for Mills & Boon—ever since she played libraries with her mother's stacks of Mills & Boon romances as a child. On her way to this dream Nina acquired an English degree, a hero of her own, three gorgeous children, and—somehow!—an accountancy qualification. She lives in Brighton and has filled her house with books—her very own *real* library.

Nina Singh lives just outside Boston, USA, with her husband, children, and a very rumbustious Yorkie. After several years in the corporate world she finally followed the advice of family and friends to 'give the writing a go, already'. She's oh-so-happy she did. When not at her keyboard she likes to spend time on the tennis court or golf course. Or immersed in a good read.

CINDERELLA'S MOROCCAN MIDNIGHT KISS

NINA MILNE

PRINCE'S PROPOSAL FOR THE CANADIAN CAMERAS

NINA SINGH

MILLS & BOON

First published in Great Britain 2025
by Mills & Boon, an imprint of HarperCollins*Publishers* Ltd,
1 London Bridge Street, London, SE1 9GF

www.harpercollins.co.uk

HarperCollins*Publishers*, Macken House, 39/40 Mayor Street Upper,
Dublin 1, D01 C9W8, Ireland

This book contains FSC™ certified paper
and other controlled sources to ensure responsible forest management.

For more information visit www.harpercollins.co.uk/green.

Printed and Bound in the UK using 100% Renewable Electricity
at CPI Group (UK) Ltd, Croydon, CR0 4YY

CINDERELLA'S MOROCCAN MIDNIGHT KISS

NINA MILNE

MILLS & BOON

To my family.

CHAPTER ONE

LILY CULPEPPER GLARED down at her phone and read the message again.

Reminder! Countdown! Ten days to go! Until… Cynthia's hen break—a sun-soaked, cocktail-filled beach break in Gran Canaria. Let's send Cynthia off into marital bliss in style! Can't wait to see you again! Julia

Followed by a string of emojis.

Lily closed her eyes, then reopened them in the hope the message had miraculously disappeared. But of course, it hadn't. After all, the original invitation hadn't vanished, nor the first reminder, so realistically it was unlikely this one would comply.

There had to be a way out of this. It was bad—no, *horrendous*—enough that she had to go to Cynthia and Tom's Valentine's Day wedding, a ceremony in which her stepsister was going to marry Lily's ex.

It was a plotline worthy of a soap opera, and remembered humiliation washed over her in a flood of mortification at the thought of the scene—two years before, on Valentine's Day no less—when Tom had rejected her in favour of the stepsister who had made her childhood a misery.

Stop. She would not take that trip down memory lane. She would not relive the pain, the sear of rejection, the sheer disbelief. And she would not show anyone that she cared; instead, she would attend the wedding, smile, laugh and act as though she was totally on board. As though the heartbreak and betrayal had never happened.

But the prospect of the hen break triggered a different sense of panic engendered by a different set of memories. Memories of a boarding school where her life had been made miserable by her stepsisters and their cohort of 'friends' and acolytes. Now she would be trapped on a 'sun-soaked' island with the same people.

Not that anyone else seemed to have given it a thought. Apparently it was all forgotten, or at least water under the bridge—a bridge constructed by others. The general consensus seemed to be that, whilst their actions had been regrettable, they'd also somehow been justifiable. After all, Lily's mum had stolen Cynthia and Gina's dad, broken up a marriage and ruined their lives. All of which might be true, but that wasn't Lily's fault, though sometimes, in some surreal way, it had felt that it was.

Lily rose to her feet and walked to the office window, needed the distraction of the busy London scene outside, the throngs of people, the red double-decker buses and the snarl of traffic. *Her* office, she reminded herself as she sought to ground herself with a reminder of where she was now, the woman she was today a long way from that frightened child.

Lily Culpepper, founder and owner of Culpepper Housekeeping Services, a niche, prestigious company that recruited housekeepers and other private staff for global clients. She looked round her London office, thought of all her plans for expansion and reminded herself of how hard she'd worked to get here.

That was what was important. As for the hen break… damn it, she didn't want to go, but she would, even if sometimes she wondered why she didn't just walk away from the whole damn fiasco.

But walking away from Cynthia and Tom would mean walking away from her mother and, despite the complexities of their relationship, Lily couldn't do that. She didn't understand Maria, and knew Maria didn't understand her—they were chalk and cheese, and always had been, but Maria was her mum and the only real family Lily had.

So she'd stuck around, also determined not to give Cynthia the satisfaction of seeing how hurt she was. At the start she'd hung on to the humiliating hope that Tom would see that he'd got it wrong, see Cynthia for who she truly was. But that hadn't happened; instead, they'd announced their engagement, and pride had dictated Lily smile and congratulate them. Now that same pride decreed she would have to face the sun-soaked island.

Well, so be it; she wouldn't run scared, she'd show up and show them all how far she'd come—prove to them and herself that they no longer had any power over her. She'd suck it up, get through it. Because, however much she might wish it, no fairy godmother was going to turn up, wave a magic wand and say, *Lily, you shall not go on the hen break!* whilst the messages on her phone all turned to pumpkin emojis.

Because magic didn't exist, and neither did fairy godmothers or happy endings. She'd believed in all that once, had fought to believe it all her life, but no longer.

A knock on the door interrupted her reflections and

she turned, a small frown on her face. Clients needed to buzz through from the foyer to be allowed in, plus she didn't have any appointments that day. Perhaps it was someone from one of the other offices.

'Come in.'

The door opened and a woman entered, not a woman Lily knew, though definitely one she recognised. A quick scan of her memory banks and the woman's identity was found—Lady Gemma Fairley-Godfrey, a woman in her sixties, incredibly wealthy, having inherited a family fortune. She'd never married, though she'd been linked with any number of celebrities, and was also known as a formidable fundraiser, renowned for her charity work.

She was also a former 'wild child' and super-model who had recently adorned the cover of the world's most prestigious fashion magazine in an outfit that could at best be described as 'revealing'. A true role model in the art of ageing gracefully, and right now she looked pretty good.

Immaculately groomed, her ash-blonde hair was expertly dyed and styled to frame a classically beautiful face with high, slanted cheekbones. Her widely spaced eyes were a clear emerald-green, adding a piquancy that the world's most renowned photographers had captured many times.

Whilst her beauty was undeniable, Lady Fairley-Godfrey had more than that. Like Lily's mother, she had an indefinable something—the 'it' factor or 'X factor' or whatever factor it was that gave beauty an additional twist, lifting it into the super-beauty category. Lily's mother had used it all her life to cajole, persuade and, in the end, ruthlessly win whichever hapless, rich male she targeted. Lily herself had inherited neither beauty nor any super-power herself; her genes presumably came from her dad's side, whoever he was. His identity a secret her mother refused to divulge.

But none of this mattered now, because Lady Fairley-Godfrey could be a prospective client and that could only add to the agency's prestige. It was well-known that only the best was good enough for this successful woman, known not to suffer fools gladly.

Lily stepped forward.

'Lily Culpepper?'

'Yes.' Lily held out a hand and the other woman shook it, a cool professional hand shake.

'Please sit down, Lady Fairley-Godfrey.'

'Thank you. And please call me Gemma. I am sorry to turn up without an appointment but I was in the area, saw your sign, remembered that you had been recommended to me and thought I'd drop in on the off chance.'

'Of course. Please sit down. How can I help?'

'I am planning a last-minute Valentine fundraiser for charity—a rehabilitation refuge that supports women and children in difficult situations, gives struggling mothers a chance to rebuild their life—perhaps saves a child from going into care. I plan to host a dinner dance for some very wealthy donors. My godson has offered his villa in Morocco, but it needs bringing up to scratch. I am planning on flying out myself to oversee things, but I need a housekeeper. Some guests will be staying, and I want to offer a five-star service.'

Lily thought rapidly. 'It's the end of January now,' she said thoughtfully. 'That's not a lot of time. But I am sure we can help. I'll need exact dates, then I can put together a shortlist of candidates for you to meet, or I can make a choice for you...'

Gemma shook her head, her green eyes holding a steely determination. 'No, you misunderstand. I want you to do it—personally.'

'Me? I'm flattered but I don't really take assignments on myself now, simply because...'

'You have a business to run. I understand that.' Gemma's voice was a touch impatient, that of a woman used to getting her own way. 'But nowadays you can do so much with technology. You could do a lot of that from Morocco, and surely you can delegate to someone here? It will only be for a week. I want the best. It's your company—I am assuming that is what you are.'

Lily's mind raced. Working for Gemma would gain Culpepper's a massive kudos boost, and oddly she didn't get the feeling Gemma was trying to push her around. It was more of a statement—she wanted the best person for the job and she had decided Lily was it. But in all honesty that wasn't Lily's prevailing thought right now—her prevailing thought was the realisation that, if she was working in Morocco, then she couldn't be on a sun-soaked island on a hen break.

And no one could question the validity of her excuse. No one would pass up the opportunity to work for Lady Fairley-Godfrey.

'I'll do it.'

Morocco, three days later

Darius Kingsleigh walked towards the villa, *his* villa, and looked at the sprawling dusk-pink terracotta walls embedded with arched latticed windows, walls that encased nine vast bedrooms, nine bathrooms, two enormous reception rooms, a dining room and a state-of-the-art kitchen. All set in an elegant mosaic courtyard enclosed by trellises. He'd purchased the villa a year ago entirely as a statement to himself, because he could. Just as he had purchased a sports car and apartments in both London and New York—with *his* money, money earned fair and square by him, from a company he'd set up himself.

A company that had nothing whatsoever to do with the Kingsleigh Hotel empire, founded over a hundred years ago, still family owned and now a global multi-billion enterprise run by his aunt and her children. Specifically not run by Darius himself, because his father, Enzo Kingsleigh, hadn't left him any shares in the business.

In point of fact, Enzo had left him nothing, not a proverbial dime. Instead, he had left his 'natural son' his 'best wishes'. An image of his father seemed to hover in the air, dark hair tinged with grey, larger than life, a man who'd denied himself nothing and had perhaps paid the price, collapsing from a massive unexpected heart attack at the age of sixty-five.

Grief, hurt, resentment, and guilt at that resentment all churned in a familiar twist in his gut, emotions that had roiled and darkened within him since Enzo's death three years ago.

Enough. Not now.

He'd moved on—moved on from Enzo, moved on from the whole Kingsleigh family. He'd made it in his own right and he damn well hoped that somehow Enzo knew that.

And then came the guilt again because, however reluctantly, however ungraciously, Enzo had accepted the truth of the DNA test and had accepted paternity and responsibility, taking Darius in. And for that he was grateful. That was why he had accepted the will, determined not to show his 'family' his true feelings. He'd left the plush, streamlined offices of the Kingsleigh lawyers and walked away. And he'd kept on walking, hadn't looked back for three years.

But soon the family drama would be exposed. He had received a courtesy call from the lawyers, informing him that probate should finally be granted in the next few weeks. Then the will would be open to public view. The whole world would know that Enzo Kingsleigh had disinherited his only son. Speculation would run rife.

Standing here now in the Moroccan sun, frustration twisted his gut. He could manage the fallout from the gossip sites. The issue was the impact on his company, the possibility of a shareholder upset, the question marks over his business prowess and his capability to run his business. The domino effect could be disastrous. Ironic that his father's opinion could matter beyond the grave.

But it could. The business world would wonder why Enzo had decided not to leave his son a single share in the Kingsleigh empire, had in fact elected to leave him nothing. It would ask if it was because Darius had proven himself to be a failure, whether he was nothing more than a playboy not to be trusted with the Kingsleigh legacy. Hurt seared again at the knowledge that Enzo hadn't trusted him, had never accepted him as a true Kingsleigh.

Darius closed his eyes, inhaling deeply. No matter; that could not be changed. But he would not let anything— speculation or gossip—impact his company. He would ride the storm. At least he had spent the past two years, since his disastrous liaison with Ruby AllStar, avoiding all publicity on a personal level, intent on ensuring all the public saw was Darius Kingsleigh, successful businessman, not a playboy.

Another deep breath and he collected his thoughts, focusing now on what lay ahead in the immediate future. He held back a sigh. In truth he did not have time for this; he should be at work, but he hadn't been able to refuse his godmother's request.

Their earlier conversation flitted through his mind.

'Darius, I need a favour.'

There'd been no small talk and no build-up, no general enquiries as to his well-being, so Darius had known his godmother's need was real. Her image on the computer screen had held unwonted signs of strain.

'Go ahead.'

'I'm due to be in Morocco later today.'

He'd nodded. 'Yup, to get the villa ready for your fundraiser. You got the keys, right?'

'Yes, I have the keys, but there's a problem. I'm needed elsewhere.'

She hadn't elaborated and Darius hadn't asked. His godmother had so many people and causes that there was always someone somewhere who needed her. He'd been one of those people himself.

'OK. What do I need to do...?'

The answer to that question had been a concise set of instructions. Now, twenty hours later, here he was.

He crossed the tiled courtyard, walked up the balustraded stairs towards the imposing arched door and frowned when he saw it was slightly ajar. Presumably the woman he was here to meet, Lily Culpepper, had already gone in, but why would she have left the door open? He entered, stood for a moment in the wide mosaic hallway, then heard a noise from the room to his right and moved towards it—just as a woman purposefully walked out, a woman with keys in hand and a cobweb in her dark-brown hair. He tried to sidestep but too late; the inevitable collision happened and he instinctively reached out to steady them both, his hands on her arms as they both stared at each other.

Arrest took him completely by surprise. There was a jolt of awareness, a spark, a sense of physical connection that shocked him into immobility. He saw a reciprocal realisation in a pair of wide, dark-blue eyes. Then he saw recognition dawn; she'd worked out who he was and her lips tightened in what was surely disapproval. Lips that, despite himself, he lingered on for a fraction of a second too long before stepping back.

'You must be Lily Culpepper,' he said, studying her properly now, trying to work out what had triggered the reaction. Dark-brown hair fell straight to her shoulders; her face was oval, with a determined chin; her best feature was her eyes, dark-blue and fringed with long, dark lashes. Her nose was a trifle long, giving her face character, and her mouth was generous.

She nodded. 'And you are Darius Kingsleigh.' Her voice was neutral but there was a fleeting look of judgment in her eyes and for some reason it caught him on the raw. He'd had more than enough judgment in his lifetime.

'Yes. I'm Gemma's godson. I assume you're expecting me and that's why the door was open? Just as a note,

I expect my staff to be security conscious. I'd prefer my villa not to be ransacked.'

Even as he said the words he wondered what the hell he was doing; he'd come across as a pompous jackass, his tone condescending, all based on a possible misinterpretation of her expression.

Before he could attempt to retrieve the situation, anger flashed across her eyes. 'Last I looked, I am not *your* staff. My company has been hired by Lady Fairley-Godfrey, and I am contracted to her. Furthermore, I'm not sure when you last visited *your* villa, or how you left it, but right now the lock is broken.'

Ah. Now he came to think of it, when he'd bought it a year ago the estate agent had said something about there being a knack to the lock. 'It took me fifteen minutes to manage to open the door and get in. I then decided to leave it open as I didn't want to lock myself in until I knew there was another way out. I left it unsecured for about two minutes. But by all means, now you are here, feel free to lock the door. I will wait for Gemma outside—she is due here any minute.'

She stepped forward, keys held out, and on automatic he reached out to take them, his fingers inadvertently brushing hers—and there it was again, an instantaneous reaction, the type that in a film would warrant little cartoon blue sparks on the screen. They both snatched their hands back and the keys fell to the ground with a clatter.

With a muttered exclamation of annoyance, she dived to get them just as he squatted down to do the same. Now they were both on the floor, practically face to face, so close he could see the smatter of freckles on the bridge of her nose, observe exactly how long her eyelashes were, smell the light floral scent she wore, and watch the sunlight coming through the crack in the door highlight the gloss of her hair.

And she was as mesmerised as he, her blue eyes darkening, her lips slightly parting, and somehow, instead of moving backwards, instead of reaching for the keys, they were both moving slightly closer to each other. For a crazy second he hoped, wished, that she would kiss him…and then the door creaked, the sound breaking the spell, and she muttered something that sounded suspiciously like, 'Idiot,' and scrambled to her feet.

Picking up the keys, he followed suit and for a moment they stood in silence. He knew he should say something, knew the longer the silence stretched the more awkward this was all becoming, but he couldn't think of anything to say. What had happened to Darius Kingsleigh, suave dater of celebrities? He'd eschewed relationships for two years, but he'd have thought some vestige of flair would have remained.

In the end it was Lily who tucked a tendril of hair behind her ear and took a step towards the door.

'I'll wait outside for Gemma.'

'No, there's no point. Gemma isn't coming.'

'Of course she is coming—her fundraiser is in less than a week and she is coming here to organise it.'

Darius took a deep breath. 'That's what I'm here to do. Gemma can't make it; she is needed elsewhere. She'll be back for the actual event, but in the meantime I'm her deputy, and she has asked if you and I can get the villa ready and plan the event.'

She took a step backwards, and then, her voice slightly strangled, she said, 'You and me?'

The 'you' was said with both disbelief and a definite
hint of horror, something he empathised with. In their
short acquaintance, Lily Culpepper had already completely unsettled him, and the situation was beginning to
grate on his already somewhat frayed nerves.

'Yes. Is that a problem?'

CHAPTER TWO

YES—IT WAS most definitely a bloody problem, with a capital P, for multiple reasons. Lily inhaled deeply, took a calming breath and wondered how on earth she'd lost such spectacular control of events.

One of her biggest strengths was her ability to remain cool and unflappable at all times—an ability she'd learnt and cultivated over the years from the moment she'd realised that she was different from other children because her mother was different. Then had honed when she'd realised the best way to face down the bullying was not to show emotion, to make them think she didn't care.

It was a trait that had stood her in good stead through the horror of Cynthia and Tom's wedding preparations, and she'd believed it to be an ingrained part of her. Yet in an instant Darius Kingsleigh had undermined all of that. That initial collision had triggered a reaction that even now she did not want to believe.

No way—*surely* no way—could she be attracted to this man. He was a man who had graced any number of celebrity magazines over the years, with any number of different women. A man often said to be a carbon copy of his father—Enzo Kingsleigh had been notorious for his party lifestyle and his son had followed suit. They both embodied everything Lily despised: people who used looks and wealth to get what they wanted. Worse than that, every affair had been brief, and no doubt Darius left broken hearts in his wake.

She could still recall his much-publicised break from the popular singer-songwriter Ruby AllStar and her accusation that he'd strung her along, promising commitment. So he might have looks, but she knew those looks were not backed up by the things Lily believed to be important—integrity, kindness, a work ethic where a person worked for what they got and didn't have it handed it to them on a silver platter.

Yet his looks were playing havoc with her hormones, which was all wrong. Lily told herself she was overreacting. She hadn't known his identity when she'd first reacted and her hormones simply hadn't caught up with events. Regardless, the most important thing was to get everything onto a professional footing. She'd been rude to her client's godson, not a good move, and an even worse move now that it turned out he was acting for the client.

She took a deep breath and tugged her jacket down in a decisive movement, looking across at Darius and seeing that his earlier anger seemed to have gone. Instead, there was a hint of amusement in his eyes. 'Did you know you have a very expressive face?' he asked.

Great. Marvellous.

'No,' she said repressively. 'I didn't know that because usually I don't.'

'Well, today you do, and I have a feeling you do have a problem with the idea of working with me—that you know what the problem is but you are trying to remind yourself to be professional and rise above it.' Now he smiled. 'How am I doing?'

Lily really wished he hadn't smiled, because the smile was doing something strange to her. It was a smile that reached his eyes, crinkled them ever so lightly and sparked them with humour and an invitation to smile back. She could feel her treacherous, expressive face wanted to do just that.

Not happening. Because now incipient panic was trickling in alongside a sense of confusion. She couldn't remember the last time anyone had read her so easily, couldn't really remember a time when anyone had been interested enough in her reactions to read them at all. And she didn't like it. With a supreme effort, she kept her face neutral. 'The problem isn't personal,' she said. 'I prefer to work alone or with a colleague of my own choosing.'

'You would have been working with my godmother.'

'That's different.'

'Why?'

Good question. 'Your godmother was the original client. She is the one I agreed to work for. And now that job spec has changed.'

'Is it about money? Gemma said she'll pay you more.'

'It's not about money.'

'You're worried you won't be able to do the new job?'

'No!' She narrowed her eyes. *Damn it.* Darius was toying with her and she could see where this was headed.

'Then it *must* be me,' he said. 'If I had been the original client, would you have refused the job?' His voice was polite, gentle even, but it was underlaid with an edge of steel. An edge that reminded Lily that, as well as being a party-loving serial dater, Darius was also an incredibly successful businessman—founder and CEO of a company that turned over billions, a company that had achieved runaway global success in the past two-and-a-half years.

'That is a hypothetical scenario,' she said.

'Yup. So let's hypothesise.'

'There is no point.'

'There is every point. Because right now I am effectively the client, so we have a choice to make: whether we can work together or not, as Gemma has requested.'

Unfortunately... 'You're right.' Could she work with this man? *Really, Lily?* Was she even asking the question, or suggesting that she couldn't work with him because she couldn't control her hormones? The sheer shallowness of the idea added an edge to her annoyance. As for personal feelings, she might not like or approve of his lifestyle, but as a professional surely she could work with him on a charity fundraiser?

'If we can't, we risk not getting the job done in time, and that wouldn't be fair to Gemma or the charity,' he pointed out. 'So I have an idea. It's nearly eight o'clock and I'm hungry. How about we go and have dinner whilst we discuss the best way forward? Gemma has given me plenty of information about what she wants us to do. Let's go and see if it's viable. If not, I'll pay you for your time so far and figure out what to do next.'

There was that edge again and Lily forced herself not to glare at him as determination solidified within her. No way was she losing this job; she was good at what she did and she was not going to let some ridiculous attraction get in the way. She was a consummate professional and now was the time to prove it. She would not let this man's looks affect her—it would be despicable. Would be almost a validation of her mother's way of life—the way she'd used her beauty as currency without caring a damn for the repercussions it had brought to so many lives, including Lily's own.

It had been enough to make her believe with all her heart that looks shouldn't matter, to make her vow always to judge people by their character. Which made it all the more mortifying to find her errant hormones betraying every one of her principles and reacting as they had to Darius Kingsleigh.

But, then again—and the thought stopped her in her tracks—he'd looked pretty poleaxed too. She shook her head. She must have imagined it, wishful thinking on her hormones' part. Darius dated beautiful celebrities, not an average-looking businesswoman whose company turned over a fraction of his wealth.

Lily had no illusions about her looks. Not since the moment her five-year-old self first overheard a conversation between two of the mothers at school.

'Isn't it odd, a beautiful woman like Maria produced such a plain little girl?'

'Maybe she's adopted.'

It had been a conversation she'd encountered countless times since, and she'd long since decided simply to accept her looks and focus on making something of her life through her achievements.

'Dinner is fine,' she said, even as instinct told her dinner sounded all wrong. 'I'd picked out a local restaurant to go to with good reviews. Does that sound OK?' She braced herself for a refusal: perhaps a small local eatery wouldn't be good enough for him.

'Works for me,' he said.

Actually, why wouldn't it? This wasn't a date; plus he'd probably be embarrassed to be spotted or snapped with someone as ordinary as her. He was studying her expression now, a slight frown on his face, as if he was trying to read her thoughts, and she kept her expression strictly neutral—there'd be no more giveaway expressions.

'Then let's go,' she said.

Darius nodded, even as he wondered why he'd extended a dinner invitation. Why he hadn't simply fired her on the spot. He was pretty sure that was what Enzo would have done.

Hell, he was through with doing what Enzo had done. He'd spent twenty years doing that, desperate to prove himself worthy of being Enzo's son. To show Enzo, show the world, that he possessed the Kingsleigh gene. He'd done what his father had, had lived his father's lifestyle, had partied, womanised and worked for the Kingsleigh empire, trying everything to show Enzo he was his true son, his blood.

All to no avail; the taste of failure was bitter on his tongue even now, three years after Enzo's death. Now it was too late, too late to win his father's love or recognition.

Perhaps it had always been too late. His father had done his duty, but love had been a step too far, and maybe that fault had lain with Darius, not Enzo. Now all he could do was focus on succeeding in his own right, on his own terms, on his own. Because that was how he liked it.

On his own, there was nothing to prove to anyone. No worry that one day the person he trusted to be there would leave without warning—the way his mother had gone. She might not have been the best mother in the world, but she'd been all he had, and he'd loved her. He'd believed she'd loved him, and his eight-year-old self had been devastated when she'd gone, even if he had the bleak knowledge and shame that he'd brought it on himself.

He took a deep breath, eyed Lily Culpepper and wondered whether it might not be better to pay her off and do this on his own. There'd be no one to answer to and, even better, no unsettling attraction to complicate things. He didn't even understand why he was attracted to her. He was pretty sure she didn't even like him, which was annoying him far more than it should. Why should he give a damn about her opinion?

'Let's go,' he agreed. With any luck, by the end of dinner she'd decide she couldn't work with him anyway.

They left the house and he pulled the door, having spent a few minutes figuring out the mechanism, before he'd managed to pull it shut. He took one last look at his statement purchase, wondering if he'd bought it in an unconscious tribute to his father—the purchase of a villa on a whim the final following of his footsteps. Though Enzo would have filled it with guests and thrown lavish parties. Darius had bought it and then left it; he could barely recall the interior. At least now it would be put to good use.

He glanced at his companion, appreciating the fact that Lily seemed content to walk in silence; there was no need for small talk as they made their way along the pavements, where the owners of small shops were putting up their shutters, until they came to a paved square full of cafés.

Lily looked down at her phone and then pointed. 'That's the one.'

Darius looked at the busy restaurant, the tiled paved outside area filled with tables interspersed with cleverly placed verdant plants in terracotta pots. 'Good choice,' he said. 'I've eaten here before. Just the once, but I do remember the food is outstanding.'

They entered the restaurant, where rows of wooden tables covered in woven rattan mats were filled with people eating and talking, the clatter of cutlery, the buzz of conversation and an array of tantalising smells all combined. Lily glanced round and bit her lip. 'It's pretty busy. I should have booked.'

Before he could answer, a woman headed towards them. 'You've come back,' she said, and smiled.

Darius blinked and wound his mind back to a year ago, recalled enjoying the meal, appreciating the quiet corner table and the excellent food. But he was pretty sure he'd never seen this woman.

He settled for, 'Yes,' and turned as the woman was joined by a man and an older lady, one he did recognise. 'You were here when I was here last,' he said and the woman nodded.

'That was me,' she said.

The man stepped forward, held out his hand. 'I am Jamal. I own the restaurant, and I'm also the chef. This is my wife, Natalia, and this is my mother. It was my mother who took a picture of you last year.'

Darius still wasn't sure where this was going.

'We had just opened and Mama put the picture in the local paper and on our website. It showed you with an empty plate in front of you, and we got lots of customers. Then we heard that you had bought the villa and we have been hoping you would come in.' Jamal's smile was apologetic. 'Mama put the picture up without telling me,' he explained. 'We know we maybe should have asked permission and...'

'We did take it all down very soon.'

It seemed clear that Jamal and Natalia were concerned, apprehensive, even. It was the sort of thing that his family would have got all strange about; they would have talked about permissions and copyrights, but not as far as Darius was concerned. 'I am pretty sure it was the excellence of your food that brought the customers in.' He smiled reassuringly. 'But, if my picture helped in any way, I am glad.'

'Thank you.' The relief was palpable as Jamal beamed at him. 'Now, come be seated. This dinner is on the house and we promise it will be one you remember.'

Natalia smiled. 'And this time no photos, we promise. We have a table all ready for you both, in a small private room. My sister has been getting it ready whilst we have been talking. Come.'

'Thank you.' It was the first time Lily had spoken, but he had been aware of her quiet presence beside him, sensing her scrutiny, and now he saw her give him a small glance of surprise. Then she turned to Natalia; soon the two women were chatting, and Darius tried not to notice the swish and gloss of Lily's brown hair or watch the grace and elegance with which she walked.

Until they arrived at the table and Lily came to a sudden halt, breaking off mid-sentence, and as he took in the scene Darius understood why.

CHAPTER THREE

LILY STARED AT the table, above which floated a massive heart-shaped helium balloon inscribed with 'Be My Valentine'. On the table there was an array of finger food arranged on heart-shaped silver plates with gleaming cutlery, a snow-white linen table cloth and red napkins with a border of…hearts…and two cocktails with heart flags resting over the rims, a scattering of rose petals.

Clearly, in their desire to create a memorable occasion, the owners had grasped entirely the wrong end of the stick and assumed this was a date. Darius was a serial dater, he was known to own the villa round the corner and had turned up in the evening with a woman—what else would they assume?

Natalia beamed at her, clearly assuming Lily's silence indicated surprised appreciation. 'I hope you like it. We will be doing a Valentine special and I had already purchased the stock. Jamal is going to prepare the Valentine menu for you too.'

It was time to set the situation straight. Lily opened her mouth to explain this was strictly business…and then she saw the expression on Darius's face: a dismay even greater than her own etched his handsome features and a sudden anger pinged inside her. Of course he was mortified; no doubt the thought of anyone thinking he would lower his standards to date someone like Lily, let alone be her valentine, horrified him.

It was reminiscent of Tom's dismay two years ago, on Valentine's Day. Memories streamed her mind of the dinner she'd prepared, every ingredient purchased with love; the table laid, complete with a heart-shaped helium balloon of her own. The whole evening was supposed to have heralded the start of the rest of her life, with the man she loved.

Instead, it had been the scene of her humiliation and rejection and all she'd been left with after Tom's shame-faced departure was the congealed food and the sauce that had bubbled away, evaporating just as all her hopes and dreams had, leaving nothing but a burnt layer on the pan and the bitter ashes of a future that was never to be.

The memory was so clear, so painful, and anger tightened inside her, transmuted into a raw sear of hurt, of fury at Darius's expression. She turned to Natalia. 'This is beautiful, and Darius and I so appreciate this early chance to celebrate Valentine's. It feels like the whole of this month should be about celebrating romance.'

Even as she spoke her brain began to catch up with her mouth. What was she doing? She was supposed to be winning over Darius Kingsleigh with her professionalism and here she was, pretending to be his date. He'd think she was a fruit loop. She *was* a fruit loop and he was no doubt about to expose her as exactly that.

Instead, a wide smile on his face, he stepped forward so he was stood next to her and she gave a small, involuntary gasp. 'Thank you—this is an unanticipated pleasure.'

'Then sit down, enjoy the champagne cocktail, make

a start on the canapés and I will bring the main course when it is ready.'

Once Natalia was gone, Darius put down his glass with a *thunk*. 'Mind telling me what all that was about?'

Lily took a small defiant sip of her cocktail and jutted out her chin. No way was she going to explain the truth. 'I thought it was a shame to rain on their parade. They'd gone to so much trouble; there didn't seem to be any harm in going along with it.'

His stare intensified, his grey eyes hard and unreadable, though she could sense anger behind the set of his lips.

'No harm?' he repeated. 'Have you considered what will happen if Jamal or Natalia or a member of staff mention to someone that we were here, or if another diner pops their head round the door by mistake?'

'Oh.' This was Darius Kingsleigh, a member of the Kingsleigh family, loved by the media for providing them with scandals and stories galore. A single picture of Darius had launched the restaurant. Darius having a romantic dinner with a woman would be seen as an event in its own right in the eyes of the gossip sites. Lily closed her eyes and wished really hard that she could rewind time, rewrite the past hour to how it should have been. But she couldn't.

'OK. Obviously, I wasn't thinking straight.' *Or at all.* Incipient panic touched her—how could she have been so unprofessional? She couldn't blame Darius for questioning her ability to do the job. Why had she even cared what Darius thought about her on a personal level? 'And I apologise. I acted on instinct. I can go and speak to Natalia and clear it up now.'

There was a silence and then he shook his head. 'Apology accepted, and no need. I think it will cause more questions than it will solve—no smoke without fire, et cetera. That's why I went along with it. Hopefully there'll be no damage. I don't think anyone noticed us when we came in and they have already promised no photographs.' He gestured at the plates. 'I think the best thing to do will be to have dinner as planned and hope we stay under the radar.'

Lily nodded, looking at the plates that adorned the table. They held plump, luscious olives, both green and a deep dark brown; delicious-looking fava beans marinated in spices and herbs; various triangular, square and rectangle pastries and an array of different condiments.

Darius pushed a plate of the pastries towards her and pointed at a bright-red paste. 'I remember from last time how incredible these pastry things are, especially dipped in the harissa sauce.'

Lily pushed down the usual sense of discomfort at eating food recommended by other people, people she didn't know or didn't trust. As always, she told herself she was being irrationally paranoid. This was food prepared by a professional chef—of course it would be fine.

'The sauce is tangy, but it's not too hot.'

Wrong thing to say, though there was no way Darius could know that. But his words triggered another throwback memory. She was back at the boarding school that her mother and stepfather had also sent her stepsisters to, so they could 'bond'.

In truth Maria had wanted to cement her new marriage and ensure she thoroughly enslaved her husband so that he didn't regret signing a pre-nup agreement that his lawyer had visibly blanched at and had advised heavily against.

So she'd come up with the boarding school idea, ignoring Lily's pleas not to send her. 'You need to toughen up. Make yourself popular and you'll be fine.'

Not advice Lily had been able to figure out, but her stepsisters had and, once they'd achieved popularity, they had made bullying Lily into their favourite group sport.

One of the games had been food-orientated; they'd doctored Lily's food with salt or spices. And then had been the worst of all—a group had surrounded her and one of the girls, one Lily had always thought was nicer than the rest, had stepped forward.

'Here,' she'd said, holding out a plate with brownies on it. 'We wanted to say sorry. It's a peace offering. Try it.'

Lily had looked round, seen no sign of either stepsister and had allowed herself to let hope trump common sense. She had taken one and bitten into it… She could still recall the pain as she'd realised it had been doctored with chilli powder. Her mouth had been set on fire, lips burning, throat scorched, eyes and nose running to the mocking laughter of the girls.

'Earth to Lily.' She blinked now and saw Darius looking at her, a small frown furrowing his brow. 'You OK?'

'Yes. Of course.' She had to get a grip. 'This does look incredible,' she added, trying to inject enthusiasm into her tone.

'I think you'll like it. From what I remember—' he pointed as he spoke '—the triangular pastries are potato-filled and the tubes are beef-filled. As for the harissa, just to be on the safe side, I'll test it first in case Jamal has changed the recipe and it's ridiculously hot.'

It was almost as if he had read her mind but she told herself that simply wasn't possible. For anyone, but particularly not a man like Darius, who judged the worth of his dinner companions by their looks and status. And yet…his words had reassured her, had calmed the irrational jitters.

He picked up a pastry and dipped it in the harissa sauce. Somehow the movement mesmerised her; the shape of his bare forearm, the strength of his wrist and the breadth of his fingers all combined to send a sudden shot of liquid desire through her veins.

'Just as good as I remember, and not too hot, I promise.' The depth of his voice shivered over her skin and she couldn't help it; she smiled and, after a moment, he smiled back with a toe-curling smile. 'The exact right level of heat and spice.'

Oh, God, was he flirting with her? Did she want him to flirt with her? Lily blinked hard, the questions wiping the smile straight off her face. This was the sort of thing Darius probably did on automatic, using charm, banter and his looks to lure women in. No way would it work on her; no way would she *let* it work on her.

She picked up a pastry, dipped it in the sauce and took a bite, relishing the crunch of the pastry, the contrast with the softness of the potato spiced with turmeric, the whole thing perfectly complemented by the tang of chilli in the harissa. 'Yup. This is really good. You were right—the food is outstanding. Maybe I can take inspiration from Jamal's menu for the dinner for the fundraiser. If we decide that I am going ahead with the job.'

Perhaps there was a smidge of relief in his eyes as he nodded. 'Time to talk business,' he agreed.

* * *

It really was, Darius reflected as he picked up another pastry, this time filled with cumin-laced beef. This whole meeting was not panning out as he'd expected, his head dizzied by the twists and turns. He still wasn't sure he bought Lily's explanation for why she'd decided to pretend this was a date but that wasn't the biggest issue.

The problem was this *felt* like a date, with a level of attraction that flared and hummed under its own control. And he didn't like that; he needed to bring this *business* meeting under his control, establish a professional footing.

'How about we start with you telling me what Gemma hired you to do, I'll then explain how that has changed and we can work out the best way forward?'

'That sounds like a plan.' She marshalled her thoughts and he couldn't help but notice the serious look in her dark-blue eyes, the small crease of concentration as she tucked a tendril of brown hair behind her ear.

'My job was to get the villa up to five-star luxury standard and then act as housekeeper, with a capital H, for all the guests who will be staying in the villa. Ensure they are supplied with everything they need, from towels, to breakfast, to picnic hampers.'

He nodded. 'As you know, the plan is to have a Valentine-themed dinner for the six couples who will be staying in the villa. After that another twenty couples will arrive for dancing, and entertainment. That now all needs to be organised.'

'So we need caterers, a menu, a band and to figure out the entertainment. Something different—your godmother is known for the uniqueness of her events.'

Darius glanced at her. 'Do you also deal with event planning?'

'No, but housekeepers tend to get involved in all sorts of social functions. I'm confident I can help with the organisational side of things.'

'What about the impact of the increased workload? Gemma mentioned you own your business.'

'I do.' Pride crossed her face, a pride he empathised with. 'I can manage—this will be a lot of work, but in a short period of time it won't be a problem. I wouldn't take it on if I thought it would impact either the fundraiser or my existing clients.'

There was sincerity and professional pride in her voice and he nodded. 'I understand why Gemma employed you—she only employs the best.'

'Thank you,' she said and there it was again—the same smile that had blindsided him earlier, a smile that lit up her face and chased away the slight reserve it held in repose, a wariness that he wasn't sure was directed at the world or just him personally.

And now his breath caught in his throat. The candlelight lit her face, showing the small smatter of freckles on the slant of her cheekbone and emphasising the character of her face and the sparkle in the blue eyes fringed by those impossibly long lashes. Of their own volition, her eyes fell to his lips and he realised that she seemed as transfixed as he was, her eyes scanning his face.

Until her phone rang out, breaking the spell as she looked away to grab it. 'Sorry. I should have switched it off or at least put it on silent.' She glanced down and quickly declined the call. Within seconds it shrilled out again, and now she pressed another button which cut the sound, though he could still hear it vibrating.

'Why don't you take it?' he asked as the door opened. 'It looks like they are bringing in the next course, so you'll have a few minutes.'

'In that case, I will. I'll be back in two minutes, give or take.' Turning, she smiled at Natalia. 'Thank you. That was all amazing so far.'

Darius forced himself not to watch her walk to the door and refused to ogle the natural grace and sway of her body. But, damn it, it was hard and he could see Natalia suppress a small smile when he turned to look at her; he realised he'd added to the whole illusory 'date' scenario.

Natalia continued to beam at him. 'Jamal asked me to explain the thinking behind the dinner.'

She started to speak and Darius resisted a groan.

CHAPTER FOUR

LILY SLIPPED INTO the bathroom and locked the door, picking up her still ringing phone.

'Hi, Mum. I am sorry, but this isn't a great time. I'm in a meeting.'

'At this time of night?' There was a sigh down the phone. 'You should be out having fun.'

'This is my idea of fun.'

'Is your meeting with Lady Fairley-Godfrey? That would at least be something.'

Lily weighed up her options, unsure what her mother would do if she told her she was having dinner with Darius Kingsleigh—combust, no doubt. So she settled for, 'It's a representative, and he is waiting at the table, so I'd better get back.'

'A representative? A man? Dinner? What are you wearing? Have you got make-up on? Is he rich?'

'I'm wearing black trousers and a top—it's a professional meeting,' Lily said repressively.

'I don't understand you and why you won't make more of yourself and opportunities like this.'

'Mum, we've been here before.'

So many times; an all too familiar frustration rolled through her. For her whole life, Lily had resisted her mother's attempts to make her follow in her footsteps, to emulate her philosophy. Maria had no objection as such to her daughter wanting a job, but she thought securing a wealthy man was way more important. 'And actually a lot more lucrative,' as she was fond of pointing out.

But Lily didn't get it, or understand why her mother didn't care about the emotional fallout her lifestyle led to. As a child, Lily had been shunted from one friend to another to keep her out of the way so her mother could give her undivided attention to her 'lucrative' man, who also happened to be married.

Then her mother had moved on to target another married man, only this time she'd upped the ante, had won him away from his wife and married him herself, thus securing a lifetime income. Maria had seen this as a triumph, seeming oblivious to the fact it had broken up a home and gained Lily two stepsisters who loathed her, and spent years tormenting her—sufficient that Lily's school life had been a living hell that she'd emerged from with no qualifications.

The result being that Lily had vowed that she would never follow in her mother's footsteps and would instead forge a real career and rely on herself for money.

Lily tuned back in to the conversation. 'Mum, I really do have to go. Why were you calling?'

'I wanted to know whether there is any way you can go to the hen event—Cynthia is very put out that you have pulled out. She thinks you should be prioritising family.'

'I can't leave this job,' Lily said firmly. She hung up, now doubly determined to close this deal. She needed this job. Professional pride aside, if she ended up on a plane home in a few days' time she would be on another plane to the sun-soaked island, pushed aboard by her mother.

The thought galvanised her into action, though it couldn't stop the *whoomph* of reaction as she approached the table and saw Darius: the dark, unruly, mid length hair; the face that was etched with a craggy strength; the breadth of his shoulder, the swell of muscle. The whole god damned package.

Enough.

Reaching the table, she sat down and looked at the spread of food on the table. 'This looks good.'

'It's a Valentine's special,' he said, a rueful tilt to his lips. 'Natalia explained it all. Jamal has put a lot of thought into it.'

'That's brilliant.' And a chance to show him that all she was thinking about was the job, *not* the tilt to his lips *or* the fine laughter lines around his eyes. 'Maybe we can use his ideas as inspiration for the fundraiser meal.'

'I'm not sure that would work.'

'Why not?' She tilted out her chin.

'Because I'm assuming our fundraiser theme is the soppy type of romance.' His voice held a hint of amusement that was reflected in his eyes, with an invitation to share the amusement that somehow warmed her, threatening to send her newly found resolve out of the window. 'This meal is more… Well, to quote Jamal, "it's saucy and steamy".'

'Oh.' *Saucy and steamy.* Heaven help her, it should sound cringe-worthy, but when Darius said it, it didn't. Instead the words sent a tingle through her whole body.

'Yup. I did promise to relay the whole spiel to you—

Natalia wants our opinion as a couple, would like feed-back at the end of the meal.'

'Oh.' *Great.* 'Go ahead.' She tried to keep her voice impersonal, as if this was simply a factual instruction.

'Here goes. Jamal suggests we start with this dish.' His voice was deep, his eyes still holding hers and, despite herself, she could feel a hum of awareness.

'Why?'

'Because it's spicy and sweet. A perfect blend—enough heat to keep things simmering and create a build-up.'

'Got it.' Her voice was a touch breathless as she watched him point to the next dish, and then his gaze was back on her, and she could see the grey eyes darken, was sure they held a promise, an invitation.

'Then he recommends we move onto this one, which packs more chillies—enough to cause a rush of heat.'

Lily forced herself to remain still, not to wriggle in her seat. She knew she had to say something, though the words that came out weren't what she'd intended.

'So all we need now,' she said, deadpan, 'is the per-fect dessert that we can share for the perfect finish—the climax to the meal.'

She met his gaze full on and saw the grey eyes go mol-ten. 'I can see you've got the hang of Jamal's thinking,' he said. Now he smiled, and this time she really couldn't stop her answering smile.

The job, remember the job. That was the focus here; she couldn't afford to get distracted by the lure of his smile, or how would she be able to do this job to the best of her ability? Unless...

'I've had an idea,' she said.

'Go ahead.'

'I'm assuming you weren't expecting to be involved in organising the fundraiser?'

'No, I wasn't.'

'I'm also assuming you are a busy man.' Lily knew that he ran a company that she assumed was an offshoot of the Kingsleigh empire, one that he'd taken to global success over the past two-and-a-half years.

'Correct.'

'Then would you prefer Culpepper's to organise the event? You could go back home and I could provide you with a daily update—keep you posted on how everything is going. What do you think?' Surely he would jump at the chance to go back to his normal life?

'No,' he said. 'I appreciate the offer, but no.'

Lily stared at him; she'd been so sure he'd agree. 'Are you sure? I am perfectly capable.'

'I'm sure you are,' he said easily. 'But that isn't the point. My godmother asked me to do this, I agreed and I intend to honour that agreement. I had already agreed to provide the villa and undertake the expenses involved as my donation. If she needs my time as well, then I will give it. Whilst I am sure you would get the job done, for me it is more than a job, it's personal. I owe my god-mother a lot—she has asked for my help and I want to give it.'

Damn it; he'd wrong-footed her and Lily could tell he was being sincere. And she couldn't help but respect him for it. It was easy for a man as rich as Darius to give money; it wasn't so easy to commit time and inconve-nience. 'I understand,' she said. 'In that case...'

'In that case I suggest we do this together, as long as you are happy to work with me rather than Gemma.'

'Happy' was pushing it, yet to her surprise anticipation fluttered through her alongside a determination to do the very best job she could. 'I'm in.'

'Then we have a deal.' He held out his hand and without thinking she put hers in it, knowing the second his hand enclosed hers that it was a mistake. She did not believe in magic, instant sparks or connections. She quite simply didn't. But his touch was doing *something* to her, sending a volt, a buzz of heat straight to her veins, and had taken the earlier awareness up a notch or three. This heat had nothing to do with sauce or spice; a shimmer of sparks seemed to have enmeshed them. Her hand was still in his and the sense of his skin on hers felt right, cool, strong and sending her a message way beyond sealing a deal.

She could sense herself leaning forward, and could see he was doing the same. Her brain seemed to have turned to mush, her entire being focused on the sensations rushing through her. Then the door opened and there was the sound of a throat clearing.

She dropped his hand, slamming back in her seat, and turned to see Jamal. Knew it was too late, that the restaurant owner had seen it all; knew too that her face was flushed and that she still looked dazed.

Jamal's face was apologetic but urgent. 'I am sorry to interrupt, but one of the diners has discovered that you are here having dinner in here. I think she is now trying to get access to the room. I wasn't sure if you minded?'

Lily saw annoyance flash across Darius's face, before he smiled. 'Thank you for the heads up. It's not your fault at all. Lily and I would rather avoid publicity, so if it's OK with you we'll slip out of a back exit. And can I just say, dinner was superb.'

'Thank you, and of course.' Jamal nodded. 'If you like, Natalia can give you a lift, rather than calling a taxi—for extra discretion.'

'That is very kind of you,' Lily said. 'And Darius is right—the dinner was superb. You will make a lot of Valentine diners very happy.'

CHAPTER FIVE

DARIUS NOTED THAT Lily elected to go in the passenger seat next to Natalia. 'You aren't a taxi,' she'd pointed out when Natalia had said they should both go in the back. He wondered if her motivation was based solely on common courtesy or whether she didn't want to risk the proximity to him.

Either way it was a good call. Proximity was definitely a bad idea; he could still feel Lily's hand in his. Her slender fingers seemed to have branded him, scorching him with a heat that had transcended all other thoughts and all common sense.

There was no point in denying the attraction—the moment of insanity when he would have acted on it and kissed Lily. What was wrong with him? He had no idea what her stance on relationships was, had set no ground rules. He had never once let attraction trump the need for rules, and never been tempted to kiss anyone without making sure those rules were in place.

Darius had always known the importance of relationship rules because he'd always known he didn't understand how relationships worked. He didn't understand how to win love, knew he didn't have the capacity to navigate a long-term relationship. Hell, he hadn't even known how to win his own parents' love.

So it seemed to him the best, the only, way for him to have a relationship was to set rules and boundaries that he *could* understand. To make sure there was no opportunity for love, no chance or expectation of it. It was always clear from the outset that any relationship could only be short term, because that was what he was capable of. That way, no one could get hurt.

Yet with Lily he'd have kissed her without a rule or boundary in place and that didn't make sense. And Darius didn't like things that didn't make sense, so the attraction needed to go.

He became aware of something nagging at his subconscious, figured out what it was as the little car slowed down to allow some pedestrians to cross the road. He turned his head to try and work out if his hunch was correct: that someone was following them.

Hard to tell—he might be overreacting but experience told him there was every chance he wasn't. Not when he knew the fascination the press had with the Kingsleigh family. Perhaps it was the sheer extent of their wealth, and the level of scandals they had generated over time—something Enzo had been particularly good at. He'd lived hard, partied wildly and grabbed headlines. Had been an erratic presence in the boardroom but, whilst he'd had flashes of business acumen that had justified his place, it was his sister Rita Kingsleigh who held sway at the helm of the Kingsleigh empire.

Rita had groomed her three children to be the Kingsleigh heirs. Unlike Darius, they had all been fast tracked to the boardroom automatically, although all three seemed to have inherited the Kingsleigh love of partying, and were a delight to the press in their own right.

As Darius himself had been: from his late teens to early twenties, Darius had tried to follow in Enzo's footsteps and prove he was his father's son. He had dated celebrities, partied and played to the camera in ways designed to echo his father's exploits. So, whilst he'd avoided any scandal in the past two years, after the extensive coverage of his break-up with Ruby AllStar—hadn't dated anyone and had focused solely on his business—he knew the press would relish any story about him all the more.

And now was not the time. The press would have a bonanza of a story in the near future once Enzo's will was made public. When that broke Darius knew he would need to prove to the world that he was a true businessman, not an untrustworthy playboy condemned by his father as not worthy to hold so much as a share in the Kingsleigh empire. So he'd take no risks now; he did not want stories about his personal life circulating.

So he kept his voice casual. 'Would you mind dropping Lily and I to Jemaa el-Fnaa? The night is young and it seems like a good idea to visit.'

He hoped the suggestion sounded natural—after all Jemaa el-Fnaa was a tourist must-see, a historic square with atmospheric appeal full of street entertainers, food and market stalls. It was meant to come alive at night.

'Of course,' Natalia said and to his relief Lily made no demur. 'If you are there, seeing as you missed dessert, go and have pancakes. Aline is part of our family and it is her first night trading there. I'll draw you a map so you can find her.'

'That sounds great. Thank you, Natalia.'

Fifteen minutes later Natalia pulled to a stop and he and Lily climbed out of the car. Lily waited until the car had receded into the distance then frowned. 'Why did you suggest this?'

'I can't be sure, but I think we were followed here from the restaurant. I reckoned, if I'm right, this is the perfect place to lose them.'

Lily glanced around. 'Do you really think someone would bother following us?'

'Possibly. Unfortunately, the press does have a massive interest in my private life and, whilst it's not a big deal, I'm sure you don't want to feature as my "mystery date", so why take the risk? Plus, this square is a must-see part of the city.'

Lily nodded. 'I have read about it and it sounds like a real experience. There are so many things to do here. I think I'll have to come back on holiday one day and go on a hot-air-balloon ride and visit the desert, but right now this sounds good.'

They stepped forward, and he was as careful as she to keep a distance between them as they approached the entrance. He heard her give a small gasp and instinctively step closer to him.

'Wow,' she said. And he knew what she meant. The square was a cacophony of noise, an overwhelming mix of people and smells that hit the senses all at once. Stalls selling food were dotted everywhere, smoke, steam and tantalising smells all rising and mingling in the air.

There were the shouts of the vendors, calling attention to their wares, English and Arabic interspersing. The number of people was mindboggling, making the whole a mass and mixture of humanity, tourists intermingled with locals. Music, drums, rock guitars and singing all blended the air with motes of noise and he closed his eyes to separate and distinguish the notes.

When he opened them, he saw Lily alight with enthusiasm, the planes and angles of her face lit by the flares of light that illuminated the darkness 'It's…amazing. I don't know where to look first or where to start or…anything.' She looked round. 'If we get separated, let's meet back here. Provided we can find it.'

In the meantime, he realised all they could do was stay close, and he steeled himself to do that without showing any reaction. He reminded himself that they were simply part of a crowd of people who were all in close proximity. But as they walked nothing, even the buzz of activity—the sight of snake charmers, people with trained monkeys, the vibrant colours and eye-catching goods on display—could completely dim his awareness of the woman by his side, the lively interest on her face, the gloss of her hair as it bobbed on the curve of her shoulder, her graceful light-footed tread or the sway of her body…

They came to a natural stop at a tent where a man stood, probably in his sixties, dressed in a long, dark-red robe, a knitted hat on his head. As they paused he stepped forward and greeted the gathering crowds.

'He's a story-teller,' a woman next to Darius said. 'He's telling the story of the Arabian nights.' A minute later, the man started to speak, his voice rich and compelling, seeming to weave the story in the air.

Darius glanced down at Lily and saw she was as transfixed as he. Somehow it didn't matter that they couldn't understand the actual words; the beauty of the language, the narrator's sweeping gestures and detailed actions all contributed to the telling of the story, painting a picture of magical hues and nuances, depth and meaning.

The story-teller was a man who had clearly done this job for decades, his grizzled hair and weather-beaten face a testament to his years and experience. His voice was low, deep and mesmerising as he spoke and the beauty of the words washed over them.

Darius was reminded of his mother's voice when she had told him stories, those few precious good moments in a childhood of uncertainty and survival. Times when she had perhaps only had a few hits of alcohol or drugs, or the best times of all, the times of hope, when she tried to stop. She'd sat with him on the tattered, stained sofa and woven him magical stories, her imagination coming up with characters he could remember to this day—daring, swashbuckling heroes and heroines who lived in worlds populated by pirates, wizards and magic. He wondered where she was now, and wished that he could turn around and see her telling a story in one of the stalls—beautiful, wistful, magical. But that wasn't going to happen.

The man came to an end and there were protests from the audience. The man next to them shook his head and turned to them. 'It's a good way of doing it. He's stopped on a cliff-hanger so we're all bound to come back tomorrow.'

'That was amazing,' Lily said.

Looking down at her, Darius wondered what she was thinking and whether this had transported her back to *her* childhood. 'Like a fairy tale.'

'No. Or at least, not like the fairy tales I used to believe in.'

He heard the slight note of bitterness in her voice. 'So you don't believe any more?'

'I'm a believer in stories where real people control their own fate and don't rely on happiness being provided by a handsome prince based on some mistaken idea of love. I mean, really? Cinderella meets the man of her dreams all because a fairy godmother waves a magic wand to transform her into someone beautiful? Do you think the handsome prince would even have noticed Cinderella if he'd walked past her in her rags, holding a mop? He wouldn't have given her a second glance, or if he had it would have been to order her to clean the floor. But once he thought she was a lady, all dressed up in a fancy gown with her hair done...when she looked beautiful...then it's different.

'On top of that they have a dance together and that's it, he falls in love? Hah! He only fell for her because she ran away from him, all because she thought he wouldn't like her if she wasn't in a proper dress. I mean, why would you fall for a man who only likes you if you're in a ball gown? And did you notice fairy tales all end with "they all lived happily ever after"? No detail... More likely the handsome prince had his head turned by another beautiful lady at the very next ball.'

She came to a halt and he studied her flushed face, sensing that her words had come straight from her heart.

'I can see you've given this some thought,' he said.

'Actually, I have. You can laugh but, whilst I think stories are incredibly important, fairy tales spin an unrealistic picture. "Happy ever after" does not need to involve love. Everyone deserves happiness, not just those who fate and genes have given good looks to.'

'I'm not laughing,' he said gently. 'I promise.' After

all, he didn't believe in fairy tales either. Think of his own story: abandoned by his mother, he'd been rescued by his father, a wealthy, handsome prince indeed; a king of an empire. That should have panned out into a happy ever after, but it had been a whole lot more complicated than that. 'I don't believe in fairy tales either. I believe in making your own happy ending on your terms.'

Now she looked up at him, perhaps caught by the unintended seriousness of his words, the hard intent he hadn't managed to hide.

There was a small frown on her face, her dark-blue eyes full of questions, her mobile face framed by the glossy hair, and there it was again: that *whoomph* of attraction; that desire to kiss her; that flare of desire that she could ignite so easily and instantaneously.

He forced himself to move and forced his lips to upturn into a light smile. 'Now, what would make me happy is a pancake,' he said. 'Shall we try and find Aline's stall?'

Lily nodded and they slipped back into the throng of people strolling through the square. But now, instead of looking at all the stalls and sights, he found his eyes dragged inexorably back to Lily. He realised that she was glancing at him, and every intercepted look, every awkward turn away, heightened the simmer of awareness, the tug and pull of a connection he didn't want or understand but couldn't seem to break.

'I think this must be it,' he said, aware his voice had an edge to it as he gestured to a stall that already had a long queue.

'It looks busy,' she said. 'That's great for Aline on her first day.'

Darius opened his mouth to answer then heard a shout

from the front of the queue. Before he could see what was happening, he heard Lily give an exclamation, and then she was off, moving towards the source of the noise.

Darius followed, hampered by the craning necks of others trying to work out what was going on. He firmly pushed his way through and came to a stop as he quickly digested the scene: two men, tourists who had clearly had a few glasses too many, were right at the edge of the stall, one of them shouting at the stall owner, a slight woman who was trying to placate them. He could see real fear in her eyes, and sensed on some level that this woman had been hurt before... A sudden memory flashed into his brain of himself as a boy, cowering before one of his mum's boyfriends.

Then from nowhere Lily emerged, clearly utterly unafraid as she strode up to the man, and Darius felt a tug of admiration.

'Is there a problem?' Her voice was crystal-clear.

'Yes, lady, there is a problem and I'm dealing with it. I've been waiting fifteen minutes. I'm fed up and I'm talking to this incompetent here, asking her what she's gonna do about it. So get out of my way.'

Lily stood her ground, seemingly not even aware as Darius stepped forward. 'I don't think so. I heard what you said to her and it was unacceptable.' Her voice was tight with outrage, etched with disdain.

'I'm warning you to mind your own business or...'

'Or what?' Darius kept his voice calm and his eye on the crowd. He saw the man's companion step forward in an aggressive lurch and heard the murmur as others too seemed ready to enter the fray. He knew security patrolled the square but he had no idea how long they would take to get here.

'Or I'll move her out of the way myself.'

Lily stepped forward. 'I don't think so,' she said, seemingly still unfazed by the man's threatening tone.

'Neither do I.' Darius raised his voice. 'But I think we all have a choice here. I don't want a fight, but I won't let you hurt anyone.' His voice was hard; he might not have been able to protect himself or his mother aged seven, but he damn well could defend himself now. 'But I'd also rather not be dragged off by security to the local police station. So how about you get back into the queue and wait for your pancake?'

There was a pause and he could see the man thinking. 'Argh! Stuff the pancakes,' he said. 'We're taking our business elsewhere. With that he left, and Darius saw Lily suddenly falter, as if the adrenalin that had been fuelling her had suddenly run dry.

'Are you OK?' he asked, moving towards her.

'Yes… I… It…' She took a deep breath. 'I'm fine. More to the point, we need to see if Aline is all right. She headed towards the stall owner and Darius followed.

'Thank you for the help,' Aline said, a faint tremble in her voice.

'No problem. We've just come from Jamal and Natalia,' Darius said. 'Natalia told us to try a pancake.'

'I am glad you were here. Please, if you will wait, I will make you both a pancake, but first…'

'First,' Lily said, 'You have a lot of customers. I think you could use some help. I'll stay until the queue gets more manageable.'

Darius blinked; a lot of women he knew would have felt they had done enough and would have suggested that Aline pack up and finish early. Instead, Lily was offering practical help. Perhaps because she knew what it was like to start out and set up a business, and so did he. Knew too the sense of despair when it felt as though an idea wasn't going to work.

'Good idea,' Darius said. 'How shall we do it? I'm happy to take orders and manage the money. Or I can help out with the pancakes?'

Surprise touched Lily's face and Darius knew she'd assumed he'd walk away. She probably thought he'd consider helping on a stall to be beneath him or something. Frustration touched him at the judgment, though perhaps he should be pleased. Her assumptions about who he was were at least a barrier to help keep attraction at bay. Yet it rankled.

Then she smiled, a smile that held a sudden warmth that seemed to flood him with a sense of happiness. 'It makes more sense if I help with the cooking,' she said.

'Sure. We can swap after a while.'

'But...' Aline looked a bit taken aback. 'You don't have to. I can manage.'

'We want to,' Darius said briskly.

Aline hesitated, looked at the queue and then nodded. 'Thank you.'

Soon enough they got into a rhythm. Darius got his head round the unfamiliar currency, and he could see that Lily and Aline had worked out the best way to work in tandem. He watched as Aline visibly relaxed, smiled even; he also saw how hard Lily worked. Never once did she look resentful, or as though she wished she were somewhere else. Respect and admiration touched him at her genuine kindness as two hours sped past, the queue started to die down and around them stall holders started to shut up shop.

'I don't know how to thank you,' Aline said softly. 'Please let me pay you or...'

'Absolutely not,' Lily said firmly. 'Your family gave us an amazing meal on the house. This can be our payback.'

Aline hesitated. 'Please do not tell Jamal about what happened. I had a helper lined up but he couldn't make it today. He will be here tomorrow, so this won't happen again, so there is no need for Jamal to worry. He is not really my family and he has already helped me and others like me so much. He runs a scheme for young adults who have had...difficulties in life.'

The young woman's voice was deliberately devoid of all emotion, the words said carefully, as if she had rehearsed them many times to try to make them more palatable. 'He takes us in and teaches us how to cook. I... owe him a lot and now I want him to see that I have succeeded, not that I am weak and need more help.'

'Needing help doesn't make you weak,' Lily said softly.

'It doesn't,' Darius said. 'But I understand you want to show Jamal that you can stand on your own two feet. So how about we make a deal? We agree not to tell Jamal, but if your helper can't make it tomorrow you either tell us and we will help out or you call Jamal and ask him.'

'Promise us that you won't do this alone tomorrow,' Lily said.

'I promise.' Aline's voice was fervent. 'Thank you for understanding. Now, really you can go.' She waved. 'I have someone coming to pick me up and take me home— here he is now. '

They waited until the man approached and greeted Aline, then they said their goodbyes and headed towards the exit.

'That was nice of you,' Lily said after a silence that had felt companionable, two people walking after a job well done.

'What was?'

'All of it—getting involved.' She puffed out a sigh. 'We were meant to be getting lost in the crowd, keeping a low profile. I'm sorry.'

'You've nothing to apologise for. You didn't ask that man to get aggressive and you didn't ask me to step in. You were doing pretty well by yourself. It was brave of you to confront him and defend Aline.' It really had been; her desire to protect a woman she didn't know had impressed itself on him, all the more because she didn't seem to rate it as unusual or praiseworthy herself.

'It wasn't brave, not really. I did it on instinct. Aline looked terrified, and that man was a bully, nothing more. Bullies prey on those they perceive to be vulnerable—the key is not to show fear even if you are feeling it. It doesn't necessarily stop them, but they feed off fear.'

She pressed her lips together, as if she'd said too much, and he wondered if she was speaking from her own experience. If Aline's experience had resonated with her in the same way it had done with him on a personal level. 'Thank you for stepping up, for supporting me.'

'Did you think I'd run away?' That truly rankled.

'No. I thought you'd go and get security rather than risk being recognised. And I definitely didn't expect you to help serve pancakes all night.' She paused. 'Why did you?'

'Why did I help? Because I wanted to help her.' It was that simple. He'd sensed a kinship with Aline, even before she'd hinted at a childhood of difficulty. He knew what that felt like. 'And I admire what she is doing. A difficult childhood sometimes leads to a lifetime of difficulty, getting into trouble. She is making something of her life, and I get that she wants to do it on her own—prove herself.'

'That she can stand on her own two feet.'

'Yes.' They looked at each other and, almost against his will, Darius smiled and Lily smiled back. He had a sudden urge to pull her into his arms, but of course he didn't. Instead, he glanced at his watch. 'We'd better get back. Where are you staying? We'll get a taxi and I'll drop you off first.'

There was a silence and Lily's eyes widened. 'Actually, I don't know. Gemma was going to sort that out and with…everything this evening I totally forgot. But it's fine. I'll stay in the villa.'

'No.' Darius had no intention of letting her do anything of the sort. 'It's nearly midnight and the lock isn't even reliable. I'll book you into my hotel.' He frowned. 'In fact, I took over Gemma's booking, so she may well have booked you a room there anyway.'

He pulled out his phone and called the hotel. 'Darius Kingsleigh here. Can I check whether Gemma Fairley-Godfrey made a booking for my colleague, Lily Culpepper?' A minute later he put his phone back in his pocket and nodded. 'All sorted. You're already on the system. Where's your luggage?'

'At the villa. But I can manage until tomorrow, assuming I can get a toothbrush from somewhere.'

'I'm sure the hotel supplies all that.'

'Then let's go.'

CHAPTER SIX

TEN MINUTES LATER they walked down a cobbled alley and into a courtyard that housed a majestic, sprawling rose-pink building more akin to a stately home than a hotel. They followed the illuminated mosaic pathway to the entrance. The lobby was an expanse of splendour with marble floors and imposing pillars tiled in tiny mosaic tiles, surrounded by intricate plaster work. The walls were covered in an opulence of mirrors and panels.

As they stood at the vast reception desk Lily tried to think, her head awhirl with the day's events as she looked at Darius. Impossible now to hold on to the original antipathy she'd felt for him, however hard she tried. Because, however dubious his morals might be in his relationships, he had exhibited nothing but courtesy and kindness to Jamal, Natalia and Aline.

He'd stood by her side and seen off the bullies, and his presence had steadied her, helped her stand her ground. She'd been aware of a warmth at seeing his protective instinct, and seeing his willingness to help Aline had helped her repel her own memories triggered by seeing Aline's fear. It had been a reminder of how fearful she had once been at the mercy of her stepsisters. But she didn't want to see Darius as a knight in shining armour, and didn't

want to like him, that would make the unwanted attraction even more complicated.

A man approached them, a smile on his face. 'Mr
Kingsleigh, it is good to see you. And you must be Ms
Culpepper. I will show you both to your suite.'

Suite? Singular?

Darius frowned. 'I assumed Ms Culpepper had a separate room booked.'

'No. Lady Fairley-Godfrey booked a suite as that was
all we had available. But there are two bedrooms and
two bathrooms. We have no other free rooms. Will this
be all right?'

Darius looked across at Lily and she tried to keep her
face composed. Two *en suite* rooms in one suite: it was
no different from having two separate rooms, not really.
Yet the idea felt too…intimate, too close, too much. But
she could hardly say that; after all, if it were any other
professional colleague she wouldn't have had an issue
with this.

'That sounds fine,' she said.

'Then I will show you the way.' They followed him
along rug-covered floors surrounded by crimson walls
and wrought-iron lanterns that illuminated the detailed
woodwork, the glass cabinets that encased vases, bowls
and sculptures, until they arrived at their suite.

The door was opened with a flourish. Lily stopped
on the threshold and blinked at the sheer splendour of
the room. Massive chandeliers hung from vaulted ceilings, and brass lanterns illuminated and shadowed the
aubergine-coloured walls adorned with art deco mirrors
with silver-and-gilt swirls. The furniture was resplendent
regency style, padded with purple velvet, whilst heavy-

swagged crimson curtains framed stained-glass windows and doors leading onto a private balcony.

The staff member walked forward and pulled open the bedroom doors to reveal similarly styled bedrooms, both containing king-size beds and walk-in wardrobes, the floors covered with Moroccan rugs and the walls stencilled with safari animals. Further inspection revealed enormous bathrooms with golden sinks, whirlpool baths and sumptuously soft towels.

'Thank you,' Lily managed. 'This all looks wonderful.'

The manager smiled and soon after he departed, leaving Lily and Darius to regard each other in silence.

Darius studied her face. 'Are you truly all right with this?'

'Yes.' She strove to put sincerity into the syllable. She refused to acknowledge that she felt edgy, not because she didn't trust him, but perhaps because she didn't trust herself. The unwanted attraction, the sense that something had shifted over the evening and a sense of intimacy were all messing with her head. But she wouldn't let it. She was a professional; Darius was a business colleague. 'Completely. I'm looking forward to getting to work.'

His grey eyes remained on her face. 'How about we start now? We could sit on the balcony and have a cup of tea.'

Lily gave a sudden smile; she couldn't help it.

'What?'

'Nothing. I just didn't associate the idea of "a cup of tea" with Darius Kingsleigh.'

'Nothing wrong with a good old-fashioned cuppa,' he said. 'Proper tea that a spoon can stand up in, that's what my mum used to say.' He caught his lip between his teeth and she sensed he hadn't meant to say that, though he continued smoothly enough. 'But, in this case, it is mint tea on offer, if that's OK?'

'That's fine, and I'd love to start planning now,' she said, suddenly aware of how little she knew about him. She knew he'd been taken in by his natural father Enzo Kingsleigh as a child. That had stuck in her head simply because it had been a childhood fantasy of her own: that her natural father would somehow discover her existence and track her down, even though she knew the impossibility of that happening. But she knew nothing about his mother; she couldn't recall any mention of Darius's life before Enzo.

She watched as Darius made the tea, looking at the deft movements, the curve of his forearm and the lithe breadth of his body. Her tummy clenched with sudden intense desire and she looked away and went out to wait on the balcony. Looked out at the view of the illuminated courtyard, complete with mosaic floors, and a water fountain providing a musical flow of water against a backdrop of potted plants and marbled pillars. The whole place was deserted and she assumed it was either closed overnight or was only for private use.

Darius brought out a tray and placed it on the table, before sitting opposite her. She concentrated on pouring the tea, hoping her hands wouldn't tremble.

'Right,' she said. 'We need to work out what order to do things in and how best to divide and share different tasks. Obviously, we need to clean the villa. I didn't have much of a chance to look over it earlier, but I could see it is quite a mammoth task. I may need to get extra help.'

'That's no problem. We can hire professional cleaners.'

'I also want to go the local souks to get local soaps and shampoos that we can try out, and then pick and choose for the guests. And I need to inventory plates, glasses and so on.'

'We also need caterers.'

Lily sipped the tea as ideas started to fizz and pop in her head. 'For the canapés, we could ask real street vendors to put up their stalls at the villa itself, perhaps in the courtyard, and we could get waiting staff to carry the food to the guests.'

'I like it.' His face lit now with an enthusiasm that mirrored her own. 'Aline could do pancakes, and maybe some of Jamal's other protégé chefs could run stalls.'

'Jamal and his team could cater the sit-down dinner.'

'We can make it a really authentic Marrakesh-themed event.'

'Yes, set a stage up, have a storyteller—maybe a local dance troupe—then clear the floor and have a band and dancing.'

Adrenalin surged through her. 'It's a plan.'

'It's better than that. It's an awesome plan.' He rose to his feet. 'And it deserves something more than tea.'

Once he'd exited the balcony, Lily rose to her feet, energised by the brainstorming session and the way they'd sparked off each other. Glancing at her watch, she saw how late it was and yet she wasn't tired. She leant against the railings, turning as he re-joined her and handed her a glass of champagne. She gestured to the view—the traditional architecture, the magical flow of the waterfall, the intricate design of the tiles— and inhaled the scent of orange blossom that pervaded the air. 'Midnight in Marrakesh,' she said. 'Isn't it beautiful?'

'Yes,' he said, his voice deep, and heat touched her face as she realised he wasn't looking at the courtyard. He was looking at her. He raised his champagne glass. 'To us.'

'To us,' she echoed. They both sipped, and now it wasn't only her brain that hummed. Moonlight glinted, highlighting his dark hair with a coppery sheen, and she could see the swell of muscle, the craggy features and his eyes, silvery-grey now as they met hers.

Something shifted, the silver-grey darkened, his eyes full of intent and promise. She could see desire and sense the swirl, pull and lure of attraction, a magnet inexorably pulling her in. Her feet moved forward without her permission, and then he also stepped forward, and somehow the glass was no longer in her hand; it was on the table and she was in his arms.

Anticipation and butterflies skittered around her tummy in a flotilla, and a shiver flitted over her skin. Then he lowered his mouth onto hers; the feel of his lips against hers unleashed a need, a yearning for more that it was impossible to deny. Not when he was so close with the scent of him, the taste of him, the feel of his body against hers.

Her lips parted and then he kissed her for real and she was lost, lost in the swirling tornado of desire and heat. She pressed against the hard, muscular length of his body and now her arms were looped round his neck.

The distant blare of a horn broke the spell and Lily pulled away, jumped back and stood still, breath ragged in the night air. What had she done? What about professionalism? Hell, she'd practically plastered herself all over him.

She had no idea what to do, what to say or how to retrieve the situation. 'Sorry,' she blurted and, turning, she half-walked, half-ran towards the suite. The best thing, the only thing, to do right now was hide. Work out a plan, a way to erase the past ten minutes: find some dignity.

Darius watched her go, and tried to work out what to do next, but his brain seemed incapable of rational thought. His whole being was still caught up in the kiss, a kiss that had blown his mind; every sense was heightened, his body still on high alert, taut with frustrated desire. A desire he had to dampen, ignore, get rid of.

He hadn't meant to kiss her, but it had been impossible not to. She'd been so beautiful, so infinitely desirable, her eyes sparkling in the moonlight, her passion for the job spilling over; she had been irresistible.

He'd broken all the rules. They were working together, and he'd known she felt uncomfortable staying in the same suite. He wouldn't blame Lily for leaving and quitting the job.

Guilt touched him. Why did this attraction have such power? Perhaps it was a simple case of timing—he hadn't been on so much as a date in the past two years. But it felt more than that—something visceral with a mind of its own—and that made him edgy. He couldn't turn back the clock, couldn't erase that kiss. But he could ensure that it wouldn't happen again. How hard could it be *not* to kiss someone?

Should he go and try and talk to her? He couldn't— to go and knock on her bedroom door would send the wrong signal completely. The only thing to do was to wait until morning. Then he'd apologise, assure her that he would not overstep the professional boundary again. And he wouldn't.

All he could do now was try to sleep…a state he eventually achieved, only to be woken by a banging on his door what seemed like minutes later.

He opened his eyes, instantly awake, and swung his legs out of the bed, tugged on his jeans, grabbed a T-shirt, made his way to the door and pulled it open.

'Are you OK? What's wrong?'

'I…' She stepped back and heat touched her cheeks as her gaze focused on his bare chest; he'd swear she gulped. 'Everything is wrong.'

'Can you be more specific?' He tugged the T-shirt over his head. 'Tell me.' Lily's blue eyes were full of panic. 'Define "everything"…'

CHAPTER SEVEN

LILY DIDN'T KNOW where to begin, but she did know everything really had gone horribly wrong.

She wasn't sure how long her phone had rung for, but she'd grabbed it, half-asleep, her head filled with fuzzy dreams featuring Darius and that kiss. She'd opened her eyes to take in the grandeur of her surroundings.

'Mum?' She'd wondered why Maria would be calling her at this hour. 'Is everything OK?'

'Well, darling, you tell me. I'm calling to congratulate you. You've finally taken my advice and made a fabulous conquest.'

'Huh?' The first tendril of panic had started to unfold.

'Darius Kingsleigh.'

'I told you I had dinner with a client. That client is Darius Kingsleigh.'

Maria had laughed, a deep and dirty chuckle. 'Well, sweetheart, if that's a client you're in a different profession than I thought. I think you should have a look at the pictures on social media.'

So Lily had done exactly that, and then she'd panicked big-time, leapt out of bed and now here they were.

'So?' Darius asked. 'What's going on?' There was a knot of impatience in his voice now and Lily gestured to the round glass table in the middle of the room, then went and sat down.

'We've been spotted. There are pictures of us from this evening…including the kiss.'

Darius did some inventive swearing, pulled out his phone, scrolled down, closed his eyes and opened them again. 'OK. This isn't good.'

'You think?' Lily shook her head. 'It's…disastrous.' Her tummy churned with horror at the situation. Everything had been bad enough before but at least then the only person she'd been hiding from was Darius. Now she wanted to hide from the whole world but there was nowhere to hide.

He drummed his fingers on the table and she took some comfort from the fact he seemed to grasp the scale of the disaster. 'Then we have to turn disaster into something palatable.'

'Palatable?' she echoed. 'There is nothing palatable about this.' She gestured to his phone, holder of the proof, pictures that even now people were looking at. 'Denial isn't going to work, is it?'

'No.'

'Then what are we going to do?' She rose to her feet and started to pace, her mind spinning. 'What am *I* going to do?' Ramifications and scenarios all whirled through her head. 'My family, my friends, my *clients* are going to see those pictures…of me plastered all over *you*. That is mortifying. They are going to think…'

That she was shallow, that she was a gold-digger, that she wanted her five seconds of fame, happy to be another proverbial notch on his bed post, another in a line of women…

Worse. 'Oh, God, you are my client. People are going to think I sleep with my clients! They may even think that I got this job because of that. My professional reputation will go down the pan.' Her stride increased with each word, hands clenched, jaw set, and then she came up against Darius. She came to a halt, looked up at him and tried to read his expression.

'Lily, slow down.'

'I can't slow down. And I can't think of a solution.' Lily inhaled deeply. It was time to pull herself together; she'd spent her life working out coping strategies. She'd coped with not knowing who her dad was, with her mother's lifestyle, with the bullying of her stepsisters and the heartbreak and humiliation of her break-up with Tom. Now it was time to stop acting like a drama queen and work out how to cope with this.

'Sorry,' she said. 'I just hate the idea that that kiss is out there being pored over, and I hate how it's going to impact my business.'

'I get that,' he said. 'Truly I do.' Lily studied his expression and heard the sincerity. 'We'll work this out,' he continued. 'But not here. If the press really decide to jump on it, they'll start making a nuisance of themselves here.'

He drummed his fingers on his thigh and she found her gaze fixated on the movement, on the strength of his fingers, the muscular sturdiness of the denim-clad muscle. 'I suggest we move.' He glanced at his watch. 'We can sneak out the back, mingle with the crowds and come up with a strategy.'

'That didn't work so well yesterday,' she pointed out.

'No, but yesterday someone at the restaurant must have tipped the photographer off...said where we were going.

Yesterday I wasn't really even sure we were being followed. Today is different, and today they know we are here.'

'Then let's get out of here.'

Fifteen minutes later Darius glanced round quickly as they left the hotel into a deserted alleyway.

'You've obviously done this before,' Lily said, pulling the brim of her sun hat down slightly.

'The important thing to do is look as though you belong, that you're just another tourist out for a look at early-morning Marrakesh.'

'OK. I'll try.'

'I know how worried you are about this.' He knew and understood her concerns. It didn't look good to be caught on camera in a thoroughly unprofessional, passionate clinch with your client, not for her and not for him. Anger at himself propelled his stride; those pictures hardly portrayed the businessman's persona he had worked so hard to show the world. Instead, they'd reignite his playboy image, and it couldn't be worse timing.

He glanced at his watch. 'Let's head to one of the city gardens,' he said. 'Find somewhere secluded to talk.'

Tickets purchased, they headed across the turquoise-blue mosaic courtyard past an array of plants. Rosemary from the hedges scented the air, along with a citrus aroma. Different hues of green contrasted and blended into a verdant oasis, succulents, grass and trees all combining to create an aura of tranquillity and peace.

'This is a good place to think,' she said as they sat on a secluded bench. 'Or at least I hope it is. Otherwise maybe I could stay right here until this all goes away.'

He could see the worry in her dark-blue eyes and guilt

touched him. Damn it—he'd known there was a risk of publicity but last night he hadn't given it a thought. Kissing Lily had seemed so right, so inevitable, and desire had taken over thought or reason.

And so he'd handed over a story all because he hadn't been able to control this damned attraction. Now they were both up the proverbial creek and he'd better find a paddle. He closed his eyes, welcoming the heat of the early-morning sunshine on his face, and allowed his mind to roam, to think. Desperation galvanised his thought process, planting the seeds of a plan. 'I've got an idea,' he said.

'Go ahead,'

'We fake a relationship. We already set the scene in the restaurant last night. Jamal and his family already believe we are a genuine couple. We say that you were hired for the role by Gemma, Gemma introduced us, *then* we became a couple, so Gemma suggested we come to Morocco together. That way you would have been hired before you even met me, when Gemma was the client.'

There was a silence and then she sighed, shaking her head. 'It's a good idea, but it wouldn't work.'

'Why not?'

'You. And me?' Another shake. 'It couldn't happen.'

'Why not?'

'Because it simply doesn't work. I wouldn't date you and you wouldn't date me.'

'I hate to be repetitive but…why not?'

'For a start, you date beautiful celebrities. I'm neither.'

There it was again, that faint but unmistakable hint of disapproval and, damn it, it still irked him, put him on the back foot. 'You're right that I've only ever dated celebrities, but there are reasons for that. When you're a millionaire, it makes sense to date women who you know aren't after your money, or only with you for the lifestyle. People who have money and status of their own. People who are used to being in the public eye and enjoy it, who aren't phased by the attention. So, yes, I deliberately chose to date people like that, but that doesn't mean I wouldn't date a non-celebrity.'

'And I'm not beautiful.' Her gaze met his full-on. 'I'm not fishing for compliments, it's a fact. Like most people, I'm not super-model material. And I don't have any "it factor".'

Darius stared at her. 'To me, you are beautiful.' Seeing the scepticism on her face, he continued, wanting her to know that was truth. 'That's what attraction is: it's nothing to do with "super-model" beauty. Sure, a few people have universal appeal because of their looks or status. They will turn heads when they enter a room, but that's neither here nor there. That's not individual "it factor", the real thing.' He looked at her, saw she was looking down at the table, knew that for some reason Lily didn't believe him. 'Look at me,' he said softly. 'That kiss last night, that was the real thing.'

And in that moment he relived it again, and so did she. He could see it in her slightly parted lips and in the widened dark-blue eyes that skimmed over his own lips and lingered before she looked back at him. She raised a hand to her lips, as if she could feel remembered sensations.

'The real thing can happen between any two people, beautiful or not, famous or not…a genuine chemistry that is unique to them. It's not explicable, but it's there, and it can be ignited by a brush of the hands, a laugh, a look, a smile…' He shrugged. 'We have that, and that is obvious. People will believe we are a couple—a proper couple.' Now his brain was firing. 'In fact, it's *better* that you aren't a celebrity.'

She eyed him with more than a hint of scepticism. 'Why?'

'Because if we portray ourselves as being in an actual real relationship, not a fling or a one-night stand but something *serious*, that takes away the stigma of being unprofessional.' It would allow him to use the publicity to counter his playboy image and show he'd evolved. 'I think we can pull this off. What do you think?'

It was a good question that Lily didn't know the answer to; her brain still fogged with the volatile swirl of emotions, a sense of the surreal, enhanced by his statement that their chemistry was real, that the kiss had been the real thing. Lily couldn't help it; that knowledge sent a thrill through her veins that the burn of need and yearning had been mutual.

What was wrong with her? This wasn't about desire; this was about salvaging her business reputation that was at stake because she'd given in to an unprofessional attraction. So, would Darius's idea work?

She closed her eyes and tried to imagine pretending to be in a relationship with Darius—the speculation, the publicity, being seen as a woman either foolish enough to fall for a playboy's charms, or a gold-digger chasing wealth and fame. The idea was abhorrent.

But the alternative was worse—being seen as a woman who slept with her clients in order to win business, or simply casually slept with them willy-nilly, with no thought of professional ethics and boundaries.

She was caught between a rock and a hard place, but in truth the choice was obvious. She would not let her business suffer, because nothing meant more to her than the business she had built up. It was solid, incontrovertible proof that she had succeeded when no one, including her, had believed she would. The bullying at school had knocked her confidence to sub-zero levels and it had had a disastrous impact on her studies. The number of times her school work had been ruined… The lack of sleep because she was too terrified to close her eyes, an inability to concentrate in class, had all resulted in grades that portrayed her as an unqualified failure.

Left behind at home whilst, thankfully, her stepsisters had gone on to further education, she'd found a job as a cleaner.

Her mother had thrown up her hands in despair yet again. 'But why, darling? Let me send you to a different type of school, with Cynthia—one where they teach you how to make the best of yourself. Then you can win yourself a man, and kaboom!'

Those words had crystallised in Lily a determination to succeed in her own right; she'd worked all hours, saved and eventually launched her own company. She'd built a reputation and a client base that now included Lady Gemma Fairley-Godfrey. No way would she jeopardise any of that—not over some hormonal reaction. If she had to fake a relationship, then so be it. She'd messed up: she'd pay the price.

'I'll do it,' she said, hearing the reluctance in her voice.

He studied her face. 'I said we *could* pull it off. We won't be able to if you feel so much antipathy to the idea.'

Lily sighed. 'You can hardly expect me to be enthusiastic,' she pointed out. 'Our attraction may exist but it's landed us in a complete mess. And I am now going to have to fake feelings for you when...'

'You don't even like me?' he suggested, and she'd swear there was a hint of hurt in his voice.

'When I don't even know you,' she said. 'But it's not that. People will class me as a fool for falling for a play-boy or believe I am a gold-digger. Then, when we end it, I will be seen as another discarded girlfriend.'

'I don't discard my girlfriends. I don't discard anyone. My relationships are short-term but that's through mutual agreement.' His voice was even, but she could hear anger in it, but knew that she couldn't let him get away with that statement.

'What about Ruby AllStar?' Lily recalled reading about the break-up, the article etched in her memory. She'd been sitting in her bed under the duvet, a tub of chocolate-chip ice-cream by her side, desperately trying not to relive the bitter humiliation of her own break-up with Tom. Trying not to let the scene replay again and again, trying not to let his words repeat on loop...

'I'm sorry, Lily, truly. I never meant this to happen.'

Her own words: 'Can't you see? Cynthia is using you... She's taken you to hurt me.'

His reply: 'Maybe. But, if I'd truly loved you, I wouldn't have been available to be taken. Whatever happens with Cynthia and I... I can't have loved you.'

His voice had been gentle and she'd seen sadness and finality in his brown eyes. And, worst of all, she'd seen pity.

When she'd read the interview with Ruby AllStar, outlining her feelings after being 'discarded' by Darius

Kingsleigh, Lily had identified with the singer's obvious heartbreak, the details resonating with her own situation.

'You broke her heart,' she said now and, seeing his lips set in a tight line, knew she'd touched a nerve. 'Led her on to believe you meant commitment. Strung her along, made promises you had no intention of keeping.'

'And you know this how—from one interview?'

Lily opened her mouth and closed it again.

'You are basing your entire opinion on one woman's version of events, letting her rewrite history.'

His words collided with her anger as their truth hit her. Letting one woman rewrite history: as her stepsisters had written theirs, making the bullying, fear and terror they'd inspired into something trivial, almost jokey. Making everyone accept their version of events so no one was inclined to listen to Lily's side, let alone believe it. Until even Lily had started to question events and her own memories.

Had that happened to Darius? As far as she knew, he'd never refuted Ruby's claims, and had never given his side, even as speculation, accusations and opinion pieces had run rife. But that didn't mean it didn't exist.

'You're right,' she said now. 'Tell me your version.'

Darius hadn't expected that, had thought Lily would double down. He'd never told anyone the truth about Ruby, but he wanted to tell Lily. To his own annoyance her accusation had set him on edge, and he suspected that this was the crux of her disapproval of him, her judgment. If they were going to fake a relationship, they had to get past it. But, more than that, he *wanted* to overturn her

judgment, remove the hint of disapproval in her deal-
ings with him.

He took a moment and then began. 'My relationship
with Ruby started like all my others. I explained up front
that all I was looking for was a short-term, fun relationship that had no chance of leading to anything serious.
And Ruby agreed to that. I wouldn't have gone on a second date if she hadn't or if I didn't believe her.'

'Then what happened?'

He hesitated. 'From my point of view, nothing. I
thought everything was on track, that we were having
fun. We got to the ten-week mark and I was about to suggest we bring things to the agreed end. Ruby was on tour
so I waited until she got back. I assumed she'd been expecting it. Instead, she got really upset. Said she thought
that, because we'd exceeded ten weeks, she thought she
was different, that I loved her and wanted something
long-term. She told me she'd changed, wanted more...
that she loved me.'

He could remember the sense of horror along with
sheer bewilderment, his weak attempts to justify, explain, when she'd asked how he could abandon her. An
echo of the question he'd asked himself about his mother
all his life.

'Didn't you realise, see any signs?' There was scepticism in Lily's tone and he couldn't really blame her.

'No, I truly didn't. If I had, I would have done something, ended it sooner at the very least. I had no intention of hurting Ruby.'

He'd never wanted to hurt any woman and he'd decided
the best way to do that was never to commit. Because
he knew he didn't get it, didn't have what it took. How

could he? He'd believed his mum loved him and she'd left; he'd spent years, decades, trying to win his father's love and had failed. Darius was bright enough to know a background like that did not give anyone a good start in the love stakes, knew he wasn't capable of long-term commitment. 'I know I got it wrong. I miscalculated.'

'This isn't about calculations, it's about feelings.'

'I don't understand feelings. I understand calculations, programming. Feelings are too messy, too complicated, too risky. I don't want any of that. Which is why I don't look for long-term relationships and why I *agree* terms up front. The other person needs to be on board too. Ruby was at the start and then she changed the rules, rewrote the terms and made it into a story, an illusion.'

'She didn't change the terms. Her feelings changed and she thought yours had too. She believed in love, believed she was loveable. Is that so wrong?' The anger was muted now, and he could see a shadow in her blue eyes, a sadness on her face, and he wanted to reach out and smooth it away.

'No.' He shook his head. 'It wasn't wrong. But she should have told me. That way, perhaps I could at least have stopped the whole misconception early. I won't change—I don't understand feelings, so I don't want love or commitment, but I don't want to hurt anyone either. That was never my intention. I thought being upfront meant I had it covered. I didn't.'

'Maybe you can't always have it covered,' she said, and now he heard a sadness in her voice. 'But I appreciate that you tried, that you try to minimise the risk of hurting someone by keeping it short-term and being honest. I am sorry for Ruby, but I do see you didn't lead her on.'

He sensed that she thinking of something in her own past, perhaps a past relationship.

'Thank you for telling me your side, and I'm sorry. I shouldn't have judged you based on a tabloid article. Shouldn't have disapproved of your lifestyle without understanding your motivations.'

The apology disarmed him; the idea someone had listened to him and come back with a positive judgment warmed him. He smiled at her; she smiled back and the impact jolted him. She looked so god damned beautiful with the sunlight glinting blonde highlights into her glossy brown hair, dappling the strands in sunlight. Her eyes sparkled, luminous, and he wished it all wasn't so complicated; he wished that he didn't have so much baggage and that he could be one of those people who understood love and commitment.

He shook his head to dislodge the absurdity of the thought, self-aware enough to know that it was generated by the unfamiliar warmth of approval and understanding. Reminded himself that he did not need validation from anyone except himself. This wasn't about validation. It was about maximising spin so that they could both protect their business reputations.

'Thank you for listening,' he said. 'And I do understand your concerns. If we go ahead with this, when we break up you can be the instigator. You will not be seen as a discarded girlfriend, I promise. For now, I suggest we go on the offensive—embrace the publicity, stress that it is early days but that we are serious, though right now our focus is on the fundraiser. We can use the publicity to promote the charity then, once the fundraiser is over, our relationship can become long distance, media interest should die down and we can fizzle out. How does that sound?'

Lily hesitated. 'That sounds…as though it could work.' She clenched her hands into fists. 'It has to.'

'Agreed.'

'So what next?' she asked.

'We should move out of the hotel. I suggest we stay in the villa—it will be easier to avoid undue press attention. I'll sort out a cleaning team now to blitz the place. That way, we can move in later today.'

She nodded. 'OK. I'd better call my mum. Before we go public, I'll try our story out on her.'

CHAPTER EIGHT

AS LILY LISTENED to the buzz of the phone, nerves strummed through her, along with a disbelief that she had agreed to this. On some level it sounded utterly bonkers, but somehow Darius had made it sound possible, believable, and a sudden unexpected frisson ran through her, along with a determination to make it work.

'Lily?' Her mum's voice was sharp. 'What's the update?'

'I didn't tell you before, I didn't tell anyone before, but Darius and I have been seeing each other. Lady Fairley-Godfrey introduced us, and when she couldn't come across to Morocco she suggested we work together. We wanted to keep it under the radar, because we didn't want any press intrusion, but obviously it's a bit late for that now.'

Lily came to a stop and held her breath, wondering if her mum would buy it, and wondering if she even wanted her to. Because telling her mum that she was dating a millionaire… That was *embarrassing*. She was doing the exact thing her mother had advised her to do and she could almost hear her mum's brain whirring and calculating.

'Hmm.' Maria's voice was thoughtful. 'Well… I hadn't expected that. I thought he kissed you because he was a bit bored and you were there and available.'

Lily gritted her teeth, wondering if there was any truth

in that. She tried to recall Darius's words, telling her the attraction was real and mutual. 'Out of interest, why did you think I kissed him?'

'Because the man is drop-dead gorgeous and you couldn't help yourself.' *Fair point.* 'But this changes things. I know you don't agree with my attitude to men, but please, for once just listen. Darius is dating you for a reason—most likely it's the novelty factor. So use this opportunity. Make the most of it. Get publicity for your business, get gifts, get *something...*'

Lily opened her mouth and closed it again. Her mother was suggesting a deal, and in truth that was exactly what this relationship was: a deal, like all her mother's relationships. Especially the one with her father, whoever he was. Lily pushed the question away; she'd accepted that her mother did not want to disclose the information; that no amount of cajoling, begging, shouting and reasoning would change her mind. Her mother had made a deal and, to give Maria her due, she kept her side of any bargain she made.

Like Darius did with his relationships. The idea, the similarities, made her edgy. Lily took a deep breath. She and Darius might have made a deal but it was not equivalent to what her mother had done. This relationship with a millionaire was strictly on paper only and, once it was over, she would tell Maria the truth.

But for now, she said, 'Mum, it's really early days. I just wanted to let you know what's going on.'

'Early days may be all you have. Make sure you get something from him.'

'I don't need anything from him. I earn my own money, good money. I have a business and a job I love.'

There was a silence and she felt the familiar frustration that her mum didn't get it; that she didn't understand Lily at all. The gulf between them was so wide she wondered if it would ever be possible to bridge it. If perhaps one day her mother would profess pride in Lily's achievements. The hope became more forlorn with each passing day.

But, all that aside, her mother was an expert on wealthy men and how to lure them in; if she had suggested that Darius had kissed her because he was bored or for the novelty factor, she was probably spot-on.

The idea was unwelcome, and Lily glanced at him, further irritated by how god damned gorgeous he was, standing in the Moroccan sunshine, phone to his ear. Her face creased into a scowl. As if sensing her scrutiny, he turned and studied her expression and then to her intense surprise he pulled a funny face. A genuine, slapstick-comedy screwing up of his features, along with a waggle of first one eyebrow than another. She couldn't help it; she smiled, the scowl chased away.

And he smiled back, a real humdinger of a smile that lit and creased his grey eyes. And now desire hummed inside her and she couldn't help but focus on the strength of his features, the shifting colours in his grey eyes, the line of his jaw and the shape of his lips. How could he make her feel like this without so much as touching her?

She didn't know, and suddenly she didn't care, recalling his voice, the way he'd looked at her when he'd told her that what they had was 'the real thing'. Maybe it didn't matter if that was generated by the novelty factor; hell, this was completely novel for her too. Nothing had prepared her for this; her body had taken on a life of its own, the common-sense part of her brain shut down by the sheer intensity of desire.

What had her mum said? To make the most of the opportunity. Her mother had meant in terms of monetary gain; well, maybe there was another way to look at it. She was stuck with this fake relationship, but she had a choice—to see it as a penance or an opportunity.

Right now, she wasn't sure exactly what that meant, but a shiver of anticipation skittered through her as he dropped his phone into his pocket and headed towards her.

'All sorted,' he said. 'Cleaners are going in to blitz the villa right now. I've also put some feelers out for a potential band.'

'Perfect. That frees us up to go shopping,' She must not forget that they were here to organise a fundraiser as well as faking a relationship. 'There is also a chance we will be recognised or snapped, so we need to look convincing at all times. Do you think we should hold hands?'

There was a pause and she sensed his reluctance, and on some level she understood it. Holding hands did denote a sense of intimacy, a connection. She'd loved holding Tom's hand, having seen it as visible proof they were together. Once he'd met Cynthia, that was one of the first things he'd stopped, telling her she was being too clingy. A sign she should have read.

'Or maybe that's a bad idea,' she said.

'No, it's not. It's a good idea. Holding hands is exactly what we should do. It's an important detail, it's what real couples do.' He held out his hand and she looked at it, at its strength and the strong shape of his fingers. 'Let's start now.'

* * *

Darius told himself to get a grip—literally. He grasped her hand and felt something…a tug, a connection…as though there was a significance to the gesture. He told himself it was just the unfamiliarity. Darius didn't hold hands, to him that was something only real couples did. The thought made him edgy and he saw Lily glance at him, then down at their entwined fingers, and he sensed her reluctance matched his own.

Telling himself he was being ridiculous, he gently tightened his hold. This was a show, a pretence… Things were complicated enough without him over-thinking a simple gesture like this.

They started walking, and as they made their way through the labyrinth of alleyways he gradually relaxed and absorbed the atmosphere, the environment, the cobbled streets, vibrant colours, the noise and the bustle.

'I am really looking forward to this,' she said. 'I did some research and the whole history of the souks is fascinating.'

'Tell me,' he said.

'You sure?' She looked surprised. 'You don't have to be polite.'

'I'm not. I want to know—knowing the history of a place makes it come alive, means you can picture how it became what it is today. A bit like people—your past shapes you, just like this place is shaped by its past.'

'OK, but stop me if I get boring.'

Looking down at her animated expression, it occurred to him that Lily was many things but boring was definitely not one of them. She tucked a tendril of hair behind her ear and started to speak,

'The souks, or trading places, all started when Marrakesh was founded in 1070, so centuries and centuries ago. Gold, ivory, metalwork…all were traded.'

As she spoke, he could see the picture she painted of laden camels crossing the desert carrying exotic goods over miles of sand, carrying news of different places and adventures.

'The city was founded by Aku Babr, who built the original gates of Marrakesh. Over the next hundred years or so the walls were built and they are roughly the same design as they are now. How incredible is that? All those years ago that basic heritage, the core trading belief, started and still lives on, and today we're part of that.'

She came to a stop at the entrance to the sprawling maze of stalls and gave a half-embarrassed smile. 'Sorry. I told you to stop me if I went on and on.'

'You told me to stop you if I got bored. I'm not…' He took her other hand in his. 'I promise.'

Their gazes meshed and all he wanted to do was pull her closer and kiss her again, wondering if she wanted him to, wondering if he should, and then the moment was gone as the crowds jostled into them, breaking them apart.

Lily opened her bag. 'I have a list of things to buy, and a map. The souks are split by types of goods on sale and I've read up on the best way to bargain.'

They stepped forward and she gave a gasp at the sprawl of goods on offer, the vibrant cacophony of smells, noise and colours that assaulted their senses. 'Look,' she said with delight as she pointed to the row of stalls. 'I wonder if I'll ever be able to buy olives from the supermarket again.'

He could see her point as they both surveyed the

mounds of glistening, plump green olives, small, wrinkly black ones and others that were a luscious purple-red, all flanked by bright-yellow lemons that filled the air with a citrus tang, overlaid with the spicy burst from piles of bright-red and dark-green chillies. Behind the fresh produce were shelves covered in columns of jars filled to the brim with a variety pickles, olives, lemons and oils.

Lily gestured to the olives. 'I'd like to buy a few to sample. I am going to put snacks in the guests' rooms and in the lounge.'

Ten minutes later, they had purchased a variety of fresh olives and she pulled out a notebook from her bag. 'I'll jot some tasting notes down.'

'In which case, you don't want to get oil on the book. Here.' He headed into a slightly less crowded bit of the souk and they stopped. He took an olive. 'Here you go,'

She hesitated then opened her mouth and he popped the olive in, felt an instant frisson as his finger brushed the softness of her lips and heard her intake of breath before she slightly stepped back, her eyes wide as she met his gaze. It was almost as if the crowds faded away, as if it were just the two of them.

Then she blinked and looked down almost absently at the notebook. 'Um…that was amazing, strong and full of flavour, and…'

He bit into one himself. 'And leaves you wanting more,' he said, and she caught her breath.

'Yes, it does. Could I try another, please?'

Her lips parted, his gaze fixed on them and he reached out and, oh, so gently rubbed a finger over them. 'I'm removing the oil,' he said, his voice husky. 'So it doesn't impede the taste of the next one.'

He dropped his hand and she looked at him, taking a step closer, and now she reached up and slid her finger over his lip, and he held his breath as sensation rocketed through him, clenching his gut with a need he saw mirrored in her eyes.

'Good idea,' she said softly.

'I'm ready.' Eyes on her, he put another olive into her mouth and then one into his own.

'This one is saltier,' she said. 'Followed by a tang of spice.'

'Chilli oil,' he said. 'It adds the spice. The salt causes a build-up of taste, of sensation, and then the heat.'

The only thing that rescued them again was the jostle of the crowds.

'I… We'd better move on,' she said.

CHAPTER NINE

As THEY WALKED Lily tried to pull her scattered senses into order—what had happened there? How could such a small gesture unleash such a sensual torrent of desire inside her?

Deep breath. She had to focus on the job in hand. Had to focus on looking around her, absorbing the sheer chaos of the atmosphere: the strident voices of the tradespeople; the good-natured bargaining and expressive hand gestures; the smiles when a deal was made. They walked along the cobbled street of another souk, this one covered with an iron trellis and crowded with tourists all examining the wares, textiles, jewellery and furniture.

But, despite all her efforts, she was also so aware of Darius that the sights and smells around her seemed slightly muted against the backdrop of sensations running through her and the tingle of her lips where he'd touched them.

Focus. She came to a stop as they entered another souk and this image did at least break through as she surveyed the row after row of pointy-toed Moroccan slippers in every imaginable colour and design in seemingly endless numbers.

'We need these,' she declared, and he looked down at her, raising his eyebrows in question.

'For the guests,' she said. 'They can wear them inside then take them away with them at the end.'

The conversation at least tracked her back some way to normalcy as they continued their journey. They stopped at the apothecary stalls where she gazed at the exotic offerings: scorpions, medicinal leeches, snails whose slime could help with wrinkles and various ingredients to mix anything, from love spells to things more sinister.

They arrived at the stalls she'd been looking for. 'Here,' she said. 'This is what I wanted—black Moroccan soap.' Picking up a sample, she inhaled the earthy, cleansing smell then passed it to him.

As he smelt it, she had an overwhelming image of rubbing it onto him, rinsing it off and then inhaling the scent from his skin. She closed her eyes, wondering if she was getting a fever.

'I like it,' he said, his voice a rumble. She nodded and slipped her hand into his as they continued to wander the souks, stopping at different food stalls. They sampled *msemen*: a flaky flatbread filled with cheese; *pastille*: filo pastry parcels dusted with sugar but filled with delicious savoury fillings; all washed down with mint tea. Then his phone beeped and he looked down.

'The villa is done,' he said.

'Then let's head back.'

As they walked and hailed a taxi, she tried to distract herself tried to focus on lists, on the villa, on everything that she needed to think about over the coming days, but to no avail.

In the end it was a relief to approach the vast villa and watch Darius pull out the keys.

'You were right,' he said softly. 'There is a knack to the

door. Let me show you.' He demonstrated and she tried
to focus on his hands, how they twisted and turned. 'You
turn and jiggle at the same time,' he said. 'Have a go.'

She stepped next to him and could smell the soap he
used, a fresh, work-like smell—coal tar, perhaps. She
tried to turn the key but couldn't, her fingers all fumble
and thumbs. He stood behind her and placed his hands
over hers, gently turning and uplifting them. Lily tried to
concentrate, she really did, but all she could feel was the
strength of his body behind her and she couldn't help but
accidentally lean back, heard his sharp intake of breath,
then the door was open and they walked in.

The fresh scent of furniture polish and clean, fresh
citrus assailed her nostrils and she took in the shine of
the floor, the cobweb-free walls and ceilings, the fresh
gleam of the door handles, and headed into the lounge.
The leather sofas had been cleaned and looked both styl-
ish and comfortable, as did the eclectic arm chairs that
she could now see were a deep-red colour. Tapestries
hung from the walls and there were low glass tables stra-
tegically placed for drinks and food.

The smells and sights acted like a welcome wake-up
call, a reminder she was here to work, and she turned to
Darius with a smile. 'They have done an incredible job
in here. I wouldn't have recognised it from yesterday.'

They walked across the corridor to the kitchen and
she noted with approval that here too everything shone,
and there was a lingering undertone of disinfectant that
indicated the clean had been deep.

'When did you buy the villa?' she asked.

'About a year ago,' he said. 'I bought it on a whim and
since then I haven't had time to get back, or decide what

to do with it.' He walked over to the fridge, pulled it open and checked the temperature. He took the olives out of the backpack and stored them inside. 'Perhaps now that it's up and running I can use it as a B&B. Give the profits to the charity.'

She glanced at him and realised another of her preconceptions about this man had been knocked away. His idea was a far cry from her assumption he'd bought it in order to throw lavish parties or entertain his celebrity girlfriends.

'Let's go and look upstairs,' he said.

Every bedroom sparkled, the bed posts had been polished, the marble floors were dust-free and the rugs looked freshly vacuumed. The bathrooms gleamed too, and Lily nodded approval, even as a sudden worry assailed her.

'I didn't expect this level of cleaning—I was planning on doing some of it. I'll reduce my fee to compensate. I don't want the fundraiser to lose money.'

'It won't. I agreed as my donation to the fund that I would donate the villa and any associated costs in getting it event-ready. This doesn't impact the money the fundraiser will make. You don't have the time to get the villa up to scratch on your own and help arrange the fundraiser. You would have had to get help in anyway, and that is partly my fault. I thought the villa was in slightly better shape than it actually was.'

Damn it—it turned out that Darius Kingsleigh really was not the man she'd believed him to be at all. He wasn't the Lothario callously leaving a scatter of broken hearts in his wake. He wasn't an idler. He was a man willing to help others with his money and his time.

And the knowledge gave her a sudden sense of warmth, even as she recognised the ramifications, the danger. One of the main reasons to hold attraction at bay had been the fact that Darius was the wrong sort of man and had the wrong sort of character. What if he wasn't? What then? It was a question she didn't know the answer to.

Seeing that he was looking at her with a question in his eyes, she tried to think and fight the urge to move over, to brush her lips against his and pull him into one of the bedrooms...

Her mind somehow scrambled back into gear. This man was paying her wages; their relationship was a fake one. 'That is very generous of you,' she said, knowing her voice sounded clipped, but it was the only way to rein herself in. 'I'd better get to work. I'll go round and inventory what else we need to buy.'

'Fine. I need to make a few calls about the band, and also about some form of security for the night as well. And release our statement, explaining our relationship status.'

His tone was all business, in line with her own, and she wasn't sure if she was glad or sad. She knew there was a part of her that wanted him to feel the same way that she did, wanted him to be as tempted, as swirled up inside.

'Sounds good,' she managed. 'Good luck with the calls.'

Darius dropped his phone back into his pocket, walked over to the open window and allowed the early-evening breeze to waft over him in the vain hope it might cool him down. He wasn't sure what was going on any more, or whether he was coming or going. The time with Lily seemed to have done something to his head: wandering hand in hand through the souks, discussing slippers, feeding each other olives... The hours had taken on a dream-like quality, a sense of an alternative reality in which he was the sort of man who did things like that.

But he wasn't, and he had to remember this was all make-believe—an alternative reality that did not and could not exist.

He turned and headed to find Lily, eventually running her to earth in a small study, sitting at a desk, her head bent over a notebook. She looked up as he entered.

'Hey,' she said.

'Hey,' he said. 'I came to give you a progress report and run something past you.'

'Go ahead,' she said, putting her pencil down.

'I may have found a band. A band that plays *gnawa*—traditional Moroccan music that dates back to the eleventh century.'

Her face scrunched in a frown as she searched her memory banks. 'I don't think I've heard of it.'

'It was brought to Morocco from further in Africa by slaves, and back then it was played in secret ceremonies—the music helped ease the suffering and created a kind of community, something that bonded the different people. The music has continued and many believe it has influenced the blues, jazz...you name it. Scores of famous musicians have incorporated the traditions and styles. The band I've found have agreed in principle to come to the event, but they have asked us to attend a venue tonight. They are playing at one of Marrakesh's top restaurants, so the idea is we go for dinner and listen to the band.'

'That sounds like a great idea...' She broke off and

looked at him and he could almost see the penny drop. 'I assume the press will be there—so this will be our first public outing as a couple.'

'Yes. I tipped the press off. It's one of Marrakesh's top restaurants, a haunt of the rich and famous, the band is up and coming so it seemed like a good place and occasion for our first public outing.' He could see a touch of anxiety cross her blue eyes.

'Do you think we're ready to go on show?'

'Yes,' he said simply.

'That's easy for you, you're used to it,' she said. 'I'm not. Any tips you want to share?'

'For me, I've always tried to be in control of publicity as much as I can—tried to use it to my advantage. A lot of my celebrity dates were trying to promote movies, so we'd use the publicity for that. Recently, I've focused all interviews and articles on my business. So focus on why the publicity is good for you, rather than it being nerve-racking or anxiety-making. You are doing this for your business and to promote a good cause—the fundraiser and the charity behind it.'

She rose to her feet, walked over to the window then turned back to him.

'But that also means if I mess up the stakes are higher.'

'You'll be fine. Just don't drop your guard or forget the part you're playing, and remember that a whole lot of it is true. You are a professional, successful woman; you are in Morocco to organise a fundraiser; you were given the job by Gemma, and she did ask us to organise it together.'

'Yes. But I am *not* dating you.' The words were said with emphasis.

'No.' Though in that moment he wondered why not,

what was stopping them. He imagined dating Lily, walking hand in hand, being able to give in to the attraction, laughing, talking…

He shook his head. Despite the pretence, he was the client; more than that, he didn't know how to date someone like Lily. What rules would he put in place? He didn't even know her relationship history, or her wishes for the future. 'We're not dating but the attraction is real.'

'So what do you suggest—I plaster myself all over you? Again.' The sarcasm was clear.

'That's not what I meant.' He tried to blink away the image of her doing just that, recalling the press of her body against his, the closeness of her.

'What do you mean?'

'We just need to show it exists so, when we look at each other, remember our kiss.'

Her eyes widened. 'Are you sure that will work?'

'Yes.' He shrugged. 'OK, no, I'm not sure. I've never tried to fake an attraction that is real. Why don't we try it?'

He reached out and took both her hands in his so they were facing each other, the breeze from the open window enveloping them in the gentle floral smells of the bursts of flowers in the courtyard below.

Suddenly Darius wasn't sure how good an idea this was as the atmosphere shifted a notch and an image of their kiss imploded in his brain. Heat climbed the slant of her cheekbones and her eyes darkened, lingering on his lips, and his gut clenched as he recalled the magic that had happened when his lips had touched hers. Now they were leaning towards each other, her eyes lit with a need that he knew mirrored his own.

The need was as irresistible as it was inevitable and now their lips met and he was lost in the sensations it evoked—he could taste mint tea, smell her light floral scent and a lingering sense of sunshine and black soap. Liquid desire pooled in his gut as he deepened the kiss, hearing her soft moan of desire, her fingers tangling in his hair, and he was lost.

Until finally they pulled back. 'I...' Lily stared at him, her hair dishevelled, her face flushed. Damn it; she looked so beautiful, his heart skipped.

'I'm sorry,' he said, then shook his head. 'No, I'm not sorry. I know I should be, and truly, I didn't intend that to happen. But I can't be sorry. It was...'

'Magical,' she said softly. 'But you're right. We shouldn't have done it.'

No, they shouldn't have. Because this couldn't go anywhere. The rules were in place. It was a pretend relationship, a fake. Messing it up could impact his business and hers, and he was already out of his depth, aware that this was different from his previous forays into arranged relationships. Before, he'd always been in control from the start. Now, the last thing he felt was in control, and it had to stop.

'No,' he agreed, but somehow the simple syllable was hard to formulate.

'I'll go and get ready,' Lily said. 'I'll meet you downstairs in about an hour, if that works time-wise.'

'Sure.' It was all he could get himself together to say.

CHAPTER TEN

LILY STARED AT the clothes in her suitcase, trying to focus on what she should wear for this fake date, but she couldn't think straight. Her whole being was consumed by that kiss. Darius was right—she couldn't feel regret, even though she knew they shouldn't have done it, it was increasingly hard for her to work out why. Because right now all she wanted was him.

Come on, Lily. The man was paying her—he was the *client.* That mattered.

Huh, said a little voice. *The whole world believes you're sleeping with him, so who cares?*

The answer to that should have been obvious: she did. But in the giddy aftermath of that kiss she didn't. And that was a problem in itself. It showed she was letting attraction mess with her professionalism, her integrity.

She dug her nails into the palms of her hands and forced herself to concentrate, pulling out a simple grey dress that should denote 'professional' and 'understated'. Which was good. After all, if everyone was going to believe this relationship was based on novelty factor, then there was no point Lily trying to compete with Darius's past flings. She didn't even want to; she didn't need to.

Because the attraction was real; she knew that now.

She had felt the urgency of his need and known it matched her own, had seen the desire blaze from his eyes, a desire that had heated her skin and clenched her insides. As she looked at herself, it almost felt transformative. Her dark-blue eyes sparkled, her skin seemed translucent and the simple grey dress seemed to shimmer.

That was it—she felt as if she were shimmering. Felt as if she were a different Lily.

She had never felt this way before. She'd believed Tom to be 'the one' but she had never once shimmered in his presence, never been so consumed with a need to touch and be touched this strong. A sneaking thought slipped into the recesses of her mind. Maybe this was how short-term relationships worked—they were all about attraction, all about the physical, about living in the moment because there was no future and that was OK. In fact that was the point.

Shaking the thoughts away, she applied the minimum of make-up, a swipe of mascara and a hint of lip gloss, and rose, feeling absurdly shy as she descended the sweeping staircase and entered the lounge.

She entered the room and again desire impacted her at the sight of him. Dressed in a dark-grey suit over a dark shirt, no tie, his dark hair slightly damp and curling against his neck he took her breath away.

'Looking good,' she said, her voice sounding shaky, the words not ones she would usually have used.

'Right back atcha,' he said, pointing both fingers at her in an exaggerated movement. Then he said, 'I don't know why I did that,' and they both looked at each other and simultaneously burst into laughter.

'Let's go,' he said. 'We can walk there—it's about half an hour—or I can call a cab.'

'Let's walk.' That way she could revel in holding his hand, and in the sheer proximity of him.

And she did, savouring every stride through the maze of alleys in the cooling dusk air. There was no need for conversation; the after-effect of the kiss seemed to have robbed them of coherence and allowed them simply to be together.

As they approached the venue, she slowed to take in the hotel's magnificence. Rose-tinted stone walls rose in a splendour of turrets in a mosaic courtyard dotted with palm trees of varying size and width, all magically il-luminated to give the whole a sense of a fairy tale. 'It's beautiful...' She breathed as they walked forward and then she became aware of the people at the entrance who turned at their arrival, cameras in hand.

Her steps faltered, but then his hand tightened round hers, offering reassurance. She walked forward, imagin-ing that this was a photo shoot for an article promoting her business, and she smiled her coolest, most business-like smile, one that mixed friendliness with profession-alism as they mounted the wide sweep of the stairs that led inside, to a lobby that had to be seen to be believed, and she didn't know where to look first.

There were glittering chandeliers suspended from a frescoed ceiling above immense, plush velvet sofas flanked by plasterwork detailed with arabesques and motifs, along which were pillars and alcoves with art deco lights and flowers arranged in bright vases, beneath which a gleaming polished marble floor stretched as far as the eye could see.

'Mr Kingsleigh, Ms Culpepper—welcome. Let me

take you to the restaurant, one of the four we are proud to harbour under our roof.'

'Thank you,'

They followed their guide through plushly decorated rooms, past intricate mosaic pillars and verdant greenery, the air scented with orange blossoms. They reached an arched doorway leading to a patio restaurant set on a courtyard that seemed enchanted. The floor was laid with mosaic tiles in earthy brown-and-red designs. Massive candles and lights illuminated pools and fountains. The tables were separated by arched trellises of flowers and leaves.

'This way, please.'

They were seated at an intimate, beautifully laid table covered with small platters of pastries and olives, and a waiter materialised to hand them heavy, tasselled menus.

'I will be back for your orders shortly,' he said.

Lily started to read. 'This all looks amazing.'

'Why don't we order a selection of items and share?'

'Good idea,'

They ordered *briouates*—pastries filled with meat or fish and cheese and lemon—served with a coriander sauce, along with Berber-style lamb tagine and a chicken couscous dish.

As the waiter walked away, a man and a woman rose from their seats and headed towards them. Darius frowned and turned to Lily. 'Business colleagues—high-powered couple Rob and Belinda Keating,' he murmured.

Lily felt a flutter of anxiety as she studied the couple. The man wasn't tall but he carried an aura of wealth, and the woman exuded confidence, her dress screaming 'designer'. Like Lily's mum, she walked with a knowledge that on her a bin bag would have looked 'designer'. The woman met her gaze and Lily saw curiosity in her green eyes. She was sure this beautiful woman was wondering what Darius was doing with Lily.

Doubt, and a memory of her stepsisters mocking her looks, mocking her intelligence, putting her down, came through her like a tsunami.

Then Darius's hand covered hers in a brief, reassuring grasp and he smiled at her, a smile full of solidarity. 'We've got this,' he said in an undertone, and the stress on the 'we' in his words gave her a much-needed jolt of confidence, reminding her they were in this together. For their professional reputations, she wouldn't let herself or Darius down.

The couple arrived at the table and Darius rose, stepping round the table to stand by her side, the bulk of his body an extra reassurance. It seemed natural to step slightly closer to him so she could catch the scent of the black soap, an added reminder of a sense of intimacy.

'Hi, Rob. Hi, Belinda. This is Lily Culpepper.'

'It's lovely to meet you, Lily. We are stakeholders in YourChoiceBookings, and of course we are also friends of Darius.'

'It's good to meet you too,' Lily said, shaking hands and smiling, aware of an undercurrent between the two men.

Rob gave a genial smile. 'Well, Lily, you make sure that you aren't keeping Darius from his duties in the boardroom. We'd rather see him gracing the columns in the *Financial Times* than the gossip pages and social media.'

Lily forced herself not to narrow her eyes and looked

up at Darius with a smile before turning a cooler smile on Rob. 'You've no need to worry about that. I don't think *anyone* could keep Darius out of the boardroom. And I wouldn't want to even if I could—I have a pretty heavy workload myself. That's why I am so glad of this opportunity to mix business and pleasure: we're organising a fundraiser together for Lady Gemma.'

'Such a wonderful woman,' Belinda cooed.

'And, believe me, we tried incredibly hard to avoid the gossip columns. But...' Lily shrugged. 'Unfortunately, that ship has sailed.'

'But we're planning to focus publicity on the fundraiser,' Darius said. 'In fact, as you're in Morocco, I could ask Gemma to add you to the guest list.'

'That would be marvellous,' Belinda said instantly. 'You're both angels. And now we'll leave you two lovebirds to it. You both look very happy together and so in tune.'

Lily sat back down just as the waiter arrived with their food.

'Phew,' she said. 'That felt like a bit of a grilling.'

'It was,' Darius said. 'Bob is an important stakeholder and a good friend, but he's a businessman first and foremost. He gave me a chance and...well... He agrees with my policy of keeping my personal life out of the papers. So that photo would have rattled him.'

They spent a few minutes admiring the food. The presentation was flawless, the vegetables of the tagine artistically arranged to completely cover the spiced meat below.

Once they had tasted everything, Lily looked across at Darius. 'Is that why you haven't had a personal life since Ruby?' she asked.

'Partly. Though in all honesty I haven't really had time, or inclination. Work has taken complete precedence and I've enjoyed every single minute.'

Curiosity touched her; she could hear the sincerity in his voice and now she questioned her blithe assumption that he was some sort of figurehead, or had been handed a business opportunity on a silver platter. 'Tell me about your company.'

'It's a booking company—a place where people can choose and book their stay somewhere, or an event venue, but the amount of detail I programmed into the system means they can really tailor their stay to them.'

'Did you do the programming?'

'Yes, I did all of it. I got the idea years ago, partly because of all the different jobs I worked at the Kingsleigh empire.' His voice was neutral but Lily was sure a shadow crossed his eyes. 'I did every job going, from porter to cleaner to receptionist, and it gave me a true insight into the detail of the hotel business.

'It got me thinking. I spoke to so many guests who loved certain things that others weren't bothered about. I spoke to one woman who loved the luxury touches, and another who went online and said she could easily bring luxuries with her. People with bad backs who wanted guaranteed comfort—soft beds rather than hard. Some people liked spending time in the room, others wanted to use it as a base. Working people versus tourists...'

He broke off. 'Sorry—I could go on for ever. The one common factor was people didn't want to trawl through lots of reviews to find out if a particular hotel suited them. So I came up with an idea and applied my computer geekiness to it.'

'You're a computer geek?'

He grinned and lifted a finger to his lips. 'It's a well-kept secret. Don't tell anyone. I have repackaged myself as a programming expert—it sounds better.'

'But really you were a high-school geek.'

The smile hardened slightly. 'It was a bit of a secret hobby. Geekiness didn't go with the Kingsleigh image.' Lily heard the faint hint of bitterness under the light-hearted tone. 'But by the time I was a teenager I could have hacked into pretty much any system, and I was fairly expert at programming and coding, so I was able to put everything together and the idea for YourChoiceBookings was born. Then it was all about research, testing, hoping and tweaking until I had it right.'

Lily nodded. 'Then it's the even scarier bit,' she said. 'When I decided to set up Culpepper's, it took me a while to get ready. I had to save up the capital, find the right premises, work out how the staffing would work, what about advertising... I made so many colour-coded plans, so many spreadsheets. That was hard work, but it wasn't scary. What was scary was actually putting the plan into action.'

'All the hopes and fears—the hope you'll realise your dream, prove yourself. The fear you won't, that you've got it wrong, or you can't do it.'

'That's exactly it.'

She'd wanted to succeed so badly to show her mother that there was a different way to make money—that a person could have a career, that looks weren't everything. She'd wanted to show her stepsisters that they had been wrong—that she'd survived their bullying and it had made her stronger. Show them that she wasn't the failure they'd taunted her with being. She'd wanted to show the world that she could stand on her own two feet and that she was worth something.

And she could hear from Darius's voice that he had felt the same. She wondered what he had had to prove, and to whom he was proving it.

He smiled at her and raised his glass of wine. 'To our companies and our success,' he said.

'I'll drink to that.' They clinked glasses and the sound of crystal on crystal seemed to symbolise something—perhaps a common understanding, a connection between them.

Stop, Lily. Remember, this is all an illusion.

She and Darius inhabited different worlds.

'Though I'm not trying to compare Culpepper's to YourChoiceBookings. You are a multi-million turnover global player. I'm not.'

'That doesn't matter.' His voice was resonant with sincerity, the depth tingling over her skin. 'Turnover doesn't matter. Culpepper's is your achievement, your idea, and you built it. You rode that roller coaster of taking an idea and believing you could make it work whilst simultaneously fighting the fear that it won't. You put in the grit, the hours and had the worries, financial and personal. That's what matters.'

'Yes, it does. Though it must be nice feeling your company was a family venture, part of an empire—I remember sometimes feeling really alone.'

'I get...' Darius broke off, his expression unreadable, and she wondered what he had been about to say. That he got that? But he couldn't. She truly believed he felt the same pride in his company that she did in hers and that he deserved to feel that pride. But he hadn't been alone; he had had untold wealth and family connections behind him.

'What you mean,' he finished. 'But the most important thing is having a vision. I had a vision and I needed to follow it through to the end, one way or the other.'

His voice was hard, full of steel determination, and again she sensed that whatever his status, whatever his family wealth, his need for success was as absolute as her own.

She studied his face, the strength of his features, the shifting colours in his grey eyes, the line of his jaw and the shape of his lips. Felt that little clutch of desire in her tummy again. His gaze met hers straight-on, and now he returned the scrutiny and she saw the steel in his eyes morph into desire. Had to resist an urge to wriggle in her seat and instead forced herself to lift her glass.

'To our visions,' she said, and again they clinked glasses.

'So what other visions do you have?' he asked. His voice was low, and seemed to hum over her. 'Apart from for your business. What do you want?'

You. The word nearly slipped out and she swallowed it down, even as she recognised its truth. She wanted him with a depth of desire she hadn't believed possible, and she wanted to do something about it, but fear held her back. Fear of rejection, fear of getting in over her head. Also a fear that she would regret it—regret the loss of integrity and professionalism.

And of course there was the ever-constant fear that she wouldn't measure up—those old insecurities resurfaced. It was safer to be alone; being with someone was a guaranteed way to heartbreak and pain. She knew that—she knew love was temporary, a shifting chimera, an illusion.

He studied her expression 'So what's your answer? What else is important to you, apart from work? What do you do for fun?'

Lily thought back over the past two years, since her split from Tom. 'Fun has been in short supply,' she said. 'I suppose work has consumed me. What about you? When's the last time you had fun?'

'Honestly?' he asked, and his smile was suddenly rueful…slightly crooked.

'Yes.'

'Here, with you. I've had fun.'

So had she, she realised: exploring the square, walking through the souks, tasting olives, choosing soap, admiring the slippers… It had all been fun.

'So have I,' she said softly, feeling absurdly shy. Looking away, she saw that the band was tuning up. A makeshift dance area had been cleared and many people had turned their chairs to face the group of men on the stage. She tried to remind herself why they were here.

'Hopefully the band are going to be right for the fundraiser,' she said, pulling out a notebook and pen from her evening bag. 'I'll take some notes.'

'Good idea. Then I have another way of assessing them.'

'Yes?'

His voice was deep, with a soupçon of amusement, a teasing note that seemed to caress her. 'Would you do me the honour of dancing with me?'

Lily tried to imagine what dancing with Darius would be like: to be allowed to be up close, to touch. 'I…'

'Actually, I don't care about assessment, I *want* to dance with you.'

As their gazes locked, all the earlier fears dissipated, dissolving under the fierce flame of desire burning dark in the grey depths of his eyes. This was real, and held a power that made her anxieties and scruples irrelevant.

'I want to dance with you too,' she said, and now anticipation swirled in her tummy as she forced herself to turn away from him, to watch as the lead singer took the mic and started to introduce the band.

CHAPTER ELEVEN

DARIUS WATCHED AS Lily's pencil skimmed over her notebook, focusing as much as he could on the words from the stage, facts that would normally have held his undivided interest. The man explained that he was a *maalem*, the lead singer, but so much more.

'To me, being a *maalem* is a way of life, an embodiment of musical and spiritual traditions and history, but also of music and meanings today. A fusion of past and present, a way of honouring both.'

Lily's face was serious now. She turned and met Darius's gaze and he knew that the *maalem*'s words resonated with her; that she understood that this man was more than a lead singer; that this was a man who had dedicated his life to his art, to his work.

The *maalem* went on briefly to describe the instruments the band would use: the *gimbri*, a three-string lute that he would play; castanets, known as *qraqeb* or *karkabas*; and double-headed drums called *tbels*, which were played with one curved and one straight stick.

'Now we will begin. We will start with some of the more traditional songs and then move on to the more modern.'

Lily turned to Darius.

'It is like we said yesterday—the past shapes the future.'

'But sometimes it is important to live in the present.'

'And to enjoy the moment,' she said. 'Maybe we've both been so caught up in work, the need to succeed, that we haven't been doing that.'

The music started and for the next ten minutes they sat transfixed along with the rest of the audience. The performers were dressed in traditional electric-blue robes and brightly coloured fezzes, and the sheer synchronicity of their movements, all somehow orchestrated by the *maalem* as he played the lute, was as hypnotic as the music itself. The twists and turns of the swaying dancers as they shook the heavy iron castanets seemed to shake beats of movement and sound into the air, with pulsating speed alongside the bass, transcendental notes of the lute and the thrum of the drums.

The words themselves were in Arabic, and they seemed to call to something in Darius, to urge exactly what Lily had said—to enjoy the moment, to seize it, take it and feel the joy of living despite, or perhaps because, life also contained pain and suffering.

And she must have felt the same, because now she rose and held out her hand to him. He took it and they headed towards the stage. Once there, he felt as though they were one, standing oh, so close but without touching, their movements in perfect synch and harmony as they moved to the music.

He was consumed by her closeness. She was so tantalisingly near that the need to touch, to feel her body against him, was excruciating, almost hurt, and yet it heightened the sense of anticipation as the beat of the music seemed to grip them in its spell.

And then the music segued into something else, into

a blues rhythm, and now they both moved forward. He heard her sigh of relief when he took her into his arms, and he'd have sworn the air sizzled as the *maalem* now sang in English. His raspy voice spoke of how this music spoke to his spirit and his soul; how it spoke of hope for the future, of freedom.

Lily laid her head against his chest and he felt as though his heart were speaking to her. The scent of her hair was more intoxicating than the glass of wine he'd drunk; the warmth of her body against his, the feel of his hand on her back, all dizzied his head.

Until the music came to an end and they stepped back and stared at each other, still caught in the spell of the lingering notes.

'Darius?' Her voice was soft, but clear and certain. 'I want to seize this moment, enjoy it. Not just this moment, but the next one and the one after that. To experience something I know I want.' Now she gave a small gurgle of laughter. 'To be clear, I want you. Not for ever, not even for long, but definitely for tonight.'

'Then let's go.' Perhaps he should stop, think, but he couldn't. He could see no hint of doubt in her eyes or voice, and knew she spoke simple truth. Not to do this would be unthinkable and so, once they had politely refused dessert and confirmed with the band that they would definitely like them to play at the fundraiser, they were finally able to leave.

Once outside, he couldn't help but laugh, a laugh of happiness as he took her hands in his. She echoed his laughter and then he picked her up and twirled her round, not caring who saw them, realising he had no idea who had taken what photos. This evening had been about Lily—for real.

As he put her down, she placed her hands on his shoulders and brushed the lightest of kisses against his lips. 'Thank you,' she said.

'For what?'

'For being you instead of the person I thought you were.'

The words warmed him.

'Now, let's get back to the villa,' she said. 'Quickly,' she added.

Clasping her hand tightly, he started to run and, half-laughing, breathless, propelled by sheer desire, they made their way back to the villa and went inside and straight up the stairs.

'My room's closer,' she said, and then they were inside. Now it was all about haste, near panic that something would happen to stop this—he didn't think he could bear that. Every sense was heightened, every part of him heated, volatile, ready for her—wanting, needing, to give and receive pleasure.

Stumbling, fumbling, in their haste, finally all their clothes were tangled on the floor and at last he could touch and feel, and then he was kissing her and they tumbled onto the silken sheets of the bed.

Lily opened her eyes, aware of an immense sense of well-being, a lightness, as memories seemed to float on the brilliant white ceiling. The images brought heat to her face as she recalled the glorious kaleidoscope of sensation; the freedom of exploring his body; of learning first hand that it was everything her imagination had believed and more.

She remembered the feel of his hands on her, his lips on her, the things they had done, the laughter, the sheer joy...

She shifted and the euphoria faded a tiny bit when she realised the space next to her was empty. Her last memory was of falling asleep, safely cocooned in his arms, in the early hours of the morning.

Don't panic, she told herself.

Perhaps he preferred to sleep alone and had simply gone back to his own room. Maybe that was how short-term, fun relationships worked. Or maybe he'd gone for a shower, or for a walk, or...

The point was it didn't matter—she would not let last night be tainted by doubts. Last night had been about phenomenal, fun sex full of laughter, passion and the type of sensations she had never experienced before. With Tom, it had been pleasant, enjoyable...but nothing like she had experienced last night and this morning. Perhaps with Tom everything had been clouded by her need for love and a happy ending, whereas strings-free sex was different: no doubts, fears or expectations.

So, whatever happened next, she'd be good with it.

Yet when she entered the kitchen half an hour later, showered and dressed in a long floral sundress, she halted on the threshold in the grip of a sudden sense of awkwardness, a shyness verging on embarrassment, when she recalled how abandoned she had been last night. How far she'd been from the professional, cool Lily Culpepper.

'Good morning,' he said and the warmth in his voice and his smile reassured her, though she saw a slight wariness in his eyes, a slight clench to his jaw as he indicated the table by the arched window. 'I'll start breakfast,' he said.

Turning, she saw he'd set the small table by the kitchen

window overlooking the mosaic-tiled courtyard where the early morning sunshine pooled, lighting the tiles with flecks of copper and gold. A vase full of flowers was in the middle along with a jug of freshly squeezed orange juice and she smiled. 'That looks lovely.'

'Thank you. I'm making an omelette with chillies and olives, if that's OK.'

'That sounds perfect. Thank you.' The words were slightly stilted as she moved closer to the hob. 'Can I help?'

As she got closer to him, she stopped. 'You used the soap,' she said, inhaling the earthy scent of the black soap.

'So did you,' he said, stepping slightly closer, and she stilled as desire churned, along with a need to bury herself into his neck and inhale his scent...

But neither of them moved closer, though she could see her own desire mirrored in his grey eyes. Instead, he cleared his throat, turned away and picked up an egg. 'You could make coffee, or tea if you prefer it. There's a cafetière, and I got some fresh coffee.'

'Sure.'

Ten minutes later, they were seated. 'This is delicious,' she said. 'Thank you for doing this. You must have got up very early to make it to the shops and back.'

'It's not a problem.'

Silence fell and Lily frowned, part of her not wanting to ask the question, but she knew she had to, her earlier euphoria starting to fade at the edges. 'Is everything all right?' she asked in the end. 'I mean, I feel like there's a problem.'

'No.' There was a pause as he pushed away his plate. 'Yes,' he amended, and now anxiety started to unfurl. Maybe she hadn't measured up... Then he went on. 'I mean, I've never done this before.'

Relief hit her and she couldn't help it—she raised her eyebrows, 'Really? In that case, last night was even better than I thought.'

This pulled a chuckle from him and lightened the tension. 'I'm glad you enjoyed it,' he said. 'So did I.'

'So that's not the problem?' She could hear the hint of a question in her tone and saw the surprise in his eyes.

'No. Emphatically no problem there. I enjoyed every second.'

'So what is the problem?' she asked.

'I've never done what we did last night without having some rules in place, rules that meant I knew how to act the next morning. I was thinking about making breakfast in bed, but I thought that might make you uncomfortable, and I don't like feeling like this—no rules, no boundaries. It's thrown me.'

Lily reached out, placing her hand over his, and wondered why he needed those rules and boundaries; why he had never once risked a real relationship. 'We didn't need any rules or boundaries to be set. I understood, I understand, that you have no wish for commitment or anything long-term. Last night was...'

She paused, trying to find words as he placed his hand over hers, and the mere touch evoked a frisson of renewed desire, reminding her of exactly how the previous night had been.

'Incredible,' he offered. 'Magical.'

'Both those things, and nothing can or should take away from that.'

But worry still flecked his eyes and her curiosity deepened along with a desire to take that worry away. 'If you're worried about what happened with Ruby repeating, please don't be. I'm completely good with this being one night only. I think your arrangements with Ruby went wrong because Ruby did want a long-term relationship with somebody one day. I don't want a long-term relationship, ever, any more than you do.'

'Why not?' he asked. 'How can you be sure? Not about us, but how can you know you don't ever want that?'

She sensed that the question was asked out of a curiosity that matched her own, perhaps along with a need for validation, a desire to understand why someone else was on the same page as him. To her own surprise, she wanted to share, to explain.

Perhaps because she trusted Darius; after all, they were in this together, both of them protecting their business reputations—a fact that had been emphasised by their meeting with his stakeholders the previous evening. Perhaps because she knew this was a bubble of time and soon enough they would go their separate ways. Maybe because Darius felt like the right person, the man who had blindsided her with an attraction she could never have imagined. A man who made her feel beautiful.

'Because... I don't believe in the traditional happy endings, for me. It's not what I want, because it requires too much trust. Yesterday, when you explained your attitude to relationships, the way you minimise the risk of hurting people and yourself, that made sense. I've seen too many people hurt, seen too often how easy it is to overturn vows of love.'

He reached out and placed his hand over hers. 'Tell me,' he said.

Lily saw the focus in his gaze and knew that here was someone who would truly listen to her in a way no one ever had before. Her mother had rarely had time to listen, or if she had she hadn't got it, and couldn't see life from any other perspective than her own. She was unable to understand or be interested in a daughter who was chalk to her cheese.

Tom… Tom had tried but he had always interrupted, or cut her short, and had never really wanted to hear anything that he deemed as negative. She looked down at their clasped hands, took reassurance from his touch and began.

'My mother is a beautiful woman, a woman with the "it" factor, X factor—every sort of factor. She fell pregnant with me when she was twenty, but I don't know who my father is. All I know is that his parents found out and they bought my mother off. They didn't want her and a baby to ruin my father's life. She took the money, moved away and changed her name.

'Then she decided the best way to live was to target a wealthy married man. She set up an arrangement with him. He bought her a house, paid her bills and he visited often. When I was ten, the liaison came to an end; my mum negotiated a lump sum last payment and moved on. This time, she decided she wanted marriage. She targeted an extremely wealthy businessman. He didn't stand a chance; he divorced his wife of twenty years with whom he had two daughters and married my mum. His wife was heartbroken.'

And his daughters had never forgiven Lily.

'What about you?' he asked. 'Where were you in all of this?'

'I wasn't, really. Mum used to send me off to "friends", and then when I was older it was a mixture of nursery and friends. It wasn't all her fault. She and I…we are so different. She wanted a different type of daughter, a pretty one. I wasn't a very pretty baby or child, really. I guess I got my dad's genes or something. I didn't like being shunted away all the time—especially because her friends didn't really want me—but I preferred it to hiding out in my room and being told to stay quiet.'

She shrugged. 'But, whatever her faults, she provided me with a roof over my head, food and security.' Lily had done her best to appreciate that, even whilst she'd sometimes wished for a more normal mum, the sort who came to sports day, the sort who asked other children round after school.

'She also showed me that fairy tales don't exist. They are illusory, unrealistic; they necessitate placing blind trust in someone with no guarantee they won't break that trust and shatter it into little pieces. Just like so many men did over my mum.'

There was a silence and she saw the intent look in Darius's grey eyes. 'It's more than that, though, isn't it?' he asked gently. 'It's not only your mum who showed you that—you've experienced it yourself.'

Lily stared at him. 'I… How do you know?' she asked.

'Because I know you,' he said. 'I can see how different you are from your mother. You've earned your own way, you've set up a successful business yourself, you're reliant on no one. You haven't followed in her footsteps. I think you would have been the same about fairy tales— you *would* have believed in them.'

Surprise washed over Lily that Darius could have worked this out about her. 'I wanted to believe in them,' she said softly. 'I wanted my mother to be the wicked witch, the wicked stepmother of fairy tales, and I would be the heroine, the princess who got true love and a happy ending. Then I met Tom and he ticked all the boxes. He was handsome, charming and I couldn't quite believe that he seemed to like me.'

She could remember the sense of gratitude she'd felt that someone like Tom would pay her any attention. The idea that she could have it all. 'We started dating and I decided he was "the one". I was determined to be the perfect girlfriend. I cooked his favourite foods, supported his football team, tried to be supportive. Then my mum asked us to dinner, and of course I said yes.' She could hear bitterness in her voice.

'Of course you did; there's nothing wrong with that.'

'But there was, really. I wanted to show him off, show her that fairy tales did exist—that love was possible, that I could win a man.' What she hadn't known was that Cynthia and Gina would be there. She could remember her instinctive recoil when they'd greeted her, and how seeing them had made her appetite disappear at the forced, manufactured politeness. 'My stepsisters were there as well.'

Darius nodded, and his eyes narrowed slightly. She wondered if he could see what was coming. What might be obvious now had seemed inconceivable to her then.

'The dinner was all right, but that's when everything changed. I just refused to see the signs.' She met his gaze. 'That's why I identified with Ruby, because I did exactly what she did—I saw what I wanted to see, rather than reality. Despite Tom cancelling dates at late notice, despite the fact he was different.'

He had called her clingy or needy. He had made excuses not to stay over. But then at other times he had been super-nice, surprising her with dinner and extravagant gifts to make up for being cross, or absent. 'So much so that I decided to propose.'

Her voice caught and remembered humiliation washed over her. 'It was Valentine's Day. I made a romantic dinner. I had a massive helium balloon, a banner that said "be my valentine". It was cringe-worthy, really—every cliché under the sun. I even had violin music playing in the background. Thankfully, before I could actually go down on one knee and ask him, he confessed—told me he'd fallen in love with Cynthia.'

As she told the story, she could taste the bitterness, feel the disbelief. 'Cynthia, who is beautiful—the sort of beauty my mother has, the universal "it" factor, and he'd fallen for it. I tried to tell him she had only targeted him to hurt me.'

She had tried to tell him about the bullying, but he'd refused to listen, the tone of dismissal absolute.

'You can't expect me to believe someone like Cynthia could do that,' he'd said. 'I understand why you are saying it but you shouldn't try to set me against Cynthia.'

The words, that he believed she would lie about something like that, had been an additional sucker-punch of hurt. And she'd vowed never to tell anyone about the bullying again, to deal with it herself.

'But he just looked at me with such pity in his eyes, and he said it didn't matter, because if he'd really loved me he wouldn't even have looked at Cynthia. And that made me feel...'

'As though somehow it was all your fault?' Darius said and she saw compassion and a genuine understanding in his eyes.

'Yes. That's exactly it. I felt as though I hadn't been good enough.'

'Not true. *Tom* wasn't good enough.'

Lily shook her head. 'It wasn't his fault he fell for Cynthia.'

'No, but not telling you, seeing her behind your back, being unfaithful, leading you on—that was his fault. You say you didn't see the signs, but you shouldn't have had to. He should have told you himself, but he didn't—his bad, not yours. His cowardice was not your fault.'

Lily heard the suppressed anger in his voice. 'And his loss.' He released one of her hands, reached out and tipped her chin so that she was looking straight at him. 'That's why I know that you were, you *are*, better than good enough.'

Lily blinked back sudden tears; it was as though some of the humiliation, the second guessing, was draining away, leaving her lighter. Now she reached out and stroked his cheek. 'Thank you,' she said softly.

A lingering doubt touched her, along with a sense of loyalty. 'And I'm sorry if I sounded negative, especially about my mum. I do know she did her best, gave me security, and I know that I am not the daughter she would have wished for.' She took a deep breath, hoping that Darius didn't think she'd been complaining. 'I just wanted to explain to you why I don't believe in fairy tales. Thank you for listening, and understanding.'

Because Darius did understand; she could see it in his eyes, hear it in what he had said and the way he had said it. She sensed a connection, a solidarity between them, and wondered if he felt the same—wondered if there was a chance he would confide a little in her.

CHAPTER TWELVE

DARIUS SAW THE sparkle of tears in her eyes, and wondered if she believed him. He wanted her to; he wanted her to see herself as he saw her—as someone who had succeeded, someone who was beautiful inside and out. He understood her decision to close her heart; how could she trust in love? But he wanted her to believe in herself, to be sure that she wasn't eschewing fairy tales because she didn't believe she was good enough to be the princess, or didn't deserve to be loved. He wanted her to know what a good person she was.

He thought about what Lily had shared with him, full of admiration for how she had handled and processed her childhood. He understood the emotions she must have experienced; for the first eight years of his life, he hadn't known who his father was either, he knew all too well how that could affect a relationship with a mother.

Looking at Lily now, seeing the pain in her eyes, he wanted to help. Strangely enough, even though he knew that meant sharing his own childhood, something he had never done with anyone, that felt all right. Because he knew he could trust Lily, and knew that soon enough their ways would diverge.

'You haven't been negative. I admire how you have

kept faith with your mother. How you handled your childhood. You should be proud about that. I wish I could have done the same.'

'Tell me,' she said, echoing his own words of earlier. 'About your childhood.'

'My mum had me when she was in her mid-twenties, and like you it was just her and me. But my mum, though I didn't really understand at the time, was an addict. Alcohol and drugs were her go-to when she was depressed, and that was a lot of the time. Looking back now, I think perhaps she was bipolar, or she'd had a traumatic childhood herself. I don't know.' He could hear the sadness in his voice, the knowledge that perhaps he never would.

'I'm sorry,' Lily said, 'That must have been hard for both of you.'

'It was—she tried her best, but when she was under the influence she couldn't help herself.' There'd been too many times with no food on the table, times when he'd come home to find his mum crashed out on the sofa, the house a tip that he'd cleaned up as best he could.

'But there were good times too—times when she'd tell me stories about pirates and wizards, magical fantasies that I loved. Times when we'd go to the park and eat ice-cream. And there was always a sense that we were in it together. I loved her and I believed she loved me.'

'That is incredibly important in itself,' she said softly. 'I never felt that; I was a duty to my mum, a responsibility she fulfilled, but I never felt we were a team. It always felt as though we were in opposition. It sounds like your mum loved you enough to try to be a good mum.'

'She did and we were managing, but…in the end I messed it up.'

Lily gently squeezed his hand. 'You were a child,' she said.

'But old enough to know better. I was obsessed with the need to know who my father was. I had this fantasy that, if I could find him, he would come and rescue us. Make my mum happy so all the times would be full of ice-cream and stories. That my father would be different from all the other men in her life.' The ones who had scared him, the ones who got drunk, the ones who had made his mum tell him to get lost and disappear, so that he'd crept out for as long as he could.

'You wanted a fairy-tale ending for her,' Lily said. 'For both of you, and you wanted your dad. That's natural. I did too. I fantasised all the time that he'd turn up one day, that he'd track us down. I used to beg my mother to contact him or to tell me who he was. But she wouldn't, and I worked out soon enough that I wouldn't be able to change her mind. So I gave up.'

'I wish I'd done the same. But I didn't. Instead, I questioned her constantly and every time she'd tell me a different story: my dad was a fireman, a footballer, a dustman... Every time she spun me a story, it felt like I had a mission. I'd go and haunt the local football ground, or accountancy offices, look for men who looked like me, even though I knew it made her angry. It was the only thing really that made her angry with me. Maybe she felt I should be happy just with her.'

'Or maybe it made her feel bad about herself,' Lily said, and he stared at her, arrested by the thought. Maybe the anger hadn't been directed so much at him but at herself.

'But you couldn't have known that.' Lily slipped her hand into his, her eyes wide. 'You were a child, trying to help, trying to change your mum's world for the better.'

'Only I got it wrong.' Sadness and self-recrimination, the guilt he had tried to hold at bay for so long, seared him. 'One day, I thought I'd found him—a firefighter, so it tied in with one of my mum's stories. In my head, I looked like him—he'd dark hair and I managed to get close enough to see he had grey eyes.

'I started to hang round the fire station; my plan was to follow him home. Only one day, it was late, he spotted me and he and a female colleague came out to see why I was there. They ended up taking me home to my mum. In my head it was going to be the grand reunion. In real life, it was a fiasco, because my mum was in the midst of a row with a boyfriend. They were both completely wrecked, and there were bottles and syringes dotted around the place. It couldn't have been worse, really. I ended up in emergency foster care. I didn't see my mum again.'

'What?' The word fell from her lips, her eyes wide with shock and consternation.

'She disappeared—cleared out the next day, they said. Left a letter for social services and a letter for me. She said I would be better off without her, and they'd take me anyway, but she'd done her best to give me what I truly wanted—a dad. The letter to social services gave four possible names: Enzo Kingsleigh was one of them. Social services approached him first and it turned out he had had a very brief relationship with my mum. They did a test and it turned out he was my biological dad. He took me in.'

'And the rest is history,' she said softly. 'You were taken in by your dad, given a home and love, security and a whole family…a dynasty.'

'Yes.' He knew his voice sounded colourless, knew too that he wouldn't refute her belief. Because he'd al-

ways pretended that had been the case in every interview he'd ever given, hoping by saying the words he'd
make them true.

'I'm sorry.' Lily's voice soft. 'I know it's been three
years since his death, but you must still miss him very
much. But at least you did find him, though I know it
came at a bitter cost.'

'I used to wish that I had never followed that firefighter. If I'd known, I wouldn't have done it. Not if I'd
know it would drive my mum away.'

Her grip tightened on his hand, giving comfort. 'And
that is a tribute to your mum, that you feel like that despite the difficulties. But it wasn't your fault. *You* didn't
drive her away.'

She reached out and touched his cheek oh, so gently.
'I know how easy that is to say, but it sounds to me as
though something else would have triggered social services to intervene. A teacher may have noticed something, or worse, there could have been an accident. All
your actions did was precipitate something that would
most likely have happened anyway.'

The words offered balm, as though she understood the
guilt he carried, but also as though she believed him. Believed that he would genuinely swap the life of wealth,
that he did truly regret what he'd done.

'It just feels wrong that she thought I'd be better off
without her; that I had been looking for my dad as a replacement for her. That she thought I wanted her to go—
that she didn't try and fight for me.'

'I'm sorry. Did social services try to find her? Did
your dad try?'

He shook his head. 'Social services tried, but I have the

impression once my dad agreed to take me in they didn't try very hard. As for my dad, he never spoke about my mum; it was as though he wanted to write that part of his life out of Kingsleigh history, out of his own history. I am not sure he even remembered very much of it himself. I think he preferred to believe that my life started aged eight.'

Lily frowned. 'So you were transferred to a completely different world and expected to fit in and forget the past eight years.'

'Pretty much. And to be grateful.' He frowned. 'Sorry, that was unfair. I was grateful. But…'

'You missed your mum.'

'I did.' He could remember now crying into his pillow, wishing, willing, her to come back. 'No one understood that except Gemma. She was in a relationship with my father when I turned up in his life, and she was wonderful; she insisted on being my godmother. But she and my dad split soon after and she disappeared from my life for a while.'

A decision made by Enzo rather than Gemma, though his godmother had re-entered his life as soon as she could. 'But everyone else seemed to think I was well rid of my mum; that she had chosen to leave and that missing her meant I didn't appreciate what I had.'

'She did choose to leave,' Lily said. 'But it sounds as though she knew that she couldn't look after you the way that she wanted to—that she left because she loved you and it was the best thing for you.'

He heard only compassion and sympathy in her voice, no judgment.

'Do you think your mum did what she did because she thought it was the best thing for you?' he asked. 'The best way to maximise security so you could have a good life?'

'She could have got a job,' Lily said. 'To be fair, she believes she did get a job—says she is a businesswoman who made lucrative deals and she has always kept her side of the bargain. She doesn't understand why I don't agree with that.'

Darius picked his words carefully. 'I don't agree with targeting men or breaking up marriages, but maybe there are reasons you don't know about. In the same way I don't know why my mother turned to alcohol and drugs or why she couldn't manage to give them up for me.'

There was a silence and then Lily reached over and put her arms around him. 'Maybe it was just too hard so instead she did something even harder—she gave you up. Maybe over the years she has made a new life for herself. Have you ever thought about tracing her?'

'I decided not to.'

'Why?' she asked.

'Because she knows where to find me. I am in the papers enough; there is no secret about where my headquarters are and there is a myriad of ways she could have got in contact.' He hoped he'd kept the hurt from his voice. 'I have to assume she has her own reasons for not wanting to make contact.'

'I can see that it would be difficult for her. She may think you don't want her to contact you, particularly if she suffers from mental health issues. Plus, she may be worried you would think she wanted money. Or she may see how happy your new life has been and she doesn't want to rock the boat. May still thinks it's best for you if she stays out of your life. It's a lot to think about, but if there is anything you want to say to her maybe you should try to trace her.'

Her words made sense; actually talking about this with someone else made a real difference. Especially as this was a topic close to her heart.

'Have you ever tried to find your father?' he asked.

'No. I thought about it a lot when I was younger but I couldn't work out how. Mum wouldn't even tell me where she was born. Then, when I was older, I decided not to. It didn't seem fair. He might be married with kids. He had no idea I existed and the reverberations would be too great. How would it affect his relationship with his parents? There are too many unknowns.'

'Or you could look at it the other way,' Darius said. 'He may welcome the knowledge. He may have no other children, or he may have children who would welcome you into the family. Especially when they see you have no expectations of them.'

If he'd found Enzo as an adult, when he was a success in his own right, would they have forged a relationship? 'You wouldn't be a responsibility—you're an adult. Maybe you should trace him. Maybe you could persuade your mother to tell you his identity, or persuade her to talk about it more and try to get some clues. Once you know who he is, his circumstances, then decide whether to contact him or not.'

There was an arrested look on her face. 'I've never thought of it like that,' she said. 'When I think about him, I revert to childhood, imagine what it would have been like to find him then. But you're right.' A smile lit her face. 'Thank you. The things you've said, the way you've listened…it's shifted something inside me.' Leaning over, she brushed her lips against his cheek and he caught his breath at her nearness.

Then something shifted; a sense of lightness, of appreciation, came into being and she was in his arms. He kissed her, a kiss that held so much—thanks and appreciation for listening, for understanding for *caring*; a sense of connection from their pasts, a reminder of the night before and a promise of what was to come. Everything intermingled and, when they finally separated, he pulled her to her feet and smiled down at her.

'We missed out on breakfast in bed but I can offer you a different activity...'

'Hmm...what sort of activity did you have in mind?'

'Why don't you come upstairs and I'll show you?' He waggled his eyebrows and she laughed, a glorious infectious laugh, and he laughed too as he tugged her towards the door.

Lily opened her eyes into an instant of confusion and saw Darius lying next to her, his face relaxed in repose. She smiled and stretched gently so as not to wake him, feeling the ache of muscles, and her smile widened as she recalled the extent of the activity of the past hour.

This time passion had been heightened by a sense of languorous exploration, a feeling that now they had more time to tease and tantalise, to scale the heights of need and desire. There'd been a sense of a new deeper connection.

She studied him now, the sunlight from the open window glinting coppery highlights on his dark hair, and she felt something twist inside her at the idea of all he had confided in her, and all she had confided in him. She felt a sense of solidarity at their joint loss: the loss of a mother who had left him, whatever her motivations; a sense of all that might have been if he hadn't gone on a quest to find his father. For her, the loss of a father she'd never known and who would never know that somewhere in the world was a daughter.

Unless she did something about it, as Darius had suggested, the idea taking root and giving her a sense of taking a step in a new direction.

Darius opened his eyes and she was rewarded with an instant sleepy smile. 'I can't remember the last time I had an afternoon nap,' he said.

'Neither can I.' She gave a small gasp. 'But now we'd better get a move on. We are supposed to be meeting Jamal and his team and then I need to go back to the souks.'

He gave a mock-groan and a salute, but she could see that he was smiling goofily, and she had a feeling her own smile was equally goofy. Because somehow it didn't feel like work—it felt like an opportunity to be with Darius.

Presumably that was how it was supposed to be—a short-term, fun relationship; a safe space in which to share confidences with someone who couldn't hurt her. Now she understood why Darius wouldn't entertain long-term relationships—he knew what it felt like to have someone who loved him, to have someone he loved leave him. So he'd set boundaries in place for protection, to protect himself and the other person. If they knew someone was going to leave, they couldn't abandon you.

He would never open himself up to that again any more than Lily would. She knew trust was too much to ask on a long-term basis and the idea of being supplanted again, being betrayed again, was unacceptable. Both of them understood that and they had both forged alternative happy endings, ones in which they were happy in their own successes.

'Darius?'

'Yes?'

'We haven't talked about…how this is going to work. I know I said this morning I was fine with it being one night, and I was, but now… Well, now we…'

'Landed back in bed without a discussion again,' he said, sitting up and moving backwards so that his back was resting against the wall. She couldn't help it; her eyes lingered on his chest, the swell and sculpt of muscle.

He grinned. 'And, if you look at me like that, we'll never leave the bed…' Heat touched her face and his grin widened as he reached out, tucked his arm around her and pulled her to his side so they sat pressed together, his strong, muscular thigh pressed against her leg.

'Tell me what you want,' he said.

'I want to have fun, to enjoy this…for a short period of time, before we go back to our normal lives. So… until the end of the fundraiser.' That was five days away. 'Does that work?'

'That definitely works. And I plan to enjoy every single minute.'

'Me too.' Happiness bubbled up in Lily at the idea of five glorious days. Yet as she looked at him, saw the warmth in his gaze as his eyes caressed her body, a sudden doubt assailed her as she thought of the time together coming to an end. She pushed the thought away. Five days: that was long enough to have fun, but short enough not to get attached in any way at all; to be protected by the boundaries, safe in the knowledge there'd be no complications or messy emotions involved.

CHAPTER THIRTEEN

LILY SURFACED RELUCTANTLY from the depths of sleep, opened her eyes and blinked as she saw Darius standing by the side of the bed, fully clothed, in jeans.

'Time to get up,' he said. She looked towards the window, saw that it was still dark and squinted at her watch. 'It's four in the morning,' she said.

'Yup. Surprise!'

She rubbed her eyes. 'You've *got dressed* and woken me up to surprise me? I can think of better ways.'

He grinned. 'Tomorrow morning I'll wake you up at four and surprise you in a different way.'

The banter triggered a jolt of happiness at the knowledge that this was a promise he would keep. 'I'll hold you to that. But seriously, what is going on now?'

'I've got a surprise for you, but you have to get up so I can take you to it.'

The excitement on his face energised her, despite the fact she'd tumbled into bed exhausted. They'd worked really hard: shopped for supplies in the souks, finalised the dinner and canapés menu with Jamal and his team, and met up with the *maalem*. But now she was wide awake, another goofy smile on her face at the idea that Darius had arranged a surprise…for her.

'Give me ten minutes.'

Soon enough she blinked in the early morning air, amazed by the quiet, only now realising how noisy Marrakesh was by day and night. She looked up at the sky tinged with the faintest anticipation of dawn, just as a car pulled up outside. They climbed in the back and Lily focused on watching the landscape go by; the streets deserted now, the shops all shuttered up, the usual fragrance of mint tea absent. Then they left the city boundaries and the road was bumpy now, the only sights a few isolated mosques until the car arrived at a base camp.

'We are going up in a hot-air balloon to see the sunrise,' he said. Moving over to Darius, Lily hugged him, holding the strong contours of his body close, cocooned in his strength.

'Thank you! That is a wonderful surprise.'

They broke apart as a woman approached them, speaking in faultless English as she offered them tea and briefed them on the safety protocols, then gestured towards the adjoining field.

'You can watch the balloon being inflated,' she suggested, and they walked over hand in hand, watching the brilliantly coloured, majestic red-and-yellow balloon billow out and upwards in a whirr of noise.

In a surprisingly short space of time the balloon was pronounced ready, and they walked towards the massive basket and scrambled in. The balloon began its ascent, slowly rising from the ground, swaying in the light breeze, the pilot expertly manoeuvring as they climbed. The ground receded, becoming smaller and smaller as they watched.

Lily felt a soaring sense of freedom as she gazed at the

expanse of sky around them, and slipped her hand into Darius's. 'Thank you for this—it is incredible. Up here, I feel as if anything is possible.'

He nodded. 'One thousand feet from the city. It truly does feel we have got away from it all.'

'It does.' Away from the tendril of doubt starting to unfurl about how she would feel at the end of this fling; worries about whether the fundraiser would be a success and the prospect of the impending wedding—watching Tom marry Cynthia, everyone's eyes on her, the knowing looks, the whispers. Up here, that didn't seem to matter.

'Look…' She pointed ahead at the jagged stretch of a mountain range.

'It's sunrise,' the pilot said.

They stood transfixed as the rays touched the looming mountain peaks, stroking and kissing the craggy outlines with hues of yellow, orange and pink as they crept across, meshing and streaking the early morning sky, gradually illuminating the vista.

'I've never seen anything like it!' She turned to look up at him.

'Neither have I,' he said softly, and she blushed slightly as he continued to look at her. What she saw in his eyes sent a glow over her, because no one had ever looked her like that—as if she was beautiful—and the idea almost overwhelmed her. She reached up slightly self-consciously and tucked a tendril of hair behind her ear.

'Have I got a mint-tea moustache?' she said lightly.

'Nope. I just like looking at you. I like the way your eyes sparkle, and the way your forehead creases when you listen.' Oh, so gently he ran a finger over her brow and Lily inhaled sharply as desire shot through her. 'And the sweep of your nose. I like the way your lips turn up when you smile.' Now his thumb rubbed over her lips and she could only gaze up at him. 'I especially like when you look at me like that,' he said.

With that she was in his arms, his lips on hers as the sun rose, burst to its zenith around them and peaked over the mountain tops. She gloried in his kiss, exhilaration and a sweet sense of happiness running through her. Until the pilot cleared his throat and they broke away, half-laughing, to see that a table had been set, laid with pastries, orange juice and tea.

'Please enjoy,' the pilot said, and they went to sit down.

Then breakfast finished, they rose and went to the side of the basket to look out at the view, the sky now a stretch of dazzling cerulean that wisped with soft, fleecy clouds as the balloon took them over clusters of settlements. The brown and red of the earth glowed russet in the early morning sun, and they could see farms dotted over the countryside. Through it all Lily was oh, so aware of the man beside her, and every so often she ran a hand over his arm and felt his fingers at her waist, or he brushed the back of her neck, each touch sending a sear of heat through her.

The minutes drifted past and they floated almost seamlessly through the sky, the imposing velvet silence occasionally intruded on by the burst and flare of the gas burners, a reminder of reality.

Then it was time to descend, and Lily felt a sudden desire to tell the pilot not to do it, to let them stay up here a little longer. But of course she didn't, and all too soon the basket was brought down on a surprisingly smooth landing. They thanked the pilot and clambered out, ready for the journey back to the villa and the day ahead.

And, as if on cue, as they turned for a last glimpse of the balloon both their phones beeped insistently. Lily smiled a rueful smile, looked down and frowned as she saw the message was from Cynthia.

She was truly back to reality with a bump. Bracing herself, she looked down, skimmed the message and frowned again, consternation superseded by anxiety.

'Everything OK?' She heard Darius's voice and quickly pulled a smile on her face.

'Absolutely,' she said. 'What about you?' She saw his frown, the worry clear in his grey eyes. 'What's wrong?'

He looked down at his phone and grimaced. 'Gemma can't make it to the fundraiser.'

'Is everything all right?' Everything Lily knew about Gemma indicated that she took her charitable work seriously. She knew that one of the perks of the fundraiser would be her formidable presence, her legendary ability to generate publicity and persuade the wealthy to part with their money. She was one of the reasons a lot of people would have bought tickets in the first place.

'I don't know,' Darius said. 'She says a close friend needs her.' His jaw tightened. 'She's asked me to take over as host and to do the speech.'

She could hear the lack of enthusiasm in his voice, and wondered at it. He was more than capable of hosting an event. Then the penny dropped and she moved towards him, taking his hands in hers.

'You'll be fine,' she said, suddenly getting that the speech would be emotive for him—talking about a charity that helped struggling mothers so they could have a shot at keeping their children. Supporting the charity in the background was one thing, giving his time and money another, but actually standing up and making a speech would be tough. 'You don't have to make it personal.'

He squeezed her hands. 'Thanks for getting it. I'll be fine. Not as good as Gemma, but I'll do my best.' He nodded at her phone. 'And you're sure you're all right?'

Recalling Cynthia's message, Lily bit her lip then nodded. 'I'm sure.'

Later that day, Darius looked up from his laptop on which he'd jotted the beginnings of his speech. He studied Lily as she stared out of the window at the courtyard beyond, her gaze seemingly focused on the exact same plant she'd been staring at the last time he'd looked up. Anxiety unfurled inside him; she'd been different since they had returned from the balloon ride. She'd seemed distracted, almost withdrawn.

Perhaps she was tired; it had been an early start, after all. Now the anxiety turned into definite jitters. Had he inadvertently done or said something to upset her...or had she changed her mind about the fling?

Chill out.

There was absolutely no point over-thinking this. He cleared his throat, and when that didn't get any response he tried her name. 'Lily?'

She gave a start, then turned towards him. 'Yes?'

'Is everything OK?'

She gave a quick look down, then back up. 'Everything is fine.' She glanced at her watch. 'Do you think we should check in with Jamal and see if he's had any more ideas for the menu or if we need to meet the team again or…?'

'No,' Darius said firmly. 'I don't think we need to do that—Jamal has it all under control.' For a moment, he wondered if Lily quite simply didn't want to be alone with him.

The unwelcome thought put him on edge and he rose to his feet. 'Come on,' he said. 'Let's go for a walk. We can climb the ramparts and watch the sunset… It seems like a good day to do it—sun rise and sunset all in the same day.'

She hesitated and then nodded. 'That does sound good.'

As they started the walk towards the city, he noticed that she was keeping a distance from him; she hadn't slipped her hand into his and he minded, which didn't make sense. He wasn't even a hand-holding guy.

They approached the ramparts. 'We can climb up from here, I think.'

They walked up in silence, both slightly breathless when they reached the top where they stood, looking over the panoramic vision of the city: the sprawling, chaotic pink-hued buildings; the ochres and earth tones; the bright splashes of colour from the people dressed in robes of yellow, red and blue; the swirling mass of humanity all surrounded by the historic walls and ramparts that enclosed this magical place.

Darius moved closer to her and, when she moved away, his own edginess ratcheted up. 'Something is bothering you,' he said. 'What's wrong?'

At first he thought she wouldn't answer, and then she sighed. 'There's nothing wrong, exactly. I got a message from Cynthia.'

'About Tom?' Scenarios raced round his head. Perhaps Cynthia had split up with Tom. Perhaps Tom had seen what a colossal idiot he had been to give Lily up and now he wanted her back. The thought clenched his hands into fists and he realised Lily was looking at him oddly.

'Sort of,' she said. 'It's from Cynthia and Tom. They've invited you to their wedding, as my plus one.'

'Their wedding?' he asked. 'You didn't mention they were getting married.'

Lily stared down at the city she had come to love in the past few days, realising he was right. She hadn't mentioned it.

'Partly because I didn't want you to feel sorry for me.' She shrugged. 'But mostly because I didn't want to think about it—like a form of denial.' She hadn't wanted to taint this magical time with a reminder of reality. 'But I'm telling you now. It's a week after the fundraiser, three days before Valentine's Day itself—a Valentine's wedding.'

'Ouch!' Darius winced. 'That's a bit bloody insensitive of them, isn't it?'

'They said they knew I would understand, as it is such a romantic idea. I think they may also see Valentine's Day as the day of Tom's lucky escape.'

'Humph. The boot's on the other foot, if you ask me. I don't even understand why you're going. Unless…you want to show everyone you're fine and you really don't give a damn.'

'That's it exactly.' She wanted to show Cynthia that, if this was another shaft in her 'make Lily pay' arsenal, it had backfired big time. She wanted to show Tom that she'd moved on and made a success of the last two years. 'I won't run away and I won't hide.' She sighed. 'But…'

'You're dreading it?'

'Yes. People will be watching me, feeling sorry for me, and the closer I get to the date the less appealing the whole thing becomes. And now…it's dawned on me that I'll also have to pretend that we're still an item.'

She hurried on, suddenly terrified that she'd sounded sad. 'I know that by the time of the wedding we won't be, but we will still be pretending…' And somehow the thought of pretending, when she'd know the fling was over, twisted her insides with misery.

'I'll come to the wedding.' His words were abrupt, as if he'd surprised himself, and she shook her head emphatically. Damn it, had she sounded needy? Clingy, as Tom had accused her of?

'No. I can't and won't ask you to do that.'

'You didn't ask. I offered.' He shook his head. 'I'm not doing this because I feel sorry for you.'

She looked away, back to the glorious vista below, as the setting rays of the sun wove tendrils of magic onto the imposing upward sweep of the city walls, causing them to glow a crimson hue. Then she met his gaze firmly.

'Then why are you offering?'

'Because I want to be there, with you, by your side. I don't like the idea of you exposed to pointing fingers and scrutiny.'

There was no denying the sincerity in his voice, and the sense of him having her back, wanting to provide a united front, warmed her, even as the temptation to let him come to the wedding escalated.

'And,' he continued, 'if you want we can extend our fling until after the wedding.'

'Is that what you want?'

'Yes.' There was no doubt in his voice; in fact, his grey eyes lit up with a glow that sent a surge of sheer exhilaration through her, a sense that the sword of Damocles had been lifted. The wedding no longer seemed as if it would be a disaster, and she muffled the voice of caution that pointed out that she was pushing the boundaries, changing the rules set up to protect her, and that that way lay danger.

Nonsense.

They were talking about a few days more, hardly anything; and, damn it, what was wrong with feeling happy about that, about having Darius by her side? What better way to show the world that she'd moved on?

'It's what I want too,' she said. 'Thank you.' Standing on tiptoe, she brushed her lips against his, against the vibrancy of the setting sun, sending shimmers and shades of red and pink across the sky. The kiss was glorious and deep, yet as she pressed her body against his Lily felt it held a bitter-sweetness she didn't understand.

CHAPTER FOURTEEN

TWO DAYS LATER Darius awoke and saw that Lily was already sitting up, her notebook propped on her knees. He shifted up the bed so he was next to her and dropped a kiss on top of her head. She stretched, her leg pressed against his, shoulder to shoulder.

'Today's the day,' he said. The day of the fundraiser.

'Todays the day,' she repeated and sighed, placing a hand on her tummy. 'I have to admit, I'm nervous. I need to tell myself that at least at this time tomorrow, one way or the other, it will be pretty much over.'

He nodded, and relief touched him that it would only be the fundraiser that would be over tomorrow, not their fling, thanks to his offer to attend the wedding. He'd been overcome by a protective instinct that would not let him leave Lily to stand alone against people who had treated her with such sheer, selfish insensitivity. Who were blithely taking for granted her courage and spirit. He would be there to shield her from pointing fingers and, as a bonus, they now had a valid reason to extend their fling.

Lily glanced at her watch. 'The villa guests will be here in a few hours. I need to be ready.'

'*We* need to be ready. We're in this together, remember?' He placed his hand over hers and she shifted closer to him, laying her head on his shoulder, her glossy hair tickling his skin.

'I know; it's just so important we get this right. To recap, we'll greet the guests as a couple, but then for the rest of the afternoon I'll be in my role as housekeeper, making sure they have everything they need. I won't join everyone for dinner, but once we get to the actual dancing and entertainment we will be hosting everything together.'

'The press will be there this evening. Gemma gave exclusive access to one particular magazine, so they'll be interviewing people and taking photos.'

Lily bit her lip. 'We haven't been on show for days, not since meeting Rob and Belinda at the restaurant.'

Could that really have been only four days ago? 'I don't think anyone will have any problem believing we are together.'

She hesitated. 'I don't think we will have a problem projecting that we are sleeping together but that's not what we want to project. Today I need to be seen as a professional, and so do you. Your stakeholders are attending. We need to get the mix right; need to make this relationship look like more than a fling.'

Lily was right; this was about being professional. 'We'll say we are attending a family wedding together in the next few days, and we'll dial down attraction and dial up…affection. Lovey-dovey isn't professional; little gestures of affection are.' Such as an occasional squeeze of the hand, a light touch on a back, a shared gaze, a quick hug—all things he could recall them doing over the past days when they *hadn't* been on show.

Unease surfaced and he pushed it away as a pointless emotion; even if there was affection, that was hardly an issue. Friends felt affection for each other.

'Gestures it is,' she said as she moved away and climbed out of bed, and he resisted the urge to pull her back. Suddenly he wished there was no fundraiser; that they were here today on a holiday, only answerable to each other. That they could stay in bed all day, entwined in each other's arms, letting desire have its way; that they could read, talk, or venture down to the kitchen to bring picnic meals upstairs.

Darius blinked. Picnic suppers in bed, staying in bed entwined…that was not how fun arrangements went, not today, not ever. And in a few days, after the wedding, this would come to an end and he would be OK with it, because he had to be. The alternative was too messy, too complicated. The unease returned and deepened and he pushed it down. There was no need for disquiet; instead, he should be glad that it would be easy to fake this relationship and that would make their job tonight easier.

Because today was about the fundraiser. He owed Gemma, owed the charity, his full focus on that. He smiled at Lily as she emerged from the bathroom fifteen minutes later,

'We'll be fine,' he said.

Ten packed hours later, Lily acknowledged that so far Darius had been right. Everything had been fine in terms of the fundraiser. The dinner had been a resounding success, Jamal and his team had excelled themselves and she didn't think anyone other than Darius had noticed that

Lily had been one of the waiting staff, standing in for one of Jamal's team, who was ill.

It had given her a chance to observe him at the table and here she'd seen a different man from the one she'd got used to over the past days—a man who cheerfully tackled plumbing problems and wielded a mop. This man fitted in with the super-wealthy. She overheard conversations about things of which she had no knowledge: clubs; fine wines; cars that cost double the cost of her London flat; properties that cost millions; private planes and yachts.

All of it was so out of her ken, but a timely reminder of how far apart their worlds were and that, once this was over, once the wedding was done, she and Darius would go back to their own separate worlds.

The idea was further reinforced by the guests' attitude to her. So far there had been no complaints about the rooms, though Lily had been to and froing with snacks and drinks, providing itineraries, making sure that everyone had everything any super-wealthy person in a luxury villa could possibly need.

And all of them had been suitably appreciative, though she had also seen the curious looks—and sensed some of the politeness at least stemmed from her position as Darius's girlfriend, rather than her position as housekeeper, or even head of Culpepper's.

But now everything was about to change. She was back in their bedroom, changing into her evening dress, ready to greet guests by Darius's side.

'You look beautiful.' Lily gave a small jump at Darius's deep voice, turning from the window as he walked towards her.

'You were looking at my back,' she pointed out.

'Doesn't matter. You always look beautiful to me.' He came to her side, lifted his hand and gently smoothed her brow. 'Don't look so worried. Everything has been amazing so far, and you've got everything covered for this evening.'

His words soothed the anxiety and made him feel less remote, more her Darius. *Whoa. Careful, Lily.* He wasn't hers, and she wasn't his. And he was right: she, they, did have everything covered. That wasn't what caused the nerves fluttering inside her. Those nerves were caused by her worry about facing all these people from his world as his girlfriend.

She glanced down at the simple black dress she'd chosen, designed not to make her too obvious, so that if need be she could slide back into her professional role and float around handing out canapés, or taking coats, and now she was glad of that. She was unsure how she was going to manage discussions about yachts and mansions—unless of course she explained the ins and outs of keeping them clean.

'You're still looking worried.' He smiled at her. 'Maybe this will distract you. I got you a gift.'

'You did?'

'Yup.' He reached into the pocket of his dinner jacket and handed her a rectangle flat box.

She opened the box and her face creased into a smile as her heart did a little loop-the-loop. 'Thank you. I love it.' She took out the charm bracelet, a delicate chain holding four charms: a hot-air balloon, a teapot, a sprig of mint and a gold star.

'To remind you of Morocco and to remind you that you are a star, the best at what you do. And that's why this evening will be a wonderful success.'

A tear threatened as she slipped the bracelet round her wrist. 'Thank you. I'll wear it tonight to bring me luck.' Now she gave him a cheeky smile. 'And I'll thank you properly tomorrow when this is all over. But, before we go down, I've got something for you too.'

She moved over to the bedside table, took out a small bag and handed it to him, feeling a sudden apprehension. The gift wasn't expensive or designer, or perhaps the sort of gift he would expect. But too late; he'd opened it and she hurried to explain.

'It's a crystal.' They both looked at the yellow-orange stone he held in his hand, smooth and multi-faceted. It glinted in the moonlight, almost as if it exuded motes of magic. 'Called "citrine". This particular one has been cut in a certain way and is of a certain carat and I thought it would fit nicely in your hand. It's supposed to bring luck and positivity and success. I thought it would be a good thing for you to have tonight, when you do your speech.' He hadn't spoken about it, but she knew it was worrying him; she had seen his face as he'd written and rewritten it, tweaked and amended it.

He closed his hand round the crystal, moved forward and pulled her to him in a hug. 'Thank you.' He hesitated. 'No one has ever given me something so thoughtful. I'll treasure it, and keep it in my pocket for later.' He sighed. 'I've made a million speeches and I've never felt nerves like this. I don't even know what I'm nervous about; all I need to do is talk about the charity and the wonderful work it does.'

'For people like your mum, who didn't get help,' she said softly. 'This is personal to you, coming from your heart.' And Darius didn't like emotions; Lily got that, as she didn't either. Feelings, emotions, got you hurt, made life complicated.

'You're right,' he said. 'And thank you again.'

'Ditto.' She gestured to the bracelet.

'So now let's go and do this,' he said, taking her hand as they left the room and headed downstairs, just as the doorbell rang...

And continued to ring as the guests arrived.

Anxiety flashed through Lily with a sense of intimidation reminiscent of years ago: how she'd felt every day at school, every classroom a potential danger; every lunch time, every evening, there'd been someone to face, and she'd been filled with fear and dread at what they had in store. But now, as then, Lily hid her nerves and refused to give in to her fear. She told herself these people were no better than her; that she could face down their curiosity, their disbelief, that Darius was with someone like her. All made easier by the man beside her with his sheer bulk and presence.

And that helped her keep a smile on her face as they greeted guests and mingled. Even when she did feel intimidated by the looks of curiosity, either veiled or direct. Or by the contrast between her attire—the simple black, high-collared, long-sleeved dress, her shoes low-heeled—and the exquisite designer dresses of the guests. Their styles were both elaborate and striking, all worn to catch the eye and be imprinted onto social media and glossy high-society magazines.

But what helped the most was the fact that Darius was clearly so at ease, so happy to introduce her as his co-host, his partner, with his arm round her waist and a private smile, a fleeting touch. He made gestures of affection and, however many times she reminded herself it was a show, damn it, it felt real.

Real enough that she was able to face the press with some level of confidence, even when a reporter asked, 'So, Lily, give me a scoop on you and Darius.'

'Not today,' she said. 'Today I am here in my professional capacity as head of Culpepper's Housekeeping Services. Today is about this fundraiser and the charity it supports. All I want is for the guests to have a wonderful time and for the charity to raise lots of money.'

'And they are having a wonderful time,' Darius said later. 'It's been a complete hit: the stalls round the sides, the storyteller, the music...everything. You did it, Lily.'

She took both his hands in hers, adrenalin and exhilaration running through her, and an emotion she didn't even try to identify as she looked up at him. 'We did it, and now all that is left is your speech. And I know that you are going to rock it.'

She slipped to the back of the seated guests as Darius climbed up onto the stage.

There was no sign of nerves as he stood before everyone, his stance upright, his expression serious. His body, the body she knew so well, was relaxed as he waited for everyone to quieten down, and then he started, delivering Gemma's apologies for her absence and joking about being a less glamorous replacement.

'But whilst I may be less glamorous, considerably so, I feel as passionate and deeply about this cause as my godmother does.' He reached into a pocket and pulled out a sheet of paper.

'This was the speech I intended to give you, and it is a

good speech—full of statistics and deserving praise for the charity. But I can summarise this in a few sentences. This charity makes a difference, a true difference, to people's lives—lives that are hard, and difficult. Lives that it is hard for people like us to envisage with our money, the yachts, the holidays, even the ability to attend events like this… If we have an addiction to booze or pills, we can afford expensive rehab facilities. If we have mental health issues, and they are serious, we have access to services, medication, counselling—access to help.

'So it is hard for us to envisage what people without money go through if they suffer from these issues. Only it isn't hard for me…'

Lily clutched the side of her chair, her whole being focused on Darius.

'Someone told me that my support for this charity comes from my heart. She is right. So I want to tell you a story—my story.'

And, up there on that stage, that was what Darius did.

'I have never spoken of my life before I was eight…' he began, and then he explained, leaving out any mention of his dad and simply detailing how hard it had been for his mum to be a good mum whilst battling addiction. 'But, however hard it was, my mum kept trying, trying to do the best she could. In the end, she decided the best she could do for me was to walk away because she had lost the fight with addiction.

'My mother was a troubled, lost soul; a woman who was prey to the downward spiral of addiction and depression; a woman who tried to pull herself up, but was unable to do so.

'But throughout the eight years I had with her I never

once doubted that she loved me, and I loved her. I wish I'd had a chance to tell her that, and most of all I wish she had been able to access the type of help this charity offers to women like her. Women who want to keep their children; who love their children but need some help. So I thank you for all you have done so far—but if you can dig deep and make an extra donation, that would help. It could help women like my mum and the little boy I once was.'

There was a silence at the end, partly stunned, and Lily she could see how moved many people were. Then a woman rose to her feet—a woman Lily recognised as another woman like Lady Gemma, a wealthy woman who tried to use her wealth for good.

'Well said,' she said. 'I wish more people had the courage to speak out as you have, Darius. I'll transfer my ticket money again.'

That set the tone, and Lily smiled to herself as more and more people pledged to do the same. Darius's voice came from the podium. 'I thank you all, as will Lady Gemma when she hears of this. Now I am done, and the band will return and the dancing can begin.'

He climbed down and headed straight towards Lily.

'You were incredible,' she said. 'And so very brave.' And now she didn't care—professional or not, she put her arms around him, stood on tiptoe and brushed her lips against his. She lost herself in the sheer sweetness, wanting him to know how much she admired what he'd done, and they only pulled apart when she became aware of the attention they had drawn. Worry touched her that they'd forgotten the rules, but as she looked round she saw that the guests were smiling at them, almost benignly, probably still caught up in the after effects of Darius's speech. Relieved, she gave him a smile and moved away to help shift the chairs ready for the dancing.

But, as she did so, she overheard two women guests.

'Hmm… Darius and that Culpepper girl—it does look real after all.'

The words made her heart give a little lurch, and for a moment she *wanted* the words to be true—for it to be real.

Then she heard the other woman answer, 'Nah, my dear. That's probably what Ruby AllStar thought.'

Lily almost slammed to a stop, because *they* were the words she needed to hear. She mustn't see things that weren't there, as she had with Tom. This was a fling and a fake relationship—no more, no less. And it was enough. Damn it, it had to be. She would not reopen her heart to a hurt she knew would come. Instead, she'd *enjoy* the next few days…the last few days.

CHAPTER FIFTEEN

THE FOLLOWING AFTERNOON, as they waved away the last of the guests, Darius watched Lily sink down onto a sofa with an exhausted but contented sigh.

'That went pretty well,' she said.

'*Amazingly* well,' he corrected, looking down at her. 'And I get you're exhausted, but there's no rest for the wicked.'

'I know.' She sighed and made to rise to her feet. 'There's still some cleaning up to do.'

'Nope, that's not what I meant. I've re-hired the cleaners to blitz the villa, and you and I are going glamping in the desert.'

Lily shook her head. 'I can't accept that.'

There was something in her tone, something he couldn't quite identify—a withdrawal, a wariness, faintly reminiscent of when they had first met. 'It's not from me,' he explained. 'Gemma arranged it as a thank-you to both of us for taking over from her. Does that make it more acceptable?'

He understood she wouldn't feel comfortable accepting expensive gifts from him; that it would make her feel as if she was following in her mother's footsteps.

'Yes, it does. Thank you for getting that. It is really generous of Gemma; it sounds absolutely incredible.'

* * *

When they arrived at the luxury camp, Darius could only agree. White rocky dunes rolled and dipped across an almost lunar expanse that stretched out across a vast, silent landscape. A silence seemed to encompass them in a bubble of timeless tranquillity. A handful of domed yurts were dotted around at more than enough distance to ensure complete privacy.

'Wow...' Lily breathed when they entered theirs. The inside was the epitome of minimalist yet comfortable chic: a massive bed; cool, cream walls; rattan lamps; a splash of colour from the Berber rugs. There was a bathroom complete with shower, and a private patio outside hosted a hot tub. The whole thing brought the sense of an oasis.

Darius glanced down at his phone. 'And dinner is being brought to us here.'

The meal lived up to the accommodation, the tagine spicy and aromatic, the couscous fluffy and tasty, all of it made even better by Lily's presence. Now the fundraiser was over, now they were no longer colleagues, something felt different as they laughed and talked, completely relaxed in each other's company.

The feeling was novel, and he suddenly wished it didn't have to end—that they could live in this yurt for ever. Instead, he would try to make this night count, because after tonight he wouldn't see Lily until the wedding. And after that... He closed the thought down.

'How about we hit the hot tub?' he suggested. 'We can sit in the starlight.'

Ten minutes later, he'd located champagne and they sat in the bubbling swirl of heated water, looking up at the star-swept sky, each pinpoint of light stark against the darkness. The whole vista utterly awe inspiring.

'It's majestic,' she said. 'It literally takes my breath away.' Just like she did to his, he thought as she turned to smile at him with the smile he'd grown to appreciate, the one that lit her eyes, her face illuminated by it. 'Gemma couldn't have picked a better place,' she said. 'But she didn't have to do this. I enjoyed every minute of this job.'

'She wanted to do it. She knows how much you did.'

'How much *we* did,' she said. 'Your speech… I meant what I said last night—it was brave, it was true and it did come from your heart. And I hope it makes your mum come forward.' She hesitated. 'It was good of you not to dwell on your dad. You acknowledged she wanted you to have a better life but you didn't detail your relationship with him—how he gave you more than wealth. How he gave you love, family, a dynasty, a chance to pursue your dreams…'

In that moment, Darius knew he couldn't let Lily keep believing the myth. For what? For whom? He trusted Lily not to betray his confidence, and here and now he didn't want to live the lie any more. Here under the stars, with the vast expanse of the desert stretching out, scorched by the rays of the sun by day and churned by camels' hooves throughout the ages. Here and now he wanted Lily to know the truth.

'It wasn't like that,' he said.

Lily turned to face him, the flicker of light from the soft fairy lights dancing on her face and highlighting the gloss of her brown hair, dancing little motes over her cheekbones and lighting up the dark-blue eyes.

'My dad didn't want to be a father. I think he hoped

when he took me in that that would change, but it didn't. He just couldn't love me. Maybe it was my fault. Maybe I tried too hard—was too needy, too clingy. But mostly he seemed to see me as someone who could have, should have, been someone else's child. I was a reminder of a time in his life when he was "in the gutter, slumming it".'

'Did he say that?' There was outrage in her voice.

'Not to me, but in my hearing. I was a quiet child. I tried to not get in the way, and it meant sometimes everyone forgot I was there and I heard things not meant for my ears. To my dad, I was never a real Kingsleigh, even though I spent every waking minute trying to prove that I was—to him.'

'And to yourself?' The question was gentle.

'Yes. I wanted to belong.'

'You were a child—of course you craved acceptance and love. I did too.'

'But you wanted acceptance on your terms,' Darius said.

'Yes, I did. But I hadn't just been catapulted into a new world where I was suddenly reliant on a new parent, one who I had craved to find all my life.' She paused. 'I assumed that once your dad found you he'd loved you and it was a fairy-tale ending, because that's what I always assumed, dreamed of, as a child. That my dad would turn up and treat me like a princess, would love me for being me. It was natural for you do anything to win your dad's acceptance and love. A love that should have been yours unconditionally.'

The knowledge that Lily truly got it comforted him, as did her sheer presence next to him in the gently bubbling water.

'I tried so hard. I looked up old photos of my father, tried to do my hair like him. When I got older, I dated, I partied and I made headlines. I went to work in the hotel, even though he didn't seem that keen. My cousins all went into management jobs from the get-go. I was told I had to "prove" myself…work my way up from the bottom. I didn't mind—that made more sense to me.'

'But it still hurts, to be treated differently. Did you get on with your cousins?'

'Not really—it wasn't all their fault. They could see how my father felt about me, and they followed suit. Said my blood was "tainted".'

Now her anger was palpable, reminded him of the time she had stood up to the men bullying Aline. 'That is horrible, unfair and cruel.'

'But they believed it and I suppose I did too. Because in the end, no matter what I did, my dad never loved me, never accepted me, never believed in me.'

'He must have been proud of your business, and the way you set it up.'

'No, he wasn't. I went to him with the idea. I thought that would prove beyond all doubt that I was a true Kingsleigh. He wouldn't give it the time of day. Said I didn't have what it took to get it off the ground anyway.'

The words had hurt and had cut him to the very quick 'So I went back to working for the Kingsleigh empire because I still hoped that that would show him I was worthy.' He shook his head. 'Ridiculous; I should have had the guts to stand up for my idea and gone and done it whilst he was still alive.'

'But you needed his backing.'

'No, I didn't. He would never have given me that. In fact, he made sure I would never have it.'

'I don't understand.'

'He left me nothing in his will. Not a penny, not a single share.' He shrugged. 'The money doesn't matter—he owed me nothing. The shares hurt, though, because it shows he truly saw me as tainted, not a true Kingsleigh. What hurt most was what he said in the will: "for my natural son, Darius, I leave my best wishes and my admiration for how hard he tried". I wish he could at least have left me his love.'

There was a long silence as the words rebounded into the vastness of the desert, the reality stretching across the miles of sand, dispersing up to the stars. The reality that Enzo Kingsleigh had not loved, respected or even liked his son had always made him believe he was unworthy of the Kingsleigh name.

'I'm sorry,' Lily said softly. 'I wish he had, but the fact that your father couldn't give you love is a reflection on him, not you. You're a good person, Darius. You tried so hard—you didn't give up trying, and there is nothing wrong with that.'

'Isn't there?' he asked. 'To try so hard and fail? That's the legacy he left me—that I tried to be a Kingsleigh, tried to win his love, and I failed on both counts.'

'No. He failed, not you. I promise you that.'

He smiled at her. 'Thank you,' he said. 'For listening, for saying the words you've said.' Though he wasn't sure he believed them.

Now Lily turned to him, her blue eyes serious and her hands clenched into small fists. 'I mean it. It's not you who is tainted, it was him. He was not worthy to have a son like you. He didn't deserve the gift he was given—the chance to be a father to someone so loyal, kind and so incredibly worthy. And I do hope he is looking down now, looking down and seeing what a success you have made without his tainted money. How you have achieved your dream. And that is something to be incredibly proud of. But you can be proud of so much more—your kindness, your compassion, being the man you are...'

Darius heard sincerity in her voice and it seemed to thaw something inside him. Lily cared on his behalf. Shifting now, he pulled her into his arms, looked into eyes that glistened with tears for him.

'Eyes like starlight,' he said softly. 'Don't cry. It's OK. In the end, I achieved my dream my way. His opinion was never going to change, and I have to accept that.'

'But that's not always easy, is it—forgiveness or acceptance? I have accepted that my mum doesn't understand me, that I'm not the daughter she wanted, but it isn't easy. I still want her acceptance—her love, even. But a parent's love should be unconditional, not based on looks or whether you are like your ancestors. If I had a child, I'd love that child unconditionally and I'd want to support them in following their dream, regardless of whether it was my dream. And I'm betting so would you.'

An image came into his head: a little boy walking in the park, scrunching leaves, eating ice-cream, hand in hand in the middle of Darius and a woman with glossy brown hair and dark-blue eyes, the three of them laughing and talking, feeding the ducks... He blinked hard, chasing the images away. That was not possible, and he knew that—not for him.

'I can't take that bet,' he said. 'I'm not planning on

being a dad. Short-term relationships don't really allow it.' The words were a reminder to himself and he saw something flit across her eyes.

'For the record, I think you would make a great dad. If not via a relationship, then maybe you could adopt.'

'You'd make a great mum,' he said softly. 'However you choose to do it.'

She gestured towards the sky. 'Look up at all those stars. I wonder, if we could read them, if they would tell us what the future holds for each of us.'

But he didn't want to think about the future. Instead, he traced the outline of her face and held it gently in his hands. As she moved forward to kiss him, something shifted inside him. This kiss held so much warmth, compassion, understanding and a weight of desire that seemed to transcend even the pleasure of their previous nights. Every touch, every sensation, was heightened, intense, beautiful and glorious as they entwined under the stars.

CHAPTER SIXTEEN

THREE DAYS LATER, Lily stared out of the window at the wintry London sunshine and gave a little shiver, despite the fact the hotel room was more than adequately heated. How far away Morocco seemed now. She and Darius had left the day after their night beneath the stars. She'd flown to London and he'd flown to LA—to their different worlds. And every day she'd woken up missing the vibrant Moroccan city with an intensity that surprised her.

Or perhaps it wasn't Morocco she missed but Darius. The thought was unwelcome; missing him had not been part of the deal. But ever since they'd fallen asleep under the stars, wrapped in each other's arms, she'd been aware of a kernel of dread inside her, a sense of impending pain that had deepened with each day apart. Each day had inexorably ticked on towards the day of the wedding—their last day, their last night, together.

And now it was here, the wedding day, and Darius was on his way from the airport.

There was a knock at the door; she went to open it and blinked in surprise.

'Gemma?'

Gemma Fairley-Godfrey stood there, a smile on her face.

'Lily. I hope you don't mind me turning up unannounced.'

'That's fine, please come in. How are you? Is everything all right?'

'Yes, it is. I wanted to thank you in person for everything you did for the fundraiser. I am sorry I couldn't be there. A dear friend of mine was very ill and he took a turn for the worse. Luckily, he is now on the mend, but it was touch and go and I couldn't leave him.'

'I am glad he is better. And thank you for the wonderful gift you gave us.'

'You deserved it. But there is another reason I am here. I have a favour to ask you, and Darius told me where I could find you. Would you mind wearing this to the wedding?' She placed a large bag on the bed and pulled it open. 'It's by a protégée of mine, an up-and-coming designer. I think you would be the perfect person to show it off.'

'Me?' Lily felt slightly bewildered. 'I'd love to help but it may not fit, or…'

'It will. I asked Darius for his help with measurements.'

'So this is Darius's idea?' Lily wasn't sure how she felt about that.

'Nope, it was my idea, and I asked him for some guidance.'

She looked at the dress she had been going to wear, lying next to the brilliant blue concoction Gemma had brought. Her grey offering looked drab, designed to make her invisible, which was exactly what she wanted to be at this wedding.

'The problem is, I'm trying to fly under the radar at this wedding.'

Lady Fairley-Godfrey gave a most unladylike snort.

'With Darius at your side? Not going to happen. Trust me, Lily, you will not be under the radar—and, if people are going to be looking at you, give 'em something to look at. That's what I've always said. Now, I must be going. Thank you again.'

With that, she was gone.

Lily stared at the dress and thought of Gemma's words, knowing that she was absolutely right. No way would she be able to escape attention, not only because of Darius, but because a good number of the guests would know she was Tom's ex and had been jilted in favour of the bride.

So she had a choice: creep around like a little mouse, trying to be invisible, or give people something to look at. Why not look good, for the world to see? And for Darius to see; after all, this was their last night, so she should make it one to remember. This was an opportunity to imprint herself on his memory banks and she wanted that.

Before she could change her mind, she pulled on the blue dress. It could have been made for her. The blue brought out the colour of her eyes and she could hear Darius's voice saying, 'eyes like starlight'. Silvery stars shimmered over the material that flared and swirled, skimming over her figure in silken folds. It was perfect—not so ostentatious that it would take attention from the bride, but enough to make her visible.

There was another knock at the door, another surprise at seeing her mother.

Maria stood in the doorway, mouth agape. And then she said, 'Thank God. You've come to your senses at last and decided to make an effort. Sit down and let me do your make-up.'

Lily opened her mouth to refuse and then suddenly recalled Darius's suggestion that perhaps her mother had reasons for her actions—reasons Lily didn't know about. She could see wariness in Maria's eyes, an expression that expected, was braced for, rejection. Yet her mother kept trying. Just like Lily did. Neither of them walking away from the other. Maybe Maria did want to connect with her daughter and this was the only way she knew how. So Lily nodded. 'OK, I'd like that. But please, nothing over the top.'

Surprise and pleasure touched her mother's perfectly made-up face, though her voice was tart. 'I know what I'm doing.'

Fifteen minutes later, Lily looked at herself and had to admit that her mother did indeed know what she was doing. The make-up was perfect, subtle but effective, making her dark-blue eyes seem larger, her lips glossy and alluring.

'There,' Maria said. 'You'll knock them all dead and no one will think you are pining away. Thank God you aren't wearing that grey dress. If people are going to be pointing fingers at you, then give them something to point at.'

Lily blinked at being given the same advice twice in five minutes by two different people. 'Thank you, Mum. And, Mum?'

'Yes?' Maria turned at the door.

'You look stunning. No one will believe you are the bride's stepmother.'

'Thank you.' Maria gave her daughter a startled look and a sudden smile before she left, and a few minutes later there was another knock. This time Darius came in, and an absurd shyness touched her as he stood stock-still and looked at her.

'You look beautiful,' he said, and her heart sung at the look of sheer appreciation in his grey eyes as they roamed over her body. And there and then she decided, the hell with it—tonight would be the one time when she'd allow herself to believe she was beautiful. A night when she'd seize the moment, let the magical dress cast a spell and allow her to revel in this moment, knowing it would be their last one together. There would be no more thoughts of sadness, just anticipation and happiness that he would be by her side.

'You're looking pretty good yourself.' In jeans and a heavy cable-knit jumper.

'I don't suppose we have time to take the dress off?' he asked.

'No.' Her voice was regretful. 'You need to change, and we need to go, but there's always later.'

'How are you doing?' he asked, and at first she wasn't sure what he meant. Then she was startled to realise that she hadn't given Tom or Cynthia a thought.

'I'm fine,' she said. 'I feel like I should be angry, or sad, but I'm not.' She'd been more caught up in thoughts of Darius than thoughts of Tom and Cynthia.

Even later in the church, as she watched Cynthia walk towards Tom, Lily felt nothing—or at least, nothing negative. She was able to watch the ceremony with equanimity, and to her surprise she could see the love on both their faces. She realised that Tom had never looked at her that way and, if she was honest, neither had she looked at him the way Cynthia did.

As they exchanged their vows all she was aware of was Darius, his strong body next to hers, his hand tightly round hers. As she looked up at him, he smiled down at her. Then it was over and they followed the bride and groom out into the fresh, crisp February afternoon, watching as confetti was thrown.

Lily studied the faces of the guests, recognised the girls from school and instinctively moved closer to Darius. She was surprised herself at the intensity of her reactions as memories threatened to surface. She told herself not to let it spoil her day, spoil the magic, ruin their last hours together.

'You OK?' Darius's voice was deep, his grey eyes searching as he looked down at her.

'Yes. But I'd like to stick close to you, if possible. I don't really want to engage in more conversation than I have to.'

'Then feel free to stick as close as you like. I won't leave your side.'

True to his word, he didn't, stayed next to her through the sit-down dinner and the speeches. Somehow with him by her side her ex-schoolmates lost their terror, and by the time the band came on Lily was filled with a sense of euphoria.

As they danced, with his hands clasping her waist, her head against his chest, the hard length of his body against hers, she allowed herself to live entirely in the moment. Lost herself in the strains of the music, in the feel of him, the scent of him and the sheer safety of him—the man who had made this day bearable.

More than bearable—almost magical.

The song finished and she stepped back. 'I need the loo, so I'll unstick myself from you for a few minutes.'

She walked away from the dance floor and saw that her mother was waiting for her, her face concerned.

'Is everything OK?'

'I don't think you're playing your cards right,' Maria said flatly. 'You're all over him. He's with you for the novelty factor, for that feeling that for once he's not being chased or cornered. If you want this to last for a while, you have to play the game, Lily. I know you don't want to hear this but a man like that…you have to work to keep. Look around you—look at the women here who are eying him up. That's part of life. Don't be foolish enough to trust Darius.'

The words made the magic start to dissipate around the edges, because it didn't matter. In a few hours, in the grey light of the morning, this would be over, all the cards played.

'Play hard to get and make sure you work out what you want from your time with him. Whatever it is—money, fun, publicity—it's a bargain. Remember that.'

Her mother of all people had hit the nail on the head. It was a bargain, one she'd entered into blithely, sure there'd be no possibility of being hurt. She watched Darius now, standing on the edge of the dance floor, Gina walking towards him. Gina, the stepsister who had hated her most, even more than Cynthia had.

Lily felt a sudden cold hand clutch her chest. There was no denying her older stepsister's beauty; it outclassed even Cynthia's. Glossy blonde hair fell in a freefall of gold to frame a face of delicate features: cornflower-blue eyes fringed with long, dark lashes; a pert, straight nose. Her figure was that of a super-model. And Lily had a sudden urge to run towards Darius, arms outstretched, stand in front of him and say, 'Mine!'

Only, he wasn't hers.

Was that why she'd wanted to stick close? Had it been some sort of possessiveness, a desire to prevent him from straying? Panic-stricken hurt churned inside her as Gina reached Darius and whispered something in her ear.

She had to calm down. Darius was not Tom. He would not flirt with anyone when he was here with Lily. But he was only with Lily for another night. This was temporary. Sure, they were going to fake a long-distance relationship for a while, but soon enough Darius would be a completely free agent. The idea of Darius with someone else sent a sear of pain straight through her, and she forced herself to turn and walk away towards the bathroom and closed herself into a cubicle.

She sat for a while, then she rose, about to exit, when she heard a group of women enter, recognised their voices and suddenly felt as if she were back at school. The people who'd made her childhood miserable were all grown up now, but it felt as though the years had not passed, and she shrank back against the wall.

'Well, I never thought I'd see this.'

'I feel sorry for her. A man like Darius Kingsleigh will never stay with her.'

'Maybe she told him about how Tom left her for Cynthia, so he's being kind.'

'He'll be quick enough to dance with Gina, given the chance, I'll bet.'

'Poor Lily. Maybe we should tell her not to be so obvious—did you see the way she looks at him?'

Lily stood frozen. How did she look at Darius? How did she feel about him? She became aware of the sudden silence from outside and knew they had noticed the closed cubicle door. She reminded herself she wasn't that frightened school girl any more, pulled in a breath and pushed open the door.

'No need to worry. I heard you all loud and clear. Thanks for the advice.'

With that, she walked out, proud at least that all their faces registered surprise at her words. They'd probably known all along that she was in there, but they didn't matter, not compared to the thoughts and emotions swirling round her brain and causing her tummy to churn in panic. How *had* she been looking at Darius?

She stepped forward and saw him still standing on the edge of the dance floor, still talking to Gina. Emotions shot through her: jealousy, panic, irrational, overriding hurt and a deep sense of possessiveness. This was an overreaction; he wasn't doing anything.

For now.

But what about the future?

She had no hold on Darius and, whilst he wouldn't be crass enough to date Gina, he would inevitably date *someone* else.

How had she looked at Darius? Like a woman in love. Her steps faltered at the sheer enormity of the realisation, as if she'd had a glass of champagne too many, even though she hadn't. She hadn't needed champagne because she'd been giddy on love, even if she hadn't known it. She'd fallen for him, for Darius Kingsleigh—just like Ruby AllStar had.

Lily closed her eyes and opened them again. She would not make a fool of herself at this wedding. She would not make a fool of herself at all. Not again, not like she had two years ago. Unlike Tom, Darius had done nothing wrong. She'd known the terms; hell, she'd instigated them herself. Now she'd see them through and would retain some dignity and self-respect. She would see out this night without letting him know what she'd so foolishly done, for her own pride and for him. He had never wanted to hurt her, and she couldn't, wouldn't, see self-recrimination in his grey eyes, nor pity.

She knew there was no hope that he would return her feelings, but even if he did, or believed he did, Lily didn't believe in for ever. Inevitably, Darius would hurt her. Their time together would be all about waiting—waiting for when the next beautiful woman came along, always looking, always circling. And she knew, of course she knew, that at some point she would lose. Her novelty factor would wear off.

Straightening up, she headed towards him where he now stood alone. She saw his face light up as she approached, and wanted to run towards him, but she didn't. Instead she forced herself to try to look like the same woman who had left the dance floor such a short time before.

'Welcome back. I missed you.' The words should have warmed her heart, but somehow made her want to cry. 'I was thinking,' he continued. 'Can we talk?' Before she could answer, the music came to a stop, a grandfather clock started to strike midnight and Lily found herself counting the chimes.

As the final bong tolled out, Cynthia entered the room, now changed into her going away outfit, to shouts of, 'Hurrah!' from the guests. Her stepsister headed straight towards her and Lily braced herself. But, to her surprise, Cynthia enveloped her in a hug, a hug that felt real. 'I want you to know I'm sorry—but I do love him. I promise.'

Cynthia stepped back, leaving Lily to process the words, words that seemed to mock her, though she truly didn't grudge Cynthia her happiness.

'I'm glad,' she managed. 'Truly, I am.' And she was. Her time with Tom now seemed muted and a long time ago, as though it all happened to a different Lily.

Then the bride and groom were gone in a swirl of well wishes and blown kisses and the guests began to disperse, heading to the bar for a final drink or to their rooms, and Lily turned to Darius, remembering his question.

'Of course we can talk. Maybe we could find a room down here somewhere?' She knew she wasn't ready yet to go back to their bedroom, needed some space, some time, to process her fevered thoughts and work out how to get through this last night, this precious last night, without betraying herself. A conversation would help that. She could only assume he wanted to discuss the plan for fizzling out their relationship.

'But first I'll go up and change.' She knew she had to get out of this dress, a dress that had used up all its magic and now symbolised nothing but the illusory promises that fairy tales made.

Turning, she headed for the exit.

Darius watched her go, a small frown on his face as he went and secured a small private lounge for them to talk. Something had shifted in the past half hour but he wasn't sure what. Perhaps it was the finality of seeing Tom marry Cynthia. It would be natural for old wounds to have reopened.

The idea caused a sharp sear of something akin to jealousy. For him, today had been magical. He'd wanted to be by Lily's side as she had requested, had been touched at the request; he'd wanted to protect her from gossip or vulgar curiosity. Wanted to show the world that Lily was a desired, beautiful woman who he appreciated. That Tom had been a fool to give her up.

Though, if Tom was a fool, then what did that make Darius? Because he too was giving Lily up after today, when there was no need. They were planning to continue the fake relationship long distance for a while, use social media and the occasional meet up to keep the ruse going, then let it all fizzle out. In which case why not carry on the fling for real? It would mean changing the boundaries, changing the rules, but they'd already done that once and there was no reason not to do it again.

As if on cue, Lily entered the room, dressed now in jeans and an oversized sweatshirt, her hair pulled back in a ponytail and face scrubbed of all make-up. To him, she looked just as beautiful now as she had in the glittering dress. 'Hey,' he said, as she came in.

'Hey.' She sat down opposite him and he poured her tea.

'What would you like to talk about?' she asked, her voice polite but wary. She was a far cry from the vital woman in the blue dress who had danced with him, laughed with him, held his hand and looked at him with sparkling eyes and a beautiful smile. Anxiety began to unfurl inside him, and he stamped down on. It had been an emotional day; she must be exhausted.

He took a sip of tea and told himself to get on with it. 'I was thinking and… I think that we should extend our fling, keep seeing each other for longer.'

His hands clenched round the arm of his chair, his heart beating faster as she met his gaze. Her blue eyes were wide with shock, but also with something he would swear was sadness.

'Why?' she asked, the syllable stark.

'Because it makes sense. We are going to continue a fake relationship—why not keep having fun? We enjoy each other's company, and we like each other, so really, why not?'

Her gaze dropped to her hands, twisted together on her lap, and now his anxiety morphed further into a sense of dread, a doomed knowledge of impending rejection.

'Because it wouldn't work. It's not what we agreed, and...' She hauled in an audible breath. 'It's not what I want.' Her gaze met his. 'It's too risky. If we make this real, there's too much risk of hurt. It's not personal,' she said. 'It's true of any relationship. We both agreed that and we both agreed to end this here, tonight.'

The words hit him with a stark force, a sucker-punch of pain that shouldn't be possible. His hands gripped around the arms of the chair as he forced his voice to remain calm, as he tried to process why this hurt so much. Every word she said made sense: stick to the rules and boundaries he'd set.

Had there been even the slightest hint of a question in her voice...? He studied her face, but there was nothing. Her expressive face, that he'd thought he could read with such ease, was shut down. She meant it: it was over. He'd never hold her again; they'd never walk hand in hand, never sit in companionable silence or discuss their hopes and dreams. It was over.

'I appreciate everything,' she said. 'It's been fun and... magical. A wonderful moment in time. But now it's time to move on.'

He'd been so sure she would want to take this further. But he'd got it wrong. Lily had been upfront about what she wanted: a short term, no-strings arrangement. She wanted magic and wonder for a few days.

If he'd thought the lines had blurred, that was his own fault.

She held out her hand, then dropped it. 'And I hope all your dreams do come true.' With that, she turned and left the room, and all Darius wanted to do was get up and go after her, persuade her to change her mind, persuade her to…

To what—to continue something she had decided she wanted to end? What would that achieve? What was the point? What did he have to offer? He had believed Lily was worth risking changing the rules for, but she didn't feel the same way about him. He wasn't really surprised. That was how these things worked—they were fun and magical for a short time. But moving on wasn't supposed to be so devastating.

He sat there staring into the fireplace, into the early hours of the morning with the bleak knowledge that it was over; that again someone had found him not worthy.

CHAPTER SEVENTEEN

L<small>ILY STARED OUT</small> of the window and tried to take heart from the weak glow of sunshine in the cloudless sky. She tried to see it as a sign that things were getting better, because surely by now the jagged tear in her heart should be healing a little bit?

She'd thought she'd known devastation when Tom had broken up with her but, looking back now to those days when she'd turned to tubs of ice-cream as solace, she could see that it hadn't been her heart that had been broken, but her pride. It had been the humiliation of it; it had been the fact that it was Cynthia who had captured Tom that had devastated her.

This feeling now went so much deeper than that. She missed Darius so much that her muscles felt clenched in constant misery. How she wished comfort could be found in a tub of ice-cream, but she knew it couldn't. Her appetite was gone, though she forced herself to eat, knew she needed the energy to keep working.

She could derive a faint glow of pride, of satisfaction, from the number of jobs that had come in thanks to Lady Gemma Fairley-Godfrey's endorsement, approval and personal recommendations. And of course Lily was pleased. At least it gave her something to do, a distraction from the gaping emptiness that hollowed inside her.

She felt a sense of regret… Why hadn't she extended their fling? Why hadn't she taken him up on the offer? Sometimes the urge to call him, say she'd changed her mind, nearly overwhelmed her. But she hadn't done it. Because, if it hurt this much now, how much more would it hurt in the future?

She forced her mind back to the proposal she was trying to put together, looking up as there was a tentative knock on the door. 'Come in.'

The door pushed inward to reveal her mother.

'Mum?' Lily rose to her feet. Maria had never visited her office. Lily was surprised she'd even been able to find it. 'Is everything OK?'

'That's what I came to ask you.' Maria glanced round the office. 'You've done a nice job here,' she said. 'Just the right amount of understated elegance to show class rather than ostentation.'

'Thank you. That's exactly what I was aiming for.'

'But I haven't come here to discuss décor. You've been ignoring my messages.'

'I've been busy. Catching up after being away. And there's been a lot of new business.'

'That's great, but that's also not why I'm here. I'm here to talk about you, and Darius. And to apologise.'

Lily had never heard her mother apologise to anyone, let alone her.

Maria took a deep breath, and another. She looked uncomfortable. 'I got it wrong. I wanted you to make the same decisions I made in my life and that's not right. I've seen how devastated you are. I can see the misery on your face, in your heart, and I know what that feels like. I never wanted to go through it again and I never wanted you to go through it at all.'

Surprise vied with shock at her mother's words. 'Tell me,' Lily said.

'Your father...' And now Maria had a dreamy look on her exquisite face as she looked back on a past she had never mentioned before. 'I loved him. I know I was young, and idealistic, but I loved him. I always knew it was doomed. Our families came from different worlds— my dad was in and out of prison, my mum drank, and your dad, he was upper-middle class, with a political family. But we fell in love.

'It was a magical year. We both kept it from our respective families, made plans about a future. He wanted a career in politics, really thought he could make a difference, and I vowed I'd support him. Then I fell pregnant and...'

Maria's voice broke. 'I went to tell him—went to his house because I didn't know what else to do. Told the housekeeper who opened the door that I was a friend. But, instead of him, his mum came to meet me. Somehow she guessed I was pregnant. I was so overwhelmed by their house—by how she looked, how she sounded—and she persuaded me. She made me believe that if I loved him the best thing I could do was leave him. That marrying into a family like mine, having a baby now, would ruin his life and his chance of achieving his political dreams. She told me about his life, the sort of girls he was used to. She offered me a massive amount of money if I would go away and not tell him about you. And I agreed.'

Lily could see the tears in her mum's eyes, knew her

own tears were imminent and reached out and took her mum's hand.

'I took the money and I left—left the house, left the city, left my family. But, please believe me, I did it because I loved him, not for the money. I needed the money for you. I had no qualifications, nothing. It turns out I am dyslexic. Back then I thought I was stupid, that I'd couldn't have a career, so yes, I took the money. But I missed him so much and it was hard, being pregnant on my own in a strange place, then being a mum.

'And when I met Max… I knew he was married, but I couldn't bring myself to care. He was kind and he was… someone. The money was running out and…'

'I understand.' And Lily did. She could picture how weary, how sad, how disillusioned her mother must have been. 'And, if Max brought you happiness and security, then I am happy for you.'

'Thank you.' She looked Lily straight in the face. 'I don't regret my time with him or after we split my marriage to Richard. Richard wasn't happy in his marriage, and if it hadn't been me it would have been someone else. And we have been—we are—happy. I have grown to love him—not the way I loved your father, but it is a real love for all that. What I do regret is my relationship with you. I know I haven't always been a good mum.'

Lily raised her hand. 'Don't, Mum. It's OK.'

'It's not, but you and I have plenty of time to sort things out.'

'I'd like that.'

'But first please listen to my advice. If you love Darius, you should tell him the truth. Don't walk away like I did, without giving him a chance. Without giving love a chance. It's a risk, but…it's a risk worth taking. I wish I had.'

Maria glanced at her watch and then rose to her feet. 'Now, darling, I have to run. I've got a facial booked in on the other side of London. Think about what I've said.'

'I will,' Lily promised, rose and pulled her mum into a hug. 'Thank you for coming here.'

Her mind whirled as her mother clicked the door shut behind her. Emotions cascaded inside her. If she told Darius she loved him, she would have to trust him. As, perhaps, her mother should have trusted her father—trusted their love, trusted that love would trump everything else.

Darius watched the last board member leave the room and hoped he'd done enough to hold their confidence. He knew he'd fought his corner. Now, as and when Enzo's will went public and the story broke, he'd at least know he'd done all he could.

And that mattered. But just weeks ago it would have been *all* that mattered. Now, he missed Lily with a depth he wouldn't have believed possible. All he wanted to do was call her, see her, share the day's news with her, and the knowledge he couldn't was bleak. But it would fade. He'd throw himself into work, and surely he would stop thinking about her? There were reminders everywhere, despite the fact Lily had never even been here with him. All it took was a song, a scent of vanilla, the bar of black soap that he couldn't bring himself to throw away, the stars at night…

He looked up as the door opened, assumed it was someone who had thought of a final question.

But instead it was Gemma, and he rose to his feet.

'Gemma.'

'Darius.' His godmother came forward, approached him hands outstretched and enveloped him in a hug—the one person who had done that consistently in his life. 'How are you?' she asked.

'Good. The meeting went well and—'

His godmother cut across his speech without compunction. 'That's not what I meant. I have full confidence that you have everything covered on the work front. I meant how are you and Lily?'

He forced himself to meet her eye. 'We are trying to keep things going long-distance, but to be honest I think its fizzling out.' He tried a laugh. 'Probably all for the best. I'm not cut out for "long term".'

There was a pause and Gemma leant forward. 'That's not true,' she said. 'You're a good man and you are cut out for the long term. I've always known that and I've been waiting for the right person to come along. I thought Lily was that person.'

'She isn't.' He tried again. 'It was good while it lasted, but both of us are committed to our work, our businesses, and neither of us wants long-term commitment.'

Gemma eyed him narrowly. 'Then why do you look so miserable?' she asked gently. 'I can see it in your eyes, Darius, the same look you had as a little boy. Perhaps you do want more with Lily.'

'It wouldn't matter if I did.' He kept his voice steady, realising he might as well tell Gemma the truth. 'She doesn't want more with me. And that is fair enough.'

'And you're happy to let it go?' Gemma asked.

Darius looked at her in surprise. 'She made it clear it was over. She said it was better that way, that it was time to move on—that it was nothing personal but it was too risky to take things further.' His voice slowed down as he considered the words.

'Did you tell her how you feel?'

'I...' How did he feel about Lily? He pictured her—pictured holding her, kissing her, walking hand in hand with her; he felt the sense of connection, the sheer happiness of being with her and the ache of missing her.

He was a fool not to have seen it—he loved Lily. The idea was both glorious and terrifying, filling him with a sense of exhilaration. 'No, I didn't.' Euphoria faded as reality sank in. 'And I won't. How would that be fair to her, to tell her I love her? She wants to move on, I need to let her do that.'

'Or you could fight for her, try to win her love, make her see that you are worth the risk of hurt. But to do that you need to believe it yourself, Darius. I believe in you. I believe you are capable of commitment and love.'

Was he? He thought of Lily. He thought again of her beautiful face, her smile, her warmth and compassion; thought about the sound of her laughter, the feel of her body against his, her hair against his chest. The way she'd listened to him, the way she'd held him. He would never hurt her; the knowledge was absolute and real. He would never abandon her.

And, damn it, she was worth fighting for. He'd given her a mealy mouthed offer of an extension of their fling, and shame ran through him at the memory. Lily was worth more than that, so much more, and he'd bottled it. He hadn't offered her his heart.

He rose to his feet, moved over to his godmother and hugged her. 'Thank you, Gemma. For being the best godmother a man could wish for.'

'You're welcome.'

* * *

Lily pulled the office door shut and set off towards the tube station. As she walked, she wondered if she'd made the right decision. Nerves skittered inside her even as she told herself she still didn't have to go through with it. She didn't have to catch the plane to LA the next day and, even if she did, she didn't have to go and see Darius. She hadn't told him she was coming. She could simply visit as a tourist and then return home. Or she could take her mother's advice, follow her heart and find the courage to tell Darius the truth. The idea, the sheer possibility, that she would see Darius filled her with a sense of anticipation and yearning…

Her thoughts broke off as she saw a man heading towards her, a tall, dark-haired man with an assured stride. Lily blinked, sure that it was another figment of her imagination. In the past days, she had 'seen' Darius so many times, only to get closer and realise it was nothing but a mirage.

Then… 'Lily.'

Her heart somersaulted, cartwheeled, and every muscle told her to run into his arms. But she forced herself to stay still and keep her face neutral, hoping he hadn't read her initial joy at seeing him.

'Darius. Is everything OK?'

He smiled at her, the smile tentative but warm, lighting his grey eyes. 'It is now,' he said. 'I was wondering, can we talk?'

Again her treacherous heart leapt and again she forced herself to stillness. This wasn't the scenario she'd planned. Perhaps he was here to discuss how to end their fake relationship.

'Of course,' she said, coolly. 'We can go back to my office or…'

'I've booked a table for dinner, if that's OK?'

'Dinner is fine.'

'Great.' Now his smile widened and she couldn't help it—she smiled back, even as she warned herself to take care.

They headed towards the road, both content with silence, a silence that strangely enough didn't feel awkward as he hailed a taxi and gave the address of a restaurant in Mayfair. Once they alighted, he gestured to a glass-fronted building. 'It's a Moroccan restaurant,' he explained. 'I've been missing Marrakesh.'

His words unfurled a small tendril of hope inside her and she allowed herself a small smile. 'So have I,' she said softly.

They entered and Lily blinked, trying to work out what was going on. There were no other diners, and the only illuminated part of the room was a table in the centre, with a chandelier overhead sending down a dim glow that showed a beautifully set table. It was strewn with rose petals and above the table was a massive helium heart-shaped balloon.

Lily gasped, trying to keep her voice level, trying to tell herself that this must be a set-up. Maybe in all the mixed emotions of the past days she'd quite simply forgotten that they'd arranged this. But then why had he asked if they could talk? 'I...don't understand,' she settled for. 'Is this...?'

'This is real,' he said. He stood and faced her and she could see the tension in his body, the set of his jaw, the deep intent focus in his eyes. 'One hundred percent real. I know it's a little late, but I am asking you if you will be my valentine—for as long as you want to be. I asked you here to talk but I want you to know from the get-go that I love you. I know you said that you want to move on, that you think this is too risky. I understand that. But you also said that it's not personal.'

He inhaled deeply. 'But it is personal and that's why I want to speak from my heart.' Just as she'd advised him to for his speech. 'I promise you that I will never intentionally hurt you, I will never leave you, I will never be unfaithful to you. I also know that those are words, words that anyone could say, but I mean every single one, and all I am asking is a chance to prove myself. We can take it as slowly as you like. I know trust had to earned, built up, but if you think there is any chance for us, any chance at all, then please say yes.'

Lily knew she should have broken in, should have stopped him before now, reassured him, told him how she felt. But she hadn't been able to. She had been listening to the words with an ever-growing sense of elation, joy and happiness. Because she knew that, as he spoke, Darius would never make promises that he couldn't keep, or make a deal he couldn't honour.

'Yes,' she said. 'Yes, I will be your valentine. Your forever valentine. Because I love you too. With all my heart.'

'You do?' Happiness suffused his face, his smile the widest she'd ever seen. 'You're sure? You're not just saying that?'

'I'm not just saying that. Look…' She pulled out her phone. 'I booked a ticket to LA. I was coming to see you to tell you I love you.' The words tumbled out of her mouth as he led her over to a velvet two-person sofa pushed against one of the restaurant walls.

They sat and she took his hand in hers, never wanting to let go. 'I knew I loved you at the wedding but I never thought that you could possibly love me. That, even if you did how, could I trust it would last for ever? But you're right—it is personal. It's not about trusting love, it's about trusting you. And I do trust you.' With all her heart.

'And…' She took a deep breath. 'It was also about trusting myself. Believing in myself.'

He nodded, his grey eyes focused on her face, and she knew that he was listening, truly listening. 'And I found that concept hard—believing you could love me for ever.

'You see, when I was younger, Cynthia and Gina resented me because of what my mum had done to their lives. They decided to take it out on me. We were all sent away to boarding school and they…made my life miserable, bullied me.' Even now she could hear the near embarrassment in her voice, as if she had done something wrong.

'It wasn't your fault.' His voice was deep and reassuring, knowing unerringly the right thing to say.

'I know, and I thought I'd worked my way through it, and achieved success through work. But I think deep down all the insecurity was still there. Because the worst thing they did wasn't the physical actions, the chillies in my food or the slugs in my bed. It was how they made me feel—ugly and stupid and small. That's why I didn't tell anyone what was happening, or why I didn't tell you. I didn't want you to think of me as a small, pathetic victim.'

Darius pulled her close. 'I could never think that of you. I have seen first hand how brave you are, how you stand up for others. I would never pity you, Lily; you are too courageous, too strong for that. But when I think of the young girl you were, and how you suffered, I am truly sorry— but it also makes my admiration for you all the greater for what you have achieved, the woman you are and the way you handled the wedding. Thank you for telling me now.'

'I'm telling you because I want you to know how much you have helped me overcome those insecurities. You make me feel beautiful and have allowed me to believe I am worthy of love. You've shown me that I can trust— trust you and trust our love.'

'And you have done the same for me. I refused to think a "for ever" love was possible for me because I was so so sure that my relationships with my parents, my upbringing, meant I would mess it up. You changed that, made me believe that I could, because I know with all my heart that my love for you is for ever and real. I know that for you I can be anyone. You listened to me, put things into perspective for me, made me see that maybe all the fault wasn't mine. That I am capable of love and being loved. Capable of being a good husband or father.'

'I know that you are. With all my heart.'

Now he dropped to one knee. 'Then please, Lily, give me the chance to be a good husband and father. Will you marry me?'

And out of his pocket came a jewellery box.

'Yes. Of course I will marry you…' Joy filled her—joy and happiness that soared through her veins along with a deep, enduring love for this man, a man whom she loved with all her heart.

She opened the box and gave a small gasp of delight. There winked up a diamond ring set with dark-blue gems in a star shape. 'To match your eyes,' he said as he slipped it onto her finger, then pulled her into his arms. And, as he kissed her in a glorious, head-spinning kiss, Lily thought she would burst with happiness.

When they finally stepped apart, he gestured to the table. 'And now I think it's time for champagne and food.'

She looked round the restaurant. 'How on earth did you manage this?'

Darius grinned. 'Once I realised I loved you, I knew I had to tell you. But I wanted to make it special. I found this restaurant, which is actually in the midst of renovations. I hired it for the week. Then I flew Jamal and his team across to make a celebratory dinner, if that was called for. They are in the kitchen waiting to be told what to do.'

Happiness bubbled inside her for this incredible, thoughtful man as they sat down at the table and raised their glasses to each other.

'And,' he said, 'I got you one more thing. Hold out your hand.'

She did and he placed something on her palm, something that made her heart overflow with love and laughter. There nestled in her hand was another charm for her bracelet—a Moroccan slipper.

'To symbolise our very own fairy-tale happy ending.'

And in that magical moment Lily knew this truly was happy ever after.

* * * * *

If you enjoyed this story,
check out these other great reads from
Nina Milne

Bound by Their Royal Baby
His Princess on Paper
Snowbound Reunion in Japan
Wedding Planner's Deal with the CEO

All available now

PRINCE'S PROPOSAL FOR THE CANADIAN CAMERAS

NINA SINGH

MILLS & BOON

To my dear Pool Mon friends.

I am so very thankful for each of you.

CHAPTER ONE

THE CALL WOULD come in any minute now. Raul knew as soon as he woke up and was alerted by his assistant to check social media.

His father, the king, would be calling him the second he got wind of the information Raul had just seen.

And he would order Raul to fix it all. Tell him to clean up another mess his sister was responsible for. Again.

Her latest mistake was quite a doozy, he had to admit. Even by Luisa's standards. Of all the ways to bring unwanted scrutiny on the family name.

Raul barely had time to wipe the sleep out of his eyes when, sure enough, his phone began to vibrate and sound the alarm he had assigned to the king.

He picked it up with a sigh. "Your Highness."

"Why do you allow her to do such things?" his father immediately responded.

"Hello to you too, Father."

"When was the last time you saw your sister?" his father demanded to know, ignoring his greeting.

Before she started all this. Or at least that's what Raul thought. But there was no way to know for sure. Just as anything else involving Luisa, his guess was as good as anyone else's

"I'm not sure, Father," Raul answered, his voice a croak both from the grogginess of sleep as well as frustration.

"Well, you should. You know what happens when she's left to her own devices."

Raul sighed, turning away from the phone. "She's a grown adult, Father. I can't very well trail her throughout her travels and escapades."

"Well, you're the only one we even have a hope of getting her to listen to. She never did heed me or your mother. Never did."

How was that his fault exactly?

His father answered his unspoken question. "I would think you'd try harder to rein her in."

Raul pinched the bridge of his nose. He'd have better luck trying to control a lightning storm. He supposed he couldn't really blame his father for being upset. The way Luisa drew unwanted attention to the royal family with her antics would drive the most patient monk to anger. But this latest escapade of hers certainly topped all the others. So far.

"You are older and wiser, after all," his father added.

Hah! As if that was any kind of argument. He was older than Luisa by a whole fifteen months. Why everyone in the kingdom seemed to forget that was beyond him.

Raul sighed. He knew full well it wasn't even worth the effort to try to make that argument. It never worked.

"Just look at the links I've sent you. Those photos are downright scandalous."

Raul reached for his tablet and called up his father's latest texts, keeping the phone to his ear. Though he hardly needed to look at the sites the links led to. He could pretty much guess what he'd be seeing. Bingo. Pictures of his sister popped up on his screen. If she knew the cameras were focused on her, she didn't seem to care.

Luisa on a yacht in a barely-there bikini, laughing at her lover. Luisa dancing in a smoky nightclub, her married boyfriend holding her about the waist. The last one was particularly racy. Luisa and the man in a deeply passionate kiss against a backdrop of a sandy beach. His sister may as well have been topless given the tiny scrap of fabric that was her swim top. The captions were as tawdry as one would expect.

Raul tossed the tablet aside. Truth be told, he was rather disappointed in Luisa himself. But his disappointment had nothing to do with his worry over salacious gossip. No. Rather, he'd thought higher of her character.

Luisa had always been a free spirit. A quality he'd actually admired and envied below the surface. Not that he would ever admit it. But she'd never been cruel or hurtful. Having a very public affair with a married man definitely qualified as being cruel. Particularly for the man's wife and children.

What in the world was she thinking?

What Luisa was doing ran far past reckless free-spiritedness.

The entire world was now having a field day with the salacious gossip. Not that Luisa cared two figs about what was said about her. But the king, well, he cared a lot. Making this whole fiasco somehow Raul's problem to solve.

"You know I can't convince Luisa to do anything she doesn't want to, Father." Even trying would have the opposite effect. His sister would only double down like a child who was being reprimanded.

"I know," the king said on a sigh so long and loud that Raul actually felt a trickle of concern. His father wasn't a young man. And he still insisted on performing his regular duties day in and day out. Any added stress wasn't good for his overall health. His doctor had already warned about the family history of various ailments his father had to watch for at his age. In fact, the king was the same age his own father, Raul's grandfather, had been when he'd suddenly and unexpectedly passed.

A shudder passed through Raul at the thought. As demanding as the king could be, he was still his father. He and Luisa had already lost one parent.

A selfish twinge of thought entered his mind. Losing his father was unbearable to contemplate. But there was something else. Raul was heir to the throne. As much responsibility as he already shouldered, he simply wasn't ready to be king just yet. The day would come soon enough. But he wanted to be more prepared.

Not to mention, the moment Raul ascended, the pressure to find a wife and procure an heir would be instantaneous. And he certainly wasn't nearly ready for any of that. Picking up his father's slack as he grew older and maintaining the investments he'd made to grow the kingdom's coffers was more than enough responsibility on him for now.

Raul swallowed a curse, pushing away the self-centered thought with no small amount of guilt. He redirected his attention back to his father on the other end of the line.

"Our only hope is to somehow take the world's attention off Luisa," his father said. "And onto something else."

"I guess we can hope for some kind of worldwide calamity," Raul quipped.

"Don't try to be cute," the king admonished. "You know that's not what I mean."

"Well, I have something of a tour coming up. That should count for something."

"That won't be enough," the king replied. "If anything,

Luisa's affair will overshadow all your efforts. You'll constantly be dodging questions about your sister."

He had a point.

"Unless…"

Uh-oh. His father's tone and hesitation was uncharacteristically coy. Alarm prickled along the surface of Raul's skin. Whatever the king was about to say, Raul wasn't going to like it. Something told him any kind of distractive calamity was going to be personally not in his favor.

"Yes?" Raul asked, already dreading the possible answer. "Unless what?"

"Unless they were asking you questions about a much safer topic."

"Such as?" Raul asked.

Something told him his father's lips had widened into a smile. "You, son."

Sir Bunbun was hardly behaving in a gentlemanly manner this morning. Sofia Nomi wasn't quick enough and received yet another splash of water to her face and torso, which took her from somewhat damp to dripping wet. She bit down on a curse and wiped her cheeks with the back of her forearm.

The not-so-subtle giggle from her assistant and best friend did nothing to lighten her mood.

"Come on, Bunbun," Sofia coaxed. "The sooner you behave, the sooner we can get this bath over with."

"It's Sir Bunbun," Agnes corrected. "His mama was very clear that we are to use his full name. You don't want to offend him now, do you?"

Sofia could only manage a grunt in response as Sir Bunbun shifted in the large tub and gave her face a wet and sloppy lick.

"Ugh!"

That wasn't the worst of it. The Great Dane– Labrador mix chose that moment to jump on his hindquarters and slosh out half the water in the utility sink. He landed his front paws with a thud on her shoulders and gave her another lick.

Sofia sucked in a breath and summoned as much patience and calm as she could muster. It wasn't much.

"Don't you dare laugh, Agnes," she warned to no avail. Her friend had her palm cupped around her mouth in an unconvincing attempt to silence her continuing giggles.

"Sorry," Agnes said. "He's just such a goofy giant," she added, giving Bunbun an affectionate scritch behind one ear. "How about I go get some more towels? The next batch should be about done."

Sofia fervently hoped so. "That would be great. Thanks."

Nothing had gone right today. She'd arrived in the morning to find that the service who cleaned and prepped for her after-hours had hired a new employee who'd neglected to launder the service towels. Her first appointment had come in particularly filthy, then a walk-in had pled with her to handle her new puppy who'd had a run-in with a skunk this morning. Sofia had reluctantly given in because of the woman's tear-filled pleas. To fit the terrier in, she'd given up her regular half hour for lunch. Her stomach reminded her of that injustice with a loud, gnawing growl even as she had the thought. Now, Sir Bunbun was behaving particularly rambunctiously, even for him. Agnes was right about him being a gentle giant. But the giant part made grooming him an adventure in patience and stamina when he wasn't behaving.

It didn't help that she was operating on very little energy or stamina after such a restless night due to yet another disquieting phone call from Phil yesterday. Her stepfather could be persistent, in a most annoying way. She supposed he had to be to achieve his level of success as a Washington, DC, businessman. As grateful as she was that her mother had finally found someone who loved her and looked out for her, Sofia couldn't help but wish Mama might have married someone a bit less ambitious.

To make matters worse, Phil's latest scheme involved using *her* as a bargaining chip! The whole idea smacked of impropriety as far as Sofia was concerned. And if her mother wasn't so in love and was instead thinking clearly, she'd see it that way too.

Sofia gave her head a shake. She would have to deal with Phil and his impossible ask later. Right now she had to get Bunbun taken care of. "Why are you being so naughty?" she chided the dog. "You really ought to be better behaved, young man."

The canine tilted his head, as if trying to understand her. Sofia couldn't help but smile. Despite all his trouble, he really was a charmer. "How about we compromise, huh?" she asked, gently removing his paws from her shoulders and setting them back down into the utility sink. "If you stop acting as you have been, I'll give you a special treat later. Our little secret," she whispered. "Just between you and me." Bunbun's mama could be a little strict with the treats. But honestly, for a dog his size, Sofia couldn't see the difference between one Graham Bone treat or two.

Sofia heard the sound of someone clearing their throat echoing from the front of the store.

"We'll be right with you," she shouted, wondering why there was anyone out there. Bunbun was her last appointment. And if it was another walk-in, Sofia would just have to put her foot down and tell the pet owner that another groom today was out of the question.

Where was Agnes? It couldn't possibly take her that long to pull towels out of the dryer.

"Perhaps you can come back tomorrow?" she shouted over the curtain. "This isn't a really great time."

"Sorry to hear that," came the response, carried on a deep, gravelly voice.

Sofia froze in the act of sponging Bunbun's haunch as a ripple of awareness ran over her skin. That voice. She would know it anywhere. But it couldn't be. Could it?

Agnes chose that moment to reappear carrying a mountainous stack of towels. Sofia grabbed the top one and began to dry her hands.

"Could you take over with Bunbun?" she asked, then turned around without waiting for an answer. She had to go see if her ears were deceiving her.

Sofia pulled the curtain to the side, trying to ignore the shaking in her hands. She had to be mistaken. There was no way Prince Raul Refik Abarra could possibly be standing in her little pet grooming shop.

"Hello, Sofia."

Sofia swallowed the brick that instantaneously formed at the base of her throat. If her ears had been deceiving her, her eyes were following along.

She somehow managed to make her mouth work. "Prince Raul. To what do I owe the honor?"

He winked at her. "No need to be so formal, Soso. It's me."

Raul wasn't expecting the figurative gut punch that struck when Sofia appeared from behind the dividing curtain. Funny, he didn't remember her being quite so...alluring. And how was that even possible, given her current state of disarray? She was soaking wet, her hair slipping out of the complicated topknot on her head and falling messily around her face.

Yet, despite her dishevelment, a surge of electricity shot through his core at the sight of her, heating him from within. Maybe he was just tired. Or suffering from some weird form of jet lag after his long flight.

"Um…what are you doing here?" she asked, clearly in shock.

"Sorry if I'm interrupting something." He'd clearly walked in when she was predisposed. Taking care of an animal. Though, for a split second when he'd first arrived and heard her words from behind the curtain, he'd thought perhaps he'd just walked in on some sort of foreplay.

A strange and unfamiliar sensation had washed over him when he'd heard her melodic voice uttering those words. A feeling he refused to believe might have bordered on jealousy. No, he'd simply felt a moment of alarm. This whole idea would be sorely hampered if Sofia was currently involved with someone. There was no plan B. His security had run a check and looked into the possibility, and assured Raul that she was single currently. Her last relationship had ended about a year ago. And it had been short enough that using the word *relationship* was a bit of a stretch.

Sofia dabbed the towel along her hairline, then lower down her neck. Raul had to resist the urge to ask her if he could take over the task.

Whoa. He really had no business thinking such thoughts. He was here for one reason. To ask her about a fake relationship. Emphasis on the *fake*. No real attraction allowed.

"I was just…uh…with a client," she said and gestured

to her soaking apron. "He was less than cooperative, as you can see."

He nodded. "I heard too. I'm guessing the offer of a special treat did the trick?"

Was it his imagination or were her cheeks beginning to flush?

"Not as well as I'd hoped," she answered. "Bunbun was much more interested in licking me than the treats in my pockets, however."

Raul figured he couldn't really blame the beast. Sofia did indeed appear quite lickable.

Damn it.

Yet another wayward thought he had no business entertaining. What was wrong with him? He couldn't remember the last time he'd felt such attraction to a woman. On one hand, it would make all the pretending that much easier. On the other hand, however, it could complicate matters in so many ways.

First thing first. Sofia had to actually agree to his offer.

"Bunbun?" he asked, trying to focus on the mundane to quell the errant emotions coursing through him.

She nodded. "Sir Bunbun, actually. We were told to use his full name."

"I see." He gestured to the back. "Can I help you perhaps? With Sir Bunbun?" He had to suppress a chuckle at the ridiculous name.

She looked horrified at the idea. Her gaze traveled him from head to toe. "I don't think that's a good idea. I wouldn't let that suit anywhere near any of the animals back there, let alone a massive beast sitting in a tub full of water. I know for a fact that what you wear is custom-made and that suit probably costs as much as a foreign sports car."

She was right, though off by several thousand dollars. He could probably buy two sports cars for what it cost.

He shrugged. "No matter. I can help if you need."

She gave her head a shake, sending droplets of water flying through the air. "Thanks. But no. And surely you didn't come here to talk about my clientele or their misbehavior."

He gave her a small bow. "You're right. As interesting a topic as that is."

"So why are you here then?" she repeated. "Are you here on official business?"

He really didn't want to get into any of the reasons for his visit here in the middle of her shop, but he supposed he had to give her something. "Yes and no."

She blinked at him. "What does that mean exactly?"

"I'm here to see you."

More confused blinks, then her features softened. "Is this about Luisa?"

"In a sense."

She squinted at him, as if studying a new breed of canine she hadn't come across before. "'Yes and no. In a sense.'" She repeated his words, then repeated herself, "What does that mean exactly?"

A loud bark sounded from behind the curtain and echoed through the air.

"I am indeed here because of my sister. I'm sure you've heard the rumors."

Her lips tightened. "She called me, tried to explain."

"Well, there is no reasonable explanation for what she's doing as far as my father is concerned."

"The king."

He nodded. "Yes, he's very concerned about the negative attention this has brought on the royal family."

"I see. But I'm not sure why any of that would bring you here."

"You're in an ideal position to help us with it."

Another loud bark from the back drowned out his last word.

"Me? How can I help? Luisa's got her own mind. There's nothing I can say or do to convince her to stop doing something she wants to do."

He waited for another round of barking before speaking again. "That's not what I mean by having you help. And I'd like to explain fully. But at a better time and a quieter place." Bunbun barked once more as if to emphasize his point. "What time do you close up shop?"

"Around five thirty."

"Do you have any plans after?"

Her answer was a very slow shake of her head. "No plans. Unless you count soaking in a hot tub and slipping into bed to stream a show."

Darned if his mind didn't automatically picture her in that tub and then bed before he shook the image away.

"Excellent. I'll have a car pick you up around seven."

She rubbed a palm down her face as if taking it all in, not quite believing it. A tremor of guilt nagged at him. He really shouldn't have shown up unannounced. But up until literally an hour ago, he wasn't even actually sure he was ready to go through with any of this.

Now, there was no turning back.

CHAPTER TWO

HER DOORMAN RANG her at 7:00 p.m. on the dot. "There's a car here for you, Sofia."

"Coming, Frank."

Sofia took one last glance in the mirror and rubbed her palm down her midriff.

So this was actually happening. She hadn't imagined Raul in her shop a few hours ago. He really had been there. And in a few short minutes, she'd be meeting him for dinner.

Part of her still couldn't quite believe it. Her phone dinged with a text message as she strode to the door.

My driver should be there to pick you up. I look forward to our meeting. R

Meeting. For some reason the last word landed with a thud as she read it. How silly of her. Of course, that's all this was. Not like Raul had asked her out on some kind of date. The man was the Prince of Vesovia, for heaven's sake. So far out of Sofia's league, he may as well be in another dimension. He'd appeared so imposing and out of place in her modest little shop. The last time she'd seen him, he'd still been harboring the leftover features of a youthful teenager. The man who'd appeared at her shop was a fully mature male.

Raul still called her Soso. She knew it was simply gentle teasing that had carried over from their teen years, but the underlying message was clear. He thought her average, mediocre, just so-so. And who could blame him? The man was set to inherit an island kingdom in the not-so-distant future.

She bathed and trimmed pets for a living.

No. He was only here because of his sister. He'd told her that he wanted to speak to her about Luisa. That she could somehow help with the latest mess her friend had gotten herself involved with. Though for the life of her, she wasn't sure what she could possibly do. True, Sofia and Luisa had become close friends during their high school years. And they'd kept in touch off and on through the years. But Luisa was as headstrong as they came. If she wasn't listening to her brother or her own father, a man who happened to be a king, how in the world could Sofia get her to see reason about her taboo relationship?

She was still pondering that very question when she made her way downstairs and out of her building. The "car" Raul had sent was a shiny black stretch limousine. Complete with a tuxedoed driver who stood by the passenger door and opened it for her when she reached him.

How the man had maneuvered such a long vehicle through her tight NoMa street, she could simply marvel at. Within minutes they were driving past the Capitol Building toward the heart of the city. She wasn't even surprised when he finally pulled up to the swankiest hotel in the DC area and stopped the car. Sofia should have known this was the place they'd be having dinner. All the dignitaries and heads of state who visited DC stayed here. She'd expect nothing less from Prince Raul Abarra of Vesovia. Only the best. As befitting a future king.

Still, she couldn't help but feel a bit like a character in a fairy tale when a uniformed attendant immediately appeared to accompany her to the front entrance and through the lobby.

A girl could get used to this.

She followed the man through the extravagant lobby and to a set of steel elevator doors. Once inside, he retrieved a key card from his pocket and swiped it along a panel on the wall. The topmost button lit up and he pushed it with a well-manicured finger. Sofia actually felt the pressure change in her ears as they climbed up. How high were they going exactly?

She got her answer when the car finally slowed a few moments later and the door swished open. To the very top, it seemed, all the way to the rooftop. The attendant nodded to her with a smile and gestured for her to exit the car. She didn't even know this hotel had a rooftop dining option. It was probably one of the well-kept secrets of the DC that only certain people knew about. People like a crown prince.

Who happened to be the only one up here. Raul stood up from where he'd been sitting at a white-clothed table and immediately strode to greet her.

Sofia's breath hitched at the sight of him. In a dark suit jacket with a silk shirt unbuttoned at the top, Raul was breathtakingly handsome. His dark hair glistened amid the backdrop of the city lights behind him and the light of the full moon above. She thought she might have stepped into a cologne ad.

He dismissed the other man without so much as a word, merely a simple glance and an almost imperceptible nod, then took Sofia by the hand. A bolt of current shot through her arm at his touch and traveled through to her core.

She really had to get a grip. She wasn't the silly school-girl who had an embarrassing crush on her best friend's older brother anymore. She didn't have to react like a love-lorn fool at the simplest touch from the man.

"Thank you for agreeing to meet me, Sofia," Raul said and led her to the table he'd just left, then pulled a chair out for her. "And on such short notice."

Sofia glanced around at the other empty tables and chairs and realized that he must have arranged for them to have the entire restaurant to themselves.

"I'll have to admit, the curiosity was eating away at me about why you asked me here."

He didn't get a chance to answer as a gentleman appeared at their side and filled their glasses with an icy pitcher of water.

"I asked the chef to prepare a Mexican-themed menu for us this evening," Raul said after the man left. "I hope that's okay."

"That sounds great." Tacos were practically a staple of her diet. Though the ones prepared here were probably a far cry from her usual food truck stop outside her grooming shop.

Raul nodded then lifted his arm. A waitress appeared with two goblets full of golden liquid. She placed one in front of Sofia first. "Our custom recipe margarita, ma-dame."

Sofia raised her hand. As tempting as the concoction looked, she was going to have to pass. "You can have mine too. No drinks for me, I'm afraid," she told Raul after the woman left.

He lifted an eyebrow. "Oh? Why's that?"

"I have an early grooming appointment tomorrow. A poodle—they're a lot of work. And this one has to be perfect or I'll have the owner come back repeatedly until she gets her exactly how she wants her."

"Can't you delegate? It is your shop after all."

She shook her head. "There's only me and Agnes. And this poodle is a two-person job."

He took a sip of his drink and studied her. "No other employees."

Sofia resisted rolling her eyes. Imagine having to explain strict budgeting to a prince who never had to worry about finances.

"I'm afraid not. I'd love to hire more qualified people. I simply can't afford it."

Raul set his drink down and leveled a look toward her she couldn't quite place. Though it had the effect of making her quake inside. As if he was about to let her in on some secret that only he knew about.

"What if I told you I could help you with that? And more."

Sofia chuckled at the question. How much more curious could this possibly get? "And how exactly would you do that?"

She wasn't prepared in the least for his answer.

She couldn't possibly have heard him correctly. In fact, maybe none of this was actually happening. Maybe she wasn't even really here. Maybe Sir Bunbun had knocked her over this afternoon and she'd managed to fall and hit her head. Perhaps she was lying on the tiled floor of her shop right at this very moment having the most elaborate of dreams.

That theory made much more sense than what she thought she'd just heard.

"I see I've shocked you," coma-induced Raul said from across the table with surprising clarity for a figment of her imagination.

"I think I may have that drink after all."

Raul nodded in the direction of the waiting server, who immediately appeared with a fresh cocktail for her.

Sofia took a sip, then gave her head a brisk shake to try to clear her thoughts. "I'm sure I misheard you. Because I really thought you just said that you wanted to hire me as part of some PR scheme for the royal palace that involves me pretending to be your fiancée." She lifted her glass for another sip. "Which can't be correct, obviously. So, either I misheard, or I'm in a coma."

The corner of his mouth lifted ever so slightly. "Those are the only two options you've come up with then?"

"They're the only ones that make a lick of sense."

Yet another waiter arrived with their food. He set a plate of empanadas that were still steaming in front of them and a serving tray with an array of sauces.

Sofia would have thought she was too distracted to eat, but her mouth watered at the aroma wafting through the air. She'd been way too tired and full of anticipation to have a snack after work despite having missed lunch. Now she realized she was starving. A loud growl sounded from the vicinity of her stomach to confirm.

Raul used the pair of tongs on a separate plate to lift an empanada and drop it on her plate. Then he took one for himself.

"Maybe we should eat first before we discuss the details. I'd prefer to do this on a full stomach."

"The details of what exactly?"

"Eat, Sofia. First thing first."

She held in a snicker. "As bossy as ever, I see." She wanted to take the words back as soon as they left her lips. That was no way to talk to royalty. What if she'd gone and offended him?

To her surprise, Raul merely chuckled in response, then popped the entire empanada in his mouth after dipping it in the thickest of the sauces. "I've told you the gist of the proposal. We'll get into the specifics once you get some food in you."

She took a forkful of her appetizer and chewed, studying him while he helped himself to another empanada.

Sofia leaned back in her chair. "Wait. So you're actually serious. About this fake-engagement idea."

He swallowed before nodding.

She put down her fork. "I'm sorry. I'm going to need you to explain sooner rather than later."

"Now who's the bossy one?"

She merely tapped her finger on the table impatiently.

"Look, this kind of thing isn't unheard-of," he began. "The fact of the matter is, Luisa is bringing a lot of scandalous attention to the royal family. The gossip has gotten out of control. My father asked me to create something of a distraction."

"By shifting all the focus on yourself."

"Correct. And in a positive way. You're the answer to it all."

"How so?"

He shrugged. "Simple. You just have to be seen with me. At three events in particular."

"What events?"

The first one right here in DC. The Washington Journalist Association dinner."

"The one with all the celebrities and politicians?"

"That's right."

"That's just three nights from now."

"I know."

Sofia inhaled a deep steadying breath. Her head was spinning. "What other events?"

"The next stop on my agenda is Canada."

Sofia practically jumped in her seat. "You want me to go to Canada with you?"

He nodded. "First stop is Toronto for a wedding. Then Montreal for the mayor's seasonal awards ball."

"Whose wedding?"

"Francesca Tate."

He had to be kidding. "*The* Francesca Tate? *That* wedding?"

"Correct."

That was the celebrity wedding of the decade. If not the century. Francesca Tate was a multi-award-winning actress known and adored the world over. And here was Raul, casually discussing taking Sofia to the event the whole world was anticipating as casually as a teenager asking to go get ice cream.

"Like I said. You're perfect as the fake fiancée who's accompanying me to it all."

If her skepticism were a tangible thing, it could take a seat at the table. "If you say so. One part of this I don't understand at all."

"What's that?"

"Why me? I mean, I'm hardly princess material."

She really didn't see it. Just how perfect she would be for what he had in mind. Sofia checked all the boxes—famil-iarity with the royal family, her devotion to his sister, nothing salacious in her past, a self-owned business. And she was beautiful to boot, that last part being an added bonus. He studied her now, the US Capitol Building looming in the distance behind her. Striking hazel eyes, hair the color of midnight. High cheekbones that were somehow always lush with color. Thick, full red lips.

Focus. She had asked him something.

"Well, first of all. You happen to be in DC. The first event is right here, in three nights, like you said."

Her lips tightened. "So, I'm convenient. Logistically."

"I prefer to think of it as serendipity."

"Kismet?"

"Exactly!"

She glanced to the side, seemingly unconvinced. "Then there's the fact that you already know the family. Went to school with my sister. And my father likes you. Always has." That last bit was probably the most relevant. The king had practically beamed at him when he'd offered up Sofia's name as a candidate. In fact, hers was the first name that came to him.

She was guileless and genuine, not interested in any kind of career that a relationship with a prince might advance. Having Sofia help with this assured that it would remain confidential.

"Look. I know how preposterous all this must sound at first."

She turned back to him. "I don't think you do, Raul."

"Do you think all those celebrity couples are really legitimately together? The ones who happen to show up at various functions together right around the time one or both of them is releasing a movie or dropping new music tracks?"

She shrugged. "Guess I hadn't really thought about it that way."

"And of course, I'll be paying you handsomely for your time. You said you couldn't afford to hire more help for your shop. I can assist with that. Think of it as a business arrangement. Nothing more."

"Nothing more," she repeated, not meeting his gaze, her eyes focused on the half-eaten empanada on her plate.

"The king and I can rest assured about your discretion. That alone is priceless as far as we're both concerned. You can name your price."

Her eyes lifted back to his face then. "I'm not even sure where I'd start with that. With any of this."

"I don't expect an answer tonight. Think about what you'd like to accomplish with your business. Any other goals you may have. What an offer like this could mean to all of those goals."

He'd struck a chord; he could tell by the expression on her face.

"It would be nice not to have to cut corners for once. And then there's the shelter."

"Shelter?"

"I volunteer my grooming services at a local animal shelter. They're always short on donations."

"Well then. Consider my first act as your fiancé to make a sizable one." He would do so regardless of her answer. But she didn't need to know that at the moment.

"I've always wondered about the journalist dinner. Plus…" She hesitated. As if unsure to share her next thought.

"Plus what?"

"It's nothing, never mind."

The way she poked at her appetizer told him it most definitely was not nothing. "Tell me," he prodded.

"It's just, there's this certain junior politician my step-father has been trying to set me up with. In order to secure a business deal he has sway over."

Raul did his best not to react. He hadn't seen this turn in the conversation coming. His security had assured him there was no other man. Something tightened in the center of his chest until he heard her next words.

"I'm absolutely not interested. But Phil has been relentless for me to accept the man's weekly dinner invitations."

"I see."

"If I show up at the dinner with…you, it might finally convince them to give up."

"I see. I'm guessing this politician will be at the dinner."

She nodded without hesitation. "Absolutely. He never misses an opportunity to be seen. In fact…" She trailed off again. Raul could guess what she'd been about to say. No doubt this politician had asked her to attend the very same dinner. Rather strange turn of events.

She rubbed a palm down her face. "What will you do if I say no?"

He released a deep sigh. "I don't really know. There is no one else as backup."

Though he'd dated and been linked to scores of women over the years, the choice to ask Sofia had been a simple one as far as he was concerned. Raul knew he could trust her to be discreet. Sofia's loyalty to Luisa alone was enough to make him comfortable that she would keep the secret. On top of all that, Sofia was simply a decent person, one he could confidently trust to keep her word. No need for the humiliation of asking her to sign nondisclosure documents.

He had no doubt that Sofia would keep the secret forever merely because she'd agreed to do so.

"You have no other options? Really?" The wide-eyed look of surprise she gave him told Raul just how unbelievable she found that to be. The truth was, he hadn't really given anyone else all that much consideration. Plus, he knew his strengths as a negotiator. Knew how convincing he could be. And he didn't sway from a decision once he'd made it.

Was there any other reason you only considered Sofia and no one else?

A subtle voice in his head mocked him with the question. He chose to ignore it.

CHAPTER THREE

"ARE YOU SURE you understood him correctly?" Agnes asked two days later as they boarded the metro train heading to the museum district. She hadn't had an opportunity to talk properly about Raul's ask with Agnes due to a packed schedule at the shop yesterday. Now, on their day off, she couldn't wait to run it all by someone else.

Sofia swiped her card at the kiosk and walked through the turnstile, her friend right behind her. "Trust me, that was my first question."

The part of DC where they were headed would be swarming with tourists this time of day on a weekday morning but Sofia didn't care. She needed to talk to someone about Raul and his "offer." He'd mentioned the importance of discretion. Sofia knew Agnes could be trusted to keep all this to herself. She was one of two people on this planet she considered her best friends. The other one being Luisa.

Sofia released a breath of frustration as their train arrived at the entry point and they boarded.

Luisa.

She was the reason this was all happening. As much as Sofia admired her wild spirit and her utter devotion to living life to the fullest, Luisa really should have practiced just a modicum of discretion regarding her affair. On the contrary, a steady flow of salacious pictures popped up featuring her and her lover whenever Sofia scrolled social media.

It took a while to find two seats together as she was right about the tourist situation. Sofia lowered her voice before speaking again. Not that anyone was really paying attention to them. A family of four with two toddlers in tow took up the row in front of them and the parents were much more concerned about containing the spill of various snacks. Everyone else either had earphones in or was focused fully on their phone screens. Often both.

"Where is this kingdom his family rules, anyway?" Agnes asked. "I don't really follow any royals."

Just the imaginary ones she watched in all those movies.

"In the North Atlantic. About a hundred miles south of Greenland. It's a small island nation that his family has ruled for generations."

"Wow. Just like last weekend's feature film."

Sofia ignored that. "I haven't given him an answer yet." Which was unfair of her, she knew. To Raul's credit, he hadn't tried to strong-arm her in response to her nonanswers when he'd called or texted. Simply told her he'd wait until she knew. But time was running out. The dinner was tomorrow night.

Sofia groaned out loud, resting her head against the glass window.

"You know, I'm not sure why you're so torn about this," Agnes said. "You're being asked to spend time with a real-life flesh-and-blood prince. Any other woman would jump at the chance. I sure would."

"It's not that simple."

"Why not? It's exactly like one of those romantic movies that one channel plays every Saturday evening. You could actually live it. Just think."

Agnes spent the rest of the train ride telling her in detail the fantasy plot of the last such movie she'd watched. Part of Sofia was annoyed about the idle chatter when she had other pressing matters on her mind. While another part was thankful for the relatively mindless distraction until they reached their stop and made their way up the escalator.

The sidewalks were packed. The line to the Smithsonian National Museum of Natural History was predictably long when they walked by. The usual line of food trucks—everything from ice cream, to taco trucks, to gyros—lined the streets. Luckily, their own destination didn't attract nearly the number of visitors. The United States Botanic Garden was the most soothing place in Washington as far as Sofia was concerned. It always helped to spend time there when she needed to clear her head or think. And she definitely needed a clear head at the moment to think on exactly what answer she was going to give Raul before tomorrow night.

Was Agnes right? Was she overthinking it all? Raul had presented her with a once-in-a-lifetime opportunity with no strings attached. Maybe she'd be a fool to turn it down.

"You know, you'd be a fool to turn him down," Agnes said, echoing her thoughts.

They reached the row of colorful agave plants on the ground floor and sat down on the nearby bench. Already the extra oxygen in the air and the vibrant array of plants helped to soothe her frazzled emotions.

"Although, I do have to admit, it's a rather unusual circumstance you've found yourself in," her friend added.

Sofia snickered. "Not according to the prince. To hear

him tell it, such arrangements are commonplace among celebrities and other elites. Us commoners wouldn't know, I guess."

"You would if you watched those Saturday-night movies with me. Did he say why he wants you in particular? This isn't some kind of come-on, is it?"

Sofia squashed the silly reaction that surfaced at Agnes's question. Raul had given absolutely zero indication that his offer had anything to do with any sort of attraction. She had no business feeling any kind of way about that.

"No. He swears it's a simple business arrangement. PR for damage control."

"Huh."

"Basically, I'm in the right place at the right time. The first event is the DC journalists' dinner. And I just happen to be in DC. Plus, there's my connection to Luisa."

Agnes nodded. "Right. You two grew close together at that private boarding school in Massachusetts."

A boarding school she'd only been able to attend because her mother was employed as a dorm mother there. For all of Luisa's faults, she was the only one who bothered to acknowledge her. Sofia had never fit in with the trust fund babies and legacy kids who attended the school.

Her inability to find her standing in such a place had had long-term effects. Sofia had always been leery of meeting new people, dating new men. Always on the outside looking in could make a girl shy and reserved.

Luisa hadn't cared that she was the daughter of a school employee. She'd befriended her anyway.

"I'm convinced Luisa's the only reason I wasn't mercilessly bullied at that school."

"And now her brother is asking for your help to take some heat off of her."

"I suppose that's part of the reason. Though I doubt Luisa much cares what people are saying about her. She never has before."

"I know what I'd say if I was the one he'd asked."

If only Sofia could be as certain. By the time the afternoon rolled around and she made her way to the animal shelter for her weekly volunteer stint, she wasn't any closer to a clear-cut decision.

Raul appeared to be a patient man. But it was only a matter of time before he'd come around and demand her answer.

Sofia looked even more shocked to see him than she had two days ago when he'd shown up at her shop. "Raul? How in the world do you keep popping up?"

Ouch. Not even remotely pleased to see him. That stung the ego a bit. "I'll have you know, I'm not even here for you."

She tapped a finger against her chin and looked him over. "Right. Why are you here then? Looking to adopt a chihuahua? They have two at the moment. Jazzy and Bob."

"Bob? Someone named their dog Bob?"

"Go figure."

"The poor thing. I might have to adopt him just to be able to change his name."

Sofia shifted her weight to one leg and crossed her arms in front of her chest. "I have a lot to do in there, Raul. At least three nail trims and one surly terrier who needs a flea bath."

"Sounds harrowing."

"It's a full afternoon. If you're not here to see me and you're not here to adopt a pet, why are you here?"

Man, she was so cute when she was annoyed. The ever-present flush to her cheeks grew rosier, her eyes somehow brighter in the afternoon sunlight. Her hair was barely contained in that same topknot from the other day. The worn loose T-shirt she had on over baggy jeans shouldn't have looked enticing in the least. Yet, somehow on her the outfit looked fetchingly sexy. He couldn't even explain it, but she looked just as captivating now as she had the other night at dinner wearing a formfitting wrap dress that hugged her curves in all the right ways.

"You said this place needed financial help. I thought I'd stop by with a donation."

"I don't understand. I thought that was a condition of me agreeing to your terms."

He shrugged. "I figured a charity that caters to animals in need shouldn't be part of any negotiations. Not in any context."

"And you decided you had to come deliver it yourself. In person, is that so?"

"It's a rather high amount. I figured I'd explain personally."

Her features softened before she frowned again a moment later. "Is this some kind of ploy to sway me toward saying yes?"

Raul couldn't resist the urge to tease her. "Depends. Is it working? Are you impressed?" In her defense, maybe there was a germ of truth to that statement. Though he'd intended to donate all along, as soon he'd heard the slight hitch in her voice when she talked about her volunteer work here.

She didn't give him a chance to answer. "Wait, how did you know I'd be here anyway? At this particular shelter."

Realization dawned behind her eyes as her jaw fell. "Did you have me investigated?"

"That can't come as a surprise. Any new hire would require a background check. And it's been a while since we were last in touch. A lot could have changed about you since then."

She practically stomped her foot. "I haven't applied to work for you!" She gave her head a shake. "I'm too tired to deal with this now." She marched around him and strode to the door, then stopped before pulling the door open. "You know, I'd be even more impressed if you gave more than your money."

Raul knew when he was being led into a trap. Everything in her demeanor gave it away. But darned if he wasn't enjoying himself. He'd follow along willingly. "What exactly did you have in mind?"

He found the answer to that soon enough when he found himself holding a wet, shivering chihuahua in a tub of water while Sofia soaped him down. He wasn't going to tell her so, but the little fella was kind of cute. In a tiny mongrel sort of way.

"He's shaking. Is he cold?"

Sofia patted the chihuahua's head. "More likely he's scared," she answered. "Poor little guy." She leaned in close to his tiny whiskered face. "It's okay, handsome boy, you can be brave."

Before Raul knew he'd even intended it, he picked up the dog and nestled him against his chest, bundling him close and wrapping his arms around the small trembling body.

Sofia snapped her head up, looked at him in surprise. "You've soaked the entire front of your shirt. And soaped it no less."

He shrugged. "Maybe being snuggled will calm him a bit."

The corners of her lips lifted ever so slightly. "Maybe."

He couldn't tell if her expression appeared amused or mocking but hoped it was the former. Though that wouldn't be all that much better.

"You're rocking," she said a moment later, her smile growing slightly.

Huh. So he was. Swaying from side to side.

If someone had told him this morning that he'd be holding a seven-pound soaking wet and soapy dog against his chest while he swayed to comfort him, Raul would have asked how much Vesovian wine they'd imbibed. But here he was doing just that very thing.

Sofia stepped closer. "Looks like it worked," she said, scratching below the pup's ear. "He's not shaking anymore."

"Well, look at that."

Sofia stood and flashed him a teasing smile. "Looks like you made a friend, Your Highness. Congratulations."

She was jesting, of course, but he did feel rather celebratory.

The man had stealth reflexes, but he wasn't quite fast enough. Sofia winced as Ceecee the calico swiped at Raul's arm yet again, this time drawing blood.

Raul swore, but to his credit, he kept his grip on the feline while Sofia clipped her final claw. She had to admit, with Raul's help, she and the other volunteers were going to be done much sooner than usual. Though his right forearm was all the worse for the experience. Ceecee was crankier than usual.

Sofia set the clippers down and reached into her apron pocket for a cat treat.

"I daresay she doesn't deserve that," Raul protested.

"You're right," she agreed. "She's a bad kitty. But she gets it anyway."

She set the cat back in her crate, then went behind the counter against the wall of the room. Grabbing several cotton balls and a bottle of antiseptic, she strode back to where he stood.

The scratch was growing angrier and redder by the second. "This may hurt."

Soaking a cotton ball, she took his hand and dabbed at the scratch.

She hadn't thought this through, had been too lackadaisical about what touching the man might do to her insides. Her stomach turned to mush while a warm sensation meandered along her spine.

Get a grip.

She was simply cleansing a cat scratch, hardly a romantic or seductive act. Though she couldn't deny it felt rather intimate. His skin felt warm against her palm, his aftershave teased her nose.

"Thanks," he said against her ear. Was it her imagination or did his voice sound strained?

Probably because he was bleeding. Nothing to do with her.

"You're welcome. And thank you for helping out."

"It was a pleasure." He cast a glance in Ceecee's direction. "Well, mostly."

"You'll find this hard to believe, but I think she actually likes you," Sofia said, gesturing toward the cat.

"Could have fooled me," Raul countered, mock indignation laced in his voice. He didn't quite hide the smile along his lips.

"She does," Sofia insisted. "Just doesn't want to show it," she added, not entirely sure she was still referring to the cat.

Three hours later they finally toweled out the last of the animals and Sofia tossed him a dry towel to clean up with. Though there was only so much a towel was going to help, between his soaked shirt and his throbbing arm.

Though it all might have been worth it to have Sofia nurse his scratched arm the way she had. The way she'd held his hand, gently brushed her fingers along his skin. He'd been sure he'd stopped breathing for several seconds.

"I'll walk you to your car," he told her, pushing away the silly thought. It made zero sense to feel grateful for a cat's scratch.

"No need. I took the metro."

"Then I'll have the driver take you to your apartment."

"I can manage, Raul. You don't have to go out of your way. Like coming here, for instance."

Raul rammed his fingers through the hair at his crown. As much fun as he had with her, despite the wet and messy—and painful—chores she'd roped him into, he didn't understand her at all. "Why are you so stubborn? About the most basic things. I simply want to see you home."

She slammed her palms on her hips. "Yeah, I'll bet."

"What's that supposed to mean?"

"I'm guessing you also want to press me about whether I'll agree to your scheme or not."

He did his best to scrounge up some patience. He couldn't recall the last time anyone had spoken to him in such a manner. Rather than feeling offended, he wanted to lift her by the waist and shake some sense into her. "Would that be so wrong of me if I did? The dinner is tomorrow."

"Yes!"

Relief soared through his chest thinking she was finally giving him an answer. Until she clarified a moment later. "Yes, it would be wrong of you. Considering how little time you gave me to decide."

His righteousness deflated like a balloon. She had a point. Truth be told, he wasn't expecting such resistance.

"Look, if you're playing hard to get to hold out for more money, I already told you, name your price."

It was the wrong thing to say; he knew it immediately by the fury that blazed behind her eyes.

She poked him in the chest none too gently. He knew his bodyguards were discreetly nearby where they'd parked the car. They had to be seeing this. Apparently, they were smart enough to realize there wasn't any real danger.

Though maybe he shouldn't be so sure.

"Of course I'm not holding out for more money. How can you think that?"

"I'm sorry," he said, fully meaning it. "It was a stupid thing to say."

Her features softened, but only slightly.

The sound of a message rang on his phone and he retrieved it, then swore out loud at what he saw there.

"What is it?" Sofia asked.

He swore yet again, a harsher word this time. "There's speculation that Luisa is expecting her married lover's baby."

"Whoa. That is not a good development, is it."

As far as understatements went, Sofia's words certainly

qualified. "Father is going to be livid. I'd better call him. This might be the final straw."

"What does that mean?"

Raul rubbed a palm down his face. "He's threatened more than once to disown her if she didn't reform her ways. If this doesn't do it, I'm not sure what will. Expecting a married man's child."

"That's a rather drastic punishment. Luisa doesn't deserve that, no matter what she's done."

His father would argue that score, no doubt. "I should get back to my hotel and call him right away. If you won't accept a ride from my driver, can I at least call you a taxi or something?"

To Raul's surprise, she merely nodded without a stubborn argument. Then she downright shocked him with the next words out of her mouth.

"I'll do it. I'll pretend to be your fiancée."

What in the world had she just agreed to?

Sofia slammed her apartment door shut and leaned back against it. Her thoughts were a jumbled mess in her head. Raul had just looked so frustrated, at the end of his rope. Then the thought of her dear friend being shunned by her own father had brought a sting to her eyes. The king couldn't be that cruel, could he? Raul sure seemed to think so. No wonder he'd been so adamant about finding a way to make Luisa's proverbial global spotlight go away as much as possible. Pulling out her phone, she brought up all the relevant sites. Luisa's possible pregnancy was the top story on every single one.

"What have you done, dear friend?"

The screen changed into an icon that belonged to her mother. Sofia released a resigned sigh. She'd avoided her mom's calls for the past several days. Any longer and she ran the risk of Ramona showing up at her door. The last thing she needed. She clicked on the accept-call button.

"Hey Mama."

Her mother's affectionate smile greeted her via video call. "Finally. I've been calling and calling you."

"I'm sorry, I've just been really busy. Haven't gotten a chance to answer or call back."

"I won't keep you then. I just wanted to see how much you were looking forward to dinner tomorrow night."

How could she know? Sofia had literally just left Raul minutes ago. For a split second, Sofia thought Ramona had somehow heard about Raul's offer. Then clarity hit. Her mother thought she'd accepted the invite from her stepfather's favorite politician. Well, did she have news for Ramona.

"Uh… I am but not in the way you think."

"I don't understand."

"I'm going to the journalist dinner. Just not with Aaron."

Even through the small screen, Sofia could see her mother's face wash with confusion. "Who else could you possibly be going with, dear?"

Sofia suppressed a groan. If Ramona only knew. She was about to explain when an incoming text interrupted the call.

There will be a package arriving at your door within minutes. Just a heads-up. R

Turned out to be more like five seconds. Her doorman rang before she'd had a chance to swipe away the text and return to the call with her mother.

Maybe she was chickening out, but she decided to take

the reprieve. "Mama, there's someone at the door. I'll call you in the morning and explain everything."

"But—"

Sofia hated to do it but she cut her off. "In the morning, Mama. I promise. I gotta go."

Frank's call came through automatically. "Uh…there's something here for you."

"Right. A package."

Frank cleared his throat. "That's not the word I would use."

Fifteen minutes later, Sofia had to wonder if there'd been something lost in translation. The "package" Raul had referred to turned out to be three racks of ball gowns, and a selection of high-heeled shoes, delivered by a team of three men.

She sent him a simple text that consisted of one question mark, and soon she had a reply.

Please pick one to wear tomorrow night.

That settled it. She was so in over her head. Here she was assuming she could throw on the simple black dress she kept in her closet for formal occasions.

Reaching for her phone, she clicked on Agnes's contact icon. Her friend answered on the first ring, didn't bother with a hello.

"I've been waiting all day for you to call. What'd you decide?"

"I'll tell you all about it soon enough. Right now you have to come over. I could use some help here."

Agnes didn't bother with a goodbye either. The call simply ended. But Sofia had no doubt her doorman would be letting her up within minutes.

Sure enough, Agnes arrived before Sofia had rifled through fewer than half of the dresses. Each one was more gorgeous than the last.

"How in the world can I possibly choose?"

"Wow," was all Agnes could come with as an answer as she lifted an emerald green gown off the rack and fingered the delicate spaghetti straps. "This one is gorgeous."

"They all are."

"There's only one thing to do," Agnes declared.

"What's that?"

"If it takes all night, you have to try every single one on." She followed the last word with what could only be described as a squeal.

"I'm glad one of us is excited."

Agnes gave her an exasperated look. "How in the world are you not more excited about this? It's like Cinderella going to the ball. Or like—"

"I know, one of those movies on Saturday nights."

"That's right. A straight fairy tale. What's really going on?"

"It's all a little overwhelming, that's all."

Agnes squinted her eyes on her. "It's more than that. It has to be. You're actually scared. I didn't recognize it at first because I've never seen you frightened about anything. Not even when that big police dog growled at us because he didn't want his nails trimmed. What's got you so spooked?"

The question brought to the forefront exactly the emotions she'd been hoping to avoid. Her friend was sharp enough to see it.

"I don't exactly have a lot of experience with men," she hedged.

Agnes shrugged. "So? What experience do you need to play pretend for a while?"

"What if I do something silly?" Like really fall for the man when she was pretending to do so? It would be just like her to do such a thing. After all, she'd had a crush on Raul since developing hormones, for heaven's sake.

"I've only had a handful of dates in college," she continued. "And one not-so-serious relationship that turned out to be a complete waste of time when he realized he still had feelings for his ex."

"That's all past history," Agnes reassured.

She had no idea. Sofia had never felt comfortable in the boarding school, where she was clearly a misfit among the offspring of the top tiers of society. Luisa was the only friend she'd made then. None of the boys deemed her worthy enough to ask out. She'd felt awkward and out of place among the elite. The awkwardness had simply followed her through to college until she'd dropped out, then later into adulthood.

"You're not really committing to him," Agnes added. "You're simply playing a part. Like an actress."

"I suppose that makes sense."

"It sure does. Live a little, try to enjoy yourself."

Easier said than done. The truth was, she *was* scared. Scared of all the ways this whole thing could backfire and leave her with a broken heart. She'd had a crush on Raul Abarra since the day she'd first laid eyes on him. Seeing him again had brought all those feelings of attraction storming back. As far as fantasy men went, Raul fit the bill in every way. She could easily lose her heart to him if she forgot for even a moment that none of this was real.

And she couldn't allow that to happen at all costs. She might never recover.

CHAPTER FOUR

RAUL WAITED IN Sofia's charming sitting room and took in her living space. Long-leafed plants hung from a ceramic pot in each corner and a Turkish rug sat in the center of the hardwood floor. Plush throws were thrown over the back cushions of each of two sofas. An upholstered rocking chair sat between them. A colorful tapestry hung on the wall by the door. The apartment suited her. It was clear she'd taken care to make it a comfortable home space that suited her personality. Funny, he'd grown up in a castle with acres and acres of land surrounding him and a beach he could see from his bedroom window. Yet he was charmed by Sofia's small apartment. It lent a coziness, a homeliness he couldn't say was afforded by any of his own residences.

She appeared out of her room and walked hesitantly to where he sat and Raul did a double take upon seeing her.

There was no doubt about it. He wouldn't be able to take his eyes off her all night. He didn't find himself speechless often but the sight of Sofia tonight quite literally took his breath away and rendered him wordless. She'd chosen an emerald green silk dress that brought out the green specks in her hazel eyes. It flowed just above her knees, the skirt slightly longer in the back. On her feet were strappy stiletto sandals that showed off her toned, shapely calves.

And how often had he even noticed a woman's calves before? Her toenails were painted a shade of green slightly darker than the dress. Her hair flowed in loose, lush curls over her shoulders.

When he finally managed to speak, he could only muster one word: "Wow."

When he'd been led up to her apartment by her doorman, he wasn't quite sure what to expect. She'd exceeded any expectations he may have had. To think, his sister took hours to get ready before any formal events and had a team of professionals whose job it was to make her picture perfect. Sofia had less than a day to prepare and had managed by herself.

"Uh…wow good?"

"Definitely, most certainly good."

"Does this work then?" she asked, doing a mini twirl.

She had no idea just how well it was all working for him. "You look amazing, Sofia. A top contender for the loveliest woman there."

She gasped out a small laugh. "Right. I heard Miss Universe is going to be there. Not to mention the latest film darling and beauty influencer."

"They'll have nothing on you—I'm sure of it."

She stepped closer to him. The smell of her perfume tickled his nose and he wanted nothing more than to lean into her and take a long deep whiff. Her flowery, fresh scent reminded him of the white gardenias his kingdom was known for.

"You don't look so bad yourself."

He mimicked the twirl she'd performed just a moment ago, making sure to exaggerate his movements in such a comical way it elicited a hearty chuckle from her.

"Thanks," she said. "I needed a bit of a laugh."

"Oh?"

She placed a palm on her chest. "I'm a bit nervous. This party isn't typically the type of event that's on my social calendar. Not even close."

"Well, I seem to recall that you had not one but two invites." As self-deprecating as she was, the fact of the matter was that a well-heeled local politician had asked her to accompany him. A real invitation unlike his fake one for the sake of paparazzi.

"Complete fluke of fate, I assure you. And an invitation that was never entertained could hardly be considered meaningful. I would have never gone with Aaron. No matter how hard my stepfather pressed the issue."

Raul was more pleased by that comment than he had any kind of right to be. This arrangement between them might not be real, but the thought of competing for Sofia's attention with another man left a sour taste on his tongue. If he'd ever had that same reaction about another woman, he couldn't recall.

He held out his arm to her. "Well, madame. Your carriage awaits. Shall we?"

She wrapped her arm in the crook of his elbow. "Yes, let's go. Let's get this over with."

He dramatically clasped his other hand against his chest. "You wound me. Is the thought of an evening spent with me so hard to endure?"

She chuckled again. He was beginning to enjoy hearing the sound of her melodic laughter. Would miss it once all this was over. He would miss *her*.

Whoa. He so couldn't go there.

Still, it was hard not to wish things between them were different. That somehow this pretense was real. That Sofia was indeed his intended princess. That their lives weren't so incompatible.

"Raul?" Sofia's voice pulled him out of his ridiculous reverie. They were from two different realities. When it came time for him to really settle down and get married, it would have to be to someone much more suited for life as a royal. Maybe someone who'd even been born into royalty herself. A few contenders came to mind. No one he particularly felt any sort of affection for or attraction to. But that was a secondary concern. Affection was a luxury for someone like him, bound to the duty and responsibility of a kingdom nation. And what good did genuine emotion do anyway? His own parents had been among the lucky few who'd really felt a real love for each other. Look how that had turned out in the end. Losing that love had left his father a defeated man, nearly crippled with grief after its loss.

Any matrimonial bond in Raul's future would merely be to serve the purpose of providing Vesovia with a ruling family and an eventual heir to keep the royal bloodline going. His future wife would be chosen based on her willingness and ability to serve the kingdom.

As disruptive as this ruse was to Sofia's life, at least it was temporary. He couldn't bear to think of her enduring the endless scrutiny and disruption actually being married to Raul Abarra might bring her.

She deserved better.

No, once all this was over, she could go back to her life, wealthier and better established to reach all her goals. In due time, the world would forget who she was and everyone would leave her alone once more.

He'd make sure of it.

She repeated his name.

He pushed away the thoughts and lowered his gaze to hers. "I'm sorry. I'm just admiring how lovely you look. And wishing I had you all to myself a while longer."

Now, why had he gone and admitted such a thing?

Her gasp of surprise nearly had him admitting even more.

"Um…thank you…?" She said the last two words as a question, confusion etched in her features.

Well, he was feeling a bit confused himself.

A different limo waited on the curb for them, this one white. The same driver stood by the passenger side and immediately opened the door for them as they approached. Raul assisted her into the spacious back seat, then sat across from her. Blue light lit up the interior. A minibar stocked with chilling champagne, sparkling water bottles and various snacks took up a quarter of the space. Soft instrumental music sounded from invisible speakers. She'd never driven in such luxury.

Raul pointed to the champagne. "Can I pour you a glass?"

Sofia immediately shook her head to decline. Her middle quaked with nervousness and excitement. She couldn't risk having her head foggy on top of that. Not that she didn't already feel somewhat heady. The way Raul had looked at her upstairs, the words he'd spoken, the clear desire in his eyes had her tingling inside in a way that had yet to subside. "Maybe just some sparkling water."

"Sure thing." He reached over to the bar, his thigh brushing hers in the process. A bolt of electricity shot through her at the contact. She didn't imagine his slight pause before he moved away. He was just as aware of the current between them. The thought made her heady and apprehensive at the same time. Twisting off the cap, he handed her a sweaty glass bottle. Sofia could only hope he didn't notice her trembling fingers as she reached for it.

No such luck. "Sofia, try to relax," he said. "This will be just a fun dinner that gives us a chance to be seen together to get all the gossip started. You'll be fine—just stick by my side."

If he only knew. Being this close to him in such tight quarters had a good deal to do with her nervousness. "I'll do my best to try," she said, forcing a smile.

"That's all I ask. It's all I will ever ask of you."

Sofia believed him. Raul wasn't a man who said or did anything lightly. Look at all the trouble he was going through to take the heat off his sister and to assuage the king.

Sofia tried to take her mind off her nerves by focusing on the lights of the city as they drove past the National Mall. A sizable crowd strolled the sidewalks given the time of day. Events in DC such as the one they were headed to always drew a secondary crowd in addition to the attendees. Support staff, family members and others. Important people tended to have entourages. Which begged a question.

"Why do you have no one around you?" she asked, striving for some sort of distraction from the churning of emotions in her gut.

If Raul was taken aback by the sudden question, he didn't show it. "What makes you think I don't?"

"I haven't seen anyone."

"Look behind you."

Sofia did as he said. Looking out the rear window, she saw nothing out of the ordinary. Just the usual heavy traffic. "I only see a sedan behind us, with the neon sign of a ride share logo."

"Look two cars behind that one."

Sofia squinted out the window once more. "There's an SUV, with rather tinted windows. They're fairly common in this city, usually following…" It dawned on her then. "Friends of yours?" she asked.

"In a sense. The driver and the passenger are two highly trained bodyguards. They've been with me the whole time."

The revelation truly surprised her. She hadn't noticed them, not even once. "Huh? I didn't realize."

The smile he sent her way held a meaning she didn't fully understand. But that made sense. Being a commoner, it hadn't even occurred to her to look for his bodyguards.

"I also have a staff occupying the suite below mine back at the hotel."

That made sense too. "You must think me so naive." There, she'd finally voiced the thought out loud.

"I think nothing of the kind. I know we exist in two rather different realities.

She knew that of course. Still, hearing the words fall from his lips drove the point home further. What did she have in common with a prince?

What if she couldn't pull this off? Nothing about this made sense. How could Raul possibly think she could play act as a princess-to-be? She had none of the qualifications. She wasn't beautiful. She wasn't elegant. She certainly didn't feel refined.

She bathed and groomed animals all day, for heaven's sake. Hardly a vocation for the likes of a princess.

Well, too late to worry about any of that at the moment. And so much for striving for any sort of calm now. She was going to stick out like a sore thumb tonight. Like

Raul said, she lived an entirely different reality than the others at this gala.

"Sofia?" Raul's voice interrupted her panic, concern laced in his voice. "You've gone rather pale. Are you all right?"

She swallowed. "I just want to make sure I say and do the right things."

He leaned over, and placed a warm palm on her knee. "You'll be fine," he told her. She knew the gesture was meant to reassure, but his touch just seemed to make her frazzled nerves all that much more splintered.

He gave her knee a gentle squeeze. "Like I said, just stick by me and follow my lead when it comes to any questions about our relationship."

Oh, God! Her panic upped several points. She hadn't even thought of answering questions. She had no idea what she'd say. "Maybe we should have gone over that. Exactly how are we supposed to have gotten together anyway?"

He shrugged and settled back in his seat. "We just stick as close to the truth as possible."

How in the world was she supposed to do that? The truth was that none of this was real.

"You seem doubtful," Raul said.

"I guess I'm not sure exactly what you mean by that."

"Simple. We say we've known each other for years through my sister. A lingering attraction between the two of us was finally acknowledged and here we are."

Well, when he put it that way...

She supposed that was rather close to the truth. The only problem was, it only held true for one of them.

She'd made a horrible mistake. Sofia's heart pounded in her chest as they pulled up to the venue and a million flashbulbs exploded outside. She couldn't go out there. She couldn't step out of this car and smile at all those cameras pretending to know what she was doing.

She turned to face Raul and tell him exactly that but he gave her such a brilliant, confident smile that the words died on her lips. She really didn't have a choice, did she? If she asked him to turn the car around and go back, she had no doubt he would do so.

"It's just paparazzi," Raul leaned over and said into her ear. "They only want to snap a few pictures. Which is exactly why we're here."

She swallowed. "Right."

"Ready?"

No. But she nodded despite herself.

He exited the car and the next thing she knew, he was escorting her out of her seat. The moment she stepped outside, she realized how soundproof the car was. A roar of noise greeted her—shouted questions, pleas to face another direction and various other commands she could hardly make out. The flash of lights was nearly blinding now.

"This will just take a second," Raul said loudly over the noise, no chance of anyone else hearing him. Sofia could barely hear the words herself. "Then we'll head inside."

Sofia used his solidness against her side to ground her. She had no idea how she managed it, but she even wrangled a smile onto her lips and angled her face from one side to another.

"That's the way," Raul told her. "You're doing great."

"Not so sure about that." But she was doing better than she might have imagined.

Mercifully, Raul took her by the elbow moments later and escorted her inside, a posse of cameramen followed them for several feet, with Raul's bodyguards making sure they kept their distance.

They entered the glass doors into a crowded lobby area with high ceilings and marble tile floor. A majestic water fountain sat in the middle. Open doors leading to a vast ballroom with hundreds of round tables sat behind it.

An elegantly dressed woman holding a microphone with a cameraman trailing behind her approached them. Raul lifted his hand almost imperceptibly to one of his guards and the man immediately had her halting in her tracks. "No interviews," he told her. The woman appeared ready to argue but wisely decided against it. With a shrug, she turned on her stiletto heels and scanned the room for another target. But not without one last, lingering look in Raul's direction.

Sofia had to wonder if her look of longing had more to do with the man himself and not so much the desire to score an interview.

Sofia could hardly blame the woman if it was the former. Raul cut a stunning figure of a man in his tuxedo. Tall and imposing, even among all these well-heeled and accomplished men, Raul stood out. A true prince, every inch of the man exuded refinement and nobility. Yet this was the same man who helped her give a terrier a flea bath yesterday. And he hadn't complained or even hinted that such a task was beneath someone of his standing.

He was going to be a tough act to follow once all this was over.

Sofia mentally paused as the thought skittered through her brain. Who was she kidding? She'd been comparing men to Raul for most of her adult life. It was no wonder she'd had no luck with any kind of real relationship. Now she'd managed to place herself in a situation that would only further exacerbate that sorry state of affairs.

"Let's get seated," he told her, placing his palm on her lower back. The now-familiar shudder of desire that ran through her body at his touch unnerved her to say the least.

Once they were at the table, Sofia finally released the hold on her breath. That had to be the hardest part. And it was thankfully over. Now all she had to do was sit through a dinner and the scheduled speeches, making sure to use the right fork. A wave of relief washed over her and the tight knot at the base of her spine began to loosen.

Maybe she could really do this after all.

Her relief was short-lived. The man who immediately approached them upon being seated was the last person Sofia wanted to see at that moment.

"Sofia! I heard you might be here. But I wasn't quite sure I believed it."

Aaron Whitmore strode his way toward them, his usual flashy white grin a bit more forced than usual. The congressman her stepfather had tried tirelessly to set her up with. The grin faltered noticeably when he clearly realized whose arm Sofia had come in on.

"Aaron, how nice to see you," she lied through a fake smile. "Please allow me to introduce you to His Royal Highness, Prince Raul Refik Abarra."

Aaron chuckled nervously. "I believe I'm supposed to bow or something, right?"

Raul thrust out his hand to shake Aaron's. "No need. Bows and curtsies are appropriate for my father. Pleased to meet you."

"Likewise," Aaron said, though he sounded anything but pleased. He turned to face her. "So, you are here after all," he said with a smile too tight to be deemed friendly in any way.

"That's right."

"Can we maybe talk?' he asked her. "Privately?"

The gall this man had. No wonder Phil had homed in on him. They appeared to be all too similar.

Aaron turned back to Raul. "No offense."

Raul ignored him, and leveled his gaze to hers. "Sofia?"

As nervous as she was about answering any questions tonight, she found herself wanting to have this particular conversation. To let Aaron know once and for all that there would be no "getting together" for drinks or dinner or anything else between the two of them. Not anytime soon. Actually, not ever.

She nodded in answer to his unspoken yet clear question. "It's okay."

He waited a beat, not even bothering to deign Aaron with another glance. "I'll find us some cocktails." The look he gave her was clear. He didn't intend to go far. Heaven help her, she might have even read a hint of possessiveness behind his eyes.

CHAPTER FIVE

RAUL COULDN'T RECALL when he'd last felt such a strong desire to grab another man by the collar and haul him outside. If this Aaron person wanted to talk privately, Raul would be happy to oblige in Sofia's stead.

Though it couldn't have been more than five minutes or so, it seemed an eternity passed before the politician finally stood up and left her side. About time.

Raul grabbed two flutes of sparkling champagne from a passing server and went back to the table, retaking his seat next to Sofia and handing her one of the drinks.

"Let me guess, the influential politician who can make your stepfather's dreams come true."

She raised the glass in the air. "You would be correct."

"The nerve of the man," he bit out, resisting the urge to curse.

"He's only partially to blame. My stepfather had no right to try and use me as a bargaining chip in his scheme to secure a business deal."

"What does your mother have to say about all this?"

A flash of hurt passed over her eyes at his question. "My mother is all too ready to follow Phil's lead. I can't really begrudge her though. She gave up a lot and worked very hard to raise me by herself as a single mother. Now that she finally has someone who loves her and treats her well, I'm afraid she's donned the proverbial rose-colored glasses. She's completely blind to his faults."

Raul didn't voice the thought in his head. Rather than protecting her daughter from being used as bait for a business deal, Sofia's mother had chosen her husband's wants instead. At least that's how things appeared from where Raul stood. But what did he know about having a devoted mother? He'd lost his at the onset of becoming a teen. Some days he had to struggle to remember her exact features.

"I see. Is it done then, do you suppose? Has Aaron finally gotten the message?"

Sofia's lips tightened. "It appears so. And hopefully he'll relay it to Phil."

"I can make sure they both fully understand your position, Sofia. Just say the word."

Sofia's eyes widened. "I don't need you to fight any battles for me, Raul. You don't have to play the concerned protector. It's not like I'm really your fiancée."

Ouch. She had a point, but still.

"I merely meant that I can explain to them that we are an item now." She had no idea how persuasive he could be.

"What makes you think I don't intend to tell my mother the truth about us?"

"Do you?"

She tugged her bottom lip with her teeth. "No. Probably not."

He'd figured as much. Sofia and her mother may have been close once, but he got the distinct feeling the stepfather had driven a wedge between them.

"Do you intend to tell Luisa?" she asked.

He shrugged. "If she asks, I'll tell her the truth. Give her an idea of the trouble she's caused. For all her faults, my sister isn't one to betray my confidence." He swirled the ice in his glass. "However, it's a moot point. Luisa's wholly preoccupied with her affair at the moment. I don't think she would concern herself with the outside world enough to notice. Whereas I'm guessing your mother will have more than a few questions for you after tonight."

Sofia took another sip of her drink. "Let's drop it for now, can we?

Avoidance. For the life of him, Raul would never understand the inclination of some people to try to sidestep an issue rather than confront it head-on. Hopefully, this little charade of theirs would work to convince her stepfather to let go of his matchmaking. But Sofia had to make him understand, in no uncertain terms, that she simply wouldn't be used as a bargaining chip to further the man's ambitions. If Raul had to guess, he'd venture that Sofia had not been firm enough about the whole thing. Probably out of her respect and devotion to her mother.

"I don't want to talk about Aaron or my stepfather anymore," she added.

Raul didn't miss the omission of her mother in that statement. She really wasn't fully acknowledging Ramona's part in all this.

He wasn't about to press. This wasn't the time. "Can I change the subject by telling you how lovely you look?"

She brightened at that. Ran a palm down her midsection. "I was so torn about which dress to go with."

He raised his glass to her. "You chose well."

"I had help. Agnes came to play Pygmalion to my flower girl." She ducked her head. "I have a confession to make."

"What is it?"

"I have to admit, I had more fun playing dress-up and trying on those gowns than I expected."

"Glad to hear it. When do you think you might wear it again? Or any of the others?"

She set her glass down to give him a quizzical look. "What do you mean? I have no intention of keeping this dress. Let alone all of them."

"Well, I certainly have no use for them. None of them are likely to fit."

His lame attempt at a joke fell flat. Sofia didn't so much as crack a smile. "I can't accept such an extravagant gift."

"You can consider it part of your compensation then."

She shook her head. "Thank you, but no. And it's not like I'll even have a use for such an addition to my wardrobe. As a pet groomer, I don't often find myself attending many galas such as this one. Unlike you, as a royal. You probably have one of these a week."

"You have no idea." Raul tossed back his drink, polishing it off.

"What's that mean?" she asked, merriment swimming behind her eyes.

"It can be a bit much."

"Oh, sure," she said dryly. "How awful it must be going from one grand event to another."

"There's more to it than just attending a party. I have to make sure to say the right things, represent the palace in a fitting way, make sure to play the role of dignitary, representative and royal family member at every moment. Not letting up for so much as a second." The part of being a prince he didn't relish, and would be loath to subject anyone else to who wasn't geared for such an existence from a young age.

"Huh. I never thought of it that way."

"You'd be surprised. It's why I'm looking forward to three weeks from now, when I can finally find some peace."

"What's in three weeks?"

"I'll be heading to Mont-Tremblant, Canada. For some much-needed isolation and peace. No one in that town cares who I am. And I have a place in the mountains. Snow, cold and quiet. The ideal prescription."

It couldn't come a moment too soon. But a nagging thought occurred to him as he studied Sofia. Their little arrangement would be over by then. She'd go back to her life in DC. Suddenly, the isolation and lack of notoriety he so looked forward to in his jaunts to Mont-Tremblant didn't hold the same appeal.

For the first time ever, maybe he didn't want to be alone there.

"How about a nightcap to celebrate the end of a perfect evening?"

Sofia settled in the back seat of the limo and rested her head against the leather. She knew she should say no, that the best course of action would be to turn down Raul's offer.

But he was right; the dinner had gone off without a hitch, even accounting for the run-in with Aaron. She'd even managed to make small talk with her table mates.

Besides, her phone was still lighting up with messages from both her mom and Phil. The urge to procrastinate returning those calls was tough to ignore.

"Sure, why not?" she answered. Though she was probably going to stick with water or juice. Enough champagne for one night.

"You've earned it. Did you happen to enjoy yourself even a little?"

She was surprised at the answer to that question. Once the food had been served and the lights dimmed, the dinner was in fact rather entertaining. The well-known comedian who'd served as emcee had been amusing and knew how to work an audience. "I did, actually. The speeches were rather funny as was the emcee. Who knew politicians and journalists could be so good at poking fun at themselves and each other."

"The jokes are definitely the highlight of these dinners."

"I thought you said you didn't enjoy these events?"

"I happened to have enjoyed this one. Must have been the company." Something flashed behind Raul's eyes as he said the words. Combined with the deepness of his tone, it sent a wave of warmth over her skin.

She gave herself a mental forehead thwack. He was merely being polite. Why was she looking any further into his words than was warranted? The last event he asked her to attend with him was in two weeks. And he'd revealed this evening that he had a solo trip planned to the Laurentian Mountains outside Montreal immediately afterward. By then, he wouldn't give her another thought. She knew she couldn't say the same about him.

Just. Stop.

That's exactly the kind of thinking she'd been concerned about when she'd hesitated to take him up on the fake-engagement ploy. No feelings could be involved.

A message dinged on his phone and he glanced at the screen. "The hotel has confirmed that the rooftop restaurant will remain open for us and the staff is awaiting our arrival."

"I hope we're not keeping any of the staff over their shift."

He sent her a handsome smile, his features thrown in shadow by the soft interior lights in the vehicle. "It's part of the arrangement when I stay there. At that particular hotel, they're to have the restaurants open with private quarters throughout the duration of my stay. Day or night."

So much of his lifestyle she would never be able to relate to. Not many people could.

Moments later they were at the front entrance of the hotel and two doormen came out to greet them. They rode the elevator to the top floor. Sure enough, a full staff awaited them when they reached the roof, uniformed and all. A minibuffet of snacks and finger foods had been set up in the center. Next to it was a round table laden with pastries and desserts, including an entire layered chocolate cake topped with raspberries. A candlelit table sat in the middle of the area with two chairs and two place settings, next to a standing tray with a bottle of wine. The lights of DC glowed in the distance.

Despite their having eaten, dinner seemed like hours ago. Not to mention, she'd hardly been able to enjoy her meal given the circumstances that had led her there.

Plus, she'd never been good at resisting sweets, particularly when it came to chocolate.

"Will this do?"

He had no idea. With the acting part of the night over, Sofia felt a loosening in the pit of her stomach. She didn't have to pretend right now, didn't have to worry about saying or doing the wrong thing. It was as if Raul had thought of that and made sure the evening ended on a pleasant note. For her.

"This is magnificent. Thank you, Raul."

"My pleasure." He shrugged off his tuxedo jacket and threw it on one of the barstools nearby. Sofia took it as a cue to kick off her high heels. Her calves ached from having them on all night. She didn't even own a pair of high heels and hadn't worn a pair since her high school prom all those years ago.

Raul's bow tie came off next. He proceeded to undo the top few buttons of his shirt, exposing a tanned vee of toned chest, then he rolled up his sleeves to reveal muscled forearms. In a matter of seconds he'd gone from a picture of refined elegance to one of rugged, hardened male. Sofia had to force her gaze away to keep from staring.

"Where shall we start?" he asked, placing his palm on the small of her back in a gesture that was now becoming all too familiar. And all too welcome. He led her toward the food.

Moments later, they were seated at the table. Sofia delved into the cake and helped herself to a forkful, heavy on the frosting. Rich, buttery cocoa flavor exploded on her tongue. She practically groaned out loud with pleasure.

"I take it you like it," Raul said with a chuckle. A goblet of red wine was balanced between his fingers.

"It's like I've stepped into chocolate nirvana."

"I'll have to make a note of it."

"Of what?" Sofia asked, resisting the urge to take another generous bite and talk with her mouth full.

"That you're particularly fond of chocolate."

"That's hardly a secret around these parts."

"Well, if we're going to spend the next couple of weeks together, it will be helpful to know what your likes and dislikes are."

Right. So he could forget about any such facts right after, when it became irrelevant what she preferred for dessert as far as he was concerned.

"That goes both ways," she told him, swallowing another forkful and washing it down with cucumber-mint water. "For instance, I wouldn't have pegged you as a movie fan."

His eyebrows lifted. "What gave you the impression that I am?"

"I just assumed, given that we'll be attending the wedding of an actress. Are you a fan of hers?"

Her tone held a tint of something she couldn't quite place. She refused to believe it was any kind of jealousy rearing its ugly head.

"Not quite. Going to that wedding has nothing to do with her."

Well, that was rather curious. "Oh?"

"I happen to be well acquainted with the groom, in fact. Rafe and I attended boarding school together in Canada. Much like you and Luisa."

"And just like us, the two of you stayed in touch all these years." She lifted her fork in a mock salute.

"To friends."

Raul raised his glass then chuckled. "Rafe and I didn't exactly start out as friends."

"Really?"

He shook his head, pointing to the small scar along his jawline that had been there since she'd known him. "No, this would be his doing actually."

She hadn't expected that. "You got that scar in a fight?"

"That's right. What would have been your guess?"

She shrugged. "I just assumed you'd taken a fall on one of your many ski trips. Or had some kind of mishap with a fishing pole. You are the outdoor type."

"Nope. It happened because of a wound courtesy of a man I consider a dear friend. In fact, he asked me to be his best man but I turned him down for his own sake. And his bride's."

"You didn't want to overshadow the main event."

He nodded once. "Precisely."

"I had no idea that scar was the result of a fight."

He smiled at her over his wineglass. "You look incredulous. Is it that hard to believe?"

"Well, yes, to be honest."

"Why's that?"

"I didn't expect the only son of the king of Vesovia to get into physical brawls."

"Yeah, well. Neither did my father. Or myself for that matter. Rafe set us both straight on that assumption."

"Just one question then. Did you deserve it?"

He didn't hesitate with his answer. "Oh, most definitely. If anything, he let me off easy. Not that I didn't land a few blows myself. We were both pretty bloody and bruised afterward."

Her jaw went slack with surprise. This was a side of Raul she'd never even considered him having. "What did you do to make him angry?"

Raul rubbed his forehead and ducked his head as if embarrassed. "I'm not proud of my behavior those first few months, after…"

He didn't need to specify. Sofia could guess he was referring to the period after he'd lost his mother. She knew Luisa had tried to cope by acting out and misbehaving. She still was. But Sofia hadn't considered Raul might have had a reactionary rebellious period of his own.

She remained silent, allowing him to discuss his lost mother further if he so desired. She wasn't going to pry in any way. Judging by what she'd heard and witnessed from Luisa, the queen's sudden death from an undiagnosed blood disorder had shocked and devastated her family.

Several beats passed in silence before Raul spoke again. "I was rather angry at the world back then. And trying to take it out on anyone who crossed my path."

"How so?"

"Ignoring my lessons. Refusing to attend functions." He tapped his scar. "Picking fights."

"People react to grief in different ways." She'd seen it firsthand. Her mother had been a shell of herself the first year after her father had left them.

"Yeah, well, my answer was to infuriate my father and try to provoke classmates. Most of them didn't dare retaliate, too afraid of the ire of the king."

"But not Rafe."

He chuckled. "Nope. Not him. He told me later he figured it would be worth expulsion to wipe that irritatingly smug look off my face."

Sofia's heart lurched in her chest at the grief-stricken young man he must have been, trying to hide behind a cloak of bravado.

"I wish I could go back and change my behavior. I'll never forgive myself for the way I let my father down. He was already grieving and suffering the loss of his wife. And Luisa and I did nothing but add to his anguish."

Sofia reached out and covered his large hand with her own. "You were both grappling with a pretty big loss yourselves."

"That's no excuse."

She gripped his hand tighter. "I'd beg to argue. It most certainly is."

"It's no wonder he sent us both away to boarding school."

Raul didn't see the discrepancy in his reasoning. As a teen, he'd lost his loving mother. Then he'd been sent away from his very home to deal with his grief on his own. She wasn't finding fault with the king or the way he'd dealt with his own loss, but there was no question he hadn't been able to find it in him to offer comfort his son or daughter.

"I think you're being too hard on yourself. And the vulnerable young man you had been back then."

He didn't respond to that. A curtain seemed to fall behind his eyes and he pulled his hand away. "All I can do is try to make it up to him. And to try and rein in Luisa as best as is humanly possible."

What a load he carried on his shoulders. As if the responsibility of being heir to a kingdom wasn't enough.

What had possessed him to get into all that? He didn't particularly care to talk about his mother or the way he'd behaved after her loss. The aftermath of their lives after she'd gone wasn't a pleasant chapter. Past history that should very well stay in the past. Something about being outside on the roof of the hotel, with the lights of the city bright on the horizon and the warm breeze in the air, it all served to have him loosening his guard and opening up to Sofia in a way he hadn't expected.

Luisa had often said Sofia was the one friend she felt most comfortable confiding in. He'd apparently fallen under the same spell.

"Can I get you anything else, sir?" A waiter had appeared by his side while Raul had been deep in his thoughts. He hadn't even seen the man approach.

"No, thank you," he answered with a look to Sofia first to confirm.

She pushed back from the table as the man began to clear their plates. "I should start making my way back home. I hadn't realized just how late it was. I must apologize to your driver for having to set out this time of night."

Did she really think he had any intention of sending her away? When he had practically a whole floor to himself here at the hotel?

"Well, you wouldn't have to do that if you just stayed here." He held a hand up to ward off the protest that was clearly coming. "I have an entire floor to myself. There's a whole suite that will sit empty. Makes no sense for you to leave at this hour."

She spread her arms, gesturing to her dress. "I have nothing with me. I can hardly sleep in this gown."

"Don't worry about that. It's already been taken care of."

She tilted her head in question. "Taken care of how?"

"Anything you may need has been delivered to my quarters downstairs. You'll find a selection of sleepwear, clothing for the morning, as well as toiletries."

She studied him, her lips pursed. Honestly, what was there to think about? They were pretending to be engaged for all the world to believe. It made no sense for her to be shy about spending the night in the same hotel.

"I guess that's reasonable. I would feel rather bad having your driver leave at this hour and then have to drive back."

He nodded, more than a little relieved that she wasn't going to fight him. She seemed pretty inclined to do so more often than not.

"Wise decision. And this will give us a chance to have breakfast together tomorrow morning and discuss our next steps."

She swallowed. "I suppose we should do that."

"By this time in three days, we'll have touched down in Toronto. The wedding is the day after we land."

Then they'd be onto the next phase. In another country where she'd be traveling with him as his fiancée.

It was well past midnight by the time they entered his suite on the penthouse floor. Sofia appeared dead on her feet.

"Let's get you into bed, shall we?" Sofia's eyes grew

wide. The words were out of his mouth before Raul registered how they could be misconstrued. He wasn't actually going to put her to bed himself. As tempting an idea as that was.

He led her to the corner of the room. "That closet is where you'll find the items that have been sent up for you."

"Thanks." Sofia opened the door and stepped inside. "Wow, this is certainly excessive. So many choices."

It so happened one of the choices in sleepwear was a lacy, skimpy number that hung right in the center of the rack. Sofia's gasp of surprise made it clear that she'd seen it just as he had.

Raul couldn't help the images that flooded his head. Sofia lying in bed, in a tangle of silk sheets, wearing the lingerie. The skirt riding up her thighs as she tossed and turned. Heaven help him, the image that followed that scene was her beckoning him to join her on the bed. Pulling her against him, wrapping her arms around his center.

He pushed the picture away and swallowed the curse on the tip of his tongue.

He should have left explicit instructions about exactly what his staff should have provided. He should have asked for thick, baggy flannel pajamas that went all the way down to her ankles. Only, Sofia would most definitely look alluring even in such attire. The thought of her in bed close by was enough to fire his libido.

Not good.

Raul cleared his throat. "I'll leave you to it then," he told her. "You should have everything you need. Good night," he added, then turned to make his way toward his own suite.

"Good night. And thank you," Sofia's soft voice came from behind him.

It was going to be a long night. One thing was for certain: he'd have to take a cold shower before trying to go to sleep. Though he doubted it would help all that much.

That theory proved correct two hours later as he lay in bed staring at the patterned ceiling. Had Sofia chosen that particular nightie to sleep in? Was she sound asleep right now? Was there any chance she might be dreaming of him, the same way he was captivated by her traveling like a temptress through his own thoughts?

He sure wasn't going to get any sleep anytime soon.

This deepening attraction to her was most inconvenient. Sure, they had to be convincing to the rest of the world to present themselves as a couple in love. But any true emotion would only complicate matters. They would be going their separate ways as soon as the ruse was over. It was bad enough he was asking her to take a temporary break from all that she had in her life. She'd left her business to Agnes's care, and she wouldn't see her friends or her home for weeks as she pretended to be something she wasn't.

He had no right to risk asking her for anything more.

Sofia rubbed a palm over her midriff, smoothing the silky material of the wisp that could hardly be called a nightgown. Why in the world had she chosen to wear this? But after Raul had left the room, she'd found herself lifting the hanger where it hung, removing the thin straps and then putting it on. It so wasn't her usual getup of loose T-shirt and baggy boy shorts. But something about the way Raul had looked at her after he'd seen it in the closet… Her skin felt aflame with the memory of that look right now.

Clearly it was the wrong choice of attire, because sleep still eluded her. Though her insomnia probably had more to do with the way her thoughts kept turning to the man sleeping in the other room. What did he wear to bed? She wasn't sure how she knew, or even if she was right. But something told her Raul wasn't the type to wear much when he slept. Perhaps a pair of comfortable pajama bottoms with nothing on top.

And he probably kept the covers low—he seemed the type to run hot at night—exposing his bare chest.

Her breath hitched and she tossed onto her back. She had to get a grip. Morning would be here before she knew it and she had yet to sleep a wink. Ironic, as this had to be the most comfortable bed she'd ever slept in. Not to mention the most luxurious room. To think, she'd be in such posh surroundings daily for the next three weeks. While she played princess. A princess in love. Though none of it was real. She couldn't risk losing sight of that. Which would be all too easy to do if she kept entertaining thoughts of Raul without a shirt on.

Turned out that was easier said than done. By the time the sun was fully shining outside her window, Sofia had only managed intermittent bouts of restless sleep. Hardly restful but there was no use in trying at this late stage. Besides, she could hear noises outside her door, telling her Raul was up and about.

With a resigned sigh, she got up and reached for the satin robe draped over the edge of the bed. To her dismay, it was much shorter than she'd realized, barely covering the tops of her thighs. Well, there was nothing for it. The robe was the only thing she'd brought into the room with her last night. It matched the nightie, making for an outfit clearly geared more toward a night of romance rather than sleep.

Maybe she could make a beeline to the closet before he caught sight of her.

No such luck. Raul, speaking into his phone, was standing mere feet away from her door when she opened it and stepped outside. She was right. He didn't sleep with any kind of shirt on. He was bare chested right now, a pair of loose cotton pajama bottoms hanging low on his hips

Speaking of romantic nights.

Just stop.

His eyes landed square on her, then lowered to her bare thighs. Sofia couldn't resist the urge to tug the bottom of the robe lower. But that small action only made things worse. The robe's collar lowered in response to reveal the lace of the nightie at her chest. Raul's eyes flashed back up to her neckline.

Great. Now he knew that she had indeed chosen that particular nightgown to wear to bed.

"Thanks," he said into the phone before clicking off the call and tossing it onto a coffee table nearby. All the while, his eyes never left her. "Good morning. How'd you sleep?"

The words were casual enough, but Sofia could swear she heard a hint of a vibration in his tone.

"Very well, thanks," she lied. Hopefully there were no dark circles under her eyes to give her away.

"I didn't expect you to be up so early," he told her.

That would explain the bare chest.

"Sorry I'm not more…uh…presentable," he added.

She forced a smile. Why was her heart pounding so hard? "I could say the same."

"You look great," he said, then flinched. "I just mean that's a nice color on you. The rose gold suits you."

"Uh…thanks?"

The conversation was becoming more and more awkward. No wonder. She wasn't exactly in the habit of waking up in a luxury hotel suite in the company of a royal prince. Or any man, for that matter. Raul had to sense her lack of experience with such things. He'd probably been seduced and charmed by some of the most beautiful women on the planet. How awkward she must seem in comparison.

For the first time in her life, she had to wonder if she might have tried harder with some of her casual dates. If only to give her some proficiency.

Sofia grasped for something else to say. "Might we get ahold of some coffee?" she asked, just as he spoke too.

"I've taken the liberty of ordering some breakfast for us," he said.

Mercifully, a knock sounded on the door at the next moment.

"There it is now," he said and headed toward the door.

A uniformed waiter rolled in a cart laden with silver covered dishes and, thank heavens, a large steaming carafe. The welcome scent of rich brewed coffee wafted through the air. Sofia's mouth watered.

"I wasn't sure what you were in the mood for," Raul said once the man had transferred his load onto the table off the kitchen area and lifted the covers. "So I tried for variety."

He certainly had. The table held everything from thick omelets to soft-boiled eggs in standing cups. A tray of various pastries sat in the center. A plate of waffles and pancakes rounded out the offerings. There was no way the two of them could eat so much food.

"I'd say you'd ordered enough for breakfast and lunch."

He smiled. "Once I get to know your preferences better, I'll be sure to only order what I know you like."

That sounded very considerate. So why did the statement send a wave of sadness over her? They were barely more than strangers. An insane part of her wished that somehow their circumstances were different. That they were indeed a real couple on the brink of a new relationship. In that exciting stage of getting to know each other and falling in lo—

She didn't let herself complete the thought. "Usually just coffee and toast. But this all looks delicious."

"Noted for next time." Without asking, he poured her a cup and handed it to her with a small pitcher of cream.

Maybe he knew a bit about her after all.

Sofia took a deep inhale of the aromatic brew before stirring in a generous drop of cream. She took the seat at the table Raul pulled out for her.

"I was just about to check online," he told her, taking a chair himself across the round table. "To see how much of an impression we made our first night being seen together."

Sofia took as large a gulp of coffee as the beverage's heat would allow and gave herself a second to savor the taste. It was divine. She would guess this particular blend was a bit further on the quality scale than the minicups she used back at home.

He pulled his phone out of his pocket and began to scroll. An expression she couldn't read crossed over his features. "Hmm."

"What is it?"

"There are plenty of pictures of us at the dinner. Along with a good amount of speculation."

"Good. That's good."

"There's more." He stood and walked over to her side of the table and handed her the phone. "See for yourself."

Sofia stared at the screen, expecting to see a picture of the two of them entering the ballroom. But the featured photo of the website wasn't taken at the event at all. No, they'd been snapped sitting head-to-head at the table on the rooftop afterward.

"I don't understand."

"Guess the tabloid sites wanted to go with a more intimate photo."

Suddenly, her appetite was totally gone. Being seen at a dinner was one thing. But the rooftop last night had felt more private. More intimate.

But rather than being bothered, Raul returned to his chair and went about eating his breakfast. He popped a piece of waffle into his mouth around a satisfied smile. In fact, he appeared rather pleased. Which begged the question...

"Wait a minute. Did you have anything to do with this photo?"

He looked up from his cup, his brows furrowed. "What do you mean?"

She pointed to the phone screen. "Was this your doing? Is this what last night on the roof was really about?"

He shook his head slowly. "I had nothing to do with it. Though I must say I don't understand why you're upset. This is precisely what we wanted. The internet is abuzz with rumors about us."

He was right. He didn't understand at all. She was indeed upset. Because a naive part of her had believed that some of those moments between them on the roof were more than a photo opportunity. That at least some part of last night might have been real.

It had been for her.

CHAPTER SIX

THIS PLANE RIDE was sure to be an uneasy one if Raul couldn't figure out a way to clear the air while they were up here.

Now, studying her across from him staring out the plane window at the clouds outside, Sofia still seemed rather miffed. He really didn't understand why. The entire day yesterday had been strained, the tension between them near tangible. He hadn't been sure what to say to make it better. Then she'd left to go by her shop to ensure everything was in place to have it run smoothly in her absence. He was half-afraid she wouldn't return.

He decided to chalk it up to nerves about leaving her business and home for the next three weeks. Though it sounded like her shop would be in good hands. Her friend Agnes had apparently recruited a cousin to help out along with a few shelter volunteers to round out the staffing needs. Still, the fact that she was leaving her business for so long to assist him served to once again trigger the nagging guilt at what he'd asked of her.

Now, to top it off, something about the photo of the two of them on the rooftop had upset her.

"Sofia."

She turned silently, one eyebrow raised in question.

He cleared his throat. It was tough to find a way to

apologize when one wasn't sure exactly what they were to be sorry for. As far as he was concerned, the posting of the unexpected snapshot had only served in their favor. It had driven gossip about Luisa out of the limelight until he and the king could figure out a long-term plan to address his sister's antics.

"I'm sorry if the photo upset you. I can have my staff look into exactly who took it and see they answer for their actions."

Her jaw fell open in surprise. "You think I'm looking to have someone punished?"

"If it will make you feel better."

Now she looked downright aghast. "Why would that make me feel better?"

Raul had to fight the urge to throw his hands in the air. Honestly, what did she want from him? She released a deep sigh and rubbed her forehead.

"Look, I guess I wasn't expecting that I would be game for that kind of intrusion at any given moment. I wasn't prepared. I will be from now on. Lesson learned."

Raul wanted to kick himself. She was right. He should have prepared her much better. He was so used to consistently and perpetually being under the proverbial microscope, it hadn't even occurred to him that level of exposure might be too much for anyone used to living a normal existence.

As if he needed another reminder that he had no business dragging someone like Sofia into such an existence for longer than absolutely necessary.

"I appreciate that," he told her, though the words were hardly adequate.

She granted him a pensive smile before turning her attention back to the clouds. Hours later, when the familiar sight of the CN Tower appeared on the horizon outside the window, he still couldn't be sure if his apology had been nearly enough.

A sleek town car awaited them when they landed in Toronto. Sofia did her best to take in the sights of the city as they drove but her mind insisted on being preoccupied.

So the second leg of their ruse was now in full live mode. By this time tomorrow night, she'd be getting ready to attend one of the most talked-about weddings of the decade. The wedding of a beautiful award-winning actress to a man who'd gone to boarding school with a prince. A prince who happened to be her date.

A small chuckle of disbelief escaped her lips.

"What's so funny?" Raul asked. He'd done that thing where he'd unbuttoned his shirt collar and rolled up his sleeves again. How did the man look so rugged yet still polished simply by undoing a few buttons?

"I'm just having a hard time believing all this," she admitted. "I guess it's finally sinking in.

As Raul leaned closer, the scent of his aftershave sent a tingling sense of longing through her center. Dangerous combination at the moment—the way he looked and the way he smelled. Given their close proximity to each other in the car, it was wreaking havoc on her faculties.

With everything going on the moment, the last thing she needed was this nonsensical attraction she felt for him to rear itself. But her senses had other ideas.

"I'm sure you'll fit in fine. You might even have fun."

Ha! Easy for him to say. "Not likely. I'll be much too nervous among all those dignitaries, world-famous entertainers and who knows who else way beyond my station."

His mouth quirked into a frown. "There will be no one

there above your station, as you call it. As for Rafe and Frannie, they're two of the most down-to-earth people you're likely to meet."

By Frannie, he meant Francesca Tate. Her last movie release had been a blockbuster. As had most of her others. Sofia had never heard her referred to as Frannie before. A nickname reserved for her inner circle, no doubt. A circle Sofia was about to crash under a false pretense.

"They'll love having you at their wedding," Raul reassured her.

He sounded so confident, but Sofia knew better. She supposed most people would seem down-to-earth to a prince in comparison. Even a world-famous Canadian actress and her groom, who happened to be heir to an electronics fortune.

"And the castle is breathtaking. Wait until you see it."

Sofia bit down a gasp. "They're getting married in a castle?"

He nodded. "Casa Loma. It's one of Toronto's most historic sights."

A castle. She really was going in blind here. What exactly did one wear to an actress and tycoon's wedding in a castle?

It was as if Raul read her thoughts. "As with the journalist dinner, you'll have an array of gowns to choose from. And you'll have some more help getting ready for this one, considering it's an affair with much more international attention."

"Help how?"

He narrowed his eyes on her, as if confused by the question. "A team. You'll have a team to assist you."

"A team?"

He nodded. "Yes. A stylist, a hair artist and other professionals to make sure you look the part."

Right. She was playing the part of a princess. A role she had no experience for, despite Raul's reassurances about how well she'd fit in.

Twenty minutes later, the car came to a stop in front of a tall high-rise. A doorman awaited them on the sidewalk just like back in DC. Would she ever get used to someone waiting on the street just to open a car door for her? Sofia doubted it.

"Is this where we're staying while we're in Toronto?" she asked Raul once they reached the marble-tiled lobby.

"Considering I own the penthouse suite, it makes the most sense." He waited until they were alone in the elevator before adding, "You'll have your own room of course."

The elevator doors opened right into his living space. A large foyer with tall green trees along the walls. The entire front wall was glass. The city skyline glittered in the distance outside. "We're by the theater district," Raul told her, leading her inside.

So he owned a cottage in the Laurentian Mountains and a penthouse in one of the country's most metropolitan cities. She recalled Luisa telling her years ago that her brother was more than a prince, that he was a successful businessman who'd grown the family's and the kingdom's wealth by several degrees. Sofia had had no idea of the true extent of his success.

She walked over to look out the glass wall. A whole city lay beneath her, lit up and bustling with nightlife. The theater district. In another reality, she might have enjoyed a romantic night on the town with a handsome date. But she was essentially here to complete a job, to playact a role. Too bad she couldn't ask Francesca Tate for thespian tips.

"Your quarters are to the right," Raul said behind her. "If you'd like to freshen up. I know it was a rather long flight."

She could certainly use the opportunity. Plus, there was another much less pleasant task she still hadn't tackled.

"Thanks. I also need to make a phone call I've been avoiding."

He braced his shoulder on the wall, leaned against it and crossed his arms. "Your mother."

"Correct." And she was most definitely not looking forward to it.

A wave of sadness hit her like a tsunami. Up until a few years ago, she had never kept anything from Mama. Let alone something as major as a fake relationship with a real prince. The idea of lying to her mother seemed so foreign and unnatural.

Yet here she was about to do exactly that. But she had no choice. Not if she wanted to abide by her promise to Raul. Anything she told to Mama, she may as well tell Phil directly. The end result would be the same.

How could one relationship change someone's personality to such a drastic extent? Her mother was no longer her own person; instead she was an extension of Sofia's stepfather now. The two of them were one unit. Which some people might find romantic. Sofia merely found it stifling and hurtful, given that the relationship had come at the cost of her own relationship with Ramona.

"I've been dodging some calls myself," Raul said from across the room.

"I take it you're referring to the king."

He nodded. "You take it right," he answered, a heavy weariness in his voice.

For the first time, it occurred to Sofia just how much

of a toll this must be taking on him as well. As busy as he was, with everything on his mind, he had to put on a happy face and present himself to the world as a man who'd recently and unexpectedly fallen in love.

Maybe they were both in over their heads.

The next day went by in a flurry of activity. Sofia had always wondered about the dogs she helped groom at the dog shows. How they managed to sit still for hours as they were prepped and primped before the competition. She figured she had a pretty good idea now.

The fashion stylist had come first to help her pick out a dress and put together the complete outfit. The woman had arrived with an actual wooden chest on wheels full of accessories. She'd left Sofia with three different options of dresses to pick from. Then came the hair stylist. As a result, Sofia was now sporting an elegant updo with tiny sparkles sprinkled throughout her tresses. Finally, a tall, rambunctiously talkative gentleman with braids down to his waist had shown up to do her makeup. He'd used no less than seven different makeup brushes and the process had taken close to an hour.

At least all the preparation helped to take her mind off the phone call with Mama yesterday. To say her mother was surprised about the turn of events regarding Sofia's love life would be a vast understatement. Sofia had no doubt that once it really sank in, her mother and Phil would try to brainstorm any way the new development might help realize her stepfather's objectives. Phil was probably giddy with the idea of a crown prince being someone he might be able to turn to for a favor or two.

Little did he know.

Now, she stood in front of the mirror in yet another silk

robe—this one blessedly longer, as it actually reached her knees—to study the end result.

She looked somehow different yet it was still her face staring back at her in the mirror. What would Raul think of the difference? He wasn't here to ask. He'd been gone most of the day, having left early to attend to some business in a local office in the city. She humphed out loud. He probably wouldn't even notice.

The professionals who'd worked on her seemed to think she looked the part. But his was the opinion that mattered, wasn't it? He'd essentially hired her to play the role of his intended princess.

If only Agnes were here. Sofia could use some feedback from her friend. Not that there was any time to backtrack any of it at this late hour. With a sigh she walked to the closet where the three dresses hung on a hanger.

Time to decide. They were all truly breathtaking. It was so hard to choose. She'd never understood why some celebrities changed into multiple outfits during the same event until now.

Eenie...meenie...

No. That was no way to pick. Funny, she wasn't typically so indecisive. In the end, she went with the first of the three. A midnight blue, tea-length number that the stylist assured complemented her figure and her coloring. Backless, it left her skin exposed down to her waist from behind. A bit more exposed than her usual taste. But these weren't exactly typical circumstances. Sofia disrobed and trailed her fingers down the fabric. As if handling delicate artwork—because in a sense that's what this dress was, a work of art—she slipped it on feet first, taking care not to mar her makeup or dislodge so much as a single hair.

She adjusted the thin spaghetti straps over her shoulders and turned to study the complete look in the mirror.

There. Transformation complete.

Those well-heeled wedding guests would never be able to guess that she made her living elbow deep in soap suds wrangling often filthy pets clean, sometimes while trying to eradicate fleas.

She tried to picture the reaction one of those guests might have if Sofia discussed how she made a living. The idea made her chuckle out loud just as a knock sounded on the door.

Raul's voice echoed from behind the wood. "Is it okay to come in? Are you decent?"

Hopefully, she was a level or two above "decent."

This was the fanciest dress she'd ever worn. The fabric felt like a light cloud over her skin. And certainly no team of professionals had ever tended to her hair or makeup before.

"I can come back later," he said a moment later when she still hadn't answered. Why was she hesitating? This was as ready as she was going to get. Except, maybe she should have gone with the red dress instead.

She could ask Raul. But that idea was nixed in an instant. He had more-important things on his mind. With a steadying breath she went to answer the door and let him in.

She caught him mid-knock. His mouth fell open when he saw her, and his eyes widened. "Wow. That was worth the wait. You look absolutely stunning."

Sofia felt her shoulders sag with relief. She wasn't even aware until that moment just how nervous she'd been about Raul's reaction. The man was used to dating international models, prima donnas and beautiful heiresses. A very real part of her worried that she wouldn't measure up as his date to this wedding, no matter how many professionals helped her prepare for it.

"So this will do then?" she asked, hating the doubt that even she heard in her voice.

He swallowed with a nod. "I'd say. Just one problem though."

Her heart sank. She knew it. Something about her was off. "A problem?"

He shook his head, eyed her from the top of her head to the strapped stiletto shoes at her feet. "There's a real risk you might upstage the actual bride."

Ha! Very little chance of that happening. "The day I upstage *the* Francesca Tate will be a day of miracles. At her own wedding, no less."

He leaned a shoulder against the doorframe, and crossed his arms in front of his chest, his gaze level on hers. "I wouldn't be so sure, Sofia. You're a vision in that dress."

She resisted the urge to squeal in delight as she felt warmth flush over her cheeks. Most likely, Raul was simply being charming. Still Sofia felt the compliment clear to her core. She wasn't used to being told she was a vision by the opposite sex, couldn't recall a single time it had happened before. To think, her first real heartfelt compliment from a man came from a crown prince.

A vision.

She could say the same for him. Dressed in a white tuxedo for this event, he looked every inch the prince that he was. Gold cuff links sparkled from his sleeves. His dark hair a striking contrast against the ivory fabric of his jacket. Regal, elegant, polished. And it all came so effortlessly.

He held his arm out to her. "If you're ready, madame, your carriage awaits."

* * *

Turned out, Raul had been quite literal with his last comment upstairs.

Instead of the limo she'd been expecting like back in DC, Raul led her out of the lobby and toward a domed wooden carriage complete with gold trim and large round wheels. A waiting driver with a top hat and tailed jacket approached them and helped Sofia up into the seat. He tipped his hat to Raul as he stepped in before going around to the front.

"I figured we'd ride in style. This will take a bit longer to get us there but it will give you a chance to take in the city."

Sofia couldn't help but feel moved by the gesture. She trailed a finger along the beige satin padding of the seat.

"If you'd rather a more conventional ride, we can summon a car instead."

"No, this is perfect. And no horses required."

He flashed her a wide smile. "That's right. It's one of those novel electric carriages. I believe this might be the first one of its kind in the city."

She'd heard about these newer vehicles. Given her love of animals, Raul had made an ideal choice as far as he was concerned. The feeling of warmth in her chest grew.

Careful.

That warm feeling could all too easily ignite into an all-out burn considering how handsome he looked and the way his knee kept brushing against hers in the tight quarters between the plush seats.

She returned his smile with a grin of her own. "I can't imagine a better transport."

Raul leaned over to give the driver the signal that they were ready to go. The man popped open the lid of a center console and pushed a button. A low humming sound echoed from the front and small fairy lights turned on by their feet and through the interior. Though it was still light outside, the lights added to the festive, happy mood.

She focused on her surroundings as the carriage moved into traffic. They'd no doubt draw a good deal of attention but it would be worth it. A nagging voice in her head wondered if the attention was Raul's true intent with the carriage idea. But she would push it aside for now. The CN Tower loomed over the city in the distance.

Raul pointed to it. "You know, you can see that tower no matter where you are in Toronto."

"That's amazing."

"And it rotates, giving observers a full view of the city scape every seventy minutes or so."

A wistful feeling swept over her as she looked at the majestic structure. Too bad they didn't have any plans to visit the landmark. Who knew when she'd ever get a chance to be back in this city. She debated asking whether they had any chance of getting there before leaving for Montreal but Raul answered her unspoken question.

"If we had more time, I would have scheduled a stop for us there. But unfortunately the agenda just doesn't allow it. We have to leave for Montreal in two days and I have another full day of meetings tomorrow. My Canada team is making sure to utilize as much of my attention as they can while I'm here." A clear note of apology interlaced his voice. She wasn't naive enough to think it might be regret.

"I understand," she told him. "It's okay, really. Maybe I'll find a way to get back here with Agnes or something."

Agnes would be the logical choice, though it would be logistically difficult for both of them to leave the shop. Even with the new hires she planned to recruit, they were the most senior and experienced. But Sofia certainly didn't anticipate having a man in her life anytime soon to go traveling with. As far as her mom…well, a few years ago, the first person she would have considered bringing back here was her mother. But Ramona was no longer the devoted, dedicated mom who dropped everything to spend time with her daughter these days. Phil had changed all that when he'd arrived in their lives. Who knew Sofia would find herself missing the borderline smothering parent Ramona had been.

Thank heavens for Agnes. The woman had started out as her part-time employee and developed into a true friend.

"And where did you just travel off to?" Raul asked.

She shrugged her shoulders and allowed herself a smile. "I'm just admiring all the sights."

That was true enough. Around them the city was bustling with activity. Sofia could hardly decide where to look as they made their way through the streets. Tourists with their phones out to snap photos or follow directions. Some who were clear locals with a clear destination in mind. A street performer stood juggling half a dozen long tubes to the delight of the circle of children watching. A long line circled around the sidewalk in front of an elegant building.

Raul followed her gaze to the building. "That's the Princess of Wales Theatre. Not sure what it's showing right now but clearly it's a popular choice.

"Clearly," Sofia agreed.

Several people turned as they passed to watch them go by. More than a few pointed or lifted their phones presumably for a photo.

For the first time since this whole charade started, Sofia actually felt like she might be in a fairy tale starring as the princess. Some kind of Cinderella. She would enjoy it while she could. Because just like Cinderella, all this would end and she would go back to her regular life working long hours grooming during the day and cleaning up at night. Followed by paperwork at home in the evening before falling asleep on her couch from exhaustion.

It was only a matter of time before the clock struck midnight.

CHAPTER SEVEN

RAUL WAS TRYING his best to play the competent tour guide; he really was. But it was so hard to concentrate on anything else with Sofia looking the way she did and with her soft, delicate perfume wafting to him even with the open-air carriage. He'd almost lost the ability to speak entirely when he'd followed her downstairs from the penthouse and seen the low-cut back of her dress. His fingers itched to trail along her neck and down her spine. And lower.

The woman could sure pull off wearing formal gowns. And he'd thought she'd looked good at the gala dinner back in DC. Tonight she looked downright jaw-dropping. He'd only been partially kidding when he'd told her she risked overshadowing the bride. She certainly would in his eyes.

She looked elegant, lovely. Kissable.

Whoa. Steady there, fella.

That was an avenue he couldn't travel down. So why couldn't he stop thinking about it? He'd hardly concentrated on anything he'd been told during his meetings, his thoughts solely focused on her and where she might be in the process of preparing for the big event. She pulled to him even when they weren't together in the same place. His thoughts drifted to her when he should have been working. Never before had a woman broken into his consciousness as often as Sofia seemed to. For the life of him he couldn't figure out why. Previous time spent with other women had been pleasurable enough. Though he didn't recall ever finding himself fantasizing about those others during his normal routines. And he and Sofia hadn't even been intimate.

Perhaps that was the issue. His imagination was focused on what he knew he couldn't have. Forbidden fruit and all.

Now he couldn't seem to stop himself from wondering what she might taste like if he took those ruby-red lips with his own. How soft she'd feel under his touch.

Maybe they should have taken separate transportation.

But watching her at the moment told him arranging for the carriage had been the right move. As they moved through downtown Toronto, she observed the city with wonder and awe. All the landmarks he himself had grown to take for granted when he visited the city he considered his second home.

"This is fantastic, Raul. Really. Thank you," she told him, her gaze still fixed on her street.

"You're welcome," he replied. She had no idea how selfish his true motives were. Sure, he'd been telling her the truth about wanting her to see the sights of the city as they made their way to Casa Loma for the wedding. But the deeper truth was that he wanted to spend some more time with her, alone, after being away most of the day and before the brouhaha that was sure to commence at the wedding of one of the biggest movie stars in the world.

And besides, she really did seem enthralled by all that she was looking at. "If you do find yourself back in Toronto in the future, I'd be happy to point out some spots you won't want to miss next time."

She turned away from the open window to look at him.

"Thanks, Raul. That would be most welcome," she said, her tone pleasant enough. But he hadn't imagined the tightening of her smile as she said the words.

"So, what should I know about these friends of yours?" she asked, jarring him somewhat with the sudden change in topic. "Aside from the fact that one is responsible for a rather angry looking scar on your chin and the other happens to be a major box office draw no matter what genre of movie she's starring in."

"Hmm. That's a fairly accurate description. I can only add that the two fell madly in love with each other and no one saw it coming, particularly the two of them."

She lifted an eyebrow in question. "Oh?"

"Rafe's firm was helping finance one of her movies set in Australia. It most definitely was not love at first sight. In fact, I've never seen Rafe so agitated by a woman before."

"You're kidding? And now they're getting married?"

It still made Raul chuckle when he thought about all the long, drawn-out phone calls he'd get from Rafe complaining about the spoiled, entitled actress who was making his life so irksome. "That's right," he answered. "They would butt heads about almost every decision. Frannie wanted the scenes to look perfect, thought it was worth the cost. Rafe, financier that he is, did analyses and formulas and pushed back whenever he thought things were getting excessive."

"I can see how that might have vexed her."

"They both did a fair amount of vexing, believe me. That's the funny thing."

"What?"

"Throughout my many conversations with Rafe when they first met, I distinctly got the impression that at some point he began to enjoy getting a rise out of her."

Sofia laughed, a soft sound that reminded him of the gentle breeze that rustled the trees back in Vesovia during early-fall mornings. He lost his train of thought before wrangling it back with no small amount of effort.

He continued, "If I had to bet, I'd guess Frannie got her own enjoyment out of the sparring. She likes a challenge and people don't often push back against anything she says or does. I think she found Rafe refreshing for not coddling her like everyone else."

"Sounds like a match made in heaven," Sofia said, her smile still solidly in place. But her eyes were distant and unfocused, and her voice held a hint of melancholy.

He couldn't read too deeply into that.

"Everyone should be so lucky," he said, surprising himself by how much he meant those words. An unfamiliar sensation churned in his gut that he refused to acknowledge as envy. Rafe deserved every bit of happiness in his life and the love of a woman like Frannie. He was honorable, loyal, and had been a good friend throughout the years.

But his friend had never had to worry about the upheaval he would bring upon a woman's life by loving her.

Raul wished he could say the same for himself.

They were headed to a verifiable castle. Complete with rising towers and a sprawling, colorful garden. Casa Loma was the most magnificent structure Sofia had ever laid eyes on. And that was saying something coming from someone who lived in DC. But while the Capitol Building, White House and One First Street were architectural marvels, Casa Loma looked like something out of a classic fairy tale.

"Your friends seem to have picked quite the setting to get married."

Raul smiled at her. "This is one of only a few standing castles in North America."

"I'd venture to guess it might be the most magnificent one."

It occurred to her then. The man beside her actually made his home in a place like this. Here she was, awestruck at this spectacular specimen of a building while to Raul, it was no different than coming home at the end of the day.

She couldn't let herself linger on that reality for too long or she might very well bid him goodbye and run back toward the theater district on foot.

Soon, they had come to a stop in front of the main door and Raul helped her out of the carriage. If Sofia had thought there'd been a lot of paparazzi at the journalists' dinner, it was scant in comparison to what they came across when they arrived at the wedding venue. There was actually a media helicopter circling in the air above.

The clicking of the numerous cameras as they made their way out of the carriage created a tidal wave of noise. Questions were being shouted at them from every direction.

"Try to relax," Raul whispered in her ear, a charming smile set on his face as he waved to the paparazzi. "We'll be inside in just a moment."

That moment couldn't come soon enough.

"No photographers in there?"

He shook his head. "Just the half a dozen or so professional wedding photographers Rafe and Frannie hired."

Half a dozen? That sounded a tad excessive. But what did she know? She wasn't an accomplished actress about to marry a successful financier. Sofia couldn't imagine the planning that must have gone into a wedding on this scale with the whole world watching.

Rafe pulled her closer to his side as he continued moving forward through the line of onlookers and cameras. So many cameras.

Sofia sucked in a breath of relief when they were finally at the entrance.

"Wow." That was all she could think to say as she took in her surroundings. The Great Hall was a spectacular sight to behold. A high ceiling that had to be at least sixty feet up. Wooden arches above. An assortment of flags hung from the walls. An indoor balcony with a circular stairway nestled in the far corner.

"Frannie fell in love with this place when she filmed a movie here a few years back," Raul told her. "It's a popular location for films. That movie about the teen wizards was filmed here, for one. As well as the fairy tale with the beastly monster who turns into a prince." He chuckled as he explained.

That's why it looked somewhat familiar.

"It's magnificent. I had no idea there was a medieval castle overlooking Toronto," she admitted.

"Reminds me a bit of Versailles in France."

"Wouldn't know. I've never been there."

"You really must go."

Sofia ignored the sinking feeling in her chest at his words. Raul kept mentioning trips she should take, like back in the carriage when he'd spoken about coming back to Toronto sometime. It never occurred to him to even offer traveling with her. Rather telling, wasn't it?

"If it's anything like this, I would love to see it someday," she said, hearing the wistfulness in her own voice.

"It's much flashier. With more gold."

A smiling woman with a tight bun atop her head wearing a sharp navy blazer and matching skirt approached them. She greeted Raul with a friendly smile. "Welcome, Your Highness," she said before turning to her. "And madame. The ceremony will be held in the Conservatory, if you'll follow me."

She led them down long, narrow corridors, her heels clicking on the hardwood floor. The sound of chatter grew louder as they walked.

"Here we are," the woman said as they entered what appeared to be a man-made indoor Eden. The ceiling above them was a colorful stained-glass dome, the floor shiny patterned tile. Tall rectangular windows behind the podium looked out to a lush green garden.

Suddenly, all the chatter seemed to gradually subside until the room grew completely quiet. She and Raul appeared to be among the last to arrive. Rows and rows of chairs were occupied by sharply dressed, impeccably coiffed guests. Sofia understood why Raul might be one of the handful of people in the world who had to arrive at events after everyone else but she could have done without all the eyes landing on them all at once and watching their every step as their greeter showed them to their seats. Their chairs were in the very first row. An older gentleman nodded his head in Raul's direction as they sat.

Then again, being seen was the point of all this, wasn't it? That was the only reason Sofia was even here to begin with. An organ began to play from behind them, a beautiful, soulful melody that Sofia had never heard before. Six men in dark tuxedos walked in from the back archway, each of them strikingly handsome. They made their way to the front of the room and stood by the podium, turning to face the guests.

The music continued as a beat later six women walked down the center aisle, holding colorful bouquets of flowers in front. Sofia recognized one of them as a talk show host who graced her TV every weekday morning with lifestyle features. She was sure the bridesmaid behind her was a fashion model she'd seen often in various magazine spreads, selling everything from high-end perfume to fashion lingerie. The woman's eyes landed on Raul and lingered just a moment longer than necessary. He tilted his head every so slightly as she passed them by.

Sofia wasn't going to let herself dwell on what any of that might mean.

She sucked in a breath as she recognized the last woman in the procession, a British duchess whose own wedding had just been covered in every major news source.

How in the world was she going to be able to converse with such people when the time came?

She really should have better prepared for this.

As if sensing her tension and panic, Raul reached for her hand next to his thigh and gave it a tight squeeze. Surprisingly, it actually helped. The warmth of his palm sent a calming wave over her skin. Her breath evened to a smoother tempo.

The music faded and then the chords of the familiar "Wedding March" began to play. A tall, elegant man with a boutonniere and a cummerbund that matched the lilac hue of the bridesmaids' dresses entered from the side and made his way to stand in front of the podium, nodding to the bridal party when he got there. The groom.

Sofia wasn't sure what she'd been expecting but if she had to pick what Raul's best friend might have looked like, she wouldn't have been too far off the mark. The two men didn't have much in common physically. Rafe was blond with softer facial features to Raul's tanned skin and dark charcoal hair. But both of them had an aura of authority and confidence that she could sense a mile away. It wasn't hard to see why they'd butted heads in school, then become close friends later. They matched each other's energy.

There was no mistaking when the bride appeared behind them. Her presence was felt before Sofia turned to the doorway. There stood one of her generation's top talents on the elbow of an older gentleman who had eyes the same shade as her famous sky-blue ones. A murmur of oohs and aahs sounded from the seated crowd as the two began to walk down the aisle, and her smile spread from ear to ear as she approached her intended. This was a woman in love. One look at Rafe's grinning face left no doubt that he was floating on a cloud of happiness at the sight of his bride.

A sharp pang jabbed in the vicinity of Sofia's chest. Hard to deny it was anything but envy. She may never have for herself the devotion she was witnessing between these two strangers. No, instead Sofia had to *pretend* she had someone in her life who felt any kind of romantic way about her. For the first time ever, she lamented the lack of a social life. Perhaps she'd given up too soon after all when a date didn't go well. Maybe she should have fought harder for the guy who'd decided to reunite with his ex four months into their courtship.

Instead, she'd been so focused on setting herself up professionally and trying to make sure she was a good daughter to the only parent she had. Look where it had left her ultimately. With no one to come home to at the end of the day and no prospects in sight. Unless one counted the many opportunistic candidates her stepfather kept throwing at her. She felt another supportive squeeze on the hand Raul still held in his. The man was growing much too tuned in to her inner emotions.

Francesca reached her groom's side and they both turned to face the officiator as the music faded to an end. The vows that followed were heartfelt and touching. Sofia might hear the echoes of those words for the rest of her life. In fact, this whole event would be ingrained in her memory for the rest of time. She was in a verifiable castle watching the wedding of the decade on the arm of a prince.

A true fairytale of a day. And just as real.

By the time the officiant spoke the words "You may kiss the bride," the crowd was already on their feet and clapping. Sofia clocked more than one guest dabbing at their eyes with a tissue. Darned if her own weren't stinging ever so slightly.

The now-married couple practically skipped down the aisle afterward, the bridal party trailing after them. The same woman shot another look their way. Sofia cast a side glance in Raul's direction for his reaction. If he noticed the look he'd been cast, he didn't acknowledge it in any way this time. In fact, his gaze was centered solely on *her*.

Sofia didn't imagine the pursing of the bridesmaids' lips as she walked by them.

"Let's get something to eat," Raul said into her ear. "I'm starving. And I'll introduce you to the couple as well as some other guests who should see us together."

Of course. While Sofia was standing here teary-eyed and touched beyond reason at the romantic moment they'd just witnessed, Raul was solely focused on performing for their ruse.

"The dinner is in the library followed by the reception outside," he added.

The other guests seemed to be waiting for the two of them to exit first. Even among this group of VIPs, Raul was given deference. Made sense, the man was a prince after all. He took her by the hand and led her out of the room, nodding to several others in greeting. They walked into a large room with dozens of tables. Glassed cabinets housing hundreds of books served as walls. The bridal party hadn't quite made it to the head table yet, lingering and talking among themselves. The other guests were slowly ambling in behind them. Raul seemed to know where he was going, and Sofia trailed behind him as he walked closer and closer to the head table.

The groom's already-wide grin grew when he spotted them. He took his new wife by the elbow and led her to where Sofia and Raul stood.

"So it takes nothing less than a wedding to get you to visit," Rafe said when he reached their side. The two men shook hands, then hugged about the shoulders.

Francesca gave her husband a playful punch on the shoulder. "Is that the only reason you married me? To get your friend here to come?"

His answer was a playful kiss on her nose.

Francesca didn't wait for an introduction, turning to her. "So glad to have you here. I'm Francesca."

As if Sofia didn't know exactly who she was. As if most of the world's population didn't know her.

"This is Rafe, my new husband," she added with a brilliant smile.

"I'm Sofia," she answered. "That was a beautiful ceremony."

"She saved her best performance for me," Rafe said on a chuckle, earning him another mock hit.

They were both so utterly charming, their inner light shining so brightly, Sofia felt as if she might be standing in the rays of a brilliant star.

Francesca turned her attention to the prince. "Raul, save a dance for me after dinner. I want to hear all about how you and Sofia got together."

Raul threw his arm over Sofia's shoulder and pulled her against his side. "It would be my delight, Frannie." The smile he flashed her was several watts strong.

Speaking of charm…he also had charm to spare. The three of them were all accomplished, worldly professionals who were obviously close. As if her feelings of being out of place weren't abundant already. Among them, Sofia felt like a third wheel. Just like she did whenever she was with Phil and her mother.

CHAPTER EIGHT

"LOOKS LIKE WE have prime seating," Sofia said as he led her to their assigned table. It was in the first row in front of where the bridal party sat. "Which makes sense," she continued. "Considering you were supposed to be the best man."

Raul had trouble concentrating on what she was saying. Her dress was the height of distraction. And temptation. The back cut low as it was, he ended up touching her bare skin whenever he reached for her. The way her skin felt under his palm was doing things to his libido he didn't want to acknowledge.

By the time they sat down and dinner was served, he'd had to curl his fingers into his palm.

"This is delicious," Sofia said, around a mouthful of food. "This has to be the most tender salmon I've ever tasted. And the glaze, I think it's pomegranate or something fruity, yet tangy."

She practically moaned in pleasure at the next bite and the images that flooded his mind had him squeezing his fists tighter to keep from reaching for her again.

She glanced at his plate. "You've barely touched your dinner. Is everything all right?"

Who could eat when he was trying to temper a different kind of appetite? A wholly inappropriate one.

He could hardly tell her the real reason he hadn't taken more than a few bites. "I'm just not thrilled about having to lie to my best friend. At his own wedding."

She set her fork down, and turned her gaze to his. "You mean about us."

He nodded. "That's right. I've never lied to him before."

"I would think you'd be able to trust him with the truth, if it's bothering you that much."

She was right of course. Rafe would keep his confidence if he asked him to.

"I'll tell him eventually. Right now is hardly the right time."

"Of course."

Several people approached their table once the plates were cleared. The curiosity around his mystery date and exactly who Sofia was to him had clearly been causing a lot of chatter throughout the dining room. The interruptions were getting tiresome at this point. Each new introduction irked him all the more. Which made no sense. It was all part of the plan after all.

A woman he recognized as Frannie's assistant approached them and handed Sofia a velvet bag. "Please let me know if the size is accurate."

"What's this?" Sofia asked, taking it from the other woman.

"We give all the women flat, comfortable shoes, miss."

Sofia blinked a question. Raul could tell she wanted badly to ask why she was being gifted footwear but didn't want to appear uninformed.

"Perfect," he said to the assistant. "We plan to do quite a bit of dancing."

The woman tossed a smile his way before making her way to the next table, handing out more shoes.

Sofia pulled out the contents of the bag and gasped in surprise. "These are Italian leather." She trailed a finger over the heel. "Soft as butter."

"I would expect nothing less from Francesca."

"She must really want a full-swing party, with lots of dancing."

He would take that as his cue. Standing from his chair, he held a hand out to her. "Well, we probably shouldn't disappoint her then. Put them on."

She kicked off her high heels and did as he'd asked. "They fit perfectly."

He'd somehow suspected they would. Frannie and her team didn't often make mistakes.

"In that case, please allow me the honor of the first dance."

When they made it outside to the reception party, the night had grown darker, with the sun setting on the horizon. The garden was lit in a cozy blue hue, the Toronto horizon framing the scene. Many of the guests were already there on the dance floor. A mini orchestra played bouncy versions of familiar pop tunes.

Raul took the liberty of removing his tuxedo jacket and tossing it on a nearby chair. He removed his cuff links and rolled up his sleeves.

"Wow. I had no idea you took dancing so seriously."

"Come on. I'll show you just how serious I can be on the dance floor."

She chuckled in response and took his hand. He didn't particularly enjoy dancing. But it surprised him how much he was looking forward to doing so with Sofia.

He gave her a twirl on the way to the dance floor, earning him another laugh. Hearing her laughter never failed to delight him like a toddler receiving a new toy. Melodic and genuine, he imagined the sound of an amused angel might sound similar.

Since when was he so poetic and fanciful about a woman's laugh? He had to get a grip already.

"Nice footwork," she told him during the first song.

"Several years of regimented dance classes being put to good use."

"Consider me impressed."

"You haven't seen anything yet," he told her, giving her another little twirl.

Essentially flirting with her despite how utterly reckless that was given their circumstances.

How much more of a Cinderella storyline could she be living? Right down to the gifted-shoes plot. Shoes that probably cost more than she might make in a month.

As for her Prince Charming, did the man have to be so good at everything? He was moving around the dance floor like a pro on that competition show she used to watch every season with her mom.

Turned out, now that the party portion of the evening had begun, she was actually enjoying herself. She'd have to be a coma patient not to have fun at such a bash.

And she couldn't ask for a better dance partner. Though he was a rather distracting one. The picture the man made whenever he took his jacket off and rolled up his shirt sleeves would be ingrained in her memory for the rest of time. Sofia couldn't even tell if her breathlessness was caused by all the dancing or the way Raul looked whenever he unbuttoned.

So that settled it. She was going to let go of the last remaining shreds of self-consciousness she'd felt since walking into the castle, stop worrying about how ill at ease and out of place she might feel. She was going to concentrate on enjoying herself. When else would she ever get a chance to dance at a famous actress's wedding reception again in this lifetime?

And the chances of dancing at her own wedding weren't looking very good at the moment. So she would keep dancing until her legs gave out. Or Raul grew tired, whichever came first.

Not that he was showing any hint of slowing down.

As if she'd tempted fate with that last thought, the music suddenly changed. The orchestra didn't stop but rather faded into a different melody. A much slower one.

Fully expecting to stop and walk off the dance floor, she was surprised when Raul held his arms out wide instead. Her breath hitched in her throat. The thought of slow dancing in Raul's arms had blood rushing to her head. She couldn't walk away of course—think of the speculation that might cause. In fact, she'd already hesitated too long. Without giving herself more time to chicken out, she stepped into his embrace and let him sway her in his arms. The now-familiar scent of his aftershave sent a heady wanting through her chest. Being so close against him, feeling his warmth in the cool evening breeze, it was all sending her senses into havoc. She missed a step and he had to grip her tighter to steady her. Heat rushed to her cheeks, leaving no doubt her face was turning red. But she was powerless to stop it. She could just imagine the sight of herself, blushing and breathless in Raul's arms while stumbling over her own feet.

Something else she should have better prepared for: the way she would react when he held her close. So far, she wasn't exactly carrying herself too well. Blessedly, the song finally came to an end. Only the next one wasn't all that much better. A classic love song full of yearning for a new romance.

"I think I could use a refreshment," she said, hearing the breathy sound of her voice.

He hesitated a fraction of a second before letting her go. "I wouldn't mind a drink myself. And maybe a break from dancing for a while."

Rafe gave them a look of question when they passed by him and Francesca on the dance floor. Raul mimicked raising a glass to his lips and Rafe nodded in acknowledgment, though the curious look never left his face. The way he held his new wife so intimately, his hands about her waist, had Sofia blushing harder. She couldn't help but imagine being held that way herself. By Raul.

By the time they reached the bar and secured two sweaty glass bottles of water, she wanted to bypass the drinking part altogether and just pour the contents over her head. Wouldn't that set the tongues wagging with gossip?

"Who? Did you say something?" Raul asked after taking a long swig straight from his bottle.

She hadn't even realized she'd spoken out loud. "I was just thinking how lovely the garden is," she fibbed. "It's an enchanting place for a wedding reception."

He held his hand out to her. "Here, let's take a stroll around. Frannie and Rafe have rented the entire castle. We can take a tour and look around. I know this place has hidden passages."

The thought of being alone in any kind of secret hallway with Raul had her heart nearly jumping out of her chest. The two of them alone in the dark, in the deep recesses of a medieval castle...

Stop right there.

"I'd just as soon avoid those," she told him. "Maybe

we could stick to the outdoors. The view is lovely from up here."

"Fair enough."

She took his hand and followed him away from the party. Along the way he reached for his jacket and shrugged it back on. Pity, she rather liked the sight of his strong and tanned forearms. Also, he'd dropped her hand and didn't reach for it again.

The noise of music and partying grew fainter behind them. The night had grown darker with a silver bright full moon casting shadows over the flower beds they passed. They'd walked behind the castle, mostly in silence. Which was fine with Sofia. For the life of her, she couldn't think of a single thing to say.

Her thoughts were a jumbled mess in her head. How could she have been so affected by simply slow dancing with a man? Had Raul felt even remotely the same level of intensity as she had?

She risked a sideways glance at him to see if his face might give her any answers.

No such luck. His profile gave nothing away. If she were a braver, more reckless woman, she might dare to ask. But she wasn't. And there would be no good way to react no matter his answer.

They'd reached a courtyard with a majestic fountain centered between more lush greenery and colorful flowers. Surrounded by immaculately trimmed bushes around the outside, several small fountains spouted water up in the air with a much larger fountain spouting higher in the center. The sound of the water drowned out what remaining noise could be heard from the party on the other side of the castle.

Not for the first time tonight, Sofia felt she might have

stepped into some kind of storybook. The beautiful garden, the rushing water. It was a scene out of some romantic movie. And the man beside her perfect in the role of love interest. She studied him now, his hands in his pant pockets, the moon highlighting the dark strands of his hair. More handsome than any man had a right to be. A shiver ran down her spine.

He turned to her. "Cold?" he asked, mistaking her reaction. He shrugged out of his jacket and draped it over her shoulders. The fabric smelled of him and his scent enveloped her. She had to stop herself from leaning into the collar and inhaling deeply.

She couldn't very well admit the real reason for her shaking.

"Do you regret turning down Rafe's request to be a groomsman tonight?" she asked, just to start some sort of conversation.

He shrugged. "If I was anyone else, I would have gladly done it. It wouldn't have been fair to take the spotlight off the wedding couple."

She'd had no idea she was going to ask the question until the words left her mouth. "Which bridesmaid do you think you'd have been paired with?" She had a feeling she could guess who the lucky lady might have been. The woman who'd sent him the smoldering look as she'd made her way down the aisle during the wedding.

He sighed and raked his fingers through his hair. "It so happens that I do happen to have a bit of a history with one of them."

Hah! She knew it!

"The model. Right?"

His eyes narrowed on her. "How did you know that? We thought we kept it rather discreet."

"Is there…anything between you now then? Still, I mean?" Why in the world was she even going down this path? It really was none of her business.

Raul stepped closer to her. "Why are you asking me that, Sofia?"

Something snapped within and she didn't have the heart to lie in answer. She'd opened herself up with her question and didn't see a way to back out now. Nor did she even think she wanted to.

"Can you not guess why?"

His eyes darkened and a muscle twitched along his jaw. "I don't want to misunderstand in any way. Help me understand."

Sofia swallowed. Was he really going to make her come out and say it? She wasn't sure how she might even find the words.

She took a breath and began to try. "I saw the way she was looking at you. Possessive. Familiar."

"And?" he prompted.

"And it made me feel a certain way."

"What kind of way?"

"Jealous," she blurted out before she could stop herself. There. She'd said it. The world seemed to stop for a moment. As if they were suspended in time. The one word hung in the air between them with no way to take it back. "I was jealous that she might have a history with you. I can't really explain why. Just that—"

He didn't let her finish the sentence. Before she could so much as register what was happening, he'd reached her and then his lips were on hers, kissing her. Heat exploded inside her belly and moved lower.

She lost track of time when he finally pulled away. Her limbs trembled with desire and disappointment. Why had he stopped and how could she get him to start once again? Right this second.

"Don't look now, but we happen to have an audience," he whispered against her mouth. "I don't know why, but Frannie's publicist just walked into the courtyard."

Sofia's blood froze in her veins. Was that why he had kissed her? To display their fake relationship to a publicist? It was just a little too perfect, too convenient.

Here she was admitting her attraction, lowering the guard on her heart. Only to wonder if it had played right into some kind of performance. The very possibility squeezed her heart in her chest. How naive of her. How careless. She'd blame the magic of this courtyard for messing with her head. The romantic atmosphere framed by the fountain and the beauty of the flowers surrounding it. All of it had made her forget why she was really here. With a crown prince she barely knew.

She stepped back away from him and shrugged off his jacket, then handed it back to him, making sure to keep her distance.

"Thanks. I'm not cold anymore." Which was a complete lie. In fact, her skin felt completely frosted, as did the area around her heart.

"We should get back," she said, doing her best to steady her voice though it wasn't easy. "You promised Francesca a dance."

Raul watched her walk away, his tuxedo jacket still draped in his hand. He would follow her back to the party of course. He just needed a minute. Maybe several minutes. The kiss had been on an impulse, one he'd been helpless to curtail. Now, he felt as if the world had somehow shifted. His insides felt like mush, his vision was blurry.

After a simple kiss. Such dangerous and treacherous territory.

In a clumsy effort to take it all back, he'd focused on the random excuse that Frannie's publicist was the real motivation behind his actions. To try to convince Sofia the kiss wasn't real. Seeing the woman approach, he'd taken it as a sign. Maybe he'd been callous. He would have to find a way to make that up to her.

But it was better than leading Sofia down any kind of false road.

CHAPTER NINE

Three days later

HE SHOULD NEVER have kissed her. The situation between them was complicated enough without blurring lines unnecessarily. And that earth-shattering kiss had definitely blurred more than a few.

Raul reread the email he'd been trying to focus on for the past ten minutes. His concentration was shot. Sofia had kept her distance since the wedding. Or, to be more accurate, since their kiss.

So she was clearly harboring some regret as well.

He wanted to kick himself. How could he have lost control that way? He had no excuse, really. No matter that Sofia had been a tempting vision in that dress that showed off all her curves. Or the way she'd felt in his arms dancing slowly, the scent of her rose perfume numbing his faculties. Or the way she'd admitted feeling jealous. About him.

He'd simply let it all snap the tight string on his control. The better approach would have been to downplay her admission. Give her a chance to back out of saying such a thing. Instead, he'd let her words go to his head and he'd given in to the relentless desires he'd been fighting for so long. So very wrong of him to toy with her emotions that way. Or his own for that matter. No good could come of any confusion, on either of their parts.

It couldn't happen again; he had to keep his distance. They still had this trip in Montreal to get through while pretending to be engaged.

He reached into the drawer of his desk and pulled out the velvet box. The original plan had been to give it to her on the jet on the way over here from Toronto but Sofia seemed much too tired and distracted. Just as well. This way, when he gave it to her, he could emphasize how much of a prop the ring was. He would tell her that they had to make sure she had it on her finger before their dinner with the mayor tomorrow night. To reiterate that the plan to convince the world they were a couple would be well on its way to completion by then.

His phone rang in his pocket, pulling him out of his reverie. His father.

"Your Highness." Raul said, clicking on the phone.

In his usual customary way, the king didn't bother with pleasantries before getting to the point. "I'm calling to say well done, son."

Raul knew immediately what he was referring to. He and Sofia were featured on a slew of gossip sites. Several photos of the two of them at the wedding were posted on all the apps that mattered. Even the one from the rooftop in DC had resurfaced.

It may have been random, but Frannie's publicists stumbling upon them during such an unguarded moment had sent the gossip mills turning at breakneck speed.

"Thank you, sir. I'm glad it's working."

"Most definitely is," the king replied with enthusiasm. "This is the first morning I haven't heard a thing about

Luisa. Every outlet that reports on us is solely focused on you and that lovely young lady you recruited."

Raul cringed inwardly at the last word. Accurate as it was, the term had an uneasy twist curling in his stomach.

"You make sure to keep it up."

"Will do, sir. In fact, the next announcement you'll see is the news that we're engaged to be married."

"Excellent. I'm glad the young lady has been so agreeable and has played her part so very well." Raul could picture the smile of satisfaction on his father's face.

"Her name is Sofia, Your Highness."

"Yes. Sofia. Please give her my thanks."

"I'll be sure to do that. Any word from Luisa?"

His father grunted in disgust. "Not a one. She isn't answering calls from anyone. Not even me. Just depleting her accounts from various parts of the world as she carries on this ridiculous affair with the man she's fallen for."

For the life of him, Raul couldn't figure out what had gotten into his sister. She'd always been a free spirit, but ignoring the king's calls was akin to self-sabotage.

"Let me know if you hear from her yourself," the king said. "Who knows, maybe all this attention you and the young lady are receiving will bring Luisa up to the surface."

"Sofia," Raul reminded him but the king had already hung up.

Owner of said name was sprawled on the couch scrolling through a tablet screen when Raul left his study after the phone call.

"Are you reading all the salacious gossip that's being written about us?" he asked.

Sofia glanced up in surprise, as if she hadn't heard him approach. "Oh, heavens no. I looked at a few photos and their captions but they were making me much too anxious."

Huh. Most of the women he knew would be grateful for such attention. Maybe Sofia hadn't been the best choice for this endeavor. She'd been uncomfortable with the scrutiny on her from the very beginning.

Not that there was much he could do about the decision now.

"All the chatter has gotten the shop some added business. There's that. Agnes said a couple of outlets called her for information about me but there really isn't much to tell." She sighed.

He leaned to look at the screen over her shoulder. "What's got you so engrossed then?"

She shifted to give him a better view of the tablet. "I'm looking at all the great attractions Montreal has to offer. What a metropolitan city."

He read her latest page. "Montreal Botanical Garden."

She nodded with clear enthusiasm. "The pictures are lovely. The DC botanical museum is one of my favorite places on earth. But it's mostly indoors." She pointed to the screen. "This place looks much larger, sprawling over acres and acres."

"Would you like to go?"

The tablet dropped to her lap. He had her full attention now. "Really?"

He shrugged. "If you want to see it, then we should plan on a visit."

Her mouth fell open before her lips curved into a wide smile. "We? You mean you'd be willing to come along?"

"Of course."

In fact, he couldn't think of a better way to spend the afternoon. They could both use a bit of a reprieve after the excitement of the wedding, then all that had followed after. Fresh air and a long walk among beautiful gardens might be just the thing to restore some of the friendly camaraderie between them that had been sorely lacking since that night at the rooftop in DC. And the kiss hadn't exactly helped.

"I have a meeting downtown followed by a few phone calls back here, but we can leave right after I'm done."

"I can hardly wait," she told him, her smile confirming her words.

The wedding seemed forever ago. Almost as if Sofia had attended it in another lifetime. Her mind registered the event as a distant memory. Except for one part.

The kiss.

That particular moment was seared in her mind as clear as the sky outside their floor-to-ceiling glass window at the luxury hotel they'd be staying in while here in Montreal. Sofia couldn't seem to stop thinking about it. The way Raul's lips had felt on hers. The taste of him. The warmth of his body as he held her tight with that magnificent fountain behind them.

Enough. Raul had only been after a publicity shot. She had to get it through her head that the kiss had meant nothing.

Not to him anyway. How foolish of her to think otherwise for even a moment.

For the umpteenth time this morning, she tried to push the images out of her head as she made her way to her private bathroom. This time last week, she wouldn't have even known that hotel lodgings could be this large and luxurious. Then again, she'd never had occasion to stay in one with an actual prince before. They were in the royal suite of the most exclusive hotel on the Golden Square Mile. Fully stocked kitchen, glass ceiling in the sitting room and not one but two massive terraces overlooking one of the most dynamic parts of the city.

She might miss the shower the most when they had to leave Montreal. Raul sure knew where to stay when he traveled.

Not that she'd seen much of him since they'd arrived. He was either out and about on what he called palace business or at the other end of the suite when he was here.

No doubt to try to avoid her. She could hardly blame him. Things had been strained between them since the night of the wedding. Their conversations had been brief and awkward. Maybe spending time in a beautiful botanical garden would clear the air between them once and for all. And then they could pretend that kiss had never happened. As if.

She should never have done it. Should have never revealed her heart that way and admitted to feeling jealous about a bridesmaid glancing his way. She cringed at the thought now, like she'd been cringing since that night.

Turning on the waterfall shower head, she flipped the switch for the chromotherapy light. The stall was immediately bathed in a soft purple hue. Sofia had never heard of chromotherapy and wasn't sure about the science behind the idea. But there was no denying the sensation of calm that washed over her along with the warm water once she stepped under the spray.

If only the feeling lasted longer than the time it took her to towel off. The problem was, any sense of calm and peace seemed to evaporate as soon as she found herself in Raul's presence. Maybe longer showers were the answer. Maybe she should stay under the water all day, until her skin pruned and her legs grew tired. Then she could just go to bed. That way she could avoid Raul altogether.

Slight problem with that approach, as tempting as it was. They were due to have dinner with the mayor tomorrow night. She probably shouldn't appear wrinkled and waterlogged for it. Oh, and she'd also asked to spend the day with Raul at the Montreal Botanical Garden. Careful what you wish for.

As much as she was looking forward to seeing the famous attraction—considered one of the finest plant and flower museums in the world—she wasn't sure how she might deal with the proverbial elephant in the room.

They couldn't avoid acknowledging what had happened between them much longer.

Could they?

Sofia sighed and turned the knob on the marble-tiled wall, getting the water as hot as she could stand. Finally, when her muscles began to feel like molten lava, she shut the spray and toweled off.

A few minutes later, she was dressed and her hair dried. Raul was waiting for her when she left her suite of rooms. She startled when she saw him, as was usually the case these days.

"Sorry," he apologized. "Didn't mean to surprise you."

"I just didn't realize you were back."

He simply nodded, his gaze bouncing around her face. "I just have to take a conference call in a few minutes. After that we can head to the gardens."

"I'm ready whenever you are."

He nodded in a jerky motion. If she didn't know him any better, she might even say he was acting nervous.

"Just one thing first," he said, reaching into his pocket

and pulling out a small item. Sofia's breath caught when she realized what it was.

"A ring," she said, surprised her mouth was working enough to get even those two simple words out.

"I figure it's time we signified to the world that the relationship is indeed serious."

Sofia had to clamp her lips from laughing hysterically at the statement. Either that or she was going to cry. Their fictitious relationship had to seem serious. So Raul was going to have her wear a ring.

He reached it out to her in the palm of his hand. Pathetic really. The first time in her life she'd be wearing an engagement ring and the man wouldn't even be slipping it on her finger. Because it meant nothing.

"Did you want to…?"

She sucked in a deep breath and lifted it out of his palm. Now that she was really looking at it, it struck her just how beautiful a specimen it was. A large square-cut diamond on a platinum band with smaller rubies on either side. It was stunning. Exactly the kind of ring she may have picked for herself.

"Where did you get this?"

He ducked his head, almost imperceptibly. "I had it ordered back when we were in Toronto. I thought it might suit you."

Sofia couldn't read too much into that statement or his intentions. The fact that he'd actually thought about what kind of ring she might like and had it ordered meant nothing. Simply another part of the act. He wasn't even going to put it on her himself, for heaven's sake.

"It's breathtaking."

His gaze was steady on her now, looking at her expectedly. What else was she supposed to say? Was one supposed to thank a guy for getting a real custom-made, clearly expensive piece of jewelry when the sentiment behind it was completely fake?

"It should fit," he said. "I asked the stylist about the jewelry you had on that night."

So that's what he was waiting for. To make sure he got her finger size right. Sofia grasped the most precious jewelry she'd ever laid her hands on and slipped it on the ring finger of her left hand.

Fighting a silly urge to cry as she did so.

She had to get some air.

Sofia watched as Raul shut the door of the room he'd been using as his office since they'd arrived to take his phone call. The ring felt heavy on her hand. A heaviness also hung around the vicinity of her chest. Making her way to the terrace that faced the Montreal skyline, she resisted the urge to glance at her ring finger yet again. It was all too easy to stare at the sparkling diamond and red rubies around it.

A cacophony of sounds echoed through the air once she stepped outside. The Golden Square Mile was rich with shops and cafés and all the trappings of a hopping metropolitan city. Another place she'd like to revisit someday under more normal circumstances. She huffed a chuckle at that. She didn't even know what was normal anymore. Kicking off her shoes, she dropped into the nearest lounge chair and stared at the tall buildings that surrounded the hotel.

She didn't know how long she sat there, simply staring at the sky and trying to process exactly what was happening. Finally, when her mind was a jumble of confusing thoughts, she pulled her phone out and clicked on Agnes's contact.

Her friend answered on the first ring. "I've been waiting with bated breath for you to call."

"I know. I've been meaning to. It's just that so much has been happening. And we're barely halfway through with…" She couldn't even come up with an adequate word. "You know."

"Tell me everything," Agnes demanded, a clear tinge of excitement in her voice. "Where are you right at this moment?"

"In the most deluxe suite of the most deluxe hotel I'll probably ever find myself in. I'm currently laying in a lounge chair on a terrace, one of two available to me at that, staring at the tallest of Montreal's buildings with a wall behind me that's covered in shrubbery and flowers."

Agnes let out a whistle as her response.

Sofia continued, "Before that, I took a shower in a marbled bathroom bathed in purple chromotherapy light."

"That sounds like heaven."

"It does, doesn't it?"

Agnes paused a beat before speaking. "So why don't you sound more like someone who's been to nirvana?"

Sofia moved the phone away from her mouth and sighed loudly. "I don't know. It's just so surreal."

"What do you mean?"

"I'm not a real princess candidate. The engagement isn't real even if the ring is."

"Whoa, whoa. Back up. Ring?"

Sofia lifted her left hand and stared at the finger sporting said ring. It was getting much too easy to keep looking at it, and her finger had become much too familiar with the added weight.

"Raul got a ring for me to wear to make this all seem more authentic."

"I bet it's gorgeous. And costs a fortune. Which leads me back to my earlier question. Why do you sound less than thrilled? Are you sad you may have to give it back someday?"

That most certainly wasn't it. Raul wasn't the type to take jewelry back no matter the circumstances. She'd insist of course. There was no reason for her to keep such a costly item.

"You know me better than that."

"You're right. So tell me why."

"I just didn't ever expect that I'd be wearing a fake engagement ring. Not that it's fake. Though he certainly could have spared the expense and gotten costume jewelry. The diamond is real enough." Sofia stopped. Now she was just rambling.

"Why don't you just try and enjoy yourself, Sof? Take the opportunity for what it is. A chance to live an alternate life for a while."

Everything Agnes said made sense of course. So why couldn't Sofia simply flip a switch and enter enjoyment mode? Why did her heart feel so heavy?

The kiss.

It had just complicated everything. Darned if she knew what to do about it.

"That makes sense. There's just a part of me that wishes things were different." That somehow this was all real.

Agnes stayed quiet for so long that Sofia glanced at the screen to make sure they hadn't lost the connection. "Oh. My. God," she finally said several moments later. "You're falling for him, aren't you?"

Oh, no. Was it that obvious in her voice?

"I mean, I can hardly blame you," Agnes added. Her friend's tone grew softer when she spoke again and sounded much more serious. "But I don't want you walking away from all this with a broken heart, Sof."

Sofia didn't say out loud the words that popped into her head. It might already be too late for that. "Don't worry about me, Agnes." She summoned the most reassuring voice she could, then added, "It's probably just a crush. The man is a handsome, successful prince. And we're pretending to be in love. I've simply gotten carried away on occasion. I'll make sure not to let it happen again."

"If you're sure."

"I am. Don't worry," she repeated, hating that she'd managed to make her friend concerned about her. That's when she noticed Raul standing by the door. A brick landed in her stomach. How thick was that glass? The thought that he might have heard any of that mortified her.

"Agnes, I have to go. Will call you later, promise." She clicked off the call without waiting for a response.

There was no telling by the expression on his face how much he may have heard, if anything. Closed book, as always. He tapped twice on the glass door before sliding it open. "Ready to go?"

She forced a smile, hoping she looked as enthusiastic as she'd been feeling this morning when looking at pictures of the gardens online. Had that really just been less than three hours ago?

"As ready as I'll ever be."

CHAPTER TEN

HE'D HANDLED THE whole ring-giving terribly.

Raul replayed the earlier scene in his head and wanted to kick himself. He'd simply wanted to give it to her without any kind of presentation. That's why he had taken the ring out of its original package. Handing Sofia an engagement ring housed in a velvet box would have made the gesture all too real. But in his attempt to make it all seem like a casual necessity that was really no big deal, he'd practically thrown the thing at her and waited until she'd put it on. As if things between them hadn't been awkward already.

All because of that damned kiss.

In hindsight, he probably should have told Sofia about his intentions when he ordered the ring to begin with. Part of him had been uncertain though about whether he would go through with it. Also, it chagrined him to acknowledge that another part of him might have actually wanted to surprise her with it. To pretend for even a moment that he was really about to propose to her, that she was really about to become his future wife. But that idea was preposterous and wholly inappropriate.

Instead, he'd just bungled the whole encounter.

He'd almost backed out of this trip to the botanical garden afterward. For a while right after he'd hung up with Vesovia's chief economist, he'd had every intention of sending Sofia off with his bodyguards to visit the gardens without him. Instead, he'd decided to face his folly and try to smooth things over. Again.

He so missed the easy camaraderie they'd had together when they'd first embarked on this trip.

To her credit, Sofia seemed to have moved on from the whole ordeal. Sitting next to him in the passenger seat of the hired sedan that was taking them out of the Golden Square Mile and toward the outskirts of the city, she enthusiastically watched the scenery outside her window and asked numerous questions about what she saw.

He'd never had such a fun travel companion, despite how unusual the circumstances were. In fact, now that they were on their way to the attraction, Raul couldn't deny feeling a rush of excitement about the outing. When was the last time he'd looked forward to a day spent essentially staring at flowers and shrubs? He couldn't recall.

Maybe that was Sofia's enthusiasm reaching him through proximity.

When they approached the front entrance and he helped her out of the car, that enthusiasm showed through in spades. Her mouth fell open as they strolled down the brick pathway to the fountain in front of the redbrick sprawling central building.

Her eyes widened when they reached the entryway and she stared at the gardens that lined the path.

"I had no idea tulips came in so many colors," she said, her voice dripping with wonder. "There must be thousands of them."

"That's just the start," he told her, draping his arm over her shoulders. A gesture he hadn't even known he'd intended. He'd never been one for outward displays of any kind of affection. Much like his father. And absolutely nothing like his very gregarious sister.

He could just picture his bodyguards smirking in surprise several feet behind them.

As casually as he could, he dropped his arm back down to his side.

"Which garden would you like to go to first?" he asked her. "There are seven of them."

She clasped her hands together in front of her chest. "I'm way too hyped to decide anything. You pick."

"You might regret that when I tell you my first choice."

She actually did a little circle twirl, her arms outstretched. "How would I possibly regret seeing anything here? Go ahead and pick."

"All right. But no take-backs."

She shook her head in mock solemness and held up a hand. "I hereby swear."

"It's settled then. Let's go."

They passed by the first garden, the Roseraie, with its majestic statue of the cast-iron lion guarding its entrance. Sofia's steps slowed and she cast her eyes about with clear hesitation. "Already regretting your offer? That didn't take long."

"Absolutely not," she answered a little too quickly, hardly sounding convinced. She looked so darned cute when she was fibbing. In fact, she looked more than cute. In a bright blue dress the color of the sky above, with another pair of strapped sandals adorning her feet, she made him yearn to do more than just throw an arm around her shoulder again. Much more. Right here in public.

"Just promise me we'll come back to see all this after wherever it is we're headed."

"Of course we will. We have all day."

Her smile widened. "We do? But you're usually so busy."

"I made sure to clear my schedule."

The area around her eyes softened, and it sent a surge of pleasure through his core. The urge to take her in his arms and kiss her senseless was nearly overwhelming.

"Thank you for doing that," she said softly.

The truth was, he should have been the one thanking her. He was actually taking a day off and enjoying himself, allowing himself to forget all the responsibility that always awaited him. At least for a little while. Instead of telling her any of that, he waved her forward to follow him.

"Come on. If we're lucky we might actually be able to see a butterfly emerging from its chrysalis.

"The insectarium, huh?" That was the first spot in the botanical garden Raul led her to. The large dome structure had displays of various insect species including several breeds of butterflies.

"Isn't it great?" Raul asked. His tone and demeanor at the moment reminded her of a little boy who'd been gifted a highly desired toy. This was a side of him she hadn't seen before. Dressed casually in khaki shorts and a silky soft short-sleeved V-neck that showed off those muscular, distracting arms. To top it off, he sported dark aviator glasses and a deep maroon baseball cap that covered his dark hair.

They'd never actually been out in public before. So this must be what he wore to disguise himself as best he could. So far, it seemed to be working. No one yet had bothered to give them a second glance.

His attire and overall look was no doubt meant to be casual, ordinary. But someone like Raul would never pull off looking anything resembling standard. Casting a quick glance at him now, she had to look away to keep from staring. Even dressed like a tourist, he was stunningly handsome.

She hadn't witnessed him having quite such fun before either. Not even at Francesca Tate's wedding. To think, all it took was thirteen displays of insects and several hundred butterflies flittering about the air from tree to tree in a domed enclosure.

After they'd taken their time going from display to display and then waiting in vain for a chrysalis emergence that unfortunately never occurred, Raul finally indicated he was ready to see the rest of the gardens.

"Okay, your turn," he said once they'd left the dome. "Where would you like to head next?"

Sofia didn't have to think twice. The picture of the beautiful rosebushes had been embedded in her mind since they'd passed them by an hour ago.

As if he could read her mind, Raul said, "Let me guess. Should we head back to the cast-iron lion statue where the rose beds are?"

"You read me so well," Sofia said. Huh, when had that come to pass anyway? Every meal they had together, each dish he'd suggested, had tasted divine. He'd ordered a ring that suited her taste to a tee. She glanced at her hand. It hadn't taken her long to get used to wearing it. Would probably take much longer to get accustomed to being without it when the time came.

"And where did you just drift off to?" he asked. Sofia dropped her hand and shifted her gaze. If only he could guess.

They'd reached the concrete path leading back to where they'd begun. "I was just thinking how the photos I saw online of the Jardin botanique didn't nearly do this place justice."

She could spend days and days here going from one garden display to another. The day had grown brighter when they made their way back to the lion statue.

"If I had to guess what heaven looks like, I'd say at least part of it would include rosebushes just like these."

"And a dome filled with butterflies." he added with a mischievous smile.

"If you say so." Sofia walked over to the nearest rosebush. The flowers were a gorgeous color somewhere between orange and yellow. "I've never seen roses this shade." She leaned to inhale their sweet scent.

They moved onto a bed of pinkish roses that smelled just as lovely yet somehow different.

"I didn't realize roses didn't all smell the same."

"They do to me."

She chuckled at his disaffected tone. "You haven't even tried to smell them. Here, give them a whiff." She gently nudged him forward toward the rosebush.

He did as she asked and when he straightened again, he tilted his head toward her. "These actually remind me of the flowers native to Vesovia that bloom every spring. And also the scent you wear."

Sofia blinked at his words. He'd noticed her perfume and associated her scent with flowers native to his kingdom. She wasn't sure what to do with that kind of information. She decided to move them along.

"How about the Japanese garden next?"

He didn't say anything for a pause, his expression impossible to read behind those dark lenses of his glasses. Something told her it was just as well she couldn't see behind his eyes. Just the way he was standing close to her, his breath rapid, it was all making her pulse skip.

Finally, just when she thought she wasn't going to be able to resist reaching for him, tracing her fingers along his lips, he spoke. "Lead the way."

Right. As if she could get her bearings at the moment to figure out where to go. "I believe it's to the left," he said, somehow sensing her quandary.

"Yes. Let's go then."

Yet neither one of them moved. Silly really. The man had rendered her near dizzy with just a few simple words telling her she smelled like wild roses he associated with his home.

With no small amount of effort, she tore her gaze away from his lips and made her feet move. She tried to make small talk as they found their way out of the rose garden and walked farther along the path. But by the time they'd reached the pathway leading to the Japanese pavilion, she'd run out of ways to say how much she loved the various flowers they passed along their stroll.

They reached a lush green area with a small stream dotted with purple-and-white trees that resembled weeping willow but in color. The sign next to it said Zen Garden. Without asking, Sofia walked over to a bench on the edge of the grass.

"I could use a few moments of Zen if you don't mind."

He smiled, taking a seat next to her. "I don't mind at all, Sofia."

Peaceful.

Raul took a deep breath and just let himself be. Whoever had designed this display sure knew what they were doing. For a rare moment in time, he wasn't running through a list of to-dos in his head. Or thinking about his next conversation with the king about Vesovia's financial outlook. Or about his sister.

The soothing sound of the running stream, the fresh air, the gentle breeze rustling the colorful leaves of the trees all served to relax him in a way he wasn't accustomed to. But those things were only part of the reasons for his current tranquil mood. The woman next to him had a lot to do with it too. Being with her somehow helped to soothe his mind and soul.

Except when he was racked with the desire to kiss her. Like he almost had back in the rose garden. Luckily, he'd come to his senses before he could reach for her and put his lips on hers.

To think he'd been trying so hard and doing so well at keeping his distance since they'd arrived in Montreal. Only to almost lose control and give in to temptation within moments of being alone with her. And out in public no less.

He had to be careful, couldn't let his attraction to her become a distraction. But that was becoming harder and harder to do with each passing day. Sofia's mere presence had added a layer to his life since she'd entered it. A layer he hadn't even known was missing.

When they'd first arrived at the Jardin, she'd actually asked him what he wanted to do first. The simple question had touched him more than he would have guessed. Despite the myriad of decisions he had to make in any given day, he wasn't often given a choice about what he wanted. No, he was more usually acting at the whim of a meticulously planned schedule or along with the demands of the king.

Being asked about his preferences was a new experience altogether.

"So, you like bugs, huh?" she asked now, a teasing quality in her voice. "Guess I learned something about you today. A couple things actually."

He gave a small laugh. No point in mentioning that one of his earliest memories involved running around the palace grounds barefoot, with his mother laughing behind him as he chased a dragonfly. The way she indulged his fascination with the strange-looking fly that he was convinced he could catch if he tried hard enough. He pushed the memory aside.

"And I learned that you really enjoy frolicking in a garden." He refrained from telling her how adorable she looked doing so. Like a cute little sprite dancing about from one bloom to another. "What's the second thing?"

"That you're pretty good at playing regular tourist guy. When you want to."

Her words were meant in jest but the underlying truth in them couldn't be denied. He was, in fact, simply playing at being some kind of regular tourist here today. His reality was much different. A factor he seemed to be forgetting all too often.

Sofia had just given him a needed reminder.

"I have to say," she began. "As much as I love most animals, I'd just as soon stay away from the insect types." She gave an exaggerated shudder.

"Admit it. You enjoyed watching the butterflies flit about at least a little."

She shrugged. "Yes, I will acknowledge that I liked that part." She raised her hand and pinched her thumb and forefinger. "But only a little. As lovely as most butterflies are, if you look too closely at them, you can still see a little insect body." Another shudder.

"Maybe that's the problem. You shouldn't be looking too closely." There was a metaphor in there somewhere, he was sure.

"Maybe," she acknowledged.

"Though I suppose you're right. Even butterflies aren't as cute as say Sir Bunbun."

That earned him a hearty laugh. "No, I suppose not."

"You really handled it well when he misbehaved. As you did the mix terrier at the shelter. Not to mention the tabby that kept trying to extract a piece of flesh with his sharp claws."

"Thanks, I've had lots of practice wrangling uncooperative pets."

"Have you always been good with animals?" he asked, genuinely curious and somewhat chagrined that he didn't know the answer and hadn't thought to ask before this.

A smile blossomed on her face. "For as long as I can remember, I've preferred their company to most humans."

"I can certainly understand that. Guess you're in the right line of work then."

"Opening the groom shop used up all my savings. I scrounged and worked double shifts at a café for years."

A sense of guilt washed over him. They hadn't seen each other in years and Raul didn't know Sofia as anything more than his sister's friend until just a couple of weeks ago. But if he'd known about her plight, he wouldn't have hesitated to help her. He would have had to up the amount they'd agreed to when she'd accepted playing the role of his fake fiancée. Probably would have done so anyway. She'd certainly earned it.

"It was the next-best thing," she said.

"Next-best thing to what'?"

She let out a small laugh. "Silly really. But when I was younger, there was nothing I wanted to do more than study to become a vet. That way I could really help animals."

"Why didn't you?" He had no doubt she would have made a great doctor for animals.

She shrugged as her smile faded. "I began the process. Looked into schools. Applied for loans. It just wasn't meant to be." Her voice had shifted lower, deep with regret.

"What happened?"

"There was never enough money. And then my mom got sick and I helped as she got better. Any extra money went to medical bills. By then I was exhausted and damned near penniless."

Luisa had never said anything about Sofia's mom getting sick. Then again, she didn't often come up as a topic of conversation.

He was really beginning to wish that wasn't the case.

CHAPTER ELEVEN

SOFIA WAS GETTING perilously close to feeling sorry for herself. It was time to move on. Both from this conversation and from the Zen garden, which was apparently relaxing enough to loosen her tongue. She hadn't talked about her thwarted dream of becoming a veterinarian since as long as she could remember. Wasn't sure why she'd even brought it up just now. She'd just been so touched and surprised that Raul actually remembered the name of the dog she'd been tending to when he'd first entered her shop. She gave a shake of her head. There she went, overplaying things again. Sir Bunbun was an unusual name. Of course he would remember.

She clapped her hands on her knees. "I think I'm ready to move on to the bonsai display."

Raul stood without hesitation and they made their way to an enclosed courtyard about an acre away. Inside was an array of small trees sprouting the characteristic branches of bonsai. Surprisingly, there were some as tall as five or six feet. Others were barely more than a few inches, displayed on stone platforms. There had to be close to a hundred trees in this one garden, making for a breathtaking scenery of lush green.

"I had no idea they could grow so big," she said, wandering to one of the taller ones.

"I've seen some even taller. In Japan."

She was going to sound like a broken record if she mentioned wanting to go there to see for herself. It seemed her newly formed list of places she wanted to visit was growing longer and longer by the day.

"That's where this one is from," came a voice behind them. A medium height gentleman wearing thick glasses and holding a pair of specialty scissors walked to where they stood. He had on a chest tag that read Phillipe Franc with the word *curator* underneath. "This is a red pine from the Atami area. I was just about to trim it."

Sofia watched in fascination as the curator began gently pruning a branch. After several moments, he turned to them with a smile. "That should do her for a few months. If you ever get a chance, you should make a trip to one of the many castles in Kyoto. The most spectacular bonsai trees," he told them before wandering off.

"He's right. The castles themselves are sights to behold."

"Trust me," Sofia said, wandering farther down the line of trees. "I'm making a mental list of all the places I've been intrigued by since we started on this little adventure together."

A silly part of her willed him to say the words she knew he never would. That he would be happy to accompany her if she ever had the opportunity to take such trips. But he'd had numerous opportunities to do so, and never even hinted at the possibility.

What did she expect? He had responsibilities. A whole kingdom to help run. One day, he'd be running it himself entirely. Raul didn't have time to gallivant around the world. Let alone with her.

And some day, probably in the not-too-distant future,

he'd be planning a honeymoon with his real fiancée. A fiancée who would match his worldliness and regality. Unlike her.

A pang struck through her core and Agnes's voice echoed in her head.

You're falling for him, aren't you?

Heaven help her, she was. With no clue as to how to stop it. But she had to figure it out. Or her heart may never recover if she fell too far.

They left the enclosure and walked farther down the path along the Japanese garden.

Two hours later after they'd meandered through the aquatic garden with its myriad of pools, Sofia realized she was parched. And starving.

Raul's next words yet again had her wondering if he could somehow read her mind. Or maybe he was growing more and more able to tune in to her moods at any given moment the more time they spent together.

What that possibility may imply was too scary to contemplate given how she was supposed to be fighting falling for him and all.

"Think it might be time for a drink and something to eat, if you're agreeable to the idea."

Her stomach answered for her with an audible rumble. How ladylike. And so not future-princess-like in any way.

"The garden has a pretty impressive outdoor restaurant," he said after a small laugh.

"Let's go."

They crossed a bridge overlooking a koi pond. Across the water, a stone lantern sat among the shrubs. Sofia watched as a group of people walked onto the field from the other side. A bridal party. The bride and groom held hands with a trail of sharply dressed people following behind them. She could make out two sets of parents, a little girl carrying a bouquet and another young woman who looked like a sibling to one of the couple. A middle-aged man with a camera rounded out the small group.

He took several pictures of the couple alone. Then the others joined in.

The bride and groom appeared so happy. Couldn't seem to stop touching each other. One of the parents picked up the little girl and pointed to the trees. More photos were taken.

A coil of longing rolled through Sofia's stomach. Francesca and Rafe's wedding had been a doozy of a soirée. And she'd loved being a guest at such a momentous event. Yet this small group of people celebrating love in such a cozy and comfortable way tugged at her, making her yearn for the slim possibility she might have such an experience herself someday.

Then her traitorous mind made things even worse by picturing just such a scene with her in the starring role of new bride. And the man standing by her side happened to be none other than Prince Raul Abarra.

She tore her gaze away from the picture-perfect scene. "I think I could use that drink now."

It wasn't lost on Raul the look on Sofia's face as the bridal party took pictures across from them while they stood on the koi pond bridge. Nor did he fail to notice how quickly she wanted to leave the Japanese garden just then.

Now, as they walked back through the aquatic garden down the pathway, she seemed content to remain silent while admiring the several pools surrounded by colorful native lilies. The garden was less crowded than she would have anticipated and they had no trouble finding a free table.

A server showed up right away to place sweaty bottles of water in front of them and to take their order.

"I would like whatever drink is considered the most popular here," Sofia said. "And the tropical salad."

Raul asked for authentic Canadian ale and the sandwich special. Plus an order of fries with gravy for them to share.

"So tell me what your favorite garden has been so far," he asked after their waiter walked away.

Sofia rubbed her chin. "It would be impossible for me to choose just one. It would be like having to pick from chocolate, ice cream or key lime pie."

He made a mental note to make sure all those items would be stocked in the fridge wherever they stayed from now on. "You're right. Why choose if you don't have to?"

She did a finger-gun motion. "Precisely. I'd say that's a good approach to life in general."

"I can't argue with that."

Their server was back in no time with his ale and he placed a fiery red drink in front Sofia.

He took a sip of his beverage just as he realized what she'd inadvertently ordered. "Sofia, don't—" But he was too late. She took a rather large gulp before sputtering out and clasping the cloth napkin to her mouth.

"Oh, my Ga—" More sputtering followed a large swig of her water. Raul was trying his best not to laugh but it was so very difficult. Her cheeks were turning that charming shade of blush again, her eyes watering. She gulped some more water.

"What is that?" she demanded to know, giving the offending beverage an evil-eye glare.

"Sorry, I realized too late to warn you."

"Warn me how? I thought it was a strawberry daiquiri or something."

"More like a Bloody Mary. But with clam juice and a heavy dose of peppery spice. It's considered a specialty drink around these parts."

Her lips curled. "Clam juice? Pepper?"

"In tangy tomato juice. It's called the Caesar."

"That fits. Because I feel about as betrayed as he was by our waiter. And he seemed so nice."

Raul laughed so loud, one of his bodyguards a couple tables over threw him a curious look. "In his defense, you did ask for the most popular drink here."

"I'll try to be much more specific next time."

He leaned over and pulled the offending drink away from her toward the side of the tale. "We'll swap it out for something fruitier."

She shook her head. "No way. I'm not taking any more chances," she said lifting the water bottle up and mimicking a toast. "I'll stick to water. Cheers."

She was turning a light shade of green. Her eyes still watering. The napkin dabbing away at her mouth. Yet she still managed to look alluringly sexy. How did the woman possibly pull that off?

There it was, the ever-present desire to take her lips with his own. And more where that came from. He'd been with more than his share of women throughout his adult life. Many of them beautiful seductresses who knew their way around pleasing a man. Yet, he couldn't recall being quite so aroused simply sitting with a woman while they had lunch.

The waiter was back with their food. "Was there something wrong with your drink, madame? I made it myself."

Rather than admonish the man for "betraying" her as

she'd described, Sofia gave him a sweet smile and actually apologized. "Sorry, it just wasn't what I was expecting so I'll need to sip a bit slow. It's really quite good."

Huh. Imagine trying to spare the feelings of a stranger over something as innocuous as a drink.

The man smiled with pleasure and left after depositing their food.

"No *'et tu Brute'* then?"

Sofia dabbed at her salad with her fork. "As you said, it was my fault for not checking before ordering. And he said he made it himself."

Raul was beginning to understand why Luisa had found such a lifelong friend in the woman sitting with him. Though the two had nothing in common.

Actually, he was beginning to understand his sister much better these days. Being tempted by forbidden fruit was not an easy struggle. Though Luisa really should have drawn the line at involvement with a married man.

"My mom would actually like that," she said, pointing her fork at the Caesar.

Her mom. He hadn't wanted to ask earlier. Figured Sofia would tell him more if she wanted to talk about it. But curiosity got the better of him. "How is your mother now? You mentioned she was sick for a while?" he asked, hoping he wasn't opening a can of worms.

She smiled with relief. "Thank heavens she's recovered fully." She set down her fork. "Physically anyway."

What a curious statement. "Oh?"

Sofia fingered the rim of her plate and stared across the patio. "She was just different afterward. Not the same woman I grew up with. She was more reckless. More forgiving of men when they didn't treat her right."

Her eyes got a faraway look as she continued to stare

at nothing. "I don't think she would have married a man like Phil before the illness."

"People change once life throws them a curve," he said, understanding better than she might have guessed. "Look at Luisa. You met her after her transformation into a wild, unmanageable teenager. As a child, she was always the respectful, well-mannered one of us. While I was the one being chastised by most everyone employed at the palace for one transgression or another."

She turned back to him, an indulgent smile on her face. "I find that hard to believe."

"It's true. My father changed as well after the loss of my mother."

The words were out of his mouth before he even knew he'd intended to say them.

Sofia reached over the table to take Raul's hand in hers. The tone of his voice sounded heavy with painful memories.

"How did the king change?"

He shrugged. "He became distant. A shell of his former self. Refused to acknowledge Luisa's cries for attention until they became extensive. Sent us both away to boarding schools instead. Then he started putting off major decisions about the castle and kingdom to the point where the staff and national councilors started coming to me instead for guidance and instruction. I wasn't even in my midtwenties yet."

Sofia could just guess the effect all that had on the man sitting before her. He'd been barely more than a teen, dealing with the loss of a parent. On top of the pain, he'd been saddled with responsibilities he was much too young and probably unprepared for.

He pulled his hand out of hers, took off his glasses and pinched the bridge of his nose. The cap came off next. Sunlight glittered in his dark hair; the hat had barely made a dent in his thick curls.

"What about you?"

"What do you mean?"

"You must have changed yourself. You'd just lost your mom."

His lips curled into a smile but it was less than convincing. "I believe I already explained how Rafe and I came to be friends. I was disruptive and incendiary. Picked a fight with anyone who crossed my path."

"You also said that was short-lived. And caused by surface anger that you eventually tackled." And what a strong young man he must have been to have done so. He clearly had no idea how resilient he'd been in the face of such turmoil. "What happened on a deeper level, Raul?"

"I don't think I know what you mean," he said, reaching for his sandwich and taking a bite then chewing quickly. Sofia had to wonder if he even tasted the food he swallowed much too fast.

"There's something I want you to know." Raul's eyes hardened as he spoke. "Luisa never told me about your mom's illness."

He was changing the subject. Clearly he regretted the vulnerable moment just now. Sofia would go along. He wasn't ready to talk any further about the loving mother he lost. Or how the tragedy had upended the life of everyone he loved.

He continued, "She also never told me that you were struggling financially. I would have found a way to make things easier on you."

Maybe he didn't know his sister as well as he thought he did. "You hardly knew me."

"Still."

She shrugged. "Thank you. But your sister offered to help us herself."

He nodded slowly. "I should have known. You turned her down, didn't you? Prideful to a fault."

"I managed to cover what we owed for my mother's medical care."

"What about tuition so you could pursue veterinary school?"

"Luisa offered that as well. But that was much too generous. There was no way I was going to accept."

Besides, what if she'd taken the money then failed her classes? She would have been humiliated to have done so on a friend's dime. With no real source of income to pay the money back.

Raul was right about her pride in that sense.

Sofia knew she didn't want to be beholden to a friend in order to pursue a career. But not for the first time, the question that was always at the edge of her mind popped to the surface once again.

What would have happened with her life if her mother had never gotten sick?

She was still pondering the question hours later when they arrived back at the hotel. Raul had been reserved on the return drive, the conversation between them sparse.

"I have some emails to catch up on," he told her. "Maybe I'll see you later if you're still up. Help yourself to anything in the fridge or feel free to order room service."

He didn't wait for a response before turning on his heel and entering his set of rooms.

Sleep would be futile for a while tonight; her emotions

were too raw. She hadn't meant for their conversation back at the garden restaurant to turn so heavy. It seemed as if all the weighted talk had sapped both of their spirits. The hour was still relatively early though. Grabbing a magazine she knew wasn't going to hold her interest, she made her way back to the terrace and lay on her favorite lounge chair, studying the night sky.

She wasn't sure how much time had passed when she was jolted awake, surprised that she'd actually drifted off after all.

Must have been all the fresh air and walking. Plus, deep conversations with a guarded prince could sure tire a girl.

Her phone was alight with missed messages on the cushion by her thigh. She scrolled the screen to find no less than three calls from her mom and half a dozen texts. They all said variations of the same thing.

What in the world is going on?

Engaged, Sofia? please answer your phone!

I'm your mother, tell me what's happening with you!

That last one was followed by several images. Her and Raul, sitting at the garden. In one photo they were smiling at each other across the table; in another they were laughing over the wrongly ordered drink. In yet another she was holding his hand on the table. A gasp sounded from her throat. That last one had zeroed in on her finger, clearly portraying her new engagement ring.

A cold wave washed over her as she processed the images. That's why he'd taken his glasses and hat off then. The whole day was nothing but a photo op. How could she have been so clueless? Just like back in DC atop the hotel after the journalists' dinner. Or when Francesca's publicist had walked in on them at the fountain. Raul wanted nothing more from their time spent together than to have his picture taken with her.

With trembling fingers she began typing out a response

I'm sorry for the shock. Things aren't always as they seem. Will explain later I promise. Please be patient though I know it's hard.

She hit Send and tossed the phone across the chair. Sheer luck kept it from bouncing onto the ground. Silently cursing Phil, she stood and began to pace. If it wasn't for her stepfather, Sofia would have no qualms about telling her mother the whole truth. But Phil was her mother's sole priority now. She couldn't rely on her mother not to betray her trust and run to tell him everything.

The thought brought tears to her eyes. Her mother used to be the one person on this earth she would have trusted with any confidence. How drastically their relationship had been altered.

And Raul. To think that just a few hours ago, she'd thought they'd passed some kind of milestone. That he'd trusted her enough to be vulnerable in her presence. But he'd clammed up immediately after and now *this*.

Raul chose that moment to step onto the concrete patio. "Is everything all right? I saw you pacing."

She strode to him and held the phone up in answer.

CHAPTER TWELVE

FOR THE LIFE of him, Raul couldn't figure out how he kept messing up so badly when it came to Sofia.

What had started out as a carefree afternoon in heavenly surroundings had turned into yet another fiasco with pictures of them splashed all over the gossip sites. So much for camaraderie.

Now, as he sat next to her after dinner in the mayor's mansion, he wished he could get another opportunity to simply talk to her. Tell her that such moments were a matter of course in his life. He couldn't always control them. That sometimes he let his guard down—like absentmindedly taking his hat and glasses off in public during a heavy conversation—and the results were immediate. Like they had been at the botanical garden. Someone who happened to be paying attention had recognized him and snapped their photos. He wanted to tell her his actions had been careless but not intentional.

But they were about to be entertained by one of Canada's top sopranos during a private performance. Hardly the time or place to try to have any kind of useful conversation.

He stole a glance in her direction. In yet another gown that showed off all her stunning qualities. The color of her dress reminded him of the lilies they'd walked by yesterday. Creamy with a hint of subtle beige everywhere the fabric folded. Her hair was loose this evening, falling in thick, flowing waves over her shoulders. He'd asked back in DC if she wanted a stylist to travel with them. She'd said no and clearly didn't need one.

Raul scanned his gaze over the other guests. She was the subject of attention for most of the other males in attendance and she had been all night.

To the point where Raul had wanted to make up an excuse and leave with her before the appetizers were served. One particular guest, a poet here to receive an award for his latest political publication, was practically leering at her as he had for most of the night. Raul knew better but couldn't help but scowl, hoping the man would notice his displeasure. He did. Leaning back in his chair, he trained his eyes on the stage before them.

Finally, the lights dimmed in the small auditorium on the ground floor of the mansion and a petite woman in a toe-length black dress came on stage.

Sofia's gasp was audible as the woman began to sing. The Abarra family had always been patrons of the arts, and his mother had been an avid opera fan. But Raul didn't have the ear it took to appreciate what he was hearing. Clearly, Sofia did. She sat leaning forward in her chair, her jaw open, her eyes fixed on the woman singing. She most likely didn't even realize it but she'd grasped his hand on the armrest. As badly as he wanted to give it a squeeze, he didn't so much as move for fear she'd notice what she'd done and pull away.

Instead, he let her enjoy the performance, watching the artist, while he let himself enjoy watching *her*.

Finally after five songs that included a very challenging piece from *Madame Butterfly*, the singer took a bow.

The audience roared with applause, everyone on their feet to deliver a standing ovation.

Sofia seemed to be the most boisterous of all with her cheering and clapping. When the lights rose again, she turned to him with glistening eyes. That telltale blush that tempted him so was back on her cheek.

"That was amazing," she said, her voice thick and breathy. "What talent." She dabbed at her eyes, surprising him that she'd actually been brought to tears. "Thank you for such an opportunity."

He wanted to respond by hauling her to him and indulging in that kiss he couldn't stop thinking or dreaming about. The desire to taste her again was keeping him awake at night.

"I'm glad you enjoyed it, Sofia," he said, meaning it down to his very bones. A bittersweet sense of regret settled over him. This was it, the last event they were to be seen at together. After this she was to head back to DC and lay low for several days until speculation died down about their engagement. While he headed to the Laurentian Mountains for some much-needed rest and leisure before a slew of obligations that would keep him busy nonstop for the next several months. A quiet announcement would then be made by the royal assistant that the union hadn't worked out after all. The gossip outlets had already moved on from their focus on Luisa.

Mission accomplished.

So why did he feel such a crushing sense of disappointment, as if all the light was about to go out of his days?

They said their goodbyes after leaving the auditorium, thanking the mayor for her hospitality.

He turned to her when they were seated in the back of the limousine. He had to get this off his chest.

"Look Sofia, I know our day at the gardens ended on a sour note. And I want to tell you that I'm deeply sorry." If his father could only hear him. The king of Vesovia and his sole heir were never expected to apologize to anyone outside of the royal family and a few select individuals on earth. But Raul knew what was right. "I should have been more thoughtful in preparing you for the possibility we might be recognized."

She smiled at him, the blue light of the interior throwing shadows over her beautiful features.

"Apology accepted," she said simply. No pouting, no angry glare or demand for further groveling like some of his previous liaisons might have done at the smallest slight.

She continued, moving him all the more. "And I should have been better about asking you to explain. I'd just been rather rattled by my mother's texts and reacted badly."

That was it then? They'd both apologized and cleared the air.

Was it really to be that simple?

It occurred to him then, a shocking realization that had his head spinning. Totally unexpected and paradigm shattering.

He was going to miss Sofia Nomi with every cell in his body.

Sofia still felt the rush of the performance she'd just experienced, such a melodic, haunting voice coming from such a small, angelic-looking woman. But if she were being honest with herself, she'd have to come to terms with the fact that her raw emotions had a lot to do with the man she'd been sitting next to all night. She would never tire of seeing the picture Raul made in his custom-tailored tuxedos.

This would be the last night she would see said picture. Hence the real reason for her charged state. By this time next week, their charade would be over and she'd be back home. More secure financially, a development she'd be forever grateful for. But sitting here in the back of a limousine with Raul's warmth and aftershave scent surrounding the air around her, she didn't feel much like celebrating her newfound wealth.

She may never see him again.

His apology just now had been nothing less than bittersweet. An apology she'd sincerely accepted because their time together was fast coming to a close. Plus, in his defense, she hadn't handled her emotions well after receiving those texts from her mother. So she'd lashed out as a result.

Apology or not, Raul was probably looking forward to finally being rid of her and going back to his regular life. Unlike her.

The stinging in her eyes intensified and she bit down on her lip to keep real tears from forming. Her time with him was nothing more than a big pretense but how in the world would she be able to avoid comparing him to every other man she may meet?

Handsome and successful. He'd spoken fluent French with the mayor. They were there because the city was recognizing him as a major contributor to a Montreal-based charity that supported world refugees. He was everything a red-blooded woman could possibly want.

A man she could never have unless it was all a fantasy.

She couldn't avoid the sniffle no matter how hard she tried.

"Still feeling the effects of the performance then," he said, completely misunderstanding her emotional state.

"I guess so," she answered, forgiving herself for the small lie. "She was very talented."

"I know it's been a long evening and you must be tired, but I wondered if we may make a stop before heading back to the hotel."

As far as a distraction, a stop along the way wouldn't be unwelcome. "What kind of a stop?"

He smiled at her. "You'll see. Do you think you're up for it?"

She nodded in agreement. "I'm not tired at all."

"That's my princess," he said, sending a jolt of lightning through her core. She was no such thing in reality.

He pulled his cell phone out of his pocket and sent off a quick message. Within minutes, they were pulling up next to a well-lit square.

Raul left the car, then came around to the side to help her out. "Notre-Dame Basilica," he told her.

Sofia looked to the majestic fountain in front of one of the grandest structures she'd laid eyes on and uttered the only two words that came to mind, "Oh, my."

"Wait till you see the inside."

The square was empty except for the two of them, the hour rather late. "We can go inside?" she asked, unable to take her eyes off the marvel she was looking at.

"Technically it's closed to the public at this hour."

He didn't need to say the rest. Someone had obliged to open the doors for him.

He took her by the hand and walked her toward the entrance. When they made it inside, Sofia had to blink to make sure she wasn't seeing things. It was like stepping into a painting. It was a struggle trying to decide where to look. Long, intricately painted columns, with wood carved statues that decorated the high walls below a spangled ceiling that seemed to reach clear to the real night sky. All bathed in a crystal blue light that reminded her of the clear blue waters of the Caribbean Sea the one time she'd been there.

Everywhere she looked was a masterpiece of art.

She was speechless, could only stay rooted in her spot as her eyes took in all the splendor.

Finally, she found her voice. "Thank you for bringing me here. I'm glad I got to see this." The basilica was a wonderful place to end her trip.

Raul had been so thoughtful to set it up for her. The perfect parting gift.

It was past midnight by the time they arrived back at the hotel. Raul held the elevator door open for Sofia and waited as she stepped inside. He wasn't ready for the night to end just yet. Not when it was their last one together.

He was trying to come up with a way to ask her about a nightcap when her phone rang.

"It's Agnes," Sofia announced, her brow furled in concern. "Wonder why she's calling so late."

He waited while she answered. Agnes's faint voice came through the tiny speaker in a mumbled torrent, though Raul couldn't make out anything she was saying. Sofia didn't speak so much as a word. Her face grew ashen as she listened.

Raul clamped down on his impatience, resisting the urge to ask her what was wrong.

Finally, she hung up, her mouth slightly agape.

"Sofia? What is it?" he asked when he couldn't stand the suspense any longer.

Before answering, she tapped the screen of her phone

several times. "See for yourself," she told him, handing him the device.

Raul was loath to tear his gaze away from her crestfallen face. When he finally did so to look at the screen, the reason for her upset was plain and clear.

"A hit piece."

She released a hysterical laugh. "On me. They're saying I'm an opportunist who has no business being engaged to a prince. A commoner who bathes animals for a living. That I'm taking advantage of your distraction with your sister to entrap you." Her voice grew higher in pitch as she spoke.

Raul bit out a curse, swearing at himself as much as at the worthless rag that had published such drivel. This was all his fault. If it wasn't for him, no one would even know who Sofia was let alone accuse her of such vile intentions.

Without thought, he stepped to her, drew her close.

"We'll handle this, Sofia. Get them to retract it. I'll get the palace press office on it right this minute."

She hiccupped. "But the damage has been done, hasn't it? The article is already out there."

He couldn't argue with her there. There was no erasing what had already found its way into cyberspace.

To his amazement, Sofia straightened in his arms and drew a deep breath. He could practically feel the strength she was summoning like some magical sprite calling upon the universe.

"But you're right," she began. "You said so yourself. Eventually they'll lose interest, won't they? This article will eventually be forgotten." The tremble in her voice sounded as if she were trying to convince herself more than looking for an answer.

He would have thought so. But now he wasn't so sure.

This was all his fault. The things they were saying about Sofia, the accusations they were throwing at her. How could he not have seen it coming? Rather than viewing their engagement as a romantic love story, the media had turned their relationship into something nefarious and they'd painted Sofia as a villain in the process.

All because of him.

She wasn't sure how long she'd been out on the terrace when she heard the sliding door swish open. Raul stepped in front of her, still wearing his tuxedo. Sofia herself hadn't bothered to undress out of her gown, her mind still processing what the world was reading about her.

He handed her a steaming mug.

"You didn't have to make me a cup of tea," she said, taking the cup. "Thank you."

"You're welcome. Though I have a secondary motive."

"What would that be?"

"To make a suggestion and see what you think."

She studied him in the moonlight. He'd rammed his hand into his pant pockets. A muscle twitched along his jaw. He seemed uncharacteristically hesitant to say his next words.

"I know we've reached the end of our agreed-upon time."

Her mouth was dry, her mind scrambling to try to figure out where he was going with all this. "I'm aware."

"I know you have to keep a low profile for a while until the spotlight on us falls, especially now. And I'll be off to Mont-Tremblant."

"Again, I'm aware," she repeated.

He tilted his head her way. "I think the media might be a bit more relentless than I first gave them credit for."

Sofia sighed and focused her attention on a twinkling star in the distant night sky. "I can handle it, Raul." What choice did she have? This was as much her fault as it was his. Neither one of them had thought to predict that at least one outlet would choose the most salacious and juicy angle.

He nodded. "I don't doubt it. But you shouldn't have to. Not by yourself."

"What does that mean?"

"Well, it occurred to me that there's no reason you have to wait out the media attention back home in DC."

Sofia scanned his face for any hint of what this conversation might really be about. He shocked her when he finally revealed the answer.

"Come with me, Sofia."

CHAPTER THIRTEEN

Mont-Tremblant, Canada

"HUH. I WOULDN'T have pegged a prince as the baking type."

Raul cut out a perfect square of the pastry he'd just pulled out of the refrigerator and plated it, handing it to Sofia with a dessert fork.

"Technically, I haven't. This is a no-bake dessert."

Sofia took a forkful and groaned in pleasure as she chewed. As much as he enjoyed her little sounds of delight and watching her enjoy her food, Raul had to look away. The temptation to replace that fork with his own lips was almost too strong to resist.

"How in the world did you learn to make these?" Sofia asked, a smidge of chocolate ganache smeared temptingly along her bottom lip.

"The sweet little old lady who owns the café in town took pity on me and gave me the recipe my last visit here. Guess she grew tired of me going by every day to buy out her entire case."

Sofia chuckled, took another bite of the Nanaimo bar, moaned again, louder this time.

She pointed the fork in his direction once she was done

swallowing. "You're a man of many talents, Crown Prince Raul Abarra. But making these might be top of my list."

The pleasure he felt at the innocuous words was enough to be considered comically embarrassing. But that was the realization that kept repeating for him since they'd arrived here after leaving Montreal—pleasing Sofia was tremendously enjoyable for him. More gratifying than growing Vesovia's national investments, or appeasing the king. Or pretty much anything else he could think of.

And wasn't that a sorry state of affairs?

Considering none of this could last. In many ways, their stay here in the charming lodge he used as his base when he stayed in Mont-Tremblant was even more pretend than their fake engagement. Their days spent walking, hiking or shopping in the quaint town. Evenings spent side by side reading quietly. It was all so cozy. So domestic.

So opposite of what his real life actually entailed.

But looking at Sofia now, as she enjoyed her dessert, the smile on her face while she savored every morsel, Raul couldn't bring himself to worry about the long term. Was it so wrong to enjoy the simplicity while it lasted? To pretend it didn't have to end?

When they finished eating, he followed her to the love seat in front of the fireplace.

"Are you going to pretend you intend on reading on your tablet again?" she asked, sitting down and curling her legs under her.

"Why, whatever do you mean?" he asked in mock confusion, though he knew full well what she was referring to.

She laughed, flipping open to her bookmarked page. "I mean that you always eventually lean over my shoulder to read my novel."

"Can't help it. Your whodunit is much more interesting than my boring spreadsheets of domestic supply chains."

She rubbed her chin. "Fair enough. Next time we're in town, we'll have to get you your own copy."

"Right. We should do that. Good idea."

He had absolutely no intention of doing any such thing. He had no idea what the plot was of the book she was reading, couldn't even name a character. The reason he sat next to her in the evenings and leaned into her shoulder had everything to do with how she smelled, the way she felt against him, the feel of her hair along his jaw.

Sometimes, as the evening grew later, he was lucky enough that she lost herself in the story and snuggled her back against his chest, let him wrap his arm around her.

He sat next to her now, then closed his tablet after less than ten minutes to lean over her shoulder.

She was, quite literally, near the top of the world. And high above ground.

Sofia took in the sights far below her feet dangling off the gondola car as it soared higher and higher along its line. A shimmering lake lay what seemed like miles below them. Lush green trees as far as the eye could see. Hiking trails that meandered down the slope. The populous town at the base of the mountain appeared like one of those miniature village models that hobby enthusiasts put together.

"I feel like I'm flying," she said on a laugh.

Raul flashed her a charming smile in response. She was referring to more than just the gondola ride. In the week since they'd left Montreal, she felt like she'd been bouncing on clouds.

Who knew she was so adventurous? So far they'd been kayaking, hiking and had slid down a synthetic luge path.

Raul certainly took his leisure time seriously. And she was so very happy to be along for the ride. The fantasy had been unexpectedly extended, and she wasn't going to overthink the unfortunate turn of events that had led her here.

Maybe accepting Raul's invitation hadn't been wise. She could have just as well hunkered down in her mom's apartment in DC, staying out of sight until the world forgot about her. But her heart would have felt empty, a hole in her life where Raul had once been.

And if she was delaying the inevitable, then so be it. Nothing would make her regret the two weeks she'd spent here in the mountains with him. Adding more days to the cherished memories she'd made in Raul's company was nothing less than a gift.

"When we come back sometime in the winter, we'll be skiing down this mountain," Raul said now loudly above the sound of the wind.

Sofia didn't trust her balance, coordination or ski skills enough to be excited about that statement. But one word he'd used caught her attention and did send a thrill down her spine.

When.

She'd lost count of the times back in Toronto and Montreal when she'd longed for Raul to hint that he might be with her on a future trip to someplace exciting. Who knew? Maybe they'd make it back to all the places on her mental travel list together after all.

They reached the top of the mountain and jumped off the car. The air felt different up here. Crisper, more energizing. And the view was one of a kind.

"Now the fun part," Raul said, guiding her by the elbow. "We hike all the way down."

It was all tremendous fun as far as she was concerned.

Sofia leaned down to tighten the laces on the special boots they'd purchased in town upon their arrival. Raul had the whole trip planned with a full schedule of activities from morning till night. Today's agenda might be the most challenging yet.

She'd known Raul was athletic and fit, but the lengths to which he drove himself simply to have some fun was exhausting to watch and impossible to keep up with.

"I'm afraid I'm going to end up slowing you down on our descent," she told him when she rose.

He tapped her playfully on the nose. "All that matters is the journey."

They appeared to be the only two people on the mountaintop. Threatening clouds had been approaching from the west but a check and recheck of the weather had assured them any pending storm would pass by the mountain entirely.

Looking in that direction now, Sofia actually crossed her fingers in hopes that was true. The sky looked awful dark out that way.

"Let's go, shall we?" Raul prompted.

They'd only made it down a few feet when Sofia's finger crossing proved futile. Within moments the sky turned dark. All those angry clouds had indeed found their way above the summit and unleashed a torrent of rain.

Raul swore next to her. "I guess the weather reports were wrong. I blame myself for trusting them blindly."

Sofia wanted to offer words of reassurance that he couldn't possibly blame himself for an unexpected shift in rain clouds, but she was too busy getting soaked.

"Here, let's try to find some shelter," he told her, wiping his face and looking around. "Most of the trails have small cottages for hikers to take a break or if they need first aid."

It was almost impossible to see. As high up as they were, the wind was surprisingly strong. Sofia actually wondered if she might tip over. "I think I see one," Raul said finally.

She could only follow him blindly, making sure her hand remained in his. After several difficult steps with the ground beneath them getting muddier and muddier, they finally reached a small wooden shedlike structure nestled between two tall trees.

It certainly wasn't much. To call it any kind of cottage would be overselling it.

The door swung open and crashed against the wall when Raul pushed it open.

"Looks like this one isn't used anymore," he said once they'd stepped inside and shut the door behind them.

"It works," she replied. "All that matters is it has a roof."

"I'm so sorry, Sofia," Raul said, his features tight. "It's no wonder we appear to be the only ones on this mountain."

She stepped closer, laid a hand on his forearm. "You only have a few days free." He'd even left his bodyguards behind on this trip, explaining to her that every time he'd been to Mont-Tremblant, no one had cared who he was or what he was doing. This place was like another world, set apart from the rest. "It's understandable you didn't want to miss out on one. And I'm also an adult—I had just as much responsibility for the decision."

His eyes scanned her face and Sofia's breath hitched in her throat. Sometimes when he looked at her that way, she wanted to curl her fingers through his hair and bring his mouth down to hers for a deep, satisfying kiss.

"You're shivering," he said, his voice a low whisper she almost didn't hear above the loud wind outside.

She may be soaked and cold, but any trembling happening at the moment was his doing. "Am I?"

He stepped closer. "You are. We might have to see about keeping you warm."

She could think of a few ways to do that where he'd be the primary operative in the endeavor.

Sofia swallowed as he stepped even closer. They were a hairbreadth apart now, and his breath felt warm on her cheek. He was so wrong about her feeling cold. Right now she felt nothing but singeing heat from the bottom of her feet to the top of her head. And everything in between.

"Would you like me to get you warm, Sofia?"

Much, much too late for the question. He already had her burning up. "Yes," she answered, surprised her tongue worked. "I would like that very much."

She barely got the last word out before his mouth was on hers. His arms wound about her waist, lifting her slightly off the ground. The taste of him was intoxicating, overwhelming her senses. She'd wanted this for so long, dreamed of it during the nights. Woke up yearning for him in the mornings. Finally. Blessedly.

All thought fled her mind. The only thing her brain registered was the feel of him against her, the taste of him. His scent surrounding her.

Her hand found its way into his shirt; feeling the hard muscle against her palm sent her desire soaring even higher. As did his responding groan.

Her other hand plunged into the hair at his neck and she pulled him closer, deeper.

Suddenly, abruptly the kiss was over. Raul tore his mouth off hers and yanked himself back.

Sofia could only blink in shock and disappointment. They both stood panting for several silent moments. She stepped toward him and he held a hand up to stop her.

The rejection came as a swift blow to her midsection. What had just happened? How could he stop so suddenly? And why? Had she thrown herself at him? How humiliating. She felt a flush rush to her face at the possibility.

She couldn't find the words to ask.

"Not like this," he said finally, his voice gravelly and thick.

Her confusion must have been clear on her face.

He leaned closer, trailed a finger down her cheek. "You can't think I don't want you." He sucked in a deep breath, squeezed his eyes shut. "But when this happens, it won't be in a dingy abandoned shack." There was that word again. *When.*

He opened his eyes again and stared straight into her soul, then he dropped a gentle kiss to her temple. "And it won't be rushed and thoughtless. You won't feel soaked to the skin with rainwater. I'll make sure you feel nothing but pure pleasure. Over and over."

Hours later, once the storm ended and they finally made their way back to the lodge, he stayed true to his word.

He'd broken every one of his rules when it came to Sofia. The sun was just rising when he felt her up against him, rustling in her sleep. Raul willed her not to wake up just yet. He didn't know what to say to her.

He didn't regret what happened between them last night. But that didn't mean he had no misgivings. For one, he should have been clearer up front about exactly what last night meant in case she had any misconstrued ideas. He should have explained that he wasn't the right man for her.

That there would be a spotlight on her at all times if she were to become involved with him romantically. Living that life might have been manageable for her for a few days of pretend, but long term was a completely different story.

As if that weren't bad enough, he had no time in his life for any kind of real relationship. The kingdom was always going to take up most of his time and energy. Which would only be a bigger factor once he actually ascended the throne. His father made it more and more clear with each passing day that he was getting ready to hand the proverbial reins over to Raul.

Sofia had a life she'd worked hard for. With the amount he'd transferred into her bank account for her assistance with Luisa's mess, Sofia wouldn't have to worry about budgeting or making ends meet in her shop. She lived in a city she loved with supportive friends and her mother nearby.

How could he ask her to give up all that for him?

He couldn't. The fact of the matter was that when he did finally settle down, it most likely wouldn't be for love. It would be for duty to the kingdom with a woman who had been raised to fit into such a life. He'd be fooling himself to think otherwise for even a moment.

Look at the havoc the attention on her had caused just for the brief time they'd pretended to be engaged. How could he ask her to deal with that for the rest of her life? She couldn't and didn't have to.

All of that should have been laid out in the open with Sofia before he'd acted on his urges and complicated everything.

He swore. In fact, even asking her here to Mont-Tremblant with him was a mistake. The first time in his life he'd acted on a whim. Driven by unplanned impulse. He couldn't even explain what had gotten into him the night of the mayoral dinner when he'd taken her to the basilica. He simply recalled that one moment he was looking forward to coming here alone, just to unwind after all that had taken place these last few weeks. The next, he couldn't bear the thought of being here without her.

Then he'd compounded the errors by not being up front with Sofia before they became intimate. He could only hope the damage wouldn't be irreparable.

She must have just missed him. Sofia awoke to find Raul's side of the bed still warm but he was nowhere to be found. It was no wonder she'd slept through his awakening this morning. Nothing less than an earthquake would have roused her after such an eventful day. And what came after later at night. Being stranded in a little shack on the side of a deserted mountain sounded like something out of one of those romantic movies Agnes was so fond of.

Her friend would never believe she'd actually lived such a storyline. Complete with the romantic interlude it had led to. With a satisfied stretch, she reached for her phone on the bedside table. He'd left her a message. Nothing from her mom, which was what she'd asked of her. But a conflicting mash of disappointment and relief washed over her that her mother hadn't tried harder to reach her after the botanical garden photos.

The only message she'd received was from Raul.

Out running on one of the mountain trails. See you soon.

A twinge of disappointment nagged at her at the straightforward message. No heart emoji or xoxo.

But that was silly. Most men didn't really do such things, did they? After all, this wasn't really a romance movie.

Honestly, how did the man have any energy to run after last night? She could barely move a muscle and felt loath to so much as get out of bed. But a cup of coffee was called for and the sun was shining bright outside. No time like right now to start the day. Plus, she was feeling rather like a relative underachiever given Raul was already out and about and strenuously exercising.

Making her way to the kitchen, she approached the new-fangled coffee contraption she was just recently getting the hang of. Making quick work of drinking the first one, she brewed a second to enjoy on the stone patio outside. The morning had only grown brighter since she'd risen.

Her coffee cup was halfway empty when Raul showed up. Dressed in a tight T-shirt that stuck to him with sweat, accentuating the toned muscles of his chest. Sofia's heart fluttered with awareness at the sight of him.

Standing, she strode the few feet to where he stood and leaned in, intending a good-morning kiss. Raul stepped back slightly but enough for her to notice, then landed a chaste peck on the side of her cheek.

An unpleasant sensation slithered down her spine.

"I'm pretty sweaty," he said by way of explanation.

She was about to reply that she didn't mind but the hardened lines around his lips and the tension in his shoulders had alarm bells ringing in her head. She saw no hint of the affectionate, passionate man she'd spent last night with. Did he regret what had happened between them last night?

The thought sent a stab of pain through her center.

Don't jump to conclusions.

Maybe he was just tired from his run.

She summoned a bright smile. "So, last full day here in Mont-Tremblant." she said just to get some kind of conversation going.

"That's right," he said. "Then it's back to reality."

She was going to ignore whatever hidden meaning such a statement might hold. "Well, as much as I miss DC and everyone back there, including Sir Bunbun, I think you've awakened the traveler in me."

He lifted an eyebrow. "Oh?"

She nodded. "That's right. I'm already planning a trip back to Toronto. I never did get to the top of the CN Tower."

He nodded once. "I remember. I think it's a great idea. You should go."

You. Not *we*.

Maybe she was being foolish, masochistic even, but she had to ask and know for sure what was happening at the moment. Though she knew she was about to risk shattering her heart. "What does your calendar look like coming up? I'd love some company."

"I don't think that would be such a good idea, Soso. I should head back to Vesovia and stay still for a while. I've been away quite long."

A brick dropped to the pit of her stomach. Not only at his words, but the reversion back to the teasing nickname he'd used for her when she'd been nothing more to him than his younger sister's pesky little friend.

Still, her heart wouldn't let her accept what her mind was clearly registering. "Oh. That makes sense. Well, I've always wanted to see your kingdom. Vesovia attracts a lot of tourists this time of year, doesn't it? Maybe I could venture out there for a quick visit."

He shook his head with zero hesitation. "I don't think that would work either."

That settled it. There was no denying now what was standing in front of her nose. He was washing his hands of her. While last night had meant the world to her, apparently Raul had merely been indulging in a last-minute fling before they each went back to their own lives.

How utterly stupid and naive of her that she hadn't even considered that possibility. After all, he'd never told her anything to the contrary. Why in the world had she assumed that one night meant anything genuine?

Because it had for her. Because she'd fallen in love with him.

While he was ready to simply walk away from her and not look back.

CHAPTER FOURTEEN

FOR THE SECOND time in a month, a royal Abarra from
the Kingdom of Vesovia entered Sofia's grooming shop
without any kind of advance warning. Princess Luisa was
beautiful as ever, sporting a golden tan and her usual mischievous smile.

Any other time, Sofia would have been thrilled to see her
friend. But her first reaction upon Luisa's arrival was how
much she wished the other sibling were here in her stead.

Luisa didn't bother with a hello, just launched into conversation as if her showing up here wasn't a complete
anomaly.

"I heard you and my brother had some kind of fling.
Only it wasn't real. Except maybe it was."

Well, that was quite a greeting. "What are you doing
here, Luisa? And why didn't you tell me you were coming?"

The princess gave a dismissive wave of her hand. "Because it was a spontaneous decision."

Par for the course.

"That answers one of my questions."

"Well, older bro has been an absolute monster lately.
Grouchy, grumpy. Seems miserable in general. I wanted
to know if you were the cause of his sudden nasty dis-
position."

Sofia rolled her eyes at the question. "I hardly think so. He was probably working on some deal for the kingdom's coffers that fell through."

Luisa shook her head, tightening her lips. "No, I don't think that's it. He's dealt with unsuccessful deals before. What he hasn't dealt with before is lost love."

Sofia couldn't bring herself to take Luisa's words seriously. And she would absolutely ignore that last word because it didn't fit.

Raul had been very clear that last morning at Mont-Tremblant. He wanted nothing to do with her once the trip was over. Whatever Luisa thought she knew, she was sorely mistaken.

"Be that as it may," she began, "I don't want to talk about your brother. I'd like to talk about you, however. You caused quite a stir for several weeks there."

Luisa gave a disaffected shrug of one elegant shoulder. "Yes, I suppose I did. I made some bad decisions and fell for a man who said all the right things but went right back to his wife when the time came to make a decision."

Sofia could certainly relate to part of that scenario. She'd made her fair share of bad decisions over the past few weeks and she'd undoubtedly fallen for the wrong man.

Luisa leaned over her counter. "But we have to talk about big bro," she declared. "It's why I'm here. He's becoming unbearable. Someone has to do something. My guess is that someone is you."

Why was Luisa not getting it? She meant nothing to Raul. She couldn't fix something she had no effect over.

Agnes chose that moment to rush out from the back office. "I've booked our tickets, Sofia." She came to a halt when she saw the princess and blinked twice. Luisa definitely didn't fit the example of their regular clientele. She looked like... Well, she looked like a royal princess in a small pet groomer shop.

Sofia made quick introductions while Agnes continued to stare at the out-of-place specimen who'd clearly honored them with her mere presence.

"Tickets to where?" Luisa wanted to know.

"Toronto," Agnes blurted out before she got a chance to answer. "We're going together in three weeks. She's been talking about returning there for another visit since she got back to DC a month ago."

Luisa tilted her head in question.

"I never got to the top of the CN Tower," Sofia said, not sure why she was bothering. She didn't really owe Luisa any kind of explanation. In fact, if it wasn't for the princess, her heart would still be intact in her chest instead of shattered into a billion pieces.

Her antics had set the entire disaster in motion.

Suddenly, her patience had grown thin and her ire not so much. "Luisa, I'm really busy. Can we please get on with the real reason you're here already?"

Luisa's eyes widened in surprise. Sofia had never so much as said a harsh word to her before. Not many people had. Maybe it was about time that changed.

"I already told you."

"And I told you that makes zero sense. Follow me, please."

This time Luisa's jaw actually snapped open in shock. Now Sofia was literally ordering her around. But she didn't really care at the moment. She'd worked hard to begin the long journey of trying to piece her heart back together. So far she hadn't been terribly successful but

Luisa's sudden appearance was picking the scabs of what little progress she'd made.

Without waiting for the princess to agree, Sofia turned on her heel and made her way to the back office. They were in between clients and her two new employees had asked for the day off, apparently to go on a date with each other.

There were only the three of them in the shop. She was rather surprised to turn around and find that the princess had, in fact, heeded her demand as she was standing in the room behind her.

She moved behind her desk and sat, motioning for Luisa to take the other chair. "I don't know what your brother told you—"

Luisa cut her off. "He didn't tell me anything. He's barely talked to me, still angry about what he calls my poor behavior and judgment."

"Maybe he's right."

"Of course he is. What's that got to do with anything?"

Sofia rubbed her forehead where a small headache was beginning.

"Luisa, I don't know what you came here expecting to get but I can't give it to you."

"I beg to differ," she said, plopping into the chair. "Did you even ask him?"

"Ask him what?"

"Ask him how he felt about you."

Sofia couldn't find the words to even respond.

"You need to ask him. And soon. He can hardly run the kingdom in the state he's in."

That did it. Of all the selfish, non-self-aware outlooks to have. "Well, then maybe *you* should step up. You're also a royal. Why is Vesovia's well-being dependent solely on Raul?"

If she'd shocked Luisa before, the princess was downright gobsmacked now. Narrowing her eyes, she stood back up and walked to the door. "Just ask him," she said, leaving the office.

"Wait!" Sofia called to her retreating back. Maybe she'd been too harsh just now but her nerves were still too raw and Luisa had never really had to answer for her often selfish behavior before. The princess was past due to hear a few truths. "You came all the way to Washington. Do you want to at least get lunch or something?"

Luisa didn't bother to turn around or so much as slow her stride. "Sure," she answered over her shoulder. "I'll have my staff call you when it's arranged."

With that she was gone.

Sofia wasn't going to hold her breath waiting on that lunch.

Leaning back in the chair, she let her head hang over the back. She felt utterly drained by Luisa's stealth visit. But as haughty and impulsive as she could be, Luisa had always been sharp as a tack. And her read of people wasn't often wrong. Especially of those people she considered loved ones.

What he hasn't dealt with before is lost love

Married life certainly seemed to suit his friend. Raul took in his friend's relaxed shoulders and wide smile and felt a pang of envy before pushing it aside. Rafe had gone to the trouble of stopping by Vesovia to see him on his way from their honeymoon and Raul owed it to him to be somewhat personable. And not a grouchy ogre as Luisa accused him of being. She was wrong of course. Raul wasn't grouchy. He was simply busy.

He turned back to his friend as one of the kitchen staff refilled their wineglasses while they dined on the terrace adjacent to the royal gardens. "And how is your lovely new bride," he asked. "Was Frannie not able to accompany you?"

"Afraid not," Rafe answered with a frown. "She had to leave right away to film on location in Hawaii."

"You miss her already," Raul said. It didn't take a magician to see what was clearly written on his friend's face.

"Like a limb," Rafe answered, a faraway look in his eyes.

His friend had it bad. At least Rafe knew he'd be reunited with the woman he was in love with.

Whoa. Raul stopped short. That wayward thought had no business scurrying around in his brain.

Raul set his glass down and stared out into the acres and acres of green grass and shrubbery. He avoided coming out here most days. The view reminded him too much of the botanical garden, which in turn reminded him of Sofia.

All she'd asked for was a simple visit. Not unlike what Rafe was here for. And he'd coldly turned her down. He hadn't even tried to come up with a way to explain why.

She must think him a selfish, callous ass.

"So where'd you just drift off to?" Rafe asked, amusement dancing in his eyes. "I must say, I don't think I've ever seen you this distracted. You still thinking about your split?"

He really must have drifted off. Raul had no idea what Rafe was referring to. "Split?"

Rafe nodded. "Yeah. I was sorry to hear things didn't work out between you and Sofia," Rafe said. "Frannie and

I really enjoyed her at the wedding. May I ask what led to the breakup? You can tell me to mind my own business if you prefer not to talk about it."

Up until hearing those words, Raul was certain he indeed did not want to talk about it. But instead of saying just that, he found himself spilling the entirety of his and Sofia's now-defunct arrangement, ending with an apology for misleading him and Frannie and at their wedding, no less.

Rafe blew out a long whistle, studying him. "But you asked her to go with you to the mountains." Funny, he hadn't so much as acknowledged the rest of the sordid tale. Or his apology, for that matter.

"Right. I should have never done that. Sofia deserves stability. A life of quiet, away from prying eyes and cameras. I can't give her that. My fate lies in marriage to a woman who's familiar with the pressure and unwanted attention that being part of the royal family requires. I should have been better at explaining all that to her."

"I don't think that's it," Rafe countered before he'd had so much as a chance to finish the sentence.

"Of course it is."

Rafe shook his head. "Man, you're one of the most levelheaded people I know. A true future king who'll do well by his people. I have no doubt."

"Why do I sense a huge 'however' about to drop my way?" Raul said around a groan of resignation.

Rafe flashed him a smile. "Bingo. Give the man a prize. The 'however' happens to be that I think you've just come up with an excuse to walk away. Because the real truth is that you're scared."

Raul could only laugh in response to the preposterous statement.

Rafe continued, "Look it's understandable. You had to step up before you were ready. I get it. The king checked out because of his grief. I respect and admire your father but you know that's the truth.

Raul shrugged. "What's that got to do with me supposedly being scared? Or with Sofia for that matter?"

Rafe leaned back in his chair with a long sigh. "Guess I'm going to have to spell it out.

"Please do."

"You're scared of becoming vulnerable. Because you saw what bccamc of your father when he lost the love of his life. And you can't bring yourself to risk the same fate happening to you. As for Sofia, I think you know how what I'm saying concerns her."

The view was just as spectacular as Raul had said. Sofia stood on the observation deck of the CN Tower watching the sparkling lights of Toronto rotate almost fifteen hundred feet below.

The scene was breathtaking really. Everything she'd imagined and more. So it made no sense that she wasn't standing here full of excitement and wonder.

In fact, she was miserable.

As great a travel companion as Agnes was, being up here felt off. Wrong somehow. Because even after the devastating morning on that patio in Mont-Tremblant, her misbehaving imagination had still insisted on conjuring him by her side whenever she pictured herself here.

All these weeks later and that sad fact hadn't changed.

Coming here was a mistake. It only served to remind her what she couldn't have. More accurately, who she couldn't have. She felt the stinging behind her eyes she thought had finally abated. Coming to the top of the tower was supposed to bring her closer. This trip was supposed to show her that she was fine without him. That she was ready to move on.

Who was she kidding? Sofia was far from fine.

She was sad and heartbroken and confused.

The ache of loneliness in her heart grew heavier with each passing day. No trip to the top of a tower was going to help heal that ache.

There was only one remedy that might.

She had to get some answers. She had to know once and for all if Raul had felt even a smidgeon of the way she felt.

If he'd grown to love her the way she'd fallen in love with him. Staring at the glimmering city below her now, she realized the trip to Toronto had been her way of delaying what was clearly inevitable.

Once and for all, she had to find out if any of it was real. As much as she begrudged to admit it, Luisa was right. She had to ask him.

Even if his answer shattered her heart for good and forever. That was a risk she was going to have to take.

Agnes appeared by her side after her latest stroll around the deck. Sofia forced a fake smile on her lips. The last thing she wanted was to mar the trip she'd talked her friend into taking with her.

"I could stay here all day and look at this skyline all night," Agnes said, clasping her hands in front of her in excitement.

Sofia couldn't bring herself to lie. She'd had enough of the view that should have brought her nothing but delight. "I think I've had enough. For tonight, I mean. We should definitely come back tomorrow." Which she would suck up and do it if that's what Agnes wanted.

"All right. But how about a quick drink in the pub downstairs first?"

Sofia really didn't have it in her, but she didn't have the heart to turn her friend down. Especially considering she was cutting the night short for both of them.

"Sure," she answered, following Agnes to the elevator. The pub was fairly empty when they made their way in. The night was relatively young still. Most tourists were out exploring or on the observation deck they'd just left. They headed to one of the empty tables in the corner.

Sofia ordered a glass of cabernet while Agnes went for the chilled ice wine Canada was known for, much sweeter than what Sofia was in the mood for. In fact, nothing about her mood felt any way sweet at the moment.

The waiter was back soon after taking their order but the drink he put down in front of her was most certainly not red wine.

"I think there's been some sort of mistake," she told the man, who had confirmed her order when he'd first taken it. "This isn't what I asked for."

She was expecting an apology and to be told that it was a simple mistake. Instead, the waiter shrugged. "Yeah, there's a gentleman that told the bartender you might want to try this first."

Sofia's radar triggered. Having strangers send a woman drinks was suspicious to say the least. Particularly when traveling. But then she realized why the cocktail looked familiar. The waiter confirmed her suspicion. "It's called the Caesar," he said, then added, "But I can take it back if you want."

Agnes sat watching the exchange, confusion clear in her chocolate brown eyes. "Sofia, what's going on?"

She wasn't sure, but she was beginning to suspect who

might have sent the drink over. Her pulse pounded under her skin, while her heart thumped like a jackhammer under her rib cage, then threatened to explode right out of her chest when Raul appeared from the corner of the darkened room.

But it couldn't be him. She had to be seeing things.

Sofia blinked and rubbed at her eyes just to be sure.

"Do you want to send the drink back then?" the waiter asked, sounding impatient.

"No, thank you. I'll keep it."

Agnes followed the direction of her gaze, then stiffened when she saw Raul. He was at their table a moment later.

"Wha-what are you doing here?" she asked him.

Agnes shot her a questioning look. She answered with a nod that it was okay. She got up and walked to a nearby table, taking her glass of ice wine.

"Fine, but I'll be right here. Watching," she yelled out in warning rather loudly before taking the chair.

For the life of her she couldn't figure out what to say. So she blurted the first thing that came to mind. "You don't look like a grouchy ogre." She wanted to suck the words back in as soon as they left her mouth.

In fact, he looked heart-shatteringly handsome. The dark eyes she'd missed so much. Those toned and muscular forearms below another shirt with rolled-up sleeves.

After an initial look of surprise at her statement, he threw his head back and laughed.

"Why are you here, Raul?"

He crouched down in front of her, taking both her hands in his own. "I'm here because I heard you would be."

"Luisa told you." She stated the obvious.

He nodded. "That's right. And I didn't want to spend another moment without you. Even though it's so unfair for me to ask that of you."

"Unfair how?"

"You will never know true privacy or anonymity ever again if you're with me. Articles like the one Agnes warned you about are sure to be written again. And again."

Sofia swallowed. The strain and concern in his voice as he spoke tugged at her heart. Concern for her. "I see."

"But I promise to do all that I can to make it all right. I'll be by your side, or we can simply go into hiding. I can try to rule from the Laurentian Mountains. Whatever you want. If you'll have me."

She shook her head, unable to quite believe what she was hearing. It was so hard to find the right words. She scrambled to try the best she could. "I don't care about running from cameras. I don't care if I have to duck paparazzi or curious bystanders for the rest of my life. All of that is worth it and more to be with you."

"That makes me the luckiest man on the planet," he said, his voice thick. "Because, somewhere along the way, when I wasn't paying attention, I fell deeply in love with you."

That settled it. She was definitely imagining all this. The air must have been too thin when she'd been up in the tower. The only explanation that made sense. Her mind was delirious due to a lack of sufficient oxygen.

She reached out to his face. If he was a ghost of her imagination, she should touch nothing but air. But her fingertips felt warm, solid flesh. He turned to drop a kiss inside her palm. The feel of his lips sent waves of hot electricity through her entire body.

"Oh, Raul. I've fallen in love with you too. Hopelessly, madly in love."

He sucked in a gasp of a breath at her words. Then, silently, he reached inside his pocket. Sofia clasped a hand to her mouth when she saw what he held.

"You left this behind," he told her, opening the small velvet box.

The beautiful ring her finger had grown so familiar wearing sat on a fluffy bed of satin. It was even lovelier than she remembered.

"Sofia Nomi. I'm a fool who doesn't deserve you and I know if you say yes, life as you know it will change forever. But I'm asking you to marry me." He paused to suck in a breath. "Please say yes."

She didn't need words to give him the answer he'd asked for.

EPILOGUE

SOFIA KNOCKED SOFTLY on the door to her husband's office and didn't wait for an answer before pushing it open. He'd been working since early morning and could use the break. Besides, she had some rather important news she had to tell him.

Raul glanced at his watch after flashing her a smile of greeting. Even after all these months, his smile sent a wave of longing through her. She couldn't resist taking a moment to stride behind his desk and lean in for a toe-curling kiss.

"Is it time to meet the king for lunch already?" he asked, then yanked her onto his lap. "I'm sure he won't mind if we're a little late," he added, taking her mouth with his once again.

Sofia lost focus as she reveled in the taste of him. Trailing her hands up his chest then around his neck, she pulled him closer and allowed herself to fully savor him. Then made herself pull away, though it wasn't easy. At this rate, she was never going to get the announcement out.

"No, it's early still," she said, breathless with happiness and the effects of the kiss. "There's another reason I'm here."

He lifted an eyebrow. "What reason?"

"I wanted to let you know about a new addition to the palace."

Raul flashed her an indulgent smile. "An addition, huh? Let me guess, we've adopted another cat from the shelter. What does that bring the number up to? Six? Seven? I've lost count."

She shook her head, hardly able to keep herself from just blurting out the news. She'd been floating on air since leaving her appointment with the palace nurse half an hour ago.

"Uh-uh. Wrong guess, my love."

He dropped a kiss to her forehead. "Another puppy then? Or a senior dog. We'll have to expand the kennels at this rate and hire another caretaker for them all."

"Wrong again."

"Oh, no. Not more bunnies. Those creatures seem to be multiplying enough on their own."

She gave another shake of her head. "You are wrong on all counts. And out of guesses."

He tilted his head in question.

She couldn't resist dropping another kiss to his lips before continuing. "This particular addition is one of the two-legged variety."

Raul's eyes grew wide and his jaw fell open. Shock flooded his eyes but it didn't last, immediately replaced with joy. And love. Pure unfiltered love.

With a whoop loud enough that the entire palace must have heard, he stood up out of the chair and lifted her in his arms.

"You mean…?"

She nodded, laughter bursting from her throat. "Yes!"

He twirled her around, then lowered her to the ground to hug her tight. Sofia mentally paused to simply savor this moment in time. That night at the CN Tower, Raul had said he was the luckiest man on earth. She was pretty lucky herself to have found him.

Her prince had given her all she could have dared to hope for. And more.

Who knew fairy tales could sometimes be real?

* * * * *

If you enjoyed this story,
check out these other great reads from
Nina Singh

Bound by the Boss's Baby
Their Accidental Marriage Deal
Part of His Royal World
The Prince's Safari Temptation

All available now

MILLS & BOON®

Coming next month

FAKING IT WITH THE BOSS
Michele Renae

'It's late, but do you have time for the entrance interviews?' the receptionist asked. 'They take about fifteen minutes and will help us to fine-tune your schedule for the week.'

Asher glanced at her and shrugged.

Maeve grabbed his hand. 'Just a second. I need to talk to my boss—er...boyfriend.' With a forced smile to the receptionist, she then tugged Asher aside near the fountain bubbling in the center of the pristine Prussian-blue-tiled lobby.

'What's up, sweetie? Sorry. Maeve.'

A momentary thrill of hearing him say her name swept through her like a cyclone, only to be followed by an even bigger, and more harrowing, disaster. 'It's this.' She waved the flyer between them. 'This is not just a couples' spa vacation.'

'What? The signs say Reconnecting Romance. Kind of cute.'

'Right, it is a spa, and about romance, but it's also focused on this.' She turned the flyer toward him and tapped the top line.

Asher read, 'Relationship *rehab*?'

Maeve swore under her breath. 'I'm so sorry, I didn't notice this when signing up. I can't believe I let that slip by me.'

'What does it mean exactly?'

'It means that not only are we faking being a couple, now we're going to have to fake relationship issues. We're here to *fix* our relationship, not relax and rejuvenate.'

Asher winked at her. 'Guess I'm calling you sweetie after all.'

He turned and told the receptionist they could do their interviews now.

Continue reading

FAKING IT WITH THE BOSS
Michele Renae

Available next month
millsandboon.co.uk

COMING SOON!

We really hope you enjoyed reading this book.
If you're looking for more romance
be sure to head to the shops when
new books are available on

Thursday 27th February

To see which titles are coming soon, please visit
millsandboon.co.uk/nextmonth

MILLS & BOON

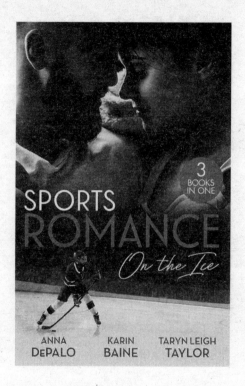

LET'S TALK

Romance

For exclusive extracts, competitions and special offers, find us online:

- 🅕 MillsandBoon
- 𝕏 @MillsandBoon
- 📷 @MillsandBoonUK
- ♪ @MillsandBoonUK

Get in touch on 01413 063 232

For all the latest titles coming soon, visit
millsandboon.co.uk/nextmonth